SNIPE

SNIPE

LILY LASHLEY
aka Etzoli

Podium

Podium

SNIPE

CHAPTER 1

Killing someone without leaving a trace is overrated.

I could do it. It just took money, patience, some skill . . . and dealing with people who couldn't care less about the police. I'd gotten pretty good at it over the years, but I'd met a lot of awful people in that time. Sitting behind the counter was yet another example. The relentless pulse of the nightclub didn't quite drown out my revulsion for the slovenly hulk I had just bribed.

His thick hands, as if he were wearing gloves underneath his dirty skin, slid the bulletproof tray around to pick up the small stack of cash I'd dropped in it, along with a messy handwritten request. The man examined the bills thoroughly with a trained eye until, satisfied, he dropped it into a plain burlap sack near the till.

"Fourth floor. Hundred more'll get you the room number, honey. You aren't his type, but I bet he'd make an exception if you put out."

I ignored him. The floor was all I needed. The Vibrato Club lay just behind the steel door next to the reception desk, the thick portal visibly buzzing from the pounding music just inside. People were dancing, getting high, and trying to ignore the world's steady descent into insanity. I couldn't blame them, but . . . couldn't they be doing *anything* else?

"You going in?"

I shook my head. A club like that was the *last* place I wanted to be. I pulled my hood low over my face and turned to leave.

"Then what was all this for?" the guy asked, gesturing toward the cash. I didn't answer—he didn't need to hear my voice. "Whatever, suit yourself . . . bitch," he muttered as I walked toward the street door.

For a moment, I hesitated. *Reputation is everything. Reputation is our power. If people think we are weak, we become weak.* If someone this low on the totem pole was mouthing off to *me*, of all people, showing so little respect to me and the people I worked for, something would have to be done.

Except in this case, my brother's advice didn't apply. I didn't look like me, for one—I'd dyed my hair and was wearing interface glasses to disguise my other eye, and I'd left my equipment across the street. For all the normal world to see, I was just like any other sixteen-year-old girl. I was wearing a thick blue hoodie with acid rain guards (not that we needed them in Cascadia, but they'd become a trend anyway), a scarf, normal clothes. Only my boots could give anything away.

Point was, I didn't want anyone to know it was me. Not being recognized was the goal.

The guy slid his VR set back onto his face as I kept walking. He had one of the semitransparent ones, where he could still see the world while getting lost in his sims. I wondered if he was one of our customers, but I didn't stick around to check. I left the building and returned to the cold night, pulling my jacket tight to keep dry in the rain.

I had a job to do.

Out of the club, across the street, I grabbed the bag I'd hidden behind a nearby dumpster and headed into an apartment building. I'd cleared the place ahead of time. The night guard was the lazy type, so I wasn't worried about the human element. Carefully, I stopped in the exact spot we'd marked out, just before the building's cameras would pick me up, and pressed my right thumb between my index and middle fingers.

The interface for my other eye appeared in midair, a ghostly projection only I could see. With tiny, quick gestures of my hand—only the right one, of course, since my left didn't have the sensor inlays—I swiped to my contact list. I had the phone number already, of course, but the encryption key shifted every two minutes, and I couldn't ever store the paired key on anything that might get stolen. It'd be pretty hard for somebody to steal my *eye* without me noticing, after all.

I pulled out a burner phone and dialed. After the connection tone, I typed in the twelve-digit key.

"Operations."

I smiled. The guy on ops tonight was Kev, one of my better partners. I don't know if I'd call us friends exactly—almost nobody in the organization knew my real name—but we had chemistry. Rapport, I guess you'd call it.

"Snipe." Snipe was my code name. I didn't pick it; neither did my brother. Somebody without much imagination had used it in the middle of my first operation, and it stuck. A sniper with the name Snipe. Well . . . at least I could *pretend* they were talking about the bird instead.

Kev never called me Snipe though. He knew I didn't really like it. "Hey, girl. Blackout time?"

"Yeah, take it down."

"You got it. Just a sec here . . ." I heard a vague rolling sound—Kev's chair most likely. He was always on speakerphone instead of his headset. "Here comes the haunting. Spooky ghosts."

The security guard just around the corner was still snoozing at his desk, or maybe he was in a sim himself. I couldn't tell yet—couldn't risk being seen by any of the cameras. Strict privacy laws prevented anything pointing toward the outside of the building owned by a private company, so I was safe just inside the doorway. But as soon as I moved even a little bit forward, I'd be spotted.

"Loops are up. You're good."

"Thanks."

I hung up and started moving. As expected, the guard was lost in his own sim, and this building wasn't connected to any of the major corps, so he was the only one around. He didn't pay me a single bit of attention, relying on his cameras and sensors to let him know if anyone was approaching—didn't want to risk his high, after all.

Up the staircase—no elevators, *never* elevators—two steps at a time, fast as I could without making noise. I'd learned the art of walking in near-silence years back when I was first inducted into the business. Darius hadn't wanted me to join, but . . . circumstances.

It was always circumstances.

I didn't blame Darius for that. He would have died if not for the fact that he had a little sister who liked guns and could get into places he couldn't. I was good at what I did and I took some kind of pride in it. I didn't *enjoy* killing, but . . . some people needed to die for the rest of us to live in peace. That was the promise between Darius and me when I started working for him.

Only people who needed to die.

It wasn't even people who *deserved* to die. There were certainly awful, horrible people in the world who probably deserved a fate as bad—or far worse—than the quick, easy death I could provide. But we weren't in the business of saving the world or righting wrongs. We were a gang. We sold drugs.

Okay, not *drugs* exactly. If they were like the drugs I used to read about, the ones mostly eradicated from Cascadia these days, I probably wouldn't be on board either. We sold hacked VR sims and modified implants. Still illegal, but . . . there's a difference.

Sometimes I wondered if I was one of those people who deserved to die.

I reached the fifth floor of the apartment complex. Another gesture from my hand and the interface reappeared. I flicked through to the visual settings and clicked thermal "on." The two primary lenses faded as the thermal camera above them booted up. I closed my left eye so I could focus better.

With only one lens and no depth perception, everything looked a lot flatter, but that was okay. I was looking for a room with no heat, somewhere empty and facing back across the street. It took half the length of the building before I found one.

The place used simple keycard locks, since it was retrofitted from an old hotel. I opened my bag, quickly deactivating the tracking device I'd sewn into the hem, and grabbed a card scrambler out of it. After only a few seconds, it transmitted the right magnetic code.

The door clicked open.

Before anyone chanced on me in the hallway, I hurried inside. The room was remarkably clean—probably unoccupied, given the empty closet. I hadn't expected it to be so spotless, but evidently the place had a cleaning staff who took more pride in their work than the security guard below. I crossed to the window and slid it open.

There were perfect sight lines from my window to every room on the fourth floor of the building opposite. Since I'd gone one floor higher, I could take an easy diagonal shot without worrying about anyone standing in the way too long, like a bodyguard. The only risk was if he stood near the far wall and never walked all the way in, but I doubted I'd get that unlucky—the drink cart and couches were near the window.

I took a breath, then began to set up. A sensor trap and a smoke grenade near the door and a quick-release rappel cord on the window gave me enough protection to feel secure. I slid the desk over to the window to make for a nice stand, since the sill wasn't wide enough to properly mount a gun. I checked again to make sure there were no cameras—officially, it would be a privacy violation, but I knew far too many hotels and apartments that ignored *that* part of the law.

The room was secure. I pulled a chair over to the desk and sat down. From my bag, I withdrew my rifle. It was a custom-made piece commissioned by my brother after six months of working for his gang. Darius had sourced its parts from all over the world and assembled it himself, making sure it was completely untraceable. I inspected it, as I always did before a job, then turned it on.

With a faint whirring sound, the rifle extended to its actual length. In the bag, it didn't even appear to be a rifle, just a smooth slab of dark gray plastic with a scope on top and a faint outline of a bird engraved into the side. When it connected to my eye software, though, I could expand it into a full-length rifle, as deadly as any.

The barrel tessellated outward, distinct from the usual sliding motion, almost seeming to create material from nothing. Extending out were a trigger and, from the rear, a shoulder brace—though I usually didn't need it, thanks to the enhancements in my arm. I tested the software, and it connected properly. I could see through the scope.

I propped the rifle up with a portable tripod, taking my first proper scan of the target room. My eye software did some calculations and came up with a range of forty-seven meters to the back wall. There was virtually no wind, and even if there was, it wouldn't affect the cartridge over such a short distance. I picked out a magazine from my bag and loaded it into the rifle.

A deep breath. I closed my eye. The other one couldn't ever close, obviously, but it *could* be shut off if I wanted it to and did so automatically when it detected me going to sleep. This was the part where most people couldn't take it; it took patience. If I was being honest, I didn't really have much either. I'd usually pull up a book on my eye software, reading the semitransparent words in midair while keeping watch on my target.

Tonight, I couldn't possibly sit still that long all on my own. I couldn't keep my mind off Darius . . . and myself. In only an instant, in a single awful moment, our relationship had been shattered into a million pieces.

When you're out there, you're never on your own.

What happens, though, Darius, when *you're* the one I'm scared of?

The serving staff arrived in the target room to start setting up. It was going to be a while. I couldn't take it. I needed *somebody* to talk to. I stayed in place, still ready to take the shot once the target showed up, but I pulled out the burner phone again and dialed.

"Operations."

"Snipe."

"Hey, girl. Thought we weren't gonna hear from you for over an hour. Did it start early?"

No doubts in Kev's mind, of course. He assumed I was already done. I was a professional. I did this for a living. In addition to the jobs I did for my brother and his gang, I contracted out to other groups, individuals with money and a vendetta . . . even some police, under the table, a couple of times. We still cleared every single target, made sure they were people who needed to die, but it gave us some extra income, built up my reputation, and also served to divorce Snipe the contract killer from certain affiliation with Darius.

A step removed. Darius was no more related to Snipe than anyone else in Seattle's underground.

Did he have any relationship to Kara, the girl behind the rifle with the eye and the messed-up arm that had to be rebuilt with state-of-the-art technology? The girl who loved to read and play pranks and would do anything for him? Were we even siblings?

"Just . . . just needed somebody to talk to."

"You got it. Quiet night here; we aren't running anything else. What's on your mind?"

I couldn't tell him *that*. He didn't even know Darius and I were related. *If* we were. Kev *was* one of the few people who knew I was completely loyal and not just a killer-for-hire, but still . . . there was so much I could never tell anyone.

"I dunno. I just feel off."

"Do we need to call off the hit?"

"No, not that. Just . . . antsy, I guess?"

Kev chuckled. "Girl, you're going in reverse on me. How's someone like you get more antsy over the years, not less?"

I winced. "Talk to me? Help me get my mind off it."

"Want me to call him?" We never said Darius's name on the line, even with how solid our encryption was. While Kev didn't know we were related, he *did* know Darius had brought me in and knew more about me than anyone else.

"Isn't he in a meeting?"

Darius was down in Portland tonight, dealing with one of our rivals. They were flooding the market with bad sims, using the same hacked implants we'd developed but without following the safety protocols we'd set up. Ours were more lax than the usual, but still . . . if you went too far, you could cause serious brain damage or end up effectively torturing somebody.

"Yeah, and bored out of his mind, I'm sure. Those guys just argue and argue for hours until they finally give in."

"But calling him away would be a huge insult to them. He'd lose face."

"True enough. You know this game better than I do; I'm just the guy on the keyboard."

Normally, I'd take that as a compliment. Who doesn't love hearing they're good at something? I prided myself on being able to navigate my brother's world so effectively, without disruption, doing as much for him as I could.

"What about you?"

"What about me?"

"How . . . how are you?"

Kev didn't answer for a moment. He knew it was a seriously weird question for the operations line, *especially* in the middle of an op. I actually fidgeted in place a little, which was completely unlike me. I never fidgeted when I was in position. Finally, just as I was starting to think he was going to call Darius anyway, he spoke up again.

"I'm not sure what's going on with you, girl, and I'm here for you for anything, but you know we can't get into personals."

Of course. What was I thinking? Kev was right—we didn't get personal. This was a business, less than legitimate but still operating on those lines. We were a team and we could have camaraderie, but we didn't go past that. None of the mess all the other gangs got into, with emotions running high, grudges everywhere, personal vendettas, the works. We had a job. We did our job. We went home at the end of the day.

Except for me; home was with Darius. I didn't have anyone else. I didn't have friends like the others did, or anyone else to connect with. Home was still part of the job, because my whole world was this.

My whole life was a lie.

"Yeah, sorry." I took another breath, clearing my throat, clearing my mind. "I'll call you later when it's done."

"You sure? I'm worried about you."

"I'm good. Thanks."

"You got it."

He hung up. Kev knew better than to question me once I got back in the zone. Not that I *was* back, but I could fake it well enough. I was still uncomfortable. I kept fidgeting, shifting around in place, though my rifle remained steady and out of sight from the window.

The guests finally started to arrive, many minutes later. One by one, they trickled in. I waited for my target. I hadn't learned his name—I usually didn't, unless I was working it solo—but I'd been given more than enough of an idea of what he did . . . and why he needed to die.

The world isn't a terrible place, but it's made worse by terrible people.

Aren't we a little bit terrible too, Darius? I kill people for a living.

I couldn't resolve it in my mind anymore. Darius's words had always been a comfort to me until now. I felt like he'd torn that away too, just as he had everything else. All his justifications, all his well-reasoned advice, echoing in his gentle voice through my mind . . . everything was just so hollow now.

The target entered the room.

I took another deep breath. My arm slid over the desk ever so slightly as I made minute adjustments, tracking him through the room. My scope worked in tandem with the range finder in my other eye, helping me aim. I could work without it most days—and I'd trained hard to make sure I could operate without if it ever broke down—but tonight, I needed it.

This man was corrupt. He'd stolen from many groups, government institutions, charities, businesses. The money went back into the child trafficking market still huge in the Midwestern States, especially after the breakup of America as a whole. Cascadia and California had done their best to stamp it out, as had the Republic of Texas, but the traffickers always found a way.

Normally, even for someone as awful as this, it wouldn't have been my job. Darius would have made a comment about how terrible he was and possibly encouraged the police to look into him, but we stayed out of public affairs. This was different though. He'd stolen from *us*, taken lobbying money Darius allocated for some reforms he supported in the legislature, and turned it for his own profits.

No one stole from us.

He walked toward the drink cart. I took a breath and held it.

Very carefully, I squeezed the trigger.

My rifle made a *pop*—even with the suppressor, it could never be totally silenced—and the window across the street shattered. The champagne glass in his hand burst. A puff of red blew out from his heart.

He fell to the ground, dead.

I let my breath out again.

It took a couple of seconds for the room to erupt into chaos. By that time, I was already packing up. My rifle contracted and went into my bag. I pulled my jacket back on, hood low and wrapped up tight in a scarf. I slid the window shut, left the room exactly as I'd found it, and exited the building without being seen.

This kill wouldn't get attributed to Darius or his gang. We had a monetary connection, and though we'd cleared every electronic communication the man ever made, Darius couldn't be sure if he'd kept a paper ledger or not. The public would assume he'd been killed for his underground connections, as soon as they came to light (with Darius's help, of course). I'd still get some credit for it, since the underground knew my rifle and my style, but I'd never claim it officially. It was clean, in and out, simple, without a trace.

Just like that, he was gone.

Just like that, Darius had erased my life too. As I hit the street level, I went into the nearest alley. I kept walking, heading toward one of my hideouts—safe houses I'd set up in abandoned or condemned buildings, places to lie low right after a job. Darius knew about some but not all of them, and right now, I needed to get away.

I pulled out my phone.

"Operations."

"It's done."

"Got it. Have a good night, girl. Don't forget to check in. Feel better, all right?"

"Okay. Thanks."

I hung up, then snapped the phone in half with my enhanced arm. It fell in two pieces, which I crushed into the pavement. I was supposed to call my brother next, let him know it was done. He'd get worried, maybe even suspicious, otherwise. But I couldn't. I broke into a sprint, against all my instincts. I needed to run.

For all my life, I'd never wondered about myself. All I remembered was living with Darius, being raised by him, though he was just eighteen and I was twelve. I'd never had friends. I'd never gone to school. I just . . . lived with Darius. My brother.

If he was even my brother.

If he hadn't changed my mind to make me think *that* too. I'd seen the data. I dug through my own implant history and found the logs, buried as they were. Darius couldn't erase the hardware evidence, though he'd scrubbed everything else clean. He'd found a way, impossible as it seemed, to change my memories.

What could I believe anymore? I'd always had an implant, as far as I knew. I'd always been his little sister. I'd always been . . . like this. A killer. Right?

I love you, Kara. Be safe.

I had to know. I had to figure out who I was, what he'd done, and who I could trust. I needed to know what was real and what was just Darius's creation. If all those hours teaching me, helping me grow into this person—someone I'd been proud of until only days before—keeping me safe, playing games with me . . . if any of it was true. I needed to know if Darius was real.

If he wasn't? If my brother was one of the terrible people? If he'd done this to me and who knew what else?

There wasn't a single thing in the world that could stop me from killing him.

CHAPTER 2

I still had to worry about cops.

One of the downsides of keeping myself sort of disconnected from Darius's gang was that I didn't get to enjoy all of its protections. Darius had an understanding with the cops. Our gang actually worked to keep the streets clean and made sure its product was safe to use. After a fashion, we were the real enforcement in these districts, since so many people were hooked. *Nobody* would dare risk getting on our bad side. If they did, they got a visit from Darius's men.

If they *really* went too far, they got a visit from me.

In turn, the cops mostly ignored us, unless any of ours stepped out of line. They had enough to deal with and already outsourced a ton of work to security firms owned by the big corps anyway. Darius worked with the police and the prosecutors, discreetly getting our people out of any jams. New cops on the force quickly got the picture from the veterans—nothing was official, but whatever Darius said, went. Even the corps knew it, and knew Darius was their best bet to keep things quiet and profitable.

Problem was, most people didn't know Snipe the assassin was part of that group.

That was by design. For one, it gave me even more of a scary reputation. If I was this good and I worked *solo*, I had some real power. Like Darius said . . . except I was trying not to think about Darius.

The cops weren't in on this latest job. Darius said they couldn't overlook murder—that was where they drew the line. Anytime I was around a cop, I always got nervous. What if they figured out I was the wanted killer they were all looking for? Everybody knew Snipe was a teenage girl with a sniper rifle. That sort of description gets *everyone's* attention.

Worse, somebody else was in town: another young female assassin. She used the same cartridge as me, a pretty uncommon new variant of the .338 Lapua, and *she* had no problem killing cops when jobs got messy. The police hadn't realized there were two different rifles, and now they assumed I was a cop killer.

It bothered me a lot. Besides the obvious—I'd never kill cops, unless they fit Darius's list—the other killer was just . . . bad. Whoever she was, all her kills were really sloppy. She was taking jobs I'd seen but turned down, and none of them were *for* cops, so all of it was just . . . unnecessary.

We're not in this for money. We're filling a need and doing it in a way that still helps everyone. If we weren't here, somebody else would do it, and they wouldn't care how many people they hurt.

Except he hurt me, and I still didn't know why—or how much.

The closest safe house was a squat, condemned apartment building at the end of the street, situated in a row of other unremarkable buildings. The whole block looked seedy, like it was just begging to get torn down and replaced with something new and shiny, like they were always doing in most of Seattle.

They had the money, after all, since most of the world still used the software and technology developed in the Silicon Forest. Cascadia was a powerhouse on the world stage, the Switzerland of the Pacific Northwest, staying out of all the erupting wars and keeping tightly secured borders. Refugee applications were an ever-growing nightmare for the government, as so many fled the civil war still raging on the East Coast or tried to escape dystopian nightmares in Asia.

At least I knew all of *that* was real.

I stole into the alleyway next to the building. The front doors were boarded up tight—and I'd added my own extra layer of security behind the wooden boards—while the alley was fenced off. I just pulled the gap aside. Sometimes, a simple fence was all I needed to keep people out.

Above the alley was an old-fashioned metal fire escape. I looked up into the rain, closing my left eye and letting the other one do the hard work. It could filter out the thick rain to let me see clearly, even as water soaked my face and hair. I ran toward the wall and then up, using a kick to propel me high enough to grab the bars. The ladder slid down, quiet and easy thanks to how often I oiled and cleaned it.

I scurried up the cold metal, wishing I'd remembered to put on my gloves. Every rain-slicked step was slippery and dripping with rain, but I made it to the top floor without any problems. The first and second floors were still boarded up, and I didn't bother to use them.

Instead, I kept to the third floor, because—thanks to the last enterprising occupant—it still had power. This was actually one of my favorite safe houses, since many of the others didn't share the same amenities. Power fed into the building through a combination of discreet, ancient solar panels still installed on the roof, plus an illegal tap into a neighbor's power supply. I'd never used enough to impact their bill, but it was good to know I had it if I needed it.

At the top of the fire escape, I drew my pistol out of my bag, just in case, and I waited. I'd pressed the button next to the door. Now, after a mental count to five, I opened it and immediately closed it. Another mental count to five, and I opened the door again. A quiet little chirp of electronics greeted me, confirming I'd disabled the security system. It was a singsong tune . . . one Darius used to hum when he tucked me in.

Everything in my life pointed to him. Wasn't there *anything* that was just me? Where was Kara in Darius's life?

This safe house was mine. I held on to that. Darius didn't know about it. He'd given me the rifle, the eye and arm, even the bag on my shoulder and the clothes on my back. I hadn't really picked any of them. I *liked* them . . . I think.

Did I like them, or was this just me convincing myself to make Darius happy?

Oh god . . .

I felt bile rising in my throat. I started walking down the hallway toward the bathroom. Like the electricity, it still functioned, though not very well. I usually tried to avoid using it, but right now, I was going to throw up. Halfway across the hall, I broke into a run.

Slamming the door open, I rushed inside, dropped the pistol on the ground, flung the toilet seat up, fell onto my knees, and let go.

An instant later, I noticed the terrified girl next to me.

She was crouched in the decrepit bathtub, eyes wide, clutching the shower curtain in a vague attempt to hide. I guessed she was probably my age, maybe a bit older. She wore ragged clothes, a few holes in her shirt, torn jeans. Only her thick jacket really seemed okay. To my surprise, though, she didn't really give off the typical homeless smell, and when I looked closer, I saw her clothes were fairly well kept, although long past their expiration date.

As I sat up a little, she flinched.

". . . Hi," I finally choked out. I dropped my bag on the bathroom tile and reached over for the toilet paper to wipe my face.

She was frozen in terror, her eyes locked onto my own. For a moment, I thought she was staring at my other eye, but I was still wearing my shaded glasses, so that couldn't be it. She couldn't see that one.

The cybernetic one.

One of those memories Darius had probably taken. As far back as I could remember, my right eye had always been that way. I'd never had a real eye there, but I didn't really mind. The cybernetic one did so much for me. It had three lenses, two for sight and one for thermals, and contained a full operating system linked to the inlays built into my right arm.

I could use it for all sorts of things. I kept books on it, notes, pictures, recordings . . . It didn't have any kind of network connection—both Darius and I thought having a device *that* connected to my body with an internet hookup besides was a terrible idea—but on the whole, it was an incredible piece of technology, and one-of-a-kind.

Cybernetics were still pretty new, even in Cascadia, and most were huge ugly pieces. My eye actually fit into my socket, even with all the additional sensors and whatnot. They'd tried to color it to match my left eye, even giving it a sort of blue tint for the center, but there was no truly concealing what it looked like, not this close up. If I didn't have the glasses on, it'd be obvious.

"How'd—" I started, but was cut off by a coughing fit. I cleared out my throat, wiped my face with another sheet of paper, and tried again. "How'd you get in here?"

The girl didn't answer. She was still frozen, though shivering slightly. I wondered if she was cold. I thought about offering her my jacket, but I didn't want to scare her any more than I already had. The pistol was still sitting on the floor next to me, so I picked it up and put it back in my bag.

"I'm not gonna hurt you, okay?" I said carefully. "I just want to know how you got in." After all, she'd gotten past my security without setting it off. No alerts, no alarms, and all my stuff was intact, even my toothbrush on the counter next to the bomb implanted in the wall.

"I watched you," she mumbled.

"Huh?"

She cleared her throat. "The last few times you've come here. I watched you go in and out. Memorized your whole thing, all the timing." The girl shrugged. "Seems kinda dumb not to have a password or anything on it. Aren't you supposed to be a big-shot assassin?"

I raised an eyebrow. "You've heard of me?" It wasn't *that* surprising, but this girl didn't really seem like the connected type.

"Snipe, right? Scary teenage girl with a sniper rifle who'll kill for a price but's super picky about jobs. Where's the big gun, anyway?" she added, glancing around. She seemed to be less scared now that we were talking. Her stringy brown hair kept falling into her mouth as she talked, and she brushed it away every time. I wondered why she didn't just put it up.

"Somewhere else." I hesitated. Something didn't quite add up. My hand tensed, ready to jump back into my bag for my pistol if I needed it. "So wait, you know who I am . . . and you were still going to try and steal from me?" It was the only explanation I could think of. I kept a good pile of emergency cash here, along with ammo and other supplies.

"I wasn't gonna steal from you," she said, a little indignant. "I just took some food, used your shower—"

"You used *that?*" I asked, dumbfounded. I'd never wanted to use it, partly because I didn't want to use that much water here and risk it being noticed, but also because it just looked gross.

"Yeah. It gets pretty warm and it's not actually dirty. It just *looks* awful. You know how hard it is to find a warm, clean, *private* shower?"

"I—"

"And of course I wouldn't take your money," she went on, barreling over me without a moment's hesitation.

Suddenly, she was getting more bold. I'd never really met someone like her. I was used to people listening to me very carefully, since they knew what I could do to them, but this girl both knew . . . and didn't care, I guess. It was weirdly refreshing.

"I bet you're great at tracking people down who don't want to be found. Stealing money from professional hit men seems like a bad life move. Err, sorry. Hit women."

I shrugged. "Probably smart."

"Besides, even if I did, how am I gonna explain carrying that much cash? I don't put out and I don't got a job. I'm just a homeless kid in public high school. If I got picked up, I'd be screwed."

I wondered what high school was like. I'd never been to one. I'd caught snippets from TV shows, but I didn't watch much TV either. Only bits and pieces occasionally when I was scoping out a target.

The girl winced. I guess some kind of look crossed my face, stealing her momentum. "So, yeah," she finished, looking cautious again. ". . . What happens to me now?"

"I haven't really decided yet," I said carefully.

Truthfully, I knew I wasn't going to kill her. Like I said before, we only killed people who needed to die. This girl didn't need to die, as far as I knew. It might be a risk and put me in real danger, but I couldn't. Darius might disagree, might put operational security above the life of a homeless teenage girl, but I wouldn't.

Especially after everything I'd learned over the last few days.

"Screw it," she said, the beginning of an outburst. Like a breached dam, words flowed out in a crashing stream, but still perfectly articulated. If nothing else, the girl was an amazing speaker, and she had lungs of *steel*. I wished I could hold my breath as long as she could.

"You're gonna kill me, right? You're the badass gangster sniper assassin. Nobody can see you up close and live to tell the tale, yeah? So here I was, going to school, living day-to-day, and saving up whatever I can. You ever lived on a single school lunch a day? God, it sucks. Then, there's the older guys kicking me out of their alleys 'cause I won't sleep with 'em but can't fight 'em off. I finally find my own alley in the middle of nowhere but still kinda close to my school, next to some godforsaken apartment, and look at that? It's got food, power, and *hot water*. I hit *gold*. But yeah, of *course* it's a weapons cache for the deadliest chick this side of I-Five, who catches me just a *day* after I move in."

She was out of breath, panting after her rant. I took the moment to jump in before she could keep going.

"I'm not gonna kill you."

"Bullshit," she shot back immediately. "Prove it."

My first instinct was to toss my gun out—but luckily, I realized how dumb that'd be. Instead, I started thinking of the real possibilities. This girl was obviously intelligent, and she knew the streets. Someone like that was an asset. She'd be too proud to take straight charity, and I didn't blame her for that, but I could pay her to work.

Besides, something about her was really growing on me. I just wanted her to keep talking. I needed someone to fill the silent, musty air of the hideout.

"You can help me."

She clearly hadn't expected that. Her eyes flicked over to the bag, where my pistol had gone, then back to me.

"Why?" she asked. "Couldn't you just kill me right now and not really have a problem?"

I shrugged. This girl was too smart for me to lie to her, and I didn't want to anyway. I'd been dealing with too many lies lately. "Yeah, probably."

She hesitated. My answer had done the trick, keeping her off-guard. "Are you gonna let me go?"

"If you want."

Again, she was thrown off. "So you'll let me leave, unharmed, even though I stole your food and you know I could just give away your hideout to the police, to other gangs besides yours, anybody who might want you dead?"

"Yes."

She grinned. "Is this the part where you tell me you're in love with me or some bullshit like that?"

I rolled my left eye. "You're not my type, sorry."

"Oh good. You had me worried for a sec. You don't want to go down that road, trust me."

"Only for a second?" I asked, trying for a joke.

"Well, the whole I-just-ran-in-here-with-a-gun-and-could-kill-you-right-now bit was pretty terrifying, but I got over it." She laughed.

I got up and strapped my bag over my arm again. I trusted her enough to turn my back and splashed some water on my face from the sink. I could still see her with my other eye, turning it upward to watch her through the mirror. She hadn't moved, but she did finally drop the shower curtain and looked a lot more relaxed.

"So you're Snipe, huh?"

"Yeah." I turned off the faucet and leaned back against the wall casually.

"How'd you get such a dumb name? No offense."

"Somebody with a dumb imagination."

"That sucks. If I were you, I'd 've come up with something way better. Something cool and intimidating. Who's scared of *Snipe*?"

"Something like what?" I asked, smiling slightly. I'd thought the same, but I'd never come up with anything. And, by this time, I was comfortable with "Snipe" anyway. Besides, it wasn't from Darius . . . Right now, that was a positive.

The girl hesitated, puzzled. "Huh. Nope, I can't think of anything. You got me. I guess it's harder than it looks, coming up with a cool name. Guess I sympathize with parents more, actually. I mean, *Faith?* Who names their kid after a concept? Some neo-hippie freaks, probably. Glad I never met 'em, child-abandoning assholes. Oh, hell," she added, glancing at me.

I *knew* a look had crossed my face that time. I glanced away, back into the hall, avoiding Faith's gaze.

"Sorry . . . I didn't mean to bring up anything rough."

"It's fine."

Faith didn't look convinced. She seemed even more uncomfortable than I was. Her eyes fell to the ground, with brief flickers toward the door. She was thinking about making a run for it.

I *really* didn't want her to leave.

"Do you want to stay here?"

Her head snapped back up. "Huh?"

I shrugged. "This place is pretty safe for now, and like you said, power, water, and food." Besides, it wasn't my most valuable hideout anyway. Just the best one Darius didn't know about. I had a couple more if I needed them.

". . . For now?" she asked pointedly. She didn't miss a beat.

"Yeah."

"Meaning . . . what, you're not sure you're good with your people?"

I glanced back at the hallway, which was still empty. Rain continued to pound on the ceiling and seemed to be getting louder, but there were only a few leaks in this building. Nothing too serious. "They don't know about this place."

"If I found it, somebody else could," Faith said thoughtfully. "That fire escape isn't super stealthy. Of course, it doesn't gotta be the only way in and out. There's another way."

"What?"

She grinned. "You never noticed? Why do you think this place smells so awful? There's a chained-up sewer grate in the basement, under all the scrap metal. It looks like it got backed up or something."

"Ugh," I groaned. That explained so much about this place. I'd seen the padlocked grating, but I'd just assumed it was a crawl space or something, not a *sewer exit*.

"Yeah, no wonder nobody ever wanted to live here." Faith shrugged. "Works for us, though, if we gotta make a getaway. Both of us are small enough to squeeze out that way, long as you got some bolt cutters in your stash." I must have made another face, because she grinned again. "Speaking of which, you cool if I grab some food? I haven't eaten dinner yet."

I nodded, glad to get off the subject of sewers. "Go for it."

Faith carefully stepped out of the tub and onto the bathroom tile and slowly made her way out of the room. I was too distracted to pay much attention, as my other eye had just flashed a low-battery warning. I started digging in my bag for one of my backups, only to realize I'd forgotten them. I'd been missing a lot of things lately . . . I'd considered calling off the job tonight, but I knew that would constitute a warning for Darius.

I couldn't risk him realizing yet. I also couldn't risk going near him. If I saw him, I don't think I could keep it in.

I walked into the hall and sat down on the dusty carpet next to an outlet, stretching out my legs. Faith peeked in a moment later, holding a box of cereal way past its expiration date. She was eating straight out of the box, clearly not bothered in the slightest by how stale it was.

"Got any milk?"

I shook my head. "It expires too fast. I don't get out here very much. But there's a bunch of water."

"*Bottled* water?" she asked, smirking. "Breaking the law, aren't ya?"

"They're reusable glass bottles," I said, rolling my left eye.

She grinned and went back to the refrigerator in the little kitchen, leaving me alone again. I felt weirdly relaxed, after how stressful the last few days had been. Something about Faith was making me feel safe. I wasn't ready to call her a *friend* or anything, but . . . this felt different, and right then, I really needed different.

The battery alert flashed on my other eye again. It still had probably a half hour to go, but I wasn't going to let it run dry. That was the *worst* feeling, suddenly losing almost all my sight. My other eye was way better than my left eye, even at just the normal seeing part. It was a part of me. I never thought of it as a cybernetic eye or anything like what Darius and the other people who saw me did. To me, it was just one of my two eyes.

I took out my charging cable and plugged it into the wall, then carefully set it into my other eye. It took a couple of hours to charge for a full week of life. I couldn't plug it in while I was asleep, so I always had to set aside a bit of time to charge. It wasn't good at quick breaks either. If I stood up without disconnecting it, it pulled at the socket *hard*. I'd had a really sore face for a long time after doing that. I went for charging it every day rather than once a week, preferring to keep the amount of power in the higher ranges and never have to stay still for too long.

Of course, this week, I'd completely forgotten. Now I had to spend a whole hour at least, if not longer, with the cord trailing out of my vision. I pulled up a book to distract myself while the tiny meter in the corner of my vision started ticking back upward.

"What the hell?"

Faith dropped the two glass bottles of water she'd just come back with. I winced, but to my relief, they didn't shatter. She ignored them, transfixed by my face. "You've got a cord sticking out of your face. You know that, right? I mean, yeah, of course you do; it's not like somebody just plugged it in without you knowing. Why do you have a cable going into your face? Are you a robot?"

I snorted. I couldn't help it. "No. I'm still human. Mostly." I waved my hand to dismiss the book.

"Okay, not a robot." Faith's shock was subsiding a bit now. "Android, then. Wait no, cyborg. That's the one. Replaced body parts. And you've got an eye replaced. Okay then. Why do you have to plug it in?"

"It's low on batteries."

It was Faith's turn to snort now. "*Low on batteries,*" she echoed. "You've got a *cybernetic eye,* and it runs on rechargeable batteries like anything else? Whose dumb idea was *that?*"

"Dunno."

"That seems super impractical. What if it runs out in the middle of a fight or whatever? Are you just suddenly blind?"

I frowned. "I've got another eye."

"Right, sorry. One-Eyed Sue, that's you." She laughed. "One-Eyed Sue with a big-ass gun." She seemed completely comfortable again. I felt a wave of unexpected relief. For whatever reason, it was super important to me that Faith was okay with my other eye. "Well, since you weren't stabbed in the eye like I thought for a second there, I guess I can keep eating."

She dropped back onto the floor, this time next to Kara. Faith carefully avoided the charging cord, digging into her cereal again. She handed over one of the water bottles.

"Any other fancy electronic bits you got, or do you want to keep 'em a bedroom surprise?"

"Huh?"

"Sorry," said Faith. "I've got terrible friends."

I shrugged and pulled up my sleeve, showing my forearm. They'd done their best to disguise it, but there were still clearly a few patches of metal mixed in with the skin, with the couple of ports where I could plug in drives for updates, along with the sensor patch.

"Shiny. Super strength?"

"Only a little. It mostly just lets me control my eye."

"B-o-o-o-o-ring. They couldn't come up with anything cooler than that?"

I frowned. "I kinda like my arm as it is, thanks."

Faith rolled her eyes. "Screw that. All this cutting-edge, top-of-the-line super-secret tech, and the best they got is a replacement for the mouse and a rechargeable battery eye. I'm genuinely disappointed in our black-market mad scientists." She gave me a sidelong glance. "That *is* where you got this stuff, right? 'Cause I've never heard of anything like this that wasn't *super* experimental."

"Yes."

Faith's eyes twinkled. "Don't suppose they could set me up with something too? I could use a boost to my legs. It's agony just walking around most days."

I glanced over, curious. I hadn't noticed anything wrong with her.

"Oh god, the Cyclops is staring at me." I rolled my left eye. She grinned. "Yeah, I've got leg issues. A car hit me way back, screwed me up. I'm more annoyed that the asshole driving didn't even slow down. I had to drag myself to the emergency room. They've never worked right since."

Faith spoke so quickly and matter-of-factly I knew it was bothering her a lot more than she let on.

"What happened to the driver?"

"Who knows?" She sighed. "Probably off living a normal life. If they can afford a car and gas, they were gonna win any court battle I might've had. So I just go on as a cripple. *C'est la vie.*" She must have noticed my unease, because her face got more serious and the half-sarcastic tone dropped. "Look, I know you're super-assassin girl and whatever, but don't bother with this. Please. I'm good. No need to go righting my wrongs or whatever."

"I wasn't planning that," I said, though truthfully I had considered it for a brief moment. It would be way below my pay grade, but I felt real anger toward this person already.

"Uh-huh. You've got that mindset. And hell, you probably could find 'em, whoever they are. But trust me, it's not worth it." Faith sighed. "Another body on the pile isn't gonna fix anything. Besides, unless I'm mistaken, you're in your own trouble right now, aren't you?"

I took a breath. "Kinda, yeah."

"Mind explaining what?"

"It's . . ." I hesitated. "It's personal."

Faith shook her head. "Okay, yeah, it might be, but your problems are now my problems too, Miss Proprietor. Besides, I might be able to help you out."

"How?" I asked. Before I could think about it, my left eye flicked down to her legs, splayed out across the hallway carpet.

Faith looked offended, and I immediately felt awful. "Hey, I might not be winning any marathons, but I'm not totally helpless. I figured you out, didn't I?"

I shrugged. She really hadn't, at least in my opinion, but she was still already closer to me than the majority of people I'd met in my life.

"Fine," said Faith. "I'll do this the long way." She flipped her stringy brown hair back and tucked it behind her ears, then drew a long, over-dramatic breath.

"You're on the run. You're also Snipe, assassin for the street gang that runs this whole district and the next one over, but you're not good with them right now. Maybe it's 'cause of one of the side jobs you do, maybe not, I dunno. Point is, you're avoiding them, so you came to a hideout they don't know about, and this happened recently 'cause you're just showing up now. More importantly—and trust me, this isn't common knowledge, but I got my sources—this runs all the way to the top, 'cause *you* run all the way to the top."

Faith paused for breath. I was already a little shocked. It wasn't common knowledge, but there was a vague sense on the street that I was more connected to Darius's gang than most others. Faith somehow knew I was directly connected to Darius himself though. How did a nobody street kid learn something like *that?*

"So if you're in hiding from the gang and you're *super* connected, we got two options: either there's a major restructuring about to go down and you're avoiding the rest of the gang to save Darius, or he's the one you're running from."

Faith took another breath, looking deadly serious. "Either way, you're in *deep* shit."

I let out my own breath, which I hadn't realized I'd been holding.

"So what's our next move?" she asked.

I shook my head. "I don't know."

"Well, can you at least tell me which of those two we're dealing with?"

". . . Running," I whispered.

Faith let out a low whistle. "Well . . . all right then."

"If you want to get out of here, I don't blame you," I said after another pause.

She grinned. "Screw that. I'm not giving up my new home that easy." Faith frowned, glancing at my bag. "When's the last time you spoke to him?"

"Yesterday."

"And you did a job tonight, right?" After I nodded, Faith glanced at the bag again. "Wouldn't you normally check in with him?"

". . . Yeah." A shock like a burst of electricity shot through me. I needed to check in. Darius *couldn't* know anything was wrong, not yet. I couldn't face him yet, but I could call. That much, I could handle for now. I tore the cable out of my other eye, ignoring Faith's wince, and dug through my bag.

My personal phone wasn't there. I started panicking. Where was it? Did I leave it somewhere? If Darius found out I'd lost my phone . . .

I dumped my bag out onto the carpet in a panic. The contents spilled across the floor—water, ammunition, my rifle, a couple of snacks, and other personal keepsakes. I didn't have time to feel embarrassed though. I should have called Darius more than an hour ago. He was meticulous about time. He'd already be worried.

"What are we looking for?" Faith asked uneasily.

"My phone."

She nodded and bent forward over the pile, avoiding moving her legs. "Well, a phone should really stand out in all *this*. Is that a hand grenade?"

"Yes," I answered impatiently, digging through the magazines. Bullets clinked against one another, but the phone wasn't buried between them. Faith lifted the grenade aside gingerly, avoiding the firing pin like it was burning.

"Definitely not a typical teenage girl's bag . . ." she muttered to herself. Faith spotted my half-open diary, the old handwritten one I used to keep before I fixed my virtual keyboard, and quickly handed it over. "I'm no spy."

I took it gratefully and put it back in the bag.

"Well . . ." Faith said dejectedly. "No phone."

I nodded. "And I don't have any other way to contact him."

"So what's our next move?"

"You're really serious about joining up with me?"

"Well, yeah, Kara, I'm on your side now."

I froze. ". . . How do you know my name?"

"Huh?"

I was more forceful. *Nobody* knew my name. "How did you find out my name?"

Faith glanced at the bag, embarrassed. "It was on one of the pages of the diary. I didn't really think it was a big deal. I mean, yeah, everybody calls you Snipe, but you said it yourself—dumb name. I figured you'd prefer Kara. Is it short for something?"

"No."

I felt exposed. Faith had a piece of information I'd kept secret for six long years now. Only two people in the whole organization knew my real name: Darius and his closest lieutenant. The diary normally never left my home—and honestly, I'd forgotten I'd ever written my name in it—but I'd brought it along tonight.

I wasn't expecting to go home ever again.

How stupid could I be, dumping out my whole bag in front of Faith? I'd had this protection my whole life, an escape Darius guaranteed for me. If I ever wanted to leave, adopt my real name and be normal, he'd made sure it was never linked to anything in our line of work. Except now . . . Faith knew it. Someone I'd only just met.

"Look," Faith said carefully. "I'm sorry. Really. I wouldn't've mentioned it, but I figure you should know I saw it. I can totally forget it too. Look, you're Snipe again. All good, yeah? No names here, just hippie-cripple-girl and dumb bird, that's us."

I finally let out a sigh. I'd live with it. And if Faith ever became a problem, or if I decided I couldn't trust her . . . well . . .

"It's okay. Just keep it to yourself."

Faith grinned. "Keep it better hidden next time, huh? But hey, secret keeping is my business. Your secret identity is safe with me."

I rolled my left eye. "You make me sound like a superhero or something."

"What kind of superhero kills people for a living?" asked Faith, her tone oddly light for a question that had been weighing on me for days, haunting my thoughts and keeping me awake long into the endless rainy nights. I killed people for a living, but I'd always considered myself a good person. Was that just something else he'd instilled in me?

Was Kara even my real name?

I didn't have an answer for Faith.

CHAPTER 3

We went back down the fire escape. I helped Faith descend—I had no idea how she'd even managed to get up in the first place. The moment she landed on the ground, her legs nearly gave out completely. As we headed back out onto the street, jackets pulled tight to ward off the rain, her rolling gait became more obvious.

It wasn't nearly as bad as I'd feared, but still, it stood out. Between one leg in pain and one that simply didn't look right in the first place, Faith walked with a perpetual limp. She did her best to hide it, and at a distance, most people probably wouldn't notice, but I was already paranoid.

I'd make do. There was no way I was abandoning her already, and she seemed to feel the exact same.

"Not that one," Faith said as we got near a convenience store. I peered through the dimly lit windows, confused—what was wrong with that store?

She shrugged. "The dick who runs the place once tried to . . . you know."

"Oh." I winced. Faith shrugged it off, never stopping for a second.

I'd offered to just go buy a phone on my own, but Faith insisted on accompanying me. I wasn't sure if it was because she was afraid I'd never come back or she felt guilty about calling me a murderer. I hadn't really minded the comment—I mean, I'm not so blind as to think I'm not a killer, but everyone I've ever taken out was part of the game—but I *did* want Faith to think well of me.

Right now, though, I needed to get in touch with Darius. I was steeling myself for that conversation already. As calm as I could manage, nothing off balance, nothing unusual. Tell him the job's done, tell him everything's okay, and get off the phone as fast as I could. He'd be finishing up the negotiations in Portland anyway and heading home. We wouldn't talk long.

We reached the next store a couple of blocks down and headed in. Faith pretended to read a magazine idly by the front door, keeping watch for anyone suspicious, while I grabbed a few prepaid phones off the rack. I went for just one model above the cheapest—the absolute bargain bins were honeypots stacked with spyware, everybody knew that. We'd piggybacked into that system ourselves.

I took them to the guy behind the counter. He barely noticed, lost in his VR sim. I had to rap on the plastic to get his attention, since I was paying cash instead of credit or coins. Grumbling, he spun the tray, took off the security locks, and spun back my change, waving me away.

Under any other circumstances, I'd be annoyed. The guy's got one *easy* job to do, and he couldn't even manage that. He didn't deserve a cent of the money I'd just laid down. Today, though, I was just grateful to get in and out with as little interaction as possible. I didn't say a word.

Faith, on the other hand, had *plenty* to complain about.

"Common decency just isn't a thing anymore," she ranted as we walked even farther from my hideout.

We were going to a nearby alley she'd declared safe—which I also knew to be a quiet zone, further validating her street knowledge—so the location would trace back far away from me, in the unlikely event the burner was tapped.

"Sure, a Seven-Eleven jerkoff was probably just as rude before the big sim revolution, but hey, at least they *acknowledged* you. Now everybody's lost in their little escapist fantasies, letting the world go to waste 'cause they barely live in it."

She stopped for breath. It was harder for her to rant while we walked, since she wasn't in great shape and her legs made every step harder. I was mostly tuning her out anyway, still watching out for possible threats. My other eye labeled everyone on the street with a faint orange square, keeping track of them for me as I swiveled. If I needed to mark a real target, they'd light up red, and I could watch them more closely.

We turned into the alley while Faith kept going. She trailed off and leaned against the wall, taking a few deep breaths to steady herself. I'd activated the phones right after we stepped out of the store, and they were finally connecting as we settled in.

After a couple of moments of fiddling, I tossed one of the phones to her.

"What?"

"Yours. I programmed the first line with this one's number"—I patted the second phone—"so you can reach me."

"Cool." She grinned and pocketed the phone with a wink. "It's about time I had a phone. Now I can finally call up that cute boy over on Fifteenth Street and get laid."

I rolled my left eye. "I didn't load it up with much. If you need more minutes, take some cash, but be discreet."

"I know, I know." Faith put on an exaggerated pout. "I'll get my boys the old-fashioned way."

I scanned the alleyway one last time, for my own paranoia's sake, then gestured to Faith. She got the hint right away and hurried down to the end, taking up a spot at the wall and launching a game on the phone, looking for all the world like a bored teenager. I crouched down in the trash-filled alley, huddling behind a dumpster.

The rain continued to drizzle, much lighter than the downpour earlier, but still creating a faint staccato beat on the metal next to me. I shivered and pulled my scarf tighter around my neck, bundling up as I pressed the cheap plastic phone up to my ear, the ringer so close it caused my skin to vibrate.

"Hello?"

I flinched. A gravelly, deep rumble of a voice had answered the phone. It wasn't Darius's. This was his bodyguard, a conniving brute who went by the name Hammer. He'd answered the phone and he was going to be as obstinate as he was to anyone who called Darius's personal number. More importantly, he'd never trusted me, seeing me as something between a rival to him and a genuine threat to Darius.

I couldn't decide if it was worse that he answered, or that Darius didn't.

"Hello?" he asked again. I should've known I wouldn't reach my brother. An unrecognized number was never going to get straight to Darius. They'd always keep him a few steps removed, in case of a sting op or ongoing hack. Hammer would answer all his calls, and nobody ever got to talk to Darius direct.

Probably not even me, but I was desperate. I needed Darius to think everything was normal.

"Let me talk to him."

". . . That you, Snipey?" I heard some shuffling in the background. Was that Darius? Something was going on, but nobody else came to the phone.

"Yes. Put him on."

"We gotta talk first. You didn't check in. It's been hours," he drawled, obviously enjoying himself.

"Phone's gone. Something came up."

"Well, what happened?"

"It's done. Clean, no trace, the usual."

"Really?" Hammer sounded surprised, which seemed off. It *had* been clean. Why was he giving me the runaround here? I should be talking to Darius already. "If it was so clean, why didn't you check in for hours?"

"It's personal. Could you just put him on already?"

"Can't. Ongoing security incident."

I hesitated. That was a pretty standard reply, but I usually got a heads-up about those. There was an automated ping, and it would have hit my backup pager, even if I didn't have my phone. I didn't know about any security incident. What was Hammer talking about?

"Well . . . tell him it's done, and that I'll call him later."

"You got it."

Hammer hung up. I pocketed the burner, more than a little confused . . . but I shook it off. If there was a security incident, I would have been pinged. Our backup paging system was rock-solid. Hammer was probably just being an asshole, and I was almost certain I'd heard Darius in the background. He'd know it was me—Hammer had used my code name out loud.

I'd get him back for this later.

"All good?" Faith asked from the front of the alley.

"Yeah."

"Cool—shit, I was doing well," she moaned as her phone made a beeping noise. "Lost my snake again."

"You were *actually* playing a game?" I asked as we started walking back down the street, taking a slightly roundabout path to the hideout.

She shrugged. "I was bored, and we're just coming off a rainstorm out here. Nobody's around. I was still keeping watch and doing the best impression of a bored teenager I could pull off."

"You mean a legitimate one?"

Faith laughed. "Exactly."

When we got back to the hideout, I helped Faith awkwardly clamber up the fire escape again. She did it without complaint, but I decided right then: either I'd figure out an easier way for her to get in and out, or we were heading to another hideout tomorrow. Once inside, she made a beeline for the bedroom, muttering something about the boy on 15th Street and how cold the bed was. I rolled my left eye, still not quite sure if her would-be paramour actually existed.

I wasn't tired yet though. The aftereffects of adrenaline were still working their way out of my system. I didn't always get a rush from a job, but tonight's had set me off. I needed exercise to flush it out, and that meant the staircase.

It was an old, rickety thing, spiraling up the side of the building, and every other wooden step creaked and groaned. I knew which ones to avoid after the third or fourth trip, exhausting myself bit by bit. As I climbed, I flicked through my eye menu, diving into recordings I'd saved. I kept a lot of them over the years in low quality, stored in the flash memory embedded in my forearm's circuits.

There was an audio jack in my arm as well—not wireless, of course. Nothing that could be connected without my knowledge. I had to climb in a slightly weird posture to make sure the buds didn't get pulled out from my arm swinging too wide, but I made it work. I needed to see and hear everything.

I went straight to the oldest recording I had—five years ago, when I was eleven, a year after I'd gotten the eye, according to Darius. My eleventh birthday, when he'd first set up the recording software. I wondered now if it'd always been there, and he'd just hidden it from me until then.

I queued it up. The video floated in front of me as I climbed up and down the stairs, my own voice as a kid, along with my brother's, filling my ears.

"Dar, can I take this out yet?"

"Keep still."

"But it feels weeeird . . ."

"I know. I had to swap out a few components on your arm to give it storage space."

"How much?"

"Enough."

"So I can take pictures and stuff now?"

"Yes, and video. Hold on a second . . . There."

The video feed flickered to life. There I was, looking at myself on a computer screen, as my other eye recorded a reflection of me.

"How do you do that?"

"Do what?"

"Make it look a different direction than your real eye."

I shrugged. "They're both real."

"Yes, but . . ." Darius sighed.

The video feed twisted around to him sitting next to me, my arm laid out on a folding workbench next to my bed. His tools were scattered all over my blankets. I sat perfectly still, my other eye now leaping around rapidly between him, his tools, the computer screen, and the mirror.

"Doesn't that make you dizzy?"

"Ki-i-inda . . ."

The feed jumped up and down a little as I shrugged.

"I dunno. I just do it."

My other eye did a quick scan of the room, obviously showing off how easily I could control it.

We were in our shared bedroom, back in our first home. His bed was across the room, surrounded by computers and servers. Mine only had a single computer, and the rest was taken up by bookshelves, a desk for my learning periods when Darius or the professor would teach me, and my reading chair in the corner with a few stuffed animals.

"That's incredible," said the doctor from off-screen. "She has perfect control and can move them independently. Her brain doesn't stop her in the slightest."

"Well, anyone can, right?"

"Yes, but it's not useful to do that. Except in her case, it is, and her brain recognizes it."

The speaker mounted near the door clicked. Darius's newest lieutenant Michael Dunham's voice echoed into the room.

"Darius, Seventh Street is gone. I shot Polarski, and we got the rest of them running. We're back on track."

Darius hurried over to the speaker to answer. After all, nobody was ever allowed in this room except for the doctor, the professor, and Darius—and the other two weren't allowed to know my name either. This was a space just for me and Darius, nobody else.

Our home.

"Thanks, Michael. I'll be down soon."

The doctor's voice, a little muffled, was full of concern. My eye was still darting around the room, but it never landed on the doctor. I was busy looking at my books, trying to see if I could read them from so far away.

"Is it all right for her to be listening to something like that?"

"To what?" I asked, still trying to read the books and not turning to look at them.

The doctor hesitated, but clearly still wasn't talking to me. "She's only eleven."

"Did he need to die, Dar?" I asked.

I spun the chair around so the back was facing the books, and leaned over it, letting my hair fall down in a curtain in front of my face. I wanted to see how well the eye was handling seeing through it now—Darius said it could calculate around the strands and reproduce the whole picture on the other side with fancy algorithms. He was still working on it, but it already seemed to do really well.

"Yes," said Darius firmly. "He did."

"Okay," I replied, and hopped off the chair. "Can we have pizza tonight?" The cord pulled taut from my arm, and with a sudden snap—

I stopped at the top of the stairs, panting a little. The recording flickered out, sliding back into the long list of archived files stored in my arm. Five years ago, I was already . . . like this. I didn't have my rifle or any guns apparently, but . . . I was completely okay with a man dying and my brother being responsible.

Back into the apartments. I briefly looked in on Faith, who was sprawled across the sheets of one of the beds, legs laid out straight and tightly bound up in a thick blanket. I slid the door closed as quietly as I could and sat down at the end of the hallway. I dug through my bag and pulled out my rifle.

Before, it was a comfort to me, as much as those stuffed animals in my childhood. I knew that already made me a bit of a freak, but the rifle held a special importance. It was one of a kind, it kept me safe, and it was a gift from my brother. He'd trusted me with something so power-ful and unique, and made sure it was wholly mine. No one else had ever laid a finger on it since he gave it to me.

I took care of it, just like it took care of me. Leaning back against the wall, I pulled out my cleaning kit and expanded the rifle to its full length. I began to polish it and clean every inch, bringing it back to its perfect state, wiping away every flaw and speck of grime until it was made new again.

There was an obvious parallel in my mind, but I refused to acknowl-edge it. I was just taking care of my rifle, nothing more. I might need it later. Who knew what might happen the next day? A major city figure had just been killed. Assassinations like that always set everyone on edge, even in our district. I was just being responsible, getting prepared.

Except for the couple of tears I had to clean off the matte plastic, I almost could have believed it.

I woke up early, long before Faith. My forehead was pressed up against the wood in the corner of the hallway, with the plastic of my rifle leav-ing a mark on my cheek. I blinked away my exhaustion and hurriedly plugged in my eye, not sure how long the battery had left before it ran out of power again, since I hadn't remembered to charge it the night before.

By the time Faith stumbled out of the bedroom, I was already back up to 75 percent or so. She headed into the kitchen with a bleary good morning, before turning right back around and coming out again.

"We're out of cereal."

I raised my eyebrows. "There were two boxes in there yesterday."

"Yeah . . . I ate them."

"You ate *all* of it?"

Faith shrugged. "I gotta maintain my figure somehow."

"How are you not fat?"

"Lucky genes from whoever-the-hell-they-were." Faith shot an apprehensive glance at the door to the fire escape. "Wanna go out?"

Normally, I would have said no. I preferred eating indoors, staying off the streets and especially out of public spaces. Today, I needed to get out of my own head, before I got lost in more self-doubt and confusion—if that were even possible. I already had no idea who I was or if any of my life was real . . . How much worse could it get?

I shuddered at the thought. I didn't want to know the answer to that question.

We ended up going out, just as she suggested. Faith was a heavy sleeper, and I'd been in-and-out all night, so it was already past noon by the time we left the safe house. Faith pointed at a few different places as we walked, but I instinctively turned each one down.

"What, too classy for fast food?"

"No, just . . ."

Faith shrugged. "It's cool. You've got money to burn. How about that?" she asked, pointing at a high-class establishment that was open for lunch. "Best Italian in the district. My guarantee."

"How would you even know that?" I asked, surprised. I mean, I had no clue if she was right or not, but . . . how could she be?

She put on a mock show of offense. "*Excusez-moi,* my dearest *Kara,* I come from the highest stock of Seattle's elite. How could you possibly impugn my refined palate as to suggest I had never been to Tortorella's? *Je suis offusquée!*"

"I . . ." I trailed off, not sure how to respond.

Faith grinned. "Nah, it's cool. I'm street trash, I know it. But seriously, if you ever go there, the *fettuccine al pomodoro* is to die for. No joke." She glanced around, then dropped her voice again. "Is it 'cause you don't want to go somewhere closed up like that?"

After a moment's consideration, I nodded. I didn't like the small restaurants, fast-food or otherwise. I needed more space to better maneuver in, just in case. Lucky for me, Faith was on top of it and had the perfect spot.

"We're going to the mall!"

". . . What?" I asked, confused. I wasn't quite sure if she was making a two-teenage-girls joke or not—and her next sentence didn't help much either.

"Well, now that I'm friends with Miss Moneybags, I want to go shopping." She winked, obviously enjoying the confusion on my face. "The food court's got a dozen options *and* a dozen exits, and it's raining again. The place is gonna be packed. Perfect place to disappear or get out in a hurry." Faith sighed. "If there's anything you can still rely on in Seattle, it's that people still gotta go shopping."

I felt taken aback by her logic. She kept surprising me at every turn . . . and it was weirdly refreshing. Faith led the way, and I followed. Soon enough, we were at the mall, and true to her words, it was *packed*.

In stark contrast to the forlorn abandonment stalking the streets I knew best, the mall was bright, clean, and full of life. Flashing screens flared in every direction, announcing the names of stores, new fashion lines, exciting technologies, makeup, anything somebody might want. I determinedly ignored every single one, but they did their absolute best to get my attention anyway.

Ad companies were always working on the next new trick, and the major malls were among the few places left not covered by strict privacy regulations. In the mall, every ad board was equipped with a dozen cameras, scanning every single shopper as they walked by. A board would reconfigure itself in moments to try and sell to each specific shopper, and they learned over time.

I'd only been here a few times, always for a job, and *still* the ad boards knew me. One of them even had an old alias I'd used for a previous kill. I resisted the urge to put a bullet in it as we walked by.

We made our way up to the food court, taking the elevators for Faith's sake, even though it bothered me. I did my best not to let it show, but I'm sure she noticed. The food court was packed, as expected. Scents of fast food, pastries, fudge, and a whole host of unrecognizable smells wafted across the room so thick I half expected to see a cloud forming above us.

"And look at that, we're in the food court." Faith grinned. "I've got you wrapped around my finger now."

"Uh-huh," I murmured, scanning the court. I was looking for familiar faces, just in case, and I didn't spot any. A few sunbeams poked through the clouds, and a burst of warmth hit my face as one dropped through the glass ceiling.

"I dunno about you, but I'm starving." Faith shot me an embarrassed look. "Don't suppose you could spot me some change, ol' buddy?"

I rolled my eye and dug into my bag, pulling out a wad of bills.

"Uhh, you know this is *way* more than I need for lunch, right?"

"Keep the extra. I've got more."

"Okay." Faith shrugged. "Cool. I'll be right back."

I wandered away, looking for a table, as she took off. My other eye was scanning as best it could, but I was still trying to hide it behind both my glasses and my hair, so it didn't have the greatest view. I found the table I wanted in a corner though—back to the wall, secluded, without anyone nearby to overhear us. I could watch everyone from that spot.

The place bustled with activity. Watching the people here, it was almost easy to forget what the world was drifting toward outside. Couples had tables to themselves. Parents struggled to control overstimulated children. Groups of teenagers wandered around, pretending to be above it all, chatting about fads. It was just the height of capitalism, totally normal.

Until I looked closer.

The clothes were all a bit more ragged than usual, made at lower standards than they used to be and for higher cost. Everyone looked a bit unkempt, a bit detached. They were all bored and disconnected. The world around them didn't really interest them anymore. Everyone was mostly here out of ritual tradition, nothing else. A trip to the mall was normal, and everybody wanted to be normal.

Nothing bad ever happened to normal people.

Once they got home, they could slip back into whatever fantasy they wanted. They'd plug themselves in and abandon the world again, avoid their jobs, their lives, everything. Some of them didn't even last that long. There were several groups of people who had plugged into the power and network outlets attached to every table, visors firmly attached to their faces. They weren't legally allowed to use the visors in a public space like the mall, in a half-hearted attempt to keep people aware of their surroundings, but who was going to follow that rule?

Nobody, obviously. They plugged in, snaked wires up baggy clothes, and covered their implants with long hair or a hood. Soon enough, they faded out into whatever sim they'd brought with them, or even the ones online if they could get a low enough latency.

Was I supposed to be one of them? Lost in a virtual world? Was that normal, and was I supposed to be normal?

"Hey, Cyclops."

I started. I hadn't even noticed her approach with two bags of hot food on a tray.

"I figured you could use something too. I haven't seen you eat anything since I met you, so . . ." She shrugged, digging out a cheeseburger from her bag and sliding the tray across to me. "Anyway, here you go."

Suddenly, I realized I *was* hungry. I'd been feeling so sick and confused over the last few days, I'd eaten far less than I needed, and it wasn't like I wasn't doing anything. I pulled open my bag and found two cheeseburgers, fries, and some water. I glanced back up at Faith, surprised.

"Hey, I'm not exactly clear on what you like to eat yet, all right?" Faith grimaced. "I grabbed the basics. You're a veggie, aren't you? Figures. I read you *totally* wrong."

I shook my head and unwrapped one of the burgers. "No, I'm not vegetarian. This is fine."

I didn't usually eat fast food, but I needed any kind of calories. Besides, it didn't taste *bad*, I just . . . well, I'd be working it off, for sure. We ate in silence for a few minutes, Faith obviously enjoying her food a lot more than I was. She downed a huge gulp of her soda and set it down, putting on a serious expression.

"How are you doing?"

My mouth was too full to answer. I just gave her a puzzled look—at least, I hoped that's what it was.

Faith shrugged, to my relief. "You just seemed super distracted when I walked up. Like, you didn't even notice me, did you? That's super abnormal for you."

"You're the expert on me already?"

"I'm pretty good at reading people. Or so they tell me. You're running circles in your head and you're way more stressed than you wanna admit. Maybe more than you actually know. Stress is funny like that."

I cleared my throat and set my food down. I looked past her into the food court, watching the crowd some more. There was a group of teens at a table across the way, laughing uproariously. They were flailing their arms in the air in unison, engaged in a multi-person sim. They leaned left and right all together. I guessed it was a roller coaster.

I didn't want to engage with Faith. If I did—if I let my mind dive into thoughts of Darius and of what was going on with me—I wasn't sure how easy it'd be to get back out again. This wasn't a safe space for that. We were in the open . . . exposed.

"All right," said Faith, swallowing another bite of burger with relish, "so we're not at the sharing-inner-thoughts stage yet. That's cool. You wanna keep it private, we're good. Just remember, you can't let it sit. You gotta deal, one way or the other."

She picked up a couple of fries, toying with them in midair. "Food rots away if you leave it out in the open. Yeah, sooner or later, it'll go away on its own, but for a long while, it's gonna stink. And it's gonna attract flies, and other, less appetizing friends." She tossed the fries into her mouth. "Best to down 'em while you can. Less goes to waste."

I stared at her, unblinking. "That metaphor kinda fell apart."

Faith grinned. "Yeah, it fell off, but it got you talking again. I'm doing the best I can as your newly appointed emotional guardian." She chomped down a few more fries, getting back to the eating business, while her food was still warm.

I looked away. Spending time with Faith was weirdly paradoxical. I'd barely known her for a day, and yet we already had a relationship I didn't understand. It was oddly comfortable, and Faith was a valuable ally. She had connections and she obviously knew way more than she was letting on. Meanwhile, I didn't know who I could trust among my old contacts. Faith was an unrelated third party.

Sure, I didn't exactly trust *her* yet, either, but I didn't think she intended me harm. If Faith wanted to hurt or kill me, she'd already had the opportunity. I was still afraid to give her anything more about myself. Faith already knew too much. She knew my *name*.

My name was my fail-safe. Darius had explained it to me very thoroughly. Nobody knew it, not even the doctor or the professor. I had my birth certificate and my identity, and at any time, I could simply vanish back into the real world as if I'd never been connected to any of them. Only Darius and Michael would ever be able to find me.

He'd even gotten into the Cascadian citizen registry databases, with untraceable hacks. No bribes, no officials, just Darius. According to the government, I was already eighteen, with a high school diploma and a sterling education, ready to go to college whenever I wanted. Until then, I was home-schooled with free online classes, but I could do it at any time.

I could disappear. I could go to a university, go down to Portland or north to Vancouver. I could do whatever I liked . . . except that Darius wasn't somebody I could trust anymore.

Was my name even really mine, or just what he chose for me?

If I left, what would he do? Would he come after me? Track me down? I knew he could. Darius had too many connections and too much power in the city, and his influence in Cascadia was only growing. He'd find me and he had more than enough muscle on his side to bring me back.

Would I even remember leaving?

A pointed reminder rolled into the mall as I spiraled inside my head. Two young guys and a girl strolled in, right through the same entrance Faith and I had just used. They were dressed in typical over-bearing ganger gear—thick black duster coats, dark jeans, tattoos, a couple of piercings. These guys weren't subtle in the slightest. They were enforcers.

In our district, they could get away with it. After all, the cops were on our side, and corpo security teams wouldn't risk messing with us. They owned this mall, more or less. The girl was leading the other two, obviously in charge of this trio, and they were moving with purpose. She had a striking tattoo, an intricate grid of lines swirling away from her brow that transitioned into a set of knives splayed outward.

They were on a mission. This wasn't just a few enforcers cruising the street. They were looking for somebody.

Was it me?

"Heads up," I murmured, nodding toward the trio. Faith twisted around with more subtlety than I expected, but I doubted she could see them yet. I was using a lot of my other eye's zoom to track them from across the mall. They were casual, walking, joking. Definitely searching, but not anything urgent. The two guys just looked bored, but the girl leading them . . . she was intense.

She checked every shop as they passed, a fierce and wild look in her eyes. The two guys had obviously already given up, but she wasn't going to. She'd probably gotten the assignment. I vaguely recognized her, but I couldn't remember exactly where from.

It was more than enough to set off a few alarm bells in my head. These were definitely our people, they were definitely searching . . . and I was the only possible person they could be looking for. But . . . how had they found us?

The burner.

I grabbed the phone out of my bag and snapped it in half.

"Uhh . . ." Faith trailed off.

"Three of them, maybe more. They just came in the south entrance. Heading our way now, slow."

"Friends of yours?" she asked uneasily.

I shook my head. "I don't have any friends," I said before realizing how awful it sounded.

With a quick twist of my hand, I shifted into thermals, trying to spot any weapons on the trio. The girl had knife-shaped gaps of heat in her front pockets, as well as a few more on her leg. The guys didn't look like they had anything, but I'd bet they had pistols in the backs of their waistbands, like any stupid enforcer probably would. I had to assume it, anyway.

"They're armed," I added. "Time to go."

We both stood up at the same time, looking around. My first exit choice, the east entrance, was blocked, as it would put us right in front of them. I needed another route, and Faith realized the problem at the same time.

"Can't use the escalator or the elevators; they're looking right at 'em," she noted, having spotted the trio now as well. Like I said, they stood out.

"Yeah. Plan C. Circle around them on this floor, hop the railing at the end, and drop down to the south entrance."

"Right," said Faith. "I'll catch up with you then."

I winced. I'd completely forgotten that Faith definitely could not manage that route. I started to search for another exit, but Faith shook her head.

"It's the right move; do it. Don't worry about me. You've got my number, right?"

I nodded. I'd memorized it and stored it in my eye, so once I picked up another phone, I could call her.

"Cool. I'll be around. Call me if, you know, you need me or whatever. Or I'll just see you back home."

"Okay."

The trio were still below, the girl examining a hunting goods store. I turned to go, but hesitated. I wasn't sure why. A moment passed, then suddenly, Faith threw her arms around me.

"Congrats, K," she murmured, "you made a friend."

I stood stiff. I wasn't sure what to do. I was torn between wanting to hug her back and wanting to push her away. Faith broke it off before I could make up my mind and sat back down again. I didn't turn to see her expression—happy, sad, confused, whatever. I just left.

I wasn't going to get attached to Faith. She was a resource I was building up. An asset. Faith having an attachment to *me* was useful, but it didn't run the other way. I couldn't risk that. It wasn't part of my job.

The mantra continued to echo through my head as I ducked past tables and circled around the top floor. I hurried over to the railing, waited until nobody was looking, and casually leaped over it. I landed just behind a food cart below, startling the young man running the stand. His eyes widened, but I hurried away before he could say a word.

I checked one last time to make sure the trio hadn't noticed, then slipped out of the mall, my would-be captors none the wiser.

FAITH

Faith watched Kara drop out of sight. She picked up the remains of her burger, chewing thoughtfully. *Something's seriously wrong with that girl,* she mused to herself, before she turned back to watch the approaching trio of gangsters.

What Kara had completely missed—and how could she possibly have known, anyway?—was a certain familiarity between Faith and the girl leading the trio. Faith wasn't unknown in this district by a long shot, but Kara operated way above her level. She wasn't surprised in the slightest that Kara had no idea who the girl was, or why she was marching toward Faith with a deadly gleam in her eyes.

The knife girl was Cassie Dunham, up-and-coming muscle and daughter of Michael, the other head of the gang. She'd recently been on the short list for a promotion in Kara's gang. Cassie would have gotten it, too, except she'd recently been thrown out of school for attempted murder. The authorities hadn't pursued charges—probably thanks to some political leanings and well-placed bribes—and officially, she was still a student in good standing, but the school wouldn't tolerate Cassie's antics anymore.

Cassie could buy herself out of any legal trouble, but she couldn't buy a better reputation, and Kara's gang operated on reputation. She wasn't ever getting that promotion, and for the time being, Cassie was stuck at the grunt level, doing enforcer work and patrols like the one she was on now. Faith could see that frustration in her eyes, boiling together with rage and hatred and all the other fun emotions she loved to see on a psychopath.

She *did* wonder how Cassie knew Faith had gotten her thrown out of school. It wasn't *exactly* true, but it was close enough. Faith's whisperers had the ear of most public officials to some degree or another, and the school board was no exception. Faith's only weapon was information, but she wielded it well whenever she could, no matter the cost to herself.

Cassie hurt her best friend. Who was Faith if not a loyal protector to her compatriots? If Cassie hadn't been drunk that night . . . Ellie definitely would have died if she'd been in more control of her knife.

Faith reminded herself of that repeatedly as Cassie stormed toward her. One wrong move, and Faith wouldn't survive the afternoon. She could only hope Cassie remembered just how much she stood to lose if Faith were to suddenly vanish.

"Afternoon, Cass," Faith said idly, twirling the paper straw around her cup. "How's it going?"

"Shut it, snitch," Cassie snapped as she scanned the restaurant line. *Huh. Not here for me. So . . . they're definitely looking for Kara, then. Tracked her phone, just like she thought.* "Watch the entrances," she added to her two enforcers. "I gotta talk to this piece of shit for a bit."

"Flattery won't buy my tongue, dearest Cassandra," said Faith, amused by the two guys. They tried to seem detached and intimidating as they took up positions out of earshot, but mostly, they just looked like goofy teenagers with seriously overinflated self-importance. *Which, yeah, they are.*

"I'm looking for someone."

"I mean, I don't think they *sell* 'em here, but I'm sure there's a soul mate somewhere in this mall. You don't care if she's not pretty, right?"

"Not looking for one of your slut friends. I'm looking for Snipe. You know her, right?"

Faith shrugged. "I think I remember something about an assassin with a lame name and a fancy gun, yeah. I can't say I know her though.

Not many actually do, unless I'm mistaken. You should probably ask the higher-ups, shouldn't you?" she added, unable to resist a brief needle at Cassie. "Doesn't she work for you?"

Cassie's eyes narrowed. Her expression had gotten darker. Let something slip, huh? Guess they didn't want anyone to know they're looking for their own. Snipe's off the leash. There's some power plays going on for sure. Internal? Kara didn't seem to have a clue, so she's not in the loop here.

Despite the danger, Faith was already enjoying this encounter. Kara had become an integral part of her world in only a fourteen-hour span. Faith could see this becoming a *very* productive relationship . . . if her instincts to protect the girl didn't get her killed in the next few minutes.

To her credit, Cassie concealed her mistake quickly enough, coming up with a cover story on the fly. "We just lost touch last night. We're trying to check in. Nothing too important."

"So, it's unimportant enough that you can carry on a casual conversation with yours truly," Faith said with a wink, "but so urgent they've got high-school-age muscle wandering the streets and invading malls to hunt her down, all in the middle of a perfectly good Saturday." She glanced up at the skylight. "Oh, wait, it's raining again. I guess you had nothing better to do after all."

Cassie glowered. "Make this quick for me. Do you know where she is?"

"Not a clue," Faith said cheerfully. "I make it my business not to be acquainted with killers. Except you, of course. I just can't resist that body. Do you work out?"

Cassie stood up, apparently trying to intimidate her. It might have worked, except Faith was already terrified. Problem was, when Faith got scared, she didn't show it, not in any traditional way.

She just talked more.

"Want some advice?" Faith asked, tossing another couple of fries into her mouth.

"What?"

"When you're trying to find somebody, it helps to ask nicely." Faith shrugged. "Just saying."

She reached for her drink, but Cassie picked it up first.

Faith frowned. "Okay, now this is just petty."

Cassie smirked and tossed the half-empty drink into the nearest bin. "I can do more than petty."

She stepped forward, and in one smooth movement, she swept her leg out. Faith's cheap plastic chair tilted over. Her world suddenly spun away from her as she crashed to the ground. Pain flared up in her legs almost immediately.

Faith groaned, awkwardly trying to push herself up again. Cassie walked around the table. A swift kick slammed into Faith's stomach. She curled around the impact, trying to protect herself, but another kick came in an instant later.

A huge burst of pain radiated down Faith's bad leg. Waves of heat crashed through her, nerves crying out. Faith whimpered, instinctively crawling away, toward the wall. All she wanted was to get away from Cassie, but the girl calmly followed her.

Pressure on her back. Cassie had knelt down, one knee pinning Faith to the floor. Faith's eyes were watering up. The girl drew a knife, and the cold metal began tracing lines on the back of her neck.

"You feel that? Just a taste. This knife is my second favorite. I won this in a throwing contest against a guy from the Republic. Real Texan steel, sharper than you can imagine. In fact . . ." She paused. A sudden line of pain opened up on the back of Faith's head, spiking through her brain. "It takes so little pressure I end up cutting people by accident all the time."

Against every desire in her body, every stubborn instinct to deny Cassie the pleasure, Faith whimpered again, even louder. As far as she could tell, not a soul in the whole mall gave them a second glance. She felt awful. Why'd she let Kara pick a location way out in the corner? They should have sat in the middle of the court, with dozens of witnesses.

Faith's mind could barely manage a thought that complex. Any plans of escape flew away before they could even begin to form. All she could do was hold on and wait for the pain to end.

"Oh, calm down. The cut's pretty minor. You're gonna be fine. I know who you are, and don't forget, I know where you hang out. And *you* know how to get in contact with me. So here's the deal: you track down Snipe for me. I know you can do it. Get her location, and you get it to me, and only me. Got it?"

Faith managed a quick nod, still reeling from the pain.

"Good."

The knee lifted off Faith's back. She tentatively reached up to the wound on the back of her neck and felt blood. She groaned again as another spike of pain shot through her skull.

"I'll be in touch."

Footsteps strolled away. Faith wouldn't have been surprised to hear Cassie whistling as she left, but she didn't even get the consolation prize of a cliché come to life. *Well, shit. Two sociopathic killers in a single day. I'm on a roll.*

Not that they were *anything* alike, of course. Kara was the other kind of sociopath, the one who didn't understand why killing was a bad thing, but wasn't exactly malicious about it. Cassie was the kind everybody knew about. *And lucky me, that's the one who hates me.*

Faith struggled back up into a chair. Cassie had done her another courtesy, shoving the rest of her food onto the floor and stepping in it as she left. She sighed. *At least I got to eat most of it.* Faith felt the beginnings of despair creeping back into her mind, but she shoved them aside. There wasn't time for that.

She was a survivor. Eighteen years on the streets made a person resilient. This was a bad day, but it wasn't her worst day. She could get through this one. She had resources and she had friends—and most importantly, she had a new tool, handed over by her newest friend.

Faith pulled out the burner phone and turned it on. There weren't any stored numbers, obviously, but she knew the important ones by heart. In her current state, Faith was desperate enough for the best help she could get, damn the consequences. She dialed the private number and waited.

After two rings, the line picked up.

"Center mall, food court. I need you."

Faith hung up, before she could be asked any questions she couldn't answer.

Twenty uneventful minutes passed. Faith watched the bustle of the mall continue unabated from her corner vantage point. Unsurprisingly, not a single person had noticed the teenage girl getting savagely beaten in the corner of the food court. The restaurant staffers were safely behind their steel-and-glass curtains while the mallgoers were lost in either VR or just their own miserable lives. Nobody noticed the girl with her legs propped up on two chairs, holding a makeshift bandage of napkins to the back of her head.

You talked yourself right into that one, Faithie. You knew she was looking for trouble and you gave it to her. Every drop of blood flowing out of your thick skull is one you probably deserve to lose.

It wasn't the first time Faith had given herself a lecture on holding back, and it definitely wouldn't be the last. She couldn't help it. Anything witty or sarcastic, anything smart or clever that came to mind, Faith had to say it. It was like she was playing to some audience that wasn't there, the star of some action flick in which she got to be the quippy heroine laughing in the face of danger.

So much for laughing. I'm barely keeping myself from crying right now. God, this hurts.

She adjusted her leg slightly, and instantly regretted it as a fresh wave of pain rolled up through her body. Faith hoped nothing was permanently damaged. Besides the usual, obviously. *Adding to your previous work, eh, Cass? Not done with the painting just yet, I see.*

Faith had lied to Kara about her injury, of course. It wasn't some nobody drunk driver who'd crippled her. No, it was Cassie Dunham, up-and-coming gangster in the district, getting her sweet revenge. Faith had been the cause of all her life woes.

Everything started with a stunt at school. In their freshman year, a rumor went around that Cassie was gay. It wouldn't have been a big deal, except Cassie vehemently denied it. She shouted down anyone who even hinted at the subject, and damn near attacked several girls who had the guts to tease her one morning before class. The school clamored for a definitive answer, one way or another—and Faith had allies to win, confederates to charm.

So, naturally, she gave them what they wanted.

It wasn't hard. Faith recruited a girl who had a secret crush on Cassie, gave her the inside track, and ensured they had frequent time alone together. Within a week, Cassie had the girl *in flagrante* in an unused classroom—and just outside, Faith had half the sophomore class parading by unnoticed. It was only thanks to the untimely intervention of an amused teacher that Cassie even saw Faith, standing at the door, a wide grin plastered on her face.

Faith would never forget her expression in that moment: confusion, quickly fading lust, and incalculable rage made an interesting mixture. She should have seen it all coming right then, but nobody had gotten in trouble. Everybody had a good laugh (except Cassie), the two girls had gotten to third base together, and nobody cared anymore. The school moved on. Nobody even mentioned it after a few days. If Cassie hadn't denied her sexuality so much, it wouldn't even have been a thing in the first place.

In Faith's mind, she'd done Cassie a favor.

Cassie returned that favor with a vicious beating, ambushing Faith on her way to her favorite overnight shelter. She wasn't into knives yet, or Faith probably wouldn't have survived, but the damage was still plenty permanent, physically and mentally. Bleeding and bruised, both legs broken, Faith had dragged herself to the nearest hospital—but without proper insurance, money, or any ID, all they could do was patch her up and send her on her way.

Faith never returned to that shelter, or even the next closest one. Her legs never finished growing properly. She ended up with her rolling limp, but she took it in stride (and took every opportunity to make that pun she could find). Faith bore her injury with pride, refusing to give Cassie the satisfaction of her defeat.

The girl *had* instilled in Faith a vicious paranoia though. Every night, on her way to whatever makeshift home she found, Faith listened for the patter of light footsteps, the tension of a quiet alley suddenly *too* quiet. The rush of air preceding a blindside punch, or the faint whistle of a knife through midair—Faith knew them all too well.

Speaking of paranoia . . .

Several suited bodyguards were casing the mall. They were subtle, but Faith could spot an experienced bodyguard a mile away. The contrast to Cassie's two bored companions from a half hour earlier was astonishing. Within only a couple of minutes, they'd canvased the entire mall and taken up guard positions at every entrance. They weren't so close they'd be obvious, but they were all within striking distance if unwanted guests showed up.

Faith almost laughed aloud at how skillful and thorough they were. It was the mall, not some high-class gala, secure government building, or private corp. Then again, they had something more worth protecting than any of those places.

She walked in. Twenty years old, tall as a mountain and graceful as an angel, moving through the crowds as though she were gliding across ice. She could have been a supermodel, a blockbuster actress, whatever she wanted—if only she didn't have the huge knife scar marring her face.

Ellie made her way across the food court, a place she clearly had no business being in, and beelined for Faith. Evidently, her bodyguards had already told her where to go. *Efficient, professional, thoughtful, like always.* Faith felt herself instinctively recoil.

The urge to flee was building up stronger with every passing second. She didn't want to talk to Ellie. She didn't want her to see Faith broken and beaten, desperate, alone.

If her leg wasn't still throbbing, her hands not stained with blood, Faith might have made a run for it. To Ellie or away from her, she'd never be sure.

Ellie saw her and immediately processed the state she was in. Within seconds, *she* broke into a run, though somehow still as graceful as ever.

Faith saw her mutter something, probably into her own implant. The nearest bodyguard broke away from his post and started moving toward them as well.

Faith groaned. *I didn't want all this.* But the moment she tried to move her leg, she knew she wasn't going anywhere for the time being.

Ellie reached her table, towering above Faith, her face etched with worry and fear . . . and so many other emotions Faith didn't want to acknowledge.

"Oh god . . ."

Faith winced. "Hi, giantess. Glad you answered."

"You're bleeding." She motioned to the bodyguard, who moved to pick Faith up. She offered token resistance but was too weak to really resist, and the guard knew how to carry her with minimal pain. "Bring her to the car, please. We're heading home right away."

Faith sighed, resigning herself to fate.

Shoulda stayed at the damn hideout.

Eleanor Maclay—daughter of the legendary Arthur and Rebecca Maclay of Maclay Technology, heiress to a fair-sized fortune, and gentle giant of the Seattle Western Public Institute of Education—owned a nice car.

Faith felt guilty to be bleeding over such tasteful seats, but the bodyguard had laid her out across them without any sort of protective sheet. The bodyguards took the front seats, and Faith was splayed out across the back, leaving Ellie in the awkward position of not having anywhere to sit. She looked dubiously down at Faith, uncertain.

Faith sighed. "It's fine."

She lifted her head up, and Ellie quickly sat down. Faith let her head drop gratefully again, perhaps a bit too quickly, but the pounding headache and the blood rushing up and down her spine wasn't giving her much of a choice. The doors slammed shut, and the car pulled away from the mall, rejoining the line of self-driving cars as it rushed through the city in emergency mode, heading back to the Maclay estate.

It was a newer model, one of the exclusive cars only available to the ultra-rich. Besides the emergency mode—which normally Faith found a travesty, but was immensely grateful for in her present state—it also had absurdly comfortable, self-warming seats and suspension so immaculate that she could barely tell they were driving over Seattle's streets. Her various aches and pains were enormously thankful.

Not that we're in my neck of the woods anyway. These roads are actually well maintained.

"Let me look at your head." Ellie's voice was gentle as always, but she'd injected a faint air of command into the sentence. *There's that future career as a doctor.* Faith didn't bother to argue as she rolled over. Ellie pulled a first-aid kit out from the back of the passenger seat and set to work stitching up Faith's neck. "I don't suppose you're going to tell me what happened?"

"Would you believe it was an accident?" said Faith, muffled a little as she spoke straight into Ellie's lap.

"Not in a million years. Jesus, Faith. You were attacked in the middle of the *mall?*"

"Not as hard as it sounds. Ow!" Faith winced.

"Sorry . . . I'm not really experienced in sewing up neck wounds. Maybe if I had my parents to help . . ." Ellie trailed off awkwardly.

"Yeah . . . well, I doubt they'd be willing to just patch me up and send me on my way." Faith winced again at another stab of pain.

Ellie paused. "Stop talking and let me finish, okay? Whenever your jaw opens, I have to deal with a moving target here."

Faith shut up. Ellie kept working in silence for a few minutes, with only the gentle engine sound filling the car. The bodyguards up front were having a muffled conversation, but the privacy screen separating the two halves of the car was remarkably effective. Faith was getting more uncomfortable with every second, and it wasn't just from the pain.

She knew they were getting closer to the Maclay estate. Sweat beaded on her forehead, dripping down into the folds of Ellie's dress.

Painful memories were coming back, one after another. Faith pushed them away, but they kept coming.

Ellie finally broke the silence while she fiddled with something in the first-aid kit. "They miss you."

Faith couldn't hold back a sardonic laugh. "Uh-huh. I remember some pretty harsh words and a very distinct order to leave and never come back."

"It was the heat of the moment. You were like a daughter to them. They felt guilty too."

"Well, they can just drop that. It was my fault. No need to share the weight here, I got it."

She sighed. "Come home with me, Faith. You'll see."

Faith remained silent. Ellie kept working, her gentle fingers stitching cleanly and quickly. Whatever she might think of her own skill, it was way above the average street doctor. Faith barely felt a thing as the threading bound her wound closed.

It was tempting—*incredibly* tempting. Just being there, lying with her head in Ellie's lap like old times, Faith felt more relaxed than she had in months. If she let her mind rest, she could imagine returning to that brief life. Living with the Maclays for a year had been a dream. She'd never wanted for food or shelter; she'd been free to wake up when she pleased on weekends; and she'd never had to reserve a spot in the soup kitchen, keep her network going, or perform any of the other dozen tasks she did every day when living on the street. All her obligations and duties beyond high school vanished, replaced with the easy bliss of high society.

Faith arrived among the social elite as though she'd been born among them. Within only a month, the Maclays found her a constant companion to Eleanor at every gathering they attended. Anything from social balls to corporate parties, if Ellie was in attendance, Faith was only a limp behind. She wore borrowed finery, hiding the scars of her street origins behind layers of silk and beads.

Her talent for networking was a boon. Faith gained the ear of many lesser operators in the city, those bureaucrats who believed themselves of too little importance to be noteworthy, but were privy to all sorts of valuable information. They were flattered and intrigued by the interest of a precocious teenager with an apparent insatiable interest in their field of employment. Faith managed to keep a few of those connections alive, but most dried up when she returned to the dirty, run-down streets she called home.

And then, of course, there was Ellie herself—the yang to her yin, her opposite and inseparable partner. Ellie was only a year older than Faith, but so shy and introverted that she'd have faded into the background of the school entirely had she not been born rich and powerful. She'd ended up with a collection of hangers-on and sycophants, none of whom she could stand, but all of whom she was too polite to get rid of.

Faith spotted her one day, ducking into the library in an attempt to avoid her gaggle of followers—much more difficult than one might suspect, since Ellie had already sprouted past six feet. Faith saw an opportunity, and managed to deflect the would-be disciples. Soon, the library was quiet and empty, and Faith made her move.

Within minutes, they were thick as thieves. Ellie hated being known only for her money and looks, not her achievements. Faith, a girl who didn't care much for either, was a godsend, and to Faith's surprise, she found something far better than a rich resource to exploit—she found a best friend. Ellie became Faith's closest ally and confidante, backing every play she made, while Faith gave Ellie the unfiltered and honest voice she'd never had before.

"I'm close to done," Ellie said finally, "but I'd be happier if I could look at this in a better light than the back seat of the car."

Faith realized she'd stopped working a while ago. She grimaced, but of course, Ellie couldn't see her face. ". . . Are they home?"

"No. They're on a business trip to Portland, won't be back 'til tomorrow morning." Ellie paused. "You can leave before they come home, if you want."

Faith nodded. She couldn't bring herself to face them. Not yet. Maybe not ever.

*   *   *

The car pulled into the Maclay estate, a small—in terms of mansions—patch of land overlooking the sound. A brief flicker of white light flashed through the car, followed by a twinge of electricity. Scanners were buzzing them to detect any unwanted guest and alert the authorities immediately if there were trespassers.

"At least I'm still on the guest list," said Faith, glancing around the grounds. Not much seemed to have changed since she left.

A symmetrical garden surrounded the perfectly circular driveway, leading up to twin garages flanking the front staircase. The mansion itself was a three-story affair, with elegant railings lining the staircase to the middle floor, while the front door was flush with the walls of the house. The entire home shimmered, the walls shifting in color and texture based on whatever angle the viewer faced.

Faith had once spent hours pacing the walls, tracing the display, trying to discern a pattern. She'd never come up with anything. Ellie's father, Arthur, always smiled mischievously when Faith's frustration finally boiled over and she asked for the solution. He'd created the wall surface himself in his spare time and delighted in watching passersby stop and stare. The only static portions were the windows, marking the dining room, the master bedroom, Ellie's room, and Faith's former room, among others.

Faith looked away before she could see anything inside her old room. The car pulled into the empty left garage, and the driver helped Faith limp into the lower floor. Her leg was getting better already, to her relief, or maybe that was the painkiller Ellie had given her. She fell onto the nearest couch, thanking him as politely as she could manage. The man bowed, with a perfect air of professionalism.

"*Arigato,* Tanaka-san," chimed in Ellie from behind them, in what sounded like perfect Japanese. "*Ie no soto de matte itekudasai.*" Tanaka bowed at her words and retreated, leaving them alone.

"Learning Japanese?" asked Faith, raising an eyebrow.

"Only a little," she replied absently, walking into the lower kitchen.

Faith rolled her eyes. Ellie was clearly mastering it just as she did pretty much anything she set her mind to. Faith grabbed the ugliest pillow she could find and laid back, trying to rest her neck comfortably.

This was one of her favorite rooms in the entire house. Several couches were laid out in a semicircle, facing inward to an elegant wooden table. Lining the walls, however, were layered shelves containing all of Arthur and Rebecca's current or failed prototypes, from Arthur's ventures into virtual reality and display technology to Rebecca's latest subdermal cybernetics. Their workshop was through the door opposite the kitchen, and this room served as a private showcase for family friends and relatives. Or, in Faith's case, it had been a room of marvelous toys and gadgets, intricate puzzles to be solved.

Ellie had never much shared her parents' love of experimentation and design, of creating systems within systems, intricately layered moving parts that formed a singular machine. She'd focused on her own studies, pursuing a life of caring and healing, wanting to be a doctor in a normal hospital when she grew up, not an inventor or an engineer or a cutting-edge scientist like them.

Faith's arrival was a breath of life into the Maclay household. They loved and supported Ellie, but they'd never quite understood her passions. Faith's mind for the interplay of systems was as insatiable as theirs, though she was more focused on social structures and power dynamics than electronics and hardware. Nonetheless, her infinite curiosity led to an endless series of puzzles and challenges as Arthur created increasingly complex toys for her to deconstruct and examine.

Her reminiscing was cut short by Ellie's return, a tiny flashlight attached to her finger and with more first-aid supplies in hand.

"Roll over, please."

"Your medical voice is getting good, Ell." Faith obediently flipped over onto her back. A fresh wince of pain was thankfully hidden by the pillow. She didn't see any blood as she laid back down, so Ellie's stitches seemed to be holding. "Nice and commanding."

"I've been volunteering as a nurse in some of the clinics. Experience helps." Ellie set to examining the wound more closely. "You should be okay. It's not deep." She leaned back, and the light flickered off seemingly on its own.

Mind-interface devices were one of Rebecca's newest inventions, piggybacking off the development of the implants and the growing research into active brain wave interpretation and interception. Ellie had one already, though they hadn't made it to market—too expensive and not user friendly enough yet.

Faith sat up as Ellie set aside the first aid and took a seat on the neighboring couch. The silence stretched out into truly uncomfortable lengths. Ellie was avoiding eye contact with Faith, apparently transfixed by the curves in the table leg she'd seen a thousand times before. Faith didn't want to speak first, and her head was still pounding anyway, so she simply waited.

"They aren't the only ones who missed you," she murmured.

Faith looked away. She'd known it was coming.

"I barely survived when you left. It hurt, a lot more than just physically."

"Ellie . . ." said Faith, her voice pained.

"I'm sorry, I just . . ." Ellie took a breath, obviously just as uncomfortable. "I was in love with my best friend in the whole world. The only person who really understood me, and you just *abandoned* me. You left me alone out here, practically while I was still bleeding. I know my parents said some things, but they didn't mean it, you know they didn't, they loved you just as much as they did me, maybe even more—"

"And I repaid that by almost getting their real daughter killed," Faith snapped. "Just by being associated with me, you got beaten and stabbed. By a lunatic sociopath, yeah, but still. For what? A dead-end romance?"

Ellie winced, and Faith hated herself even more, but she had to say it.

"You're practically my sister, Ell. Besides, I don't bat for the other team. So you confess your love to me, I can't return it, and instead I let somebody hack a blade into your face. Leave you . . . like this."

Ellie winced again, her hand unconsciously going to the scar on her face.

"I couldn't—" Faith's voice caught in her throat. She swallowed, trying to force the words out. "I couldn't be around you anymore. Art and Becca were right. I'm just dangerous street trash. I don't deserve to live here. Not in your world. And you deserve way better than me."

Tears filled Ellie's eyes. She looked away, and Faith felt a grim defeated satisfaction at the result.

"I'm sorry I called you. I should've just found a clinic." Faith stood up, but she stumbled on her bad leg.

Ellie reacted instantly. She was on her feet, right at Faith's side, arm around her shoulder and helping her stand upright.

Faith pushed it away, against every instinct in her body and her heart. You're my long-lost sister, Ell. I can't be what you want me to be, in more ways than one here.

"I have to go, Ell."

Faith started limping back to the garage. From behind her, she heard the faint sound of Ellie subvocalizing. The door to the garage swung open, and Tanaka stepped back into the room.

There's that phone built into her now, too, or some kind of voice command thing. Another one of Becca's experiments. Becca had already been theorizing it when the attack happened, and afterward it was a sure thing. Ellie could call any of a set number of people with implants embedded in her body, speak to them in less than a whisper, transmit anything she heard nearby, let them track her.

All because of me.

Faith looked over her shoulder, prepared to at least offer a thank-you, but Ellie was already disappearing into the kitchen. She could hear her crying from all the way out here. Faith sighed, her heart sinking even further.

"Where to, ma'am?" asked Tanaka. His Japanese accent was the perfect balance of audible yet unintrusive, adding even more to his professional demeanor. The Maclays could afford the best, after all, and this was one of Ellie's personal guards. Faith could trust him without question.

Where to go though? Faith needed to get back in touch with her network. Her allies and informants were out there, and Faith needed information. She needed to know what was happening with Kara, and more importantly, with her gang. Something was going down, and Faith had a feeling it was going to rock the whole district to its core.

Besides which, Faith had grown rather fond of the girl over a very short span of time. Kara had been nice to Faith without any reason to be. Even after Faith broke into her safe house, Kara gave her shelter, food, money, and some companionship.

And most importantly, Kara needed help. She needed the kind of help a low-life street urchin like Faith could provide. Faith was eager to get back to that life, to the muck and grime where she had her own kind of power. It wasn't pretty, but it was power she'd earned, through long, hard work and dedication.

She rattled off the address of Kara's hideout. Without comment, Tanaka nodded and helped her limp into the car. In moments, they were off again.

Back to where I belong.

CHAPTER 4

I left the mall without a particular direction in mind. The trio hadn't been hard to avoid, but it was still really unsettling. Why were they looking for me? There couldn't be any other explanation for their presence at the mall, well outside our territory. I hadn't checked in with Darius on time, sure, but did that merit sending out enforcers to hunt me down?

It *had* to be something else.

Was it Darius, afraid I'd found out the truth?

I'd always been cautious on the streets—even if I *was* a top assassin for the most powerful gang in this part of Seattle, most people I ran across weren't exactly going to know that offhand. To them, I just looked like any other teenage girl. So, as any other teenage girl in the city would, I watched my back with every step.

There's a big difference, though, between standard caution and active paranoia. I'd moved into the second category now. Just like people on the street might never have a clue it was Snipe walking next to them, I wouldn't recognize most of our own gang—but they'd definitely recognize *me*. Every single person I passed could suddenly be an active threat hunting me down, and in this part of the city, the streets were empty.

I needed to get out of here.

I needed open air, crowds, and clear sight lines. Darius wouldn't authorize a strike in broad daylight, not with our reputation to uphold.

Drawing my jacket tighter around my shoulders, I hurried down the wide street toward the waterfront. It was past lunch now, so the market would be packed with tourists and normal shoppers alike. The rain was picking up again. In the alleyways I passed, people were ducking beneath makeshift shelters and putting on anything protective they could find. They'd remain under cover until the rain cleared, when corpo security would sweep through again.

Seattle's homelessness problem had been growing since the turn of the millennium. As the largest city in Cascadia, it took in far more of the refugees fleeing the eastern wars than anyone else. Though the local government did its best, there simply wasn't enough space for everyone to have a proper home. They filled the spaces between the city blocks, stuck between a home too dangerous to return to and the unfulfilled promise of a new life.

All told, I felt awful about it, but I had no idea how to solve such a thing. Just like Darius said, their lives shouldn't be terrible—we'd solved a lot of the problems plaguing the early half of the twentieth century. Even climate change saw a remarkable reversal, and projections for the world weren't quite as apocalyptic as they used to be. Automation, self-driving cars, robots . . . everything was getting safer. All that needed to improve was the people themselves. The tools were all there.

It wasn't my job to fix any of that though, thank god. The ministers and secretaries of this and that were in charge. I was on the other side of the legal fence.

An hour or so after I left the mall, taking care to stick with crowds and move through the neutral zones, I finally made it to the waterfront market. As I hoped, it was packed. Letting the crowd push me where it wanted, I slipped into a store and picked up another burner phone, just in case, but I tried to stick to the main thoroughfare. Tourists were here, scattered among the locals, to see the famous fish tossing, now approaching a full century of tradition. I often came down here to find new clothes or other little oddities, usually while killing time until the next job.

Normally, I hate crowds. The horrible paradox of my life is that crowds are the best thing for me—after a kill, vanishing into the crowd is ideal for losing any possible tail. It wasn't often I had to get up close for a hit, but when I did, blending in was a valuable skill. As long as I had my glasses or could wear my hair down, I had no distinct characteristics. Even better, I knew how to move through a crowd almost invisibly, showing no indication I was trying to avoid anyone.

On top of that, I'd picked up a prickly sense of danger, what my brother called "sniper's intuition." Occasionally, I'd feel it—electricity buzzing on the back of my neck. I trusted that feeling without question. The moment I felt it, I ducked for cover, and more than once, it preceded a bullet that absolutely would have scattered my brain on the nearest wall.

My brother berated me for each and every one of those, in his mix of abject fear and overwhelming concern for my safety. I learned to conceal my position better, to slide through crowds unnoticed, to sit back much farther in a room so my rifle wasn't visible to the outside, and so many other techniques for keeping myself safe. I was a ghost in the crowd, flitting by barely noticed by anyone.

For a moment, I considered trying to achieve this with Faith at my side.

She'd give me away in a heartbeat. Faith's walk was distinctive, but even worse, *she* was distinctive. She stuck out in every way, from her voice to her attitude to the perpetual half smirk she now wore around me at all times. If I were trying to escape pursuit or hide, Faith was the *last* person I'd ever want with me.

And yet . . .

And yet, after only a day of knowing her and being apart for just an hour now, I already missed her. Maybe it was because she was the first person I'd met since . . . since I found out. Or, maybe, it was something about her personality, how she spoke her mind and didn't hold back because of opsec or legal consequences, or merely to get an advantage over someone.

Maybe I was just desperate for a friend. I'd never really had one—that I knew of.

I shook my head, trying to unjumble my mind back into focus. There were more important things to worry about. I still hadn't checked in with Darius, not properly . . . and I needed to, if I was ever going to get answers. Trying to find my phone was pointless by now—the moment I'd reported it lost to Hammer, he would have sent a brick signal. The phone would have melted itself in moments, to the surprise of whichever hapless thief had picked it up.

Or, more likely, there was a fresh steaming pile of useless metal and silicon on my bedside table, right where I left it as I rushed out of my home.

The only way I could get in touch with Darius was through someone else in the gang. I needed somebody with high enough clearance. If they were already searching for me, the gang would have put Darius and the ops center on lockdown. Nobody was getting anywhere *near* him, or even a clue as to *where* he was. I'd have to track down any of them, get them to help—or just steal their phones, I guess. I started coming up with plans, but only a few minutes later, I slowed down again. After all, once I got in touch with Darius . . . what then?

What was I supposed to say? Hey, big brother, thanks for mind-raping me?

Would I ask him why? Could I possibly expect a straight answer? Would I believe anything he told me anyway?

Except . . . Darius cared about me, didn't he? As I moved through the crowds at the market, aimlessly letting the flow of people lead me around, the very instructions he'd once given about keeping quiet in a crowd resurfaced. When I'd nearly been killed in return fire, or caught by rival gangs, Darius had showed true concern. It wasn't just caring about an asset—he was genuinely worried for me.

If I understood *anything* about sibling relationships, I knew we were really siblings. I felt that same affection and concern in return, but I was annoyed or frustrated with him just as often. We argued, we fought, we disagreed, but we *always* had each other's backs. There was a connection there, way deeper than anyone else in the world . . . wasn't there?

I needed more information. I couldn't trust my own memories anymore, even my own impressions of Darius or anyone I'd met before. Video evidence might not be as foolproof as it once was, but the files in my own arm were as unmodified as I could possibly find. I'd written a lot of that code. I knew they hadn't been edited—and I knew Darius couldn't get around that log, given his fingerprints all over my implant.

As I walked, I put in my earbuds and queued up another video. The player floated in midair, a translucent overlay on the crowded market. Trusting my feet and my body to keep me moving and blending in, I dove back into my own life once more, desperate to figure out exactly who Darius was—and who I might have been.

The feed only showed darkness.

". . . Kara?" my brother asked from somewhere off camera.

"Yeah?"

The recording had started due to the sudden sound, a safety feature implemented by Darius in case anything ever happened to me while I was asleep. I was twelve now, according to the video time stamp. This year, Darius would introduce me to my new teacher. I hadn't had my own teacher until I was twelve—before that, Darius had just taught me himself, as far as I knew.

"You awake?"

The light clicked on. My hand retracted from the bedside lamp and out of sight. The camera spun around to face Darius, before rolling over and looking out the window. I was watching him with my left eye as my other eye watched the raindrops roll down the windows. Sometimes, I would challenge myself to keep my focus while my other eye tracked individual raindrops at increasingly high zoom levels.

In this particular video, I was only four steps below max. The camera moved dizzyingly fast to keep up with each drop, and I could make out tiny bits of debris carried down along the windowpane as they went.

"Hi, Dar. It's not time yet, is it?"

"Not quite. I wanted to show you something first."

Suddenly, I was looking at Darius. He wore a serious expression—who was I kidding? His face was always serious. Darius only showed any sense of humor when we were totally alone, playing games or just spending time together. Right now, I couldn't see or hear anyone else in the video, but he was still serious as always.

And Darius held a rifle in his hands.

It wasn't my rifle—I wouldn't get that for nine months, as my thirteenth birthday present. This was just a simple air rifle.

"That's a gun," I said—and winced at my past self.

"Yes."

He rolled his chair over to my bed. With obvious reluctance, the camera inched up to a sitting position, as my long-lost fuzzy blanket slid off camera. Darius held the rifle out slightly, letting it rest on my knees. Even in the present, I could feel the sudden weight and cold wood texture on the skin of my knees. It wasn't a good rifle . . . but it was my first.

"Kara, you know that I work with weapons a lot."

"Yeah." Darius's face bobbed up and down as I nodded. I didn't have the automatic stabilization for my other eye yet. "They protect you. And they protect me too."

"Yes, but they also kill people." Darius set the rifle next to me on the bed, then got up and sat down on the bed as well. The video didn't turn to face him, now back to examining the raindrops on the window again. "Guns are always going to be a part of your life, even if you don't like them. I think it's important you know how to use them."

"I don't mind," I replied. I wondered if I was looking at the gun at this point or at Darius.

The rifle lifted up again, and now my hands—small, but definitely growing bigger every day—grasped it. I winced at how badly I held it: how I didn't prop it against my shoulder properly, or how my hands were in the completely wrong spots for a steady aim, how my other eye was way off-center and wouldn't ever hit anything.

"Does it feel okay?" asked Darius.

"I guess so. It's lighter than I thought it was gonna be."

"That's your arm." His hand reached out and tapped on the metal visible in my forearm. I winced in the present as I did in the past, though of course I didn't feel a thing. "It's stronger than a normal girl's."

"So I'm not normal?"

I sounded so . . . casual asking it. Like I didn't care. Truth was . . . I didn't, until today.

Darius though . . . he didn't sound casual. He sounded nervous. "No, Kara. You're normal. You just have a few things most girls don't."

"Cool." The rifle lowered again. "How long until the doctor gets here?"

"Not for a while. Do you want to play something?"

"Yeah!"

Darius got up and pulled out one of the board games, the cool ones with pieces that had holographic overlays built in. My eye rendered them into actual figures, with effects and everything, on the fly. Each piece had an identifying set of markers. Darius had programmed the whole thing with some of his sim developers, though they had no idea what they were working on—just an AR experiment that didn't end up going anywhere.

He couldn't see the effects, but he didn't seem to mind. Every time I laughed or got excited, he seemed happy.

I sped up the video. I didn't need to see this. Seeing us happy was too confusing right now.

A knock at the door.

"Hello?" called Darius. I immediately fell silent, as usual.

"It's me," called the voice of the doctor.

Darius looked over at the computer screen, then back to me. "Why didn't you tell me?" he asked jokingly.

My arms moved slightly. I assume I shrugged, but I couldn't be sure. "I turned off the clock on my eye."

"Why? I'd love to always see the time."

"I dunno. I just don't like being rushed, I guess."

Darius nodded. "Well, if you finish things ahead of time, you're never worried about running out of it. Remember when we talked about not getting your homework done on time and the consequences? The clock will help you remember how much you have left. I think you should keep it on." He smiled. "I wasted time, and now doth time waste me."

"Huh?"

"A man named William Shakespeare wrote that. I'll teach you about him someday." He raised his voice. "Come in, Doctor!"

A creak as the door swung open.

"Darius, what—"

The camera feed swung around to look at her, though my head hadn't moved from the game. She was staring with her jaw open in shock. Barely in view, I could see my legs curled up next to me, with a couple of toes idly poking at the wooden stock. To the doctor, I imagined this was . . . unsettling, to say the least.

". . . Dr. Maclay?" asked Darius, sounding confused. In the present day, my eye went wide, and I walked into the tourist in front of me. They made a grunt of annoyance, but I slipped by easily enough and got moving again before anything more dramatic occurred.

I'd forgotten her name . . . or maybe it had been erased. The doctor, the one who always worked on my eye and my implant, who visited me and Darius regularly and with whom Darius worked on all sorts of other projects.

Dr. Rebecca Maclay.

Darius and the doctor retreated out of the room, and though my past self was completely ignoring them in favor of examining the rifle more closely, I could still hear them now, thanks to the recording and being able to pump up the volume.

"A rifle?"

"It's only an air rifle."

"But—"

"You know the life I lead, Rebecca. She'll always be in danger, no matter what happens. She needs to learn gun safety, and to use one if she needs to."

"You aren't going to—"

"God, no!"

". . . Darius, I respect you and what you're trying to accomplish. I know you care for your sister, and I'm shocked at how well you've managed to isolate her from all of this. I don't even know her name, for God's sake. But . . . you raising her totally alone just isn't right. She needs peers. She needs socialization and a proper education."

"I'm teaching her."

"If it were anyone else, I would have stepped in years ago. But . . . at some point, she has to leave the nest."

"Nobody else can ever—"

"If I find someone. If I vet them, and you vet them, and we make it incredibly clear how much they have to lose . . . would you consider it?"

"How does that socialize her?"

"She only ever interacts with two people. We start easing her into more."

Darius's voice dropped lower. "It's not like she's never been around other kids . . . She knows how to talk to them."

"I . . ." Dr. Maclay trailed off, as if she were going to say something else but had decided against it.

My brother sighed. "If you find someone, let me know. I'll consider it."

"Thank you."

"Let's start the appointment, then? I've been trying to teach her about time management and keeping to a schedule, and this isn't exactly what I had in mind."

She laughed a little. "All right. Lead the way."

As they walked back toward me, the camera swung around to focus on the approaching footsteps. "Time for another appointment?" I asked, a little glum.

"I'm sorry," said the doctor. "I know it's not pleasant. If I could do anything about that, I would."

She gestured toward the chair near the table. I got up and followed her over there. As I sat down, I started shutting down software in preparation for the next update and diagnostics check.

"Darius, would you give us girls a minu—"

*   *   *

The abrupt end of the recording shocked me back into life. At some point, I'd stopped walking, and was leaning against a wooden post with a view over the bay. Far more striking, though, was a new idea that came to my mind: there were two people who'd ever interacted with my other eye, not just one.

Darius and Dr. Maclay.

One of them had erased my memories. I'd assumed it was Darius this whole time, but now, I couldn't be sure anymore. The logs didn't have a user fingerprint—my eye's operating system didn't actually have multiple users, just an administrator account. The erasure had been performed using that account, tied as it was to the implant system to piggyback onto the brainstem. No sense being more invasive on the nervous system than absolutely necessary.

Both of them had access to it, as did I. She had done diagnostics on my eye so many times . . . She had ample opportunity. I needed to be sure. My brother could be innocent, and our life could go back to . . . well, we'd never be normal, but . . . *something*, at least.

I'd been given a clue to find out about the original hack. Someone had placed the idea in my mind, let it simmer, and allowed me to draw my own conclusions. There weren't a lot of people privy to my direct connection to Darius, but a few did know, and one of them had given me a tip that shattered my whole life into pieces.

I needed to talk to Jack Monroe, kingpin of the coast.

The man who had indirectly broken my life apart operated near here, barely a couple of miles from where I was standing. I knew without a doubt I'd subconsciously walked this way for a reason, planning to get more information out of him. With a newfound sense of purpose, I started moving back through the market with one goal overriding every other thought in my mind—persuade him to talk.

*   *   *

I didn't find him. His men found me.

It's not easy to sneak up on me. Like I mentioned before, I had a sniper's intuition for danger—problem was, it was going off every single second of the day now. I *always* felt in danger, and it was hard to detect the little extra bit of stress on top of all the normal stress piled up.

Even with that, I was still pretty hyperaware. Paranoia kept me constantly alert, and I have a distinct advantage over normal people: I can look in two directions at once. My other eye was always dancing around, checking corners, zooming in on possible threats, switching to thermal on the fly, and generally giving me way wider peripheral vision than any typical human.

My hand probably looked like I was a tweaker, one of the types who'd long since been driven out of our district. Of course, many of them ended up over here in Jack's territory. He brought in drugs on barges from the PRC, ready and willing to fulfill the market we'd driven away. We still made more money, since we didn't have to deal with an active police presence (and our product was practically risk-free now that implants were so ubiquitous and safe), but Jack certainly lived comfortably.

He also employed a *lot* of muscle.

By the time I realized I was surrounded, it was way too late. They'd already taken every single alleyway on my right, and to my left, there were just the docks, the barges, and beyond . . . Elliott Bay. I pretty much only had three options: fight my way out (and probably die, since I don't do straight fights), keep walking and let them herd me to Jack, or swim.

Darius never taught me how to swim.

I steeled myself and kept walking as if I hadn't noticed them. I needed to stay confident. This wasn't typical protocol at *all*—assassins didn't just approach leaders in the open for jobs. We had a system. There was a website, well-secured, open source and on distributed hosting. No one controlled it, and everyone could come and go freely. Jobs were posted and accepted in public, though our names were never attached, and money paid out through an automatic, smart-contract cryptocurrency system.

It was a pretty active market. Everybody needed someone killed sooner or later. I was more exclusive than most on who I chose to go after, but everyone knew I always got it done, and always did it clean and untraceable.

Jack had hired me twice before. The first was a pretty straightforward target, a rival of his trying to encroach on his territory. Jack needed him gone, and Darius and I agreed. The guy was insane—setting people on fire in public, robbing local stores at random, pushing dirty drugs that killed as many as they got high. He needed to die.

He was gone within two weeks of arriving in Seattle. My bullet shoved his body into the bay all on its own.

The second time . . . was a lot stranger, and Darius never learned of it. The man hadn't seemed connected to the game at all—he was just an ordinary doctor who lived up north in Vancouver. Jack wanted him killed and specifically wanted me to do it. He said he wouldn't accept anything less than the best and would pay any price. Jack meant it, too, offering a handsome fortune—the highest paying contract I'd ever taken.

I refused at first. Jack didn't give up. He determined—in ways I still haven't figured out—my connection to Darius's gang and came back to me with that. With implied blackmail hanging over my head, I still refused to violate my principle . . . but Jack showed me what this doctor had done. He'd blinded so many people . . . horrible experiments for god-knew-why.

To be clear, I don't have any special affinity for eye injury vendettas. Like I said, I've always had my other eye as far as I know. I don't feel inhibited in the slightest. I'm not saying I'd necessarily want *two* of them, but I'm totally okay as I am. Still . . . the idea of losing your sight because some doctor—someone who's supposed to *heal* you—decided you were the next guinea pig in his sick experiment?

He died two days later, one hour before his next patient.

As I walked into the warehouse at the end of the docks, I kept all of that in mind. Jack was a drug pusher, but he had morals. He had principles, like me. We tolerated him because—even if he was selling something we despised—he kept it clean. Nobody innocent got caught in the crossfire; no one pushed dirty batches. Hell, he even kept the tweakers responsible and had them on schedules. There were almost no overdoses in his whole district last quarter.

It was still exploitative, but . . . it was something.

It could be worse, I reminded myself. Jack's two largest enforcers were now obviously escorting me down the interior walk of the warehouse, alongside the waves of the bay lapping against the planks of the wharf. Water dripped from the ceiling and slapped my face, cold as ice. I wiped it off, grateful as always my eye was waterproof, and headed straight into Jack's temporary office. The muscle stayed outside.

My right hand was immediately in my bag as I crossed the threshold. Jack was better than most, but he *was* a drug-dealing kingpin. He was a killer, even more so than I was. I wasn't going to let down my guard—or let go of my pistol—for a second while I faced off with him.

Likewise, Jack had a pistol lying openly on the desk, next to a closed laptop with a plugged-in flash drive. He didn't touch either, leaning back in his chair with an unlit cigar and a bemused smile, but the respect was clear. The room was almost spartan otherwise. Nobody else in the room—just Jack, me, one cheap laptop, and a couple of guns.

"Hi," I said finally, after neither of us had spoken for a few minutes.

"Hello yourself, dear."

Jack, in one of his many oddities, maintained a British accent despite being born and raised in the New Confederate States. From what Darius could dig up, he'd emigrated to Cascadia at ten with his family, who all died shortly afterward from overdoses in a small town on the Oregon coast.

"You brought me here . . ." I said a little lamely.

Jack shrugged. "In a manner of speaking. I've been waiting. Honestly, I expected you sooner."

"I need more," I blurted out, tired of the runaround already. "You already knew, right?"

"Knew what?" he asked, his eyes twinkling.

I shook my head, and emotions got the better of me. "Don't give me any crap today. Just tell me. *Do* you have more?"

"You sound an awful lot like one of my customers . . ."

"Last time we talked," I said, gritting my teeth slightly in frustration, "you said you had everything I ever needed to know. What you told me before wasn't enough. I need to know more."

Jack leaned forward, rolling the unlit cigar in his mouth. The scar across his face stood out prominently as he rubbed his chin. I knew he was trying to be theatrical, put on a show for me, but I was impatient. I shouldn't have shown it, not in a negotiation, but this was different.

This wasn't a kill; this wasn't to gain money or territory. This was my life.

"Quid pro quo, my feathered friend," Jack said pensively. "I need something from you as well."

"I already gave you money."

He sighed. "I have money. More than you, I'd imagine. I'm looking for a favor."

I hesitated. Favors were powerful. I'd never given one out, but I knew how much they were respected in our city's underground. Breaking a favor was akin to suicide. If I accepted . . . who knew what Jack would request? But . . . like I said, I was desperate.

". . . If I did, I'm not—" I cut off as Jack leaned forward, his eyes even wider. I took a breath, starting again as I got myself together. "My rules still apply. Even for a favor."

"Of course," said Jack, leaning back again, twirling his cigar. I didn't smell it at all, just the brine of the bay, so he hadn't even been smoking before I came in. "I'm a man of principle and I can respect a young woman doing the same."

"So . . ." I prompted.

"For the rest of what I know, without restraint, I require a job. A hit, as you prefer, free of charge, on the target I'll supply."

I shook my head. "I can't agree to that without knowing the target."

"Knowing if they deserve to die?" Jack asked knowingly. *Not exactly,* I replied mentally, but he went on. "Once you see what I've seen, you will not hesitate. I've never witnessed a crime such as this, and it haunts me to my core. This man deserves to die."

". . . What's the name?" I asked.

Jack shook his head. "Watch the evidence first," he said, spinning the laptop around to me. He stood to leave. My hand gripped the pistol again, but he'd already holstered his own. "You'll see your target dossier on the computer as well." He looked strangely sympathetic to me, which I didn't understand. "Good luck, my dear."

I didn't answer. Jack left, and I heard his muscle leaving as well. After a few minutes, I checked—and to my surprise, they'd all completely vanished. The warehouse was empty, only the gentle tap of a single empty boat at the end of the dock and the continued waves against the wharf filling the huge metal space. I went back into the office again . . . terrified of what I would find.

If Jack was so certain this person needed to die . . . what had they done? What was I about to see? If I didn't agree, could I still bring myself to kill them, in exchange for everything Jack knew? He was a man of his word and he respected favors as much as anyone else. I knew he'd give me an honest deal. But . . . could I live with it?

I had to know. I was already living in a world of misinformation where I couldn't even believe what was in my own head.

The laptop was open before I could think about it another second. I clicked play on the video, and in that tiny room at the end of the docks, all alone, I learned the truth.

It was a small operating theater. The label on the wall said Maclay Technology—Biomedical Engineering Wing. Dr. Rebecca Maclay, accompanied by a small team of lab-coated and masked individuals, leaned over a young girl strapped to a table. She was dressed in a white hospital gown, but with the sleeves cut away to expose her arms more clearly. The girl was propped up on her side, with the gown open to provide better access to her neck and back.

From another camera angle, the girl's right arm could be seen laid out on the table. It was bloody and split open, with wires and tubes snaking away and intersecting a table full of mechanical parts. Metal replacements for bones of various sizes were laid out nearby, each with all sorts of electronic circuitry built in.

On the girl's arm, more circuitry and wiring ran up the side, disappearing underneath her skin as it approached the shoulder. As it reached her back, the circuitry reappeared, connecting to the black plastic and metal implant placed into the base of her neck. From there, the cables continued off to a computer terminal with several monitors, breaking out vital signs and other statistics. In the corner of one monitor, barely visible at the resolution of the camera, was a progress bar with only two words attached—Implant Process.

The girl's face could be seen reflected in a mirror visible to the camera. She was conscious. Tears streamed down her face, but she was otherwise paralyzed by whatever medication had been given to calm her and allow the procedure. She already had the other eye. The silvery-gray metallic orb was set into her socket, where it would stay for years and years to come, lenses not yet opened for the first time.

Darius stood in the far corner.

His hands were folded behind his back, his face masked in shadow. His face never turned away from the girl's gaze. He didn't budge through the entire video while the small surgery team worked through the final steps of the procedure. The girl's remaining real eye was locked onto his, still crying even as she couldn't move or speak.

They were skilled, and the arm surgery was completed in a remarkably short time. Dr. Maclay left the table and hurried to the terminal. She typed in a few commands, and suddenly, the girl's other eye whirred to life. It spun rapidly, looking in what seemed like eight directions at once.

Dr. Maclay hurried to the girl's side. She knelt down, speaking softly, soothing the girl. The girl's real eye was wide and panicked while the other one kept spinning as if completely out of control, switching targets every few milliseconds. The doctor kept talking, a steady stream of comfort and calm, explaining to the girl she'd lost her eye in an accident. She explained how she'd gotten a new one, and the basics of controlling it, never losing that calm and even tone.

Slowly, the girl managed to gain control. The other eye started moving with purpose again, and the girl reined it in until it stood completely still. Her real eye was still wide, but it didn't seem quite so urgent. Dr. Maclay never stopped her slow, steady stream of words to keep the girl calm. As the team around her finished up, she gave them a signal behind her back.

One of the team took an IV and gently inserted it into a tube on the girl's arm. Within moments, her real eye began to droop. After a couple of minutes, she had drifted away completely—and only then did the doctor finally stop talking.

Darius walked forward.

His face was calm and clear. Dr. Maclay stood up, and they began to talk while the team continued to clean up around them. Their voices weren't loud, and the bang of instruments around the unconscious girl was distracting, but they were still audible.

"Did she have to be awake for all of that?" asked Darius. His voice was so quiet, any sense of emotion was completely absent.

"I don't think it would be effective during sleep," said the doctor, switching from her comforting tone to a clinical, analytical voice. "The device latches on to and modifies active brain waves. We might have been able to accomplish it during a REM cycle, but if it hadn't lasted long enough, we could have caused permanent damage to her brain."

Darius nodded. "Yes, of course. I forgot."

Dr. Maclay shook her head. "It's okay. That looked worse than it really was. She'll be fine," she added, though her face as she glanced down at the girl suggested otherwise.

"And she won't remember a thing?" asked Darius.

"Nothing," said the doctor. "Her brain took the procedure very well. Brain waves were all within safe parameters, and we were able to fully realize the neurons. We managed a deep modification. Even if anything related to her past is mentioned, those neurons were completely erased. She won't recognize anything from the events and connections we removed."

She paused, and her air of professionalism vanished. "Was this right?"

Darius's eyes hadn't left the girl's through the entire video and still hadn't. He took a very long time to respond.

"She'll be happier this way. She'll have a future. I'll take care of her. It's the best thing we could have done."

Dr. Maclay nodded. The team had left by now, and only the two of them remained in the operating theater. Darius took the girl's hand. The doctor walked over to the terminal, picking up a dictation microphone, and her clinical voice returned.

"Memory operation completed successfully as of three sixteen on September the twenty second. The patient appears to be in strong physical condition. Ninety-five percent recovery is expected within two weeks. Brain scans and activity monitors indicate one hundred percent success in stated objectives. The operation was performed by Rebecca Maclay with associated team in unofficial capacity. Operation concluded."

She pressed a few keys on the console, and without warning, the video cut to black.

CHAPTER 5

I hadn't moved for ten minutes at least. The hard metal edges of the chair dug into my legs. Chilly air off the bay swirled into the room from cracks in the cheap walls. I was getting cold. I really needed to start moving, get my blood flowing, warm up, and get back to doing something . . . doing *anything*.

Except there he was. Darius, unmistakably, participating in—and *admitting to*—erasing my memory. My brother.

This couldn't be faked. There was no way Jack—or anyone else for that matter—had enough reference material to convincingly simulate my brother's face and voice. Dr. Maclay, maybe. She was on the news often enough for her company. But . . . why bother if Darius himself was right there, giving the order?

Taking away my life.

He *erased* my life.

It could still be fake, I reminded myself. Jack had more than enough motivation to undermine my relationship with Darius. I needed to be certain.

The laptop he'd left had an internet connection. I logged into one of our remote repo servers and started downloading diagnostic and forensic tools. We could access—and even contributed code to—the best available forensic software in Cascadia, generally only available to the federal investigations and cybersecurity departments. I had the best possible resources to check for fraud.

Every single one returned a clean result.

The video was unmodified by every standard we knew how to check. It even still had the date and location metadata attached—right in the Maclay Technology lab, as it looked. The video was almost *too* unmodified, which didn't help my paranoia at *all*. It was clean, there was no artificial grain, no odd jump-cuts, the recording started and stopped naturally, all the frames were in the right places. Regular, consistent keyframes exactly as would be expected for a standard video encode from a security camera suite.

My only remaining doubt: Why would they have recorded it at all? Was it just standard procedure, a habit from someone else on the team? Maybe Rebecca recorded it as blackmail for Darius someday? Was it my brother, feeling guilty and wanting to show me someday?

I had no idea and I needed one. I couldn't keep myself together without knowing.

Except . . . I still had no way to contact my brother.

I took a deep breath, then copied the video file out onto a portable drive, along with everything else Jack left in the laptop. I wasn't about to move it onto my own storage—if this *was* a trap from Jack, and I was still sure it was in *some* way—I didn't want to risk a zero-day embedded in the video somehow. After the transfer completed, I took out my pistol and fired three shots directly through the laptop and the table beneath.

The whole thing shattered and burst. I picked up the twisted remains of the laptop and tossed them out the window into the bay.

I didn't need to see Jack's favor. I already knew.

Jack wanted me to kill my brother, and he had just given me the motivation to do it.

If I couldn't contact Darius remotely, I'd need to do it in person. With that—and the recent group of our own gang hunting me through the mall—in mind, I started heading back toward the district we con-trolled. I'd have to stick to the shadows and alleys, but I'd always liked them best anyway. Sunlight stung my eye and added lens flare all over my other eye, and with my light skin, I burned easily.

When you have to lie still for hours at a time to land a hit, sunburn becomes a serious concern. I burned through a *lot* of sunscreen when-ever I had a job that required me to be outside, on a fire escape or a rooftop or some other similar perch, if I didn't bring the right clothes.

It was getting toward evening now, as the sun started to dip toward the bay. I was moving away, back into the city at large, so I didn't have to worry about much of that. Instead, I felt a little thrill of fear and adrenaline every time someone looked at me for more than a second, every time someone seemed to be following me down the street. Behind my hair and my hood, my other eye danced wildly, trying to track as many possible threats at once as I could.

Almost immediately upon entering our district border again, I started feeling those prickles on the back of my neck. Something was off. I was being watched, from more angles than usual.

I spotted them easily enough—as soon as I switched to thermal, I saw a few people in the same shadows I'd use, watching every inroad and alley into the district. In fact, I might have trained a few of them, indirectly anyway. Darius had once asked me to teach some of his enforcers how to move through the city like I did.

They were too alert. Usually, we relied on our cameras and recogni-tion software more than human eyes. Darius didn't trust humans like he did computers.

A computer will always do exactly as it is told. Computers cannot act unless instructed. The trick is that you may not know who's instructing it.

I didn't know who was instructing them. They were following our protocols, and they certainly seemed like our people, but why would they be on alert? If they were, why wasn't I paged? This sort of deployment suggested we were in serious trouble. Why was I out of the loop?

I ducked into an alley none of them had eyes on—taking a mental note to remind Darius of the gap—and rushed across the street to a nearby electronics store. The staff barely took note of me as they went about their business—no bulletproof glass here, not in our district. I went straight to one of the demo laptops and signed in with an admin account I had stored in my other eye's database.

First, I tried to connect to one of our private networks, but I got rejected. This wasn't too surprising—we regularly blacklisted IP blocks from public computers. Problem was, when I tried to run our tunneling software to connect again . . . I still got rejected, with just as generic a message.

The prickling on my neck got worse.

I brushed my hair back and hooked a nearby chair with my foot, pulling it over so I could sit down. The computer wasn't the fastest, especially after the regular use it got from homeless people, for whom it was their only internet connection, but it should have been enough for me. I tried loading up a different connection, another tunnel to a private website—the assassin board.

Oh my god . . .

There it was. Right at the top of the board, with a massive bounty and a "claimed" mark.

Darius.

I sat back in the chair, blood rushing through my skull. Adrenaline was already spiking again through my veins.

Jack had made it public. There was a hit on Darius, and it was already in motion.

No wonder our whole gang was on high alert. *Nobody* placed hits on us. They all knew doing so was practically suicide. The last time someone tried, putting a hit on Darius's closest lieutenant Michael, it ended quite abruptly. They were traced back, a hit placed on them in return, and they died within days, clean and easy. I should know—I was the one who shot them.

I logged the computer out and wiped it. The staff could deal with rebuilding it. I wasn't about to leave any trace, known or otherwise. I hurried out of the building and down the street—straight away from our territory.

Few in our gang were aware of my pseudo-membership. If I tried to get in directly and find Darius, I'd probably get shot before I got anywhere near him. With no way to contact him and the whole gang watching for possible shooters . . .

Oh god.

They think it's me.

The hit was posted yesterday. In the cafeteria, the knife girl—Cassie, I remembered suddenly—had been actively searching for someone, yet I hadn't known about anything we might be searching for. I was locked out of our systems with no specific error.

I was getting iced out.

A gunshot echoed through the street. People screamed. Crowds on the street scattered in every direction as another gunshot flew overhead, and I could *hear* it whistle past me.

My face stung. I whipped around, and flecks of blood flew off.

Someone had just shot at me. I spotted them—and they were one of ours.

Idiot, I thought, completely incongruously. You're aiming for my head. You're supposed to aim for center mass. Headshots are overrated. And in the middle of a crowded street? This isn't how we do things.

As the guy adjusted his aim, ducked behind the lip of a balcony, I made a split-second decision. I wasn't going to try and fire back. These were our guys, and if I had any hope of surviving and getting back to my old life, I couldn't engage.

I ran.

Another gunshot flew out, and I felt a stinging sensation on my stomach and another in my shoulder, but I didn't stop. I kept sprinting as a fourth and fifth shot followed me away. I saw the bullets strike the pavement in front of me and bounce off, my other eye tracking them and tracing back rough trajectories to find the shooter.

In a few minutes, I was out of our territory again and I was safe . . . for the moment.

I found a quiet alley and fell to my knees. Leaning up against the wall, I pulled myself together, little by little. I needed to get a plan in motion. Something—*anything*—to get me in touch with Darius. But I had no resources. My connections with the gang were obviously shot, and anything even remotely connected to Darius would have been warned about me by now.

They . . . they shot at me. On sight.

Oh my god.

I'd never actually had a kill order on me before. Despite how many high-profile kills I had—or maybe *because* of them—I'd always been insulated from this sort of hunt. I knew how to evade someone chasing me, and I'd escaped hot spots before . . . but this was different. The whole district seemed to be awake and watching out for me.

A drop of blood landed on my hand.

I dug into my bag and pulled out a hand mirror to look at the damage. There was a shallow graze on my face, actively bleeding, but it wasn't too deep. Wincing, I pulled up my shirt to look at my stomach—and to my relief, it wasn't too bad either. The shoulder was a bit worse—a bullet seemed to have taken a small chunk out—but it was all surface level. I felt a stab of pain with every motion, and walking wasn't going to be pleasant, but I could manage it. Downing a pair of painkillers, I started bandaging up.

My face was already fixing itself up. I cleaned up the blood, but there was still an obvious streak of injured skin across my cheek where the bullet nearly took my head off.

I almost died just now . . .

I'd never come that close. I'd been shot before, but only once. It was way more painful, but I'd been with a team, and they'd gotten me out right away. Somehow, despite a bullet hole clean through my shoulder that time, I felt more safe and secure than I did now.

It was too much. I needed time to collect myself.

The alley I'd picked was secluded enough and cleaner than I expected. I was on the ground behind a dumpster. As the air got even colder, I wrapped myself up in my coat, tied my scarf tight around my neck, and pulled out my gloves. I'd take a few minutes to warm up and refocus.

As I leaned back against the wall, I flicked through my video storage and pulled up another memory, one which sprung to mind after the firefight. I wasn't expecting to find any better evidence about Darius—I remembered everything since that night pretty well. It was clear to me now: Darius had simply erased everything before that day. I'd never noticed, because how do you notice something you've always assumed was totally normal?

I'd never had memories before twelve years old and I'd never really cared, until I realized they'd been taken away.

"It's on," I said, giving Darius a thumbs-up.

We were in the middle of the forest, well outside Seattle. A truck was just off-screen, though I remembered it perfectly as if it were yesterday. In front of me, an overturned log held a variety of guns, from tiny pistols through to sniper rifles. It didn't have my rifle yet—I wouldn't get that until my birthday later that year. These were just normal guns from the gang's armory.

"Why am I recording this?"

"Because we'll be learning a lot and we don't have a lot of time. If we get noticed, we may have to get out of here very quickly." Darius glanced around, though they were deep inside the forest, and I had my doubts anyone would ever show up. "I'd rather you be able to go back and reference this video if you need to."

"Okay." I reached out toward the first gun in the line—a tiny pistol, one that actually fit in my small hands at the time. I was only twelve. Most of the others would be awkward for me to use until I grew a little more, and the recoil was always something I had to worry about. "What's this one?"

"A Ruger LCP II .380," said Darius. "You'd keep that one in your bag at all times, even if you have another bigger gun."

"Why?"

"You never know when you might need it." Darius sounded uncomfortable, and his eyes screwed up. He didn't seem to want to look at me. After a few moments, while my hands turned the little pistol over and over in my hands, Darius finally spoke again. "Kara, there will be people who want to kill you."

"Huh?"

The video jumped up as both eyes focused on Darius. I tended to do that more often when I was younger, when something completely grabbed my attention. These days, I only put both eyes on someone when I wanted them to be sure I wasn't ignoring them, though I didn't really have trouble listening and still watching every direction at the same time.

"What do you mean?" I still held the pistol, but I was obviously ignoring it now. "I'm not someone who needs to die, am I?"

"No, of course not," Darius said quickly, his voice a little pained. "But not everybody thinks like that."

"So why would they want to kill me?"

Darius reached out and took the gun from my hand, setting it back on the log. He walked over and sat down next to me, putting an arm around my shoulder. In the present, I could almost feel the weight. I didn't like it then and I still didn't now, but I'd give anything for him to be doing so—if only because it would mean we were okay again.

"All sorts of reasons. None of them are good. They might because you're connected to me, because I'm someone who people would want to kill."

"Why would they want to kill you?" I asked, obviously even more confused.

Darius sighed. "I promised you I'd never lie to you, Kara."

"Yeah?"

"What I do is illegal. I run a gang. We sell something illegal and we break the law in more ways than one doing it. To keep our group running, we use violence, just like everybody else. I like to think I do better than most,

but . . ." Darius shook his head, though it was barely visible at the edge of the camera view. "I'm not a good person."

"I think you are," I said stubbornly. "And if anybody wants to kill you, I'd kill them first."

Darius didn't respond. My arms reached forward and picked up the next gun in the line.

"What's this one?"

I jerked back to the present. I'd fallen asleep during the video. It was nearly at the end, when Darius and I were about to pack up the guns. He'd ask which was my favorite, I'd tell him the rifle at the end—even though it was so hard for me to handle, but I never admitted that. Six months later, he'd base *my* rifle off that model.

With a gesture of my hand, I cut it off. I didn't need to see the rest. I didn't need to see the beginning either, but . . . in a way, it comforted me a little. Darius cared about me. I still cared about him, too, even if my own feelings were so mixed up right now.

There was only one option. I needed to get in touch with Darius. Until I actually talked with my brother, I'd be running in circles without any information. I couldn't kill him, not until I was sure if he needed to die.

I needed someone who could get through to my brother, no matter what.

My eye flashed up a low-battery warning. I winced, realizing I hadn't let it charge long enough the last time Faith and I had been at the hideout. Between the heavier use I was putting it through, with more thermal and video playback than usual, and the lack of real charge time, I was dangerously low. I could plug into a public outlet . . . but I didn't want to risk being tied down.

The eye flash also brought my attention to my eye socket. It felt dry and a bit sore, common enough after long stretches. They'd had to remove the tear duct from that side, and it couldn't really lubricate itself well. I dug into my bag for my eyedrops . . . and my hand bumped into my burner phone.

It couldn't get in touch with Darius, but . . . I *could* reach somebody else.

Suddenly, I'd found myself without any allies. Most of my contacts were either too close to my brother to trust right now, or too far removed to *ever* trust. I really only had the one person left who didn't seem connected in any way.

Could I really trust Faith though?

So far, she hadn't given me much reason *not* to trust her. Faith could have killed me, or given away my hideout, or tried to stall me back at the cafeteria. She also knew way more than she was letting on . . . yet those secrets remained secret. Faith even knew I was directly connected to Darius—and if I were her, I'd be guessing the sibling connection pretty soon too—but I hadn't heard a whiff of blackmail.

Faith was my only contact. Even if it backfired later, I needed *something* right now. I needed a resource, and Faith seemed to have plenty, while somehow staying outside everyone's radar.

Worst case, I could definitely take her in a fight.

I pulled the number for Faith's burner out of my database and dialed.

Faith answered on the sixth ring. She sounded a bit sniffly, as though she had a cold.

"Hello?"

"It's me," I replied. I figured she'd get it, and I really didn't want to say my name out loud right now, real or otherwise.

Who knew if either of them were really mine?

"Are you all right?"

I couldn't answer that to *myself*, much less to her. "I'm alone."

". . . Not what I asked, but okay. What's up?"

Suddenly, I realized—was Faith actually willing to go through with anything I might ask? Sure, she was adjacent to our world and moved in some of the same circles, but this was on a whole new level. I'd be bringing her into the middle of a conflict and I doubted she'd ever been in a fight.

"How far are you willing to go with me?"

Faith didn't answer for a few moments. I thought I heard another sniffle, but I couldn't be sure. Finally, just as I was about to give up, Faith spoke.

"You've seen my life, K. I've got nothing else worth doing."

"That's not good enough," I said firmly. "There's a lot on the line here."

"Well, screw that," snapped Faith. "I'm already in this mess. I want to help you. You're in deep shit and you already helped me. It wouldn't be right if I didn't return that."

I didn't know what to say to that. Quid pro quo was the name of the game in my world, but I hadn't really given Faith shelter in expectation of anything. For Faith to actually return the favor was . . . refreshing, in a way. Just like everything else about her.

"K?" asked Faith.

". . . Okay," I said finally.

"Good," she said, and I could hear her voice brighten a little as I accepted. "What do you need?"

"I need to talk to Darius, one-on-one."

"And you can't just waltz in like normal, I'm guessing."

"Yeah. He'll be in hiding at this point. There's . . ." I swallowed. "There's a hit out on him, and they're going to think I'm the one who took it."

"Well . . . shit. Okay. Any idea where he might be?"

"No." I sighed. "Could be a bunch of different lockdown spots we've got. I know someone who *would* though. If I give you a name and a description, could you find him?"

I swear I could hear Faith smirking through the phone. "*Can* I, K? Have you no *faith* in me yet?"

I rolled my eye, though of course she couldn't see it.

"Who's the guy?" she asked.

"Goes by Hammer. Darius's main bodyguard."

"I know him. I'll call you back soon." She paused. "Stay safe, K."

The phone clicked off.

I dropped it in my bag, and as I did, a plan began to form in my mind. I'd need some supplies, but it could be done. We'd need to trap him, and Hammer wasn't the easiest guy to hold down. It'd have to be a complete blind side.

Now *I* was smiling. I was really good at blind sides.

CHAPTER 6

If I was going to steal a phone off Hammer *without* setting off alarms throughout the gang—more than the ones already happening, anyway—I needed to make it look like something else and make sure Hammer couldn't get in contact with anyone for a while. With that in mind, I'd gone to a few retail stores, buying some heavy ropes and some more . . . festive material.

As I was leaving the last store with a few paper bags in hand, my phone beeped. I noted Faith's number and flipped it open.

"Go ahead."

Faith snorted. "Ooh, talk to me all businesslike, K."

". . . Sorry," I muttered.

"Don't worry," she said, her voice softening. "I get it. Anyway, we found him. He's out at a bar right now, missing the entire point of going to bars."

"We?"

"A few of my homeless friends. We help each other out sometimes on jobs for quick cash. I bought them a couple of phones with the stash money to stay in touch. They're watching him right now." I heard a beep through the speaker. "Yeah, he's still there."

"Can you trust these friends?" I asked carefully.

"*Hell* no," said Faith. "But they don't know anything. Probably just think I'm marking him for a con or something. Super common. And the phones were dirt cheap, they can't exactly resell them for anything worth it."

Relief ebbed through my body. Faith knew how to run an operation, and the first step was already done. If anything, she'd found Hammer faster than our own enforcers usually managed. When someone was out in our blind spots, we had to rely on ground troops to pick someone up—and they were grunts, easily distracted by their own business or pleasure. I was lucky to get within a half hour's accuracy.

"Can I get the location?"

Faith rattled off the name of a bar and an address. Outside our district, thankfully—but what was Hammer doing out there if the rest of the gang seemed to be on high alert?

She cleared her throat. "What are you planning to do to him?"

"Nothing permanent."

"Nice," she laughed. "Need any help?"

I paused. I'd planned to do it myself, but if Hammer spotted me, that'd give away the trick. If I could make him think the phone theft was just a random gutter kid, instead of a targeted pick-off, he'd be slower to report it stolen and get it wiped. I could get more time on the clock.

More importantly, I wasn't in a good spot for a fight. I'd been shot, for one. It still stung, but I was managing. Any sort of remove from the front line was good for me. Faith couldn't do it though, not with her leg . . .

"Any chance your associates want a little extra cash?"

"You're set up?" I asked. My mind was already slipping into focus. I had a specific job to do. I had a mission. As long as I could focus on that, I wasn't spending my time dwelling on the uncertainties.

"Yeah, we're good," said Faith. "Ready whenever you are."

I checked the ropes again, just to make sure they were tight enough. It wasn't the most ingenious trap or anything, but I was confident it'd hold Hammer long enough. Setting it up had been harder than I expected, as my shoulders twinged with every movement. We'd picked an alley between two dirt-cheap apartment blocks, the sort that were usually just used by streetwalkers for the night. I didn't need anything special . . . and with how much I was hurting physically, I'd take anything adequate.

It's never hurt this bad before . . . has it? I looked so bad on that operating table . . . Was that because they were putting in the cybernetics, or because I was already seriously injured?

The confusion was getting to me again. I shook my head and tried to return to focus. I needed to clear my mind, go back to the place where I could take the shot, make the kill, do my job. I leaned in against the apartment window and checked my shot again. My other eye did the calculations, lining it up, and I confirmed it with my eye.

"Okay, go."

"They're off."

Faith had hired a couple of young pickpockets to piss Hammer off as he left the bar. They were screwing around just outside pretending to smoke and be stupid teenagers. I couldn't see them from my angle, but from what I could hear, they were doing a pitch-perfect job of blending in—so well, I was about to ask Faith if they were *actually* doing their job.

She was down at the corner of the alley on the sidewalk, wrapped up in a blanket and looking for all the world like a bored homeless girl trying to get some cash. Faith even had a cardboard sign, To Everyone Still Paying Attention, You're the Real Heroes. She'd decorated with drawings of sunshine and rainbows, a strong contrast to the perpetual cloudy skies and downpours we'd been seeing lately.

It seemed too detailed for her to have made it just in the last couple of hours.

"Does that sign work?"

"Nah," said Faith. She shrugged, a movement I could barely read from two stories up and down the alleyway. "You gotta actually ask for money to get money, and give 'em a way bigger sob story."

"But—"

She shook her head. "It's my fault. I don't deserve charity for it." Faith's head turned toward my building, and I winced. *She shouldn't give my position away like that . . .* "You good up there?"

"Yes."

Faith had a tip from someone that this room hadn't been used in months, and it showed. The place was covered in dust, but otherwise remarkably clean. Compared to the hallway—and some of the other rooms—it was almost cozy. I wouldn't want to live here, but . . . for a perch, it wasn't bad.

"He's outside now," Faith reported suddenly. I tensed and took a deep breath to relax myself again. I focused on the ropes I'd laid out and shifted my other eye into thermals. We'd dipped the ropes in boiling water just before we started, and they shone in a clear outline despite the deep shadows of the alley at nighttime. Meanwhile, Faith's face was lit up in a circle of white sticking out from her blanket.

I settled in, finger on the trigger and ready to go.

"They're closing on him. Jenny's playing the idiot, as usual. I think they're still pretty covered though. He hasn't reacted yet. Closer . . . closer . . . oh *shit*. Okay, we're on," Faith said before I even had time to worry about the curse.

I could just barely hear a shout around the corner—it was definitely Hammer.

"They made the pull. Coming our way. They've got a great lead. Coming in now."

Two shining faces entered the alley. They sprinted past, and I could just *barely* make out the leader tossing a small object to Faith as he rounded the corner. Faith buried it in her blanket and returned to normal, just as Hammer came into view.

He was *furious*—though it was hard to tell on the slab of meat that made up his face. Hammer had a crooked nose, broken from a lifelong career of bar fights, and a seemingly constant shifting pattern of colorful bruises. As far as I knew, he got in a fight nearly every night he wasn't working, seemingly for no reason at all. Hammer just sought them out.

More importantly, he *won* them. Hammer wasn't particularly tall, but by every other measure, he was a human tank. Broad-shouldered, arms that were bursting out of their sleeves, not a speck of fat to be found. He was a beast—and we'd just pissed him off.

Faith's friends were nearly at the other end of the alley, and Hammer was barreling forward right into the circle of heated rope. Faith had already exited the alley as soon as Hammer passed her by. I took a breath, and just as Hammer's foot landed in the circle, I let it out—and pulled the trigger.

The pistol I carried, so silent I doubted Hammer would even notice under the shouts and taunts below, loosed a bullet across the alley. It struck the rope and released a counterweight I'd strung up. The ropes suddenly pulled taut, wrapping Hammer up tight.

With a comical yelp, he slammed to the ground, thoroughly restrained.

I hurried out of the room, before he managed to roll over and realize where the trap came from. As I headed downstairs, I put the phone back to my ear.

"You got it?"

"Yeah. Already gone." Faith sounded exhilarated and out of breath, likely from the sprint down the street on her leg. "He didn't even glance at me. We're good. Kevin and Jenny are probably long gone."

"Okay." I paused. "Meet me at that abandoned store?"

"You got it."

Faith's voice crackled, and then the phone went dead. I silenced it and dropped it back in my bag. With Hammer's phone, I had a direct line to Darius—one of the very few, besides my own missing phone. All I had to do now was . . . call.

Steel shutters and lease notices had long since lined the windows of our meeting place. It had been closed ever since the last global market crash before Cascadia seceded, and no one ever bothered to buy it up again, not in *this* neighborhood. However, the abandoned store retained one very useful thing for my needs: it still had power.

I crouched down and pulled out a screwdriver from my bag. The door lock was a newer model and not one I had backup codes for in my database. I pried it open and found the tiny backup pins normally used by maintenance worker—eight of them, each with eight possible positions. If I wanted to do this manually, I'd be here for hours.

We created computers to work for us, not control us. Never forget they are tools, but do not be afraid of them. A computer can make seemingly impossible tasks trivial in moments. It is all up to the user.

Darius was right. I had the tools to do this, I just needed to use them right.

I pulled out the burner phone and an adapter cable. It took some quick wire stripping, but I managed to get the pins to line up with the interface on the lock. With a quick download from another one of our software repos, I'd loaded up a keygen and set it humming. The lock only had simple brute force protections, so as long as I didn't make too many tries per second, it shouldn't be a problem.

"Uhh . . ."

Faith's voice was so close to my eye, I jumped. I nearly lost the connection on the wire and barely managed to hang on. How had she gotten so close without me noticing?

"What are you doing?"

"Hacking," I replied, checking the phone to make sure it was still running the brute force app. Faith didn't ask anything else, to my relief. At the moment, with the upcoming phone call hanging over my head and the hunt no doubt still progressing through the city, I had too much anxiety already to pay attention to anything else.

The door clicked open. I disconnected the wire, replaced the casing, and pocketed my phone. Faith hadn't noticed I was done, looking away as though trying to avoid embarrassing me. I shoved the door open and pulled her inside before we were seen.

As it slid closed behind us, the lights flickered on. I sprinted across the room to the light switches. As I leaped over the sales counter, the edge clipped my shoulder. I groaned involuntarily from the pain, but still managed to flip the lights off before anyone noticed we were here.

I sat down on the floor behind the counter, leaning up against the wall, trying to catch my breath. Between the pain and the anxiety, I was *seriously* off-balance and I hated it. I was never off-balance. My life had always been straightforward and simple—take a job, finish the job, spend time with my brother, attend online classes in my spare time. I hadn't really cared much about the last part, but Darius always insisted.

Now everything was wrapped up in one confusing bundle. My current job was my brother, and I hadn't even chosen it. I was supposed to kill him. I *wanted* to kill him, didn't I?

"Kara?" asked Faith.

I looked up, startled by the mention of my name. "Huh?"

"You're bleeding." She pointed at my shoulder.

It *was* bleeding. I shrugged off my jacket and peeled the sleeve away, wincing with every movement. The bandage had been ripped apart. I needed to replace it. To my relief, it didn't look any worse, but still—better safe than sorry. I grabbed my first-aid stuff out of my bag and started working.

". . . Ow," Faith said sympathetically as I dabbed alcohol on the wound. I winced, but I managed to keep myself silent. "So . . . you got shot."

"Yes."

"Were you gonna tell me?" She sounded genuinely concerned . . . almost like Darius in a lot of ways. *Why? Is it just because she thinks I'm her meal ticket? Why does she care?*

"It's nothing."

". . . Yeah, you're just casually walking around with a bullet hole in your shoulder and another one in your belly. Totally nothing. You're bleeding there too," she added, pointing. I glanced down and realized she was right.

"I'm fine."

"Kara, you're a lot of things, but you are definitely *not* fine," said Faith. She sat down across from me, against the sales counter. "You were already off this morning, but this is like ten times worse. No assassin's gonna cut it if she can't even notice she got *shot*."

"I *noticed*," I pointed out. "I bandaged it earlier."

"Uh-huh." She rolled her eyes. "What happened?"

"I got shot."

". . . Work with me, K," said Faith, exasperated. She pulled out Hammer's phone from her pocket and set it next to me. "Tell me *something*, at least?"

I hesitated. She's been loyal so far. She's been helpful, when most people would've cut their losses, taken my cash, and ran. Faith's still here. She even knows my real name and hasn't tried to blackmail me. So . . . what?

"It was my people. They shot me as I was walking back into our district."

"Well . . ." Faith cocked her head to the side. "Guess they're stepping it up a notch. They don't normally shoot in the middle of the street."

"They think . . ." I trailed off, uncomfortable again. I didn't normally reveal my clients or contacts. It was a code that kept me safe. But . . . these were special circumstances, and *technically*, I hadn't actually agreed to the job—not that he'd see it that way. "Do you know Jack Monroe?"

"The kingpin of the coast? 'Course I do. But why would he be mixed up here? Figured you two had a solid relationship."

I didn't say anything. In fact, I was a little shocked she even knew we had a relationship. It was only two jobs, plus the other couple of casual contacts. Well, what passed for casual in our line of work, anyway.

". . . If he's related, you took a job from him," said Faith, starting her deduction routine from the day before. "Which means you accepted a job against someone in your own crew."

"I didn't *accept* it," I shot back defensively.

"So he's blackmailing you?"

". . . No." I finished bandaging myself and put everything away. Hammer's phone lay on the floor between us. I reached forward to grab it, but Faith slid it away. "What are you doing?"

"You took a job from Jack. You're on the run from your own gang. We just pulled a job to steal a phone off a top-ranking member." Faith shook her head. "I'm in this with you, Kara, but you gotta tell me *everything*. Or at least, you gotta tell me who's involved. I can help you, but we're working around a lot of dangerous people." She sighed. "One of my friends who just helped us jack Hammer's phone works for . . . well, Jack."

Faith gave a crooked smile at her bad wordplay, but I was *not* amused. "What?"

"Don't worry. It's pretty low-level, just the occasional drug run. I don't think it'll be an issue. But . . . in the future . . ." She trailed off pointedly.

I sighed. She was right. If we were going to work together—and I *did* want to keep working with her—Faith needed to be in the loop. If she made a bad call, involved the wrong person, because I hadn't given her all the details, we could die.

Information is everything. The world runs on information, and the best-laid plans will fail if you do not understand the whole picture. Only by everyone seeing everything can true progress be made.

"All right," I said finally. "I'm sorry. You'll get the info."

"Cool," said Faith. She smiled. "So . . . anything else I should know? Any big enemies you're hiding?"

The battery meter flashed up, a ghostly red warning in the corner of my vision. I leaned back and plugged in my other eye to the nearest wall socket, with a sigh of relief as the meter began to refill.

"Just the cops," I replied as Faith pulled herself together after watching me jab a wire into my face.

She tore her gaze away from my other eye, apparently shocked. "I thought you didn't go after cops."

"They go after me now." I sighed and closed my eye, letting it rest for a while. The other one could still function when it was plugged in, though there was a black wire hanging in midair over one lens.

"Oh . . ." Faith closed her eyes too. "Those three who got offed a few months ago people blamed you for?"

"Yes. There's somebody here who uses the same cartridge as me making a mess. She left them in alleys and caused a panic, and I guess they got a glimpse of her on the last one." I shrugged. "Really amateur."

"And you can't just get a rifle like that in Cascadia," said Faith, nodding. "Shit. That sucks. I'm sorry."

I shrugged. "It hasn't been a big deal yet. They don't know what I look like, and my rifle's easy to hide."

"Okay. Anybody else?"

"I don't exactly make a habit of having enemies . . ."

Faith grinned. "Leaving them alive, anyway." She opened her eyes and immediately winced.

"What?"

"Sorry. I'm just . . . not quite used to that eye of yours."

Now I felt even worse. I felt . . . uncomfortable. I'd never cared about my other eye and how strange it must look to most people, but Faith wasn't most people. Her discomfort was reflecting right back onto me. I swept my hair forward to let it cover up the offending half.

Faith winced again. "Oh god, please, no. You don't have to do that. Shit. I'm sorry. I'm an idiot."

I ignored her. "Any other questions?"

To her credit, Faith looked upset now. I wasn't sure how to feel about that, but at least she wasn't treating me like a freak. She needed some time to adjust, but . . . I didn't know if I could give that to her.

She shrugged. "Nope, nothing."

I leaned forward again, and this time, Faith didn't pull Hammer's phone away. She didn't avert her eyes from my other eye, either, as my hair fell back again to reveal it. I appreciated that, but my mind was focused again now.

That phone would get me in touch with Darius. I could call him right now . . . except I needed to talk to him in person, if I could. A video call would be best, and I needed it to be private. Me and him. My brother and me.

Nobody else.

I unlocked the phone with a backup code, one only known to myself and Darius. Hammer's contacts were all in code, but it was crude enough that I could figure it out—with an emphasis on crude. I recognized my own phone number under the heading "Attack Bitch." Disgusted, I found Darius's number under the name Persia.

No way Hammer put that one into the phone. He's not smart enough to come up with that reference.

I sent my brother a text message, doing my best to imitate Hammer's writing "style."

Hammer: need 2 speak privately. can u vid

Persia: Yes. Give me a minute. We're moving to station three right now.

Station three already? He's really scared, then . . . This had only been going on for a day, and Darius was already moving through lockdown procedures like they were nothing. Our normal level of lockdown should be enough . . . *Is this how much he respects me as a killer? Or . . .*

Hammer: problem?

Persia: Maybe. We've gotten word of movement from the Pirate.

The Pirate is Jack. Is Darius already aware of our connection? The job to kill him hasn't been up that long yet. I thought I'd have more time. Is this me, or something else?

Hammer: what about other problem?

Persia: She can wait.

Not me, then. It was as close as I dared to press by text. I didn't want to reveal my access to this phone until I'd actually spoken to Darius directly. The station change shouldn't take much longer, if I was guessing the timing correctly. Ten minutes, maybe, at most.

Ten minutes, and I'd be face-to-face with my brother.

Tension boiled in my chest. My throat seized up; my head got dizzy. A mess of emotions roiled inside me. I tried to force them away, went through my usual routines, but they kept coming back. Stress threatened to grab me tight and choke me alive. I coughed, trying to clear my throat and bring back the calm, but it wouldn't go away.

Deep breaths. Focus on the target.

I didn't have a target, but I did have . . . Faith.

My eye snapped open, and both lenses on my other eye locked onto her. Faith was watching me carefully and, suddenly, I was doing the same. To my relief, she didn't wince or look away. She matched my gaze.

"You okay?" she asked softly.

"It's working," I replied.

Faith looked surprised. "He's going to call?"

"Yes." I kept my eyes locked on a spot below her face, as if I were going to take her out, even though I had no weapon in my hands. "Ten minutes, give or take."

"Okay."

Faith started to move, and—quite unexpectedly—shifted around to sit next to me. I felt a strange burst of comfort from having her nearby . . . something I'd always felt whenever Darius was close. All at once, I felt more safe, more relaxed. I let my eye close again, listening to the rain trickle off the roof and land on the street outside. Any minute, Darius would call, and this would be over.

"I miss them," Faith said after a minute's silence. I didn't move, prompting her to continue. "My parents."

A ping of suspicion bounced through my mind. Something was inconsistent. "I thought you never met them." I didn't say it as an accusation, just . . . curious.

"Yeah," said Faith. "I never met my birth parents. They ditched me with a birth certificate and a blanket on the doorstep of an orphanage. But . . . I found some people a few years ago. They took me in. *That's who I miss,*" she went on. "My real parents. They were my real family, you know? That's what I miss. Family."

I didn't answer, lost in my own thoughts.

Was Darius my "real parent"? He raised me, taught me everything I needed to know to stay alive. He'd introduced me to guns, taught me about the world, provided for me, cared about me. By all conventional wisdom, that was parenting . . . Not the *best* parenting. Certainly better than abandonment, but still, he'd brought me into a life of killing.

Except . . . I'd never felt more alive than when I landed a perfect shot and walked away clean. I was proud of how good I was at this career and I'd practically perfected it. I could lay a trap, I could slip through the shadows unseen, I could hit a man from two thousand meters without blinking an eye—quite literally. Without Darius, I would never have experienced that.

Except . . . he'd spurned our way of living. *He* broke us, not me.

The reminder jarred me back to the present. Darius had rejected our family of two. He'd done the unforgivable, betraying me. He'd stolen my life away, shaped me into . . . this. Into whatever I was now. We weren't family anymore.

My discomfort returned tenfold as I looked at Faith again. Suddenly, I didn't want her anywhere near me. This was too personal, and Faith was suddenly the last person I wanted around. She desperately wanted a family and was latching onto me. Meanwhile, I was about to lose mine, and I had to choose to save it—or end it forever.

I'd only met her yesterday. She'd broken into my home. I couldn't trust her with my life. She'd helped me, but this was different. This was family.

"Leave."

Faith stiffened up. "What?"

"You got what you wanted," I said, voice steady and quiet. "The hideout's yours, and nobody's gonna find it. I won't come back to it."

". . . That's it?" asked Faith, her voice breaking slightly. "You're just . . . *dismissing* me?"

I shrugged.

She looked crestfallen. "Kara . . ."

I ignored her and pulled my rifle out of my bag, beginning to polish it. Faith got the message right away.

She didn't say another word. Her face, mixed with so many emotions, was nearly unreadable. The odd thing, though, was that she didn't seem angry. I'd expected her to be angry. She was *hurt,* certainly, but . . . this was a girl clearly not afraid to speak her mind, and I'd rendered her totally silent.

Faith got to her feet and hobbled out on her good leg. I had my other eye follow her every step out while my eye watched the phone on the ground. With every limp away, I felt a little more conflicted about my choice to send her out.

The door swung closed behind her. Faith stepped out into the downpour outside. Her silhouette wandered away outlined by the streetlights against the shutters, sliding across until it disappeared entirely. I sat back against the wall and let out a deep breath, trying to figure out why I suddenly felt so very alone.

CHAPTER 7

Persia: Okay, we're all set. Call me whenever you're ready.
Hammer: youre alone?
Persia: Yes. Guards are outside, but I'm alone.

My adrenaline spiked like a rocket. I couldn't keep my hand from shaking as I lifted the phone up to my face. I glanced at the camera, just to make sure it took in my entire face, but also blocked out anything of note behind me. Every location option on the phone was disabled, including the secret ones Darius loaded onto all of our phones.

If my brother had figured it out, or if Hammer had called it in, they weren't going to find me fast. We *did* have access to the cell networks, so they could eventually triangulate me, but this was an internet call and not through traditional cell service, so I could easily bounce it a few times before it went out. I should have enough time to talk . . . and enough time to figure out if he needed to die.

I pressed call.

Text raced across the screen as the application bounced through seven different proxy servers, each employing a different encryption protocol. I'd never be able to call Darius without one of our phones. There were simply too many security layers we'd added to our system, and our phones were absolutely secure.

It rang twice. Darius *always* picked up before the third ring. I tensed up as it started to sound the third—and suddenly, there he was.

His eyes, half visible behind his glasses, went wide.

"Don't hang up."

I spoke so quickly the words ran together. Darius took a visible second to comprehend what I'd said, his expression full of caution.

". . . What are you doing, Kara?" he asked. His voice was quiet and firm, and I knew for certain—if he was using my real name, he was alone. I could see another desktop machine behind him in the corner near an empty cot, and Darius sat in a simple office chair. Besides that, the room was quite bare. Our lockdown hideouts weren't exactly designed for comfort, after all.

"I needed to talk to you."

"So you stole my bodyguard's phone?"

I felt a twinge of embarrassment, despite everything. "Well . . . I lost mine."

"That's really not like you." His voice held an undercurrent of disapproval, a tone Darius had become infamous for. Hearing it in his voice generally meant you were about to meet a very swift end.

I took a breath. "It's already been nuked. Our opsec is secure."

Darius frowned. "Kara, the phone doesn't matter. Please stop avoiding the topic."

"I'm not avoiding it," I said, though of course I was. "I'm . . ." *Trying to figure out how to ask if you violated my brain and erased my life. If you've been manipulating me all these years. If you're really my brother.*

"You took a job to kill me."

"I didn't."

"Two nights ago, at the conference above the Vibrato, you killed one of our men," Darius went on. A brief shock rolled through me, but Darius kept going before I could respond. "There's a hit out on me, and it was claimed by one of your aliases. You never checked in. Your phone wasn't responding."

I shook my head, but my voice caught in my throat.

"I trust you see the pattern," said Darius, oddly calm for the list he'd just rattled off.

"What do you mean, killed one of our men?" I finally managed.

"It shouldn't be a surprise. I've never known you to miss, Kara. Even on your very first job . . ." He shook his head. "Why do you want to kill me?"

"I . . . I don't." *Or maybe I do. I don't know anymore. I . . . What is going on?*

Darius raised an eyebrow. "What, then?"

". . . Why?"

He sighed. "Why what, Kara? Specify."

Darius had the same air of annoyance as when he used to teach me, before he brought in the professor. Seeing that same restrained frustration, that familiarity, pushed me over the edge.

"Why did you erase my life?" I snapped.

He froze up. I waited while Darius slowly brought himself back together. I could barely see his eyes, but his whole face was like a statue, totally stuck. It was his turn to come up empty.

"You erased my memory, Dar . . ." My voice cracked, but I forced myself to keep going. "You changed me. I don't know who I am anymore. I don't know . . . anything. Am I me? Did you just . . . make all this up? How can I know?"

He shook his head. "Everything you remember is real," Darius said firmly. "Memories can't be created or altered. All . . . all we could do was hide them." His voice was quiet and steady, but I could tell he was uncomfortable too. He was blinking more often. His head tilted more. He twitched slightly and focused his gaze away from the screen.

My mind was racing, trying to find answers that made sense, but nothing came to mind. "Why?"

"Specify, Kara," he said again.

"Why did you do this to me?"

"I can't tell you why."

"You *can't?*" I snapped. "I can't remember who I am! I don't know if Kara is even my name! Are you even my real brother? Is *any* of it true?"

"Yes. It is. All of it. I never lied to you."

"You *violated my mind!*" I shouted. "Tell me *why!*"

"Because you asked me to!" cried Darius, his face bulging with emotions—terror chief among them.

I dropped the phone. My world stopped.

What did *that* mean? I'd *asked* for this?

My anger melted away, lost in a morass of a thousand emotions. I was confused. I was afraid. I was hopeless and lost and desperate and stressed and trapped and lonely and terrified. Panic and anxiety began to swallow me up, taking every emotion and amplifying it tenfold. I needed to move. I needed an exit.

Except . . . it was all in my mind. How could I get away from my own mind?

The phone chirped on the ground. Something else was happening on Darius's end. I rocked back and forth, trying to breathe, trying to think. A few words floated through my ears from the phone: "Hammer," "lowlife," "killed," "Jack"—and abruptly, the call disconnected.

My panic increased tenfold. I slammed my heel into the phone and shattered it.

That wouldn't be enough though. I got to my feet, head pounding. They could be coming for me. I had no way of knowing if I'd been traced. Without a moment to lose, I sprinted for the door, heedless of the continuing spikes of pain from the gunshot wounds. I needed to get away.

But where? My hideouts could be compromised too . . .

Night had truly fallen by now, and there weren't many people outside. I bolted outside, slammed by the curtain of water falling from the sky, and rushed onto the street. There weren't many people around, but I heard shouting. Someone stood out—a man, face darkened by a hat, a long overcoat hugging his shoulders. He could be concealing any number of weapons. The man's hand withdrew from one and lifted to his ear.

Was he calling Darius? Calling Hammer? Calling Jack?

I had no idea and I wasn't about to find out. I drew my pistol and shouted—a meaningless sound, a rage and confusion-fueled primal roar of pain.

He dropped the phone and bolted, practically screaming, into the nearest alleyway. I reached his phone and picked it up. The number was 911, and he'd just pressed call. He wasn't involved . . . but the cops would be on their way. I needed to get moving, either way.

I let out a huge breath. My heart kept racing and my head kept thumping, as if I'd just run a dozen miles, but I seemed to be in the clear for now. I started moving, a bit less frenzied this time, more controlled, more purposeful.

The back of my neck was prickling so much now, it might as well have a porcupine stuck to it.

Another voice called out behind me, something I didn't quite understand. For the briefest moment, I thought it sounded familiar, but I didn't dare turn around to check. If it was familiar, it could be someone from our gang. I needed to get out of there. Taking a page out of Faith's book, I ducked into an alley and immediately broke into another sprint.

By the time I went through two more alleys, I was pretty sure nobody was following me.

I took a moment to catch my breath. My bag was too loose, bouncing against my leg as I ran. I tightened it and double-checked my bandages again to make sure I wasn't bleeding all over the place. They'd probably never heal at this rate, with how little time I had to rest and recover. My other eye was never going to get fully charged, either, as it perpetually hung in the lower third of its battery life.

My hideout. I need to get to my hideout.

Getting there wouldn't be easy. I wasn't in our district, nor was my hideout, but I'd have to get pretty close. Either that, or I'd be heading into a part of the city where I was probably worse off—the richest sector, where the cops made regular patrols twenty-four hours a day, along with tons of corporate security. They'd scan the guns I was carrying and take me out in no time at all.

I didn't have another choice. I started off, moving between city blocks, desperate to reach my hideout and some measure of safety. I wanted something familiar and safe, but Darius had taken everything else away. All I had were the few places I'd made for myself, and the rifle tucked safe in the bag at my hip.

My rifle.

It wasn't Darius's rifle. It was mine. I could trust that, if nothing else. Even if he'd had it designed for me, custom-built with technologies most militaries didn't even have access to, I wouldn't let him have that part of me.

I heard a gunshot.

Instinctively, I dove to the ground, though it hadn't been near me. There was a good block or two between me and the source of the shot, but in my current state, I was on a hair trigger for *everything*. As I crouched in cover, watching down the street, I heard screams.

It was coming from our district.

People began diving for cover, screaming and panicking. Gunfire in our district was practically unheard of. It was why I'd been so shocked that our people started firing in the open when I'd gotten near. We kept the peace and we'd been too strong for anyone to challenge. Except . . . apparently somebody was, right now. It couldn't be a coincidence.

I moved forward, darting around the townhouse steps one by one, keeping to the darkest parts of the street. I saw a streetlamp pop ahead as someone shot it out. It disgusted me. I hated seeing this sort of public terror, watching dark shapes rushing through the city night, gunning for one another in the open.

Guns were a private thing. They shouldn't have been brought into the public like this. Firearms were for taking out threats and keeping the peace, not for this sort of wanton violence. The public wasn't ever supposed to see something like this. We had rules. They were unspoken, unwritten rules, but it was a code, and nobody broke it.

Until now.

I dove to the wall as an SUV spun around the corner ahead. From cover, I watched the windows burst open as gunfire peppered the sides. Flashes of fire shot back out, the chatter of an automatic weapon. They fired indiscriminately into the street, and I was almost certain they'd hit the bystanders cowering behind cover.

Above the sidewalk, the windows of the apartment building shattered. People were firing back—*our* people. I even recognized one of them, silhouetted in the light from his bedroom. They took out the gunners in the car, but more were arriving. This was erupting into a full-on battle in the middle of the night—and I was stuck in it.

A car was driving straight down the street toward me. I pulled out my rifle and slammed the button to expand it. One shot, straight into the front tire.

It burst. The car skidded off to the side and slammed into a fire hydrant. Water burst into the air, mixing with the pouring rain.

I dropped my rifle back into my bag and turned away. I couldn't get to my hideout. This was only getting bigger. We'd never had a real street war in Seattle. Most disputes here got settled with words or money. If that wasn't enough, someone like me was employed. We kept things civil, compared to some of the other urban sprawls at any rate. Every gang maintained a respectable armory, but it was all about intimidation. Nobody ever expected to use it.

Well . . . guess it was bound to happen sooner or later.

Who was going after us though? My first thought was Jack, of course . . . but we'd been on solid terms with him. More importantly, he didn't have the best relationship with the other major gangs of the city. We kept them in line, which let Jack operate in relative peace on the coast. If he was attacking us, it put him in just as much risk.

More gunfire erupted in front of me. The streets echoed in every direction with bullets crackling and ricocheting off stone walls. I couldn't get anywhere now. This wasn't just one battle. This was a whole war, just like I'd thought, and I was trapped in the middle of it.

I could go into an apartment complex, but I didn't want to tangle with the residents. For now, I was still just another anonymous civilian, a nobody in the crowd as long as I didn't draw my weapons. My hand was in my bag clutching the grip of my pistol at all times, just in case, but outwardly I just looked like anyone else on the street.

A shop. I could see corner stores starting to close up, metal security shutters slamming down, the occupants praying they were bulletproof enough to protect against stray gunfire.

Wouldn't work against my rifle, but everything else . . .

I sprinted toward the nearest open shop. It was a bar set into the corner of the block. The lights were on, and I could see a man rushing down the stairs to reach a button on the wall.

The metal shutter began to slide closed behind the doors while every window in the place matched it. I reached the door and yanked it open. The shutters were over halfway down. I dove.

I only barely made it inside. As I landed on the tile floor, a sharp wave of pain rushed through my body. I cried out against every instinct, and a huge wave of nausea cascaded down into my stomach. It was too much. Between the stress, the adrenaline, the sharp waves of agony and nausea, I fell apart.

As my world faded away into pitch-black, I only vaguely made out the face of an old man walking toward me, saying something I couldn't possibly understand.

I still felt groggy, and pain in my shoulder and stomach was flaring up again. The whole world was dark and cloudy, as though I were trapped in a huge fog—except for my other eye. It was giving me something totally different. I saw something . . . spinning. It kept moving in circles, over and over, leaving and coming back around again way above my head. It took me a few minutes to figure out what it was.

A ceiling fan. I'm in a bar. Middle of the night. There's a war going on.

My eye snapped back into focus. I felt like my brain was a solid rock, a huge weight instead of the sharp muscle I relied on every day. I struggled to catch up to where I was, focusing on the environment around me.

A faint *whumph* signaled an explosion of some kind, muffled by the metal shutters around us. More *tap-taps*, bullets plinking off random parts of the street. The battle continued in earnest outside, but I seemed to be safe for now.

Old man.

The guy who owned the bar suddenly popped into my brain. I felt around and realized I'd been moved onto the bench of a booth nearby. My bag lay next to me . . . and my guns were still inside. I breathed a sigh of relief.

"You awake?" asked a voice nearby, nervous and shaking.

I stiffened. My hand grabbed my pistol without thinking. I took aim, but I didn't see him anywhere.

"I don't want any trouble," he said.

"I—" A cough overtook me. I had to clear my throat, struggling to breathe properly. It wasn't easy still laying on my back, so I struggled upright—and found myself staring down a double-barreled shotgun.

". . . You gonna be trouble?" asked the old man, shaking a little.

"No," I said, doing my best not to move.

"You got a gun."

"So do you," I pointed out. "Most people can't get guns in Seattle."

"Gotta protect myself," he said. "Dangerous 'round here."

". . . You're from the Republic?" I asked, trying to ease him back a little. It was audible in his accent—a Texan lilt just under the surface. Most Texan transplants tried to hide it. There was a prejudice against them in parts of Cascadia, and though the law protected them from discrimination, that didn't stop people from treating Texans like outsiders.

"Born and raised," he said proudly, and the shotgun lowered a little. "So don't think I don't know how to use this, Miss."

"I'm just trying to hide," I said as calmly as I could manage. "I don't want any trouble either."

". . . Okay," he said finally, lifting the gun away. He glanced at the door, still securely locked behind the metal shutter.

I coughed a few more times and finally struggled fully upright. "Is anybody else here?"

"Nope. I was gonna close down for the night when everythin' started explodin'." He squinted at me. "What the hell's goin' on out there?"

"I don't know," I answered honestly.

I had a few rough ideas, but right now, I felt as clueless as he did. I felt like Jack had to be involved . . . and I felt like I was being used somehow. I didn't like it. I needed more information, and now that I had a safe place for a little bit, I could actually start getting some.

The old man had lowered his shotgun completely, though he hadn't let go of it yet. I still had to step carefully around him.

"Do you have a computer I could borrow, please?" I asked as politely as I could.

He snapped back to look at me, eyes narrowed. "What d'ya need a computer for?"

"I want to message a friend and let them know I'm safe. Also, not to come out this way tonight . . ."

His eyes softened. I felt weirdly uncomfortable taking advantage of him like this, but . . . I wasn't going to really do anything bad here.

"I'll go get my niece's laptop," he said finally. "You wait right here."

"Okay."

As soon as he left, I wished he'd come back. The moment he'd disappeared upstairs, the full weight of what I'd heard back in the abandoned store started to hit me.

Darius said . . . said I asked for it?

He had to be lying . . . except Darius never lied to me. That part I felt was true, and he'd reaffirmed it. Yet . . . he'd done this to me. Which was I supposed to believe?

He should have told me. But . . . if he told me, I'd ask to know what I didn't want to remember. Do I . . . do I want to remember it still?

I needed to know. Not knowing was worse, I could say that with certainty now. Nothing could be worse than being trapped inside my own skull, feeling like pieces were missing from my life, and never being sure which parts were true and which were a construction.

He said they couldn't make new memories. Do I believe him?

If he was telling the truth, maybe I could find real answers. If he was lying . . . did it matter? I wasn't sure. Either my whole life was a fake, and I'd kill Darius, or . . . he'd just construct new memories again, and I'd never know. If I was going to stay sane, I had to believe the memories in my head were real. Anything else, and I'd fall apart completely.

The barkeep returned with a laptop plastered with giant flower stickers. I took it gratefully and plugged in at the table. To my relief, he had solid internet. Immediately, I copied out all the files I'd taken off Jack's laptop from my portable drive, so I could start investigating them more thoroughly.

There was . . . a *lot*. All of it had to do with Darius . . . and most of it wasn't good.

The old man was back behind his bar now, polishing glasses between glances at me and at the door. He still seemed nervous, but I got the impression it was more to do with the outside than with me. Thankfully, the gunfire had finally died down, though we still heard more shouting and the occasional shot—the war definitely wasn't over.

I couldn't bear to look at the contents anymore. I'd learned more about Darius's operations than I'd ever known in mere minutes. He was my brother. I'd worked for him for years now, at the top of his gang . . . or so I thought.

This could still be false. I don't know where this all came from. I need proof.

The forensic tools did their job. Most of the metadata was scrubbed clean, but I found a server origin point buried within the directory structure on a few hidden files. Jack wasn't good with computers— I doubt he had a clue how to clean most of this—but someone else *had* cleaned it. They'd missed one or two *tiny* pieces, barely identifiable crumbs.

I recognized those crumbs. I knew *exactly* where Jack got all his info from, because I used the same secret broker.

There were few people in the city with the kind of connections to get any kind of info you needed at a moment's notice. We had one in our gang, but when I was working an outside job, or I didn't want Darius to know what I was doing, I used Jerome. Everybody did, because Jerome was the best-connected scum in the city.

I hated him. Everyone hated him. But he did his job well, he did it fast, and he charged a pretty reasonable price, so everybody used him. Now, as I was fast learning, "everybody" included Jack.

Guess I'm going to give Jerome a visit.

As I got to my feet, I felt dizzy. I nearly fell over and had to drop back onto the booth bench again, clutching my stomach.

"You okay?" the barkeep asked nervously.

"Just . . . just need a minute," I choked out. After a few minutes, though, it became clear I needed rest more than anything. With reluctance, I glanced up at him. "Can I sleep here tonight?"

". . . Anyone after you?"

I shook my head. "No." *Not right now, anyway . . . Darius specifically said I could wait, and Jack is waiting on me to go after Darius. Everybody's gonna be distracted with whatever's going on outside. I should be safe for the night.*

". . . Okay." He glanced at the door upstairs. "I'm gonna lock the door though. You stay down here. If you want somethin' to eat, it's yours, but . . . you're gone in the mornin', ya hear?"

I nodded, and immediately regretted the motion. "I'll leave money on the counter."

"Don' worry about it," he muttered, retreating upstairs to leave me alone.

When he was gone, I laid back down again. I normally wouldn't be able to sleep in a strange place without any assurance of security . . . but these were unusual circumstances, and I felt like I was in *way* over my head.

The most important person to rely upon is you. All the friends and allies in the world cannot help you if you can't trust yourself to get the job done.

Darius's words echoed endlessly in my head, a never-ending parade of platitudes and advice. Even now, when I wasn't sure if I hated him, if I could trust him, if I wanted to kill him . . . I still took his advice to heart. If nothing else, I trusted myself now. I trusted my own memories, though they abruptly stopped four years ago.

My brother had raised me to take care of myself in every situation, and now, stuck in a booth in some no-name bar, while a street war continued all around me, I felt the results of his pseudo-parentage more than ever. As I drifted back to sleep, pistol gripped tight in my hand, I held tight to that single thought—that I could take care of myself.

DARIUS

K ara, are you listening?"

"Huh?"

Darius made a *tsk* sound, glancing at his sister. "Please, Kara. Pay attention. This is important. It's history." He turned back to the laptop and pressed play to resume the lesson.

"Amid growing discontent between scandals, foreign policy nightmares, and overwhelming dissent between the regions of the country, the beginnings of the Californian Independence Party formed out of Los Angeles. Their rhetoric, a nonstop barrage of messages against the US government and the controlling political party, would inflame the disenfranchised Californian population to action."

A cartoon map began illustrating the various regions as they broke away.

"California eventually declared secession, and the region broke away from the country. Soon after, the Republic of Texas followed suit, maintaining a well-equipped armed forces and declaring neutrality in the brewing civil war of the eastern states. The Cascadian National Council met for the first time a year later in Seattle, Washington. Only a week after, they, too, declared independence, emulating the Texans in their neutrality while maintaining strong overseas relationships to keep their economic dominance . . ."

Darius glanced over as the lecture continued and saw Kara had fallen asleep. Her cybernetic eye was stationary while her real eye had slipped closed. She'd always had trouble following history or politics and most of her coursework, in fact. It just wasn't very interesting for her. He knew it wasn't the adult-level of the course—Kara had demonstrated more than a few times her precocious intelligence and ease at grasping high-level topics. Something about school though . . . it bored her.

She tried to fake it. Through every lesson, Darius had tried to engage her, and while she managed to project a false enthusiasm for a short time, it died out as the weeks went by. At first, he'd wondered if it was him—if some residual resentment meant she couldn't latch onto his lessons. He'd tried bringing in tutors, and there, he'd seen a *real* change come over her.

While Kara wasn't interested in his lessons, she *did* engage with him. The tutors though . . . Kara gave them the cold shoulder at best. He'd hired them discreetly from the best private schools in Seattle and beyond, but none of them knew how to handle a passive, obliquely hostile, potentially lethal one-eyed teenager with a chilling firearm obsession, whose name they were never permitted to learn.

The last tutor he hired, a psychology professor with a specialization in high schoolers, had given Darius a horrified report—Kara was mentally unstable and extremely dangerous. She was a violent sociopath waiting to happen, and Darius was enabling her.

He agreed with most of that diagnosis. The only part the psychology had wrong was the "waiting to happen" part.

Darius dismissed the tutors eventually, and instead had Kara enrolled in online courses. She took classes with a huge group of other students, under her real name—the only tie to her birth identity Darius permitted in her life. She would get an education, get a *degree* in her real name, and someday, she'd be able to escape this life. Darius had no idea what she'd do in their world, but . . . it had to be better than this.

Kara terrified him, in more ways than one. Darius had seen the results of her work firsthand, many times over. He bribed her to do well in class by promising access to more guns, more weapons, more power. It worked, and that frightened him even more. Kara started getting perfect grades in her community college courses in exchange for more lessons.

She was studying on her own, but she wasn't social. Kara had no friends, no connections beyond the tutors, Dr. Maclay, and Darius himself. He wasn't sure if she was better off that way—would friends help socialize her, familiarize her with a less violent world than the one Darius inhabited . . . or would she bring that violence into the complicated and confusing social structure of high school?

Darius didn't know what to decide, and so he went with the easiest choice. Kara would stay with him, where she could be properly cared for, where he could make sure her eye was working, that she was fed, that she stayed in shape, was well educated . . . was happy.

And she *was* happy. Darius saw that more often than not, and every time, it reaffirmed his choice. His sister, the most precious thing to him in the world, was happy and at peace, when he'd never believed that possible again. Every time she smiled, or laughed during one of their games, or showed a thrill of triumph when she mastered a new skill—Darius existed for those moments.

He knew his world wasn't a good one, but it provided for Kara's every need. He could live with himself if she was happy.

A *ping* on his cell phone signaled the arrival of Kara's present. Darius nudged her, still asleep in front of the laptop. It had paused automatically, waiting for an input from her. She spluttered awake.

"I'm listening," she yawned. Her real eye fluttered open and quickly found the screen again. Meanwhile, the cybernetic eye did the same as it always did whenever Kara woke up—a rapid scan of the entire room, so fast Darius couldn't comprehend how she possibly got anything useful out of it. Yet he'd tested her, and she'd proven it; Kara truly could look at everything in a room that quickly.

Kara leaned forward and pressed a button. The laptop confirmed the correct answer, and it proceeded to the next part of the lecture.

Darius raised an eyebrow. "I thought you were asleep."

"No," said Kara, shaking her head. "I was totally paying attention."

He frowned, suspecting some other form of cheating, but it wasn't the time to accuse her. Meanwhile, he was shocked to see how steady the cybernetic eye kept its gaze even as her head moved in all directions. She'd taken to the unnatural piece of hardware so fast, it unnerved him, just as so many other things about his sister did.

Rebecca had warned him most users never gained full motor function on the eye. The brain simply wouldn't rewire to operate the foreign device properly. At best, they occasionally got jerky, unsteady movements, but usually it operated as a forward-facing camera with a remote control they could attach to a hand.

Kara was an exception beyond their wildest projections. Rebecca speculated it might be due to her age, or perhaps some other factor they hadn't calculated, but Kara accepted it fully within a few months. She'd even learned to use it as a separate entity from her real eye, granting her incredible peripheral vision. The circuits in her arm had given her more irritation, and she'd complained for much longer, but given how well she'd adapted to the cybernetic eye, Darius had no doubt she'd acclimate soon enough.

"It's fine. No more lectures tonight. I've got a surprise for you."

He walked to the door. The package was in the delivery chamber, a one-way pneumatic chute that pulled the delivery up from one of his subordinates on the floor below. Darius plucked it out, and Kara's real eye widened slightly. He brought it back to the desk and set it in front of her.

"It's a little early, but I think you've earned it." He gestured at the case.

Kara glanced at it dubiously. "It's locked."

Darius didn't answer, simply raising an eyebrow.

She took the hint and began to examine the lock. It was a fairly simple deadbolt combined with modern electronic circuitry. One of Kara's recent fascinations was lock picking, and she enjoyed puzzles in general, so Darius had crafted this one especially for her. Kara quickly pried off the case and found an interface port. Without hesitating, she plugged it into the laptop and started querying the lock for more details.

Darius smiled as the first piece of the puzzle came up—the name of the device, which he'd encoded to word *thirteenth*. Kara, never one to give up easily, found the embedded unlock program after a bit of digging, which was simply named "happy," and prompted for an unlock code. Kara tried to run the usual keygens and brute-force attacks on it, but nothing worked.

She glanced at him, but he only shrugged.

Kara sat back in her chair, thinking for a moment—and finally, it hit her. She leaned forward and typed in the password: birthday.

The case popped open.

It was precisely as Darius ordered it, to his satisfaction. Kara looked over every inch of it, excited by the new rifle, one completely unique and designed just for her. It was collapsible without losing power or stability, quiet without overheating, easy to conceal and light enough for her to carry without much effort.

"This is . . . wow," said Kara, a little lost for words.

"It's yours," said Darius.

". . . What?" she asked. "But . . . you said—"

"This one is yours," he repeated firmly. "It's registered to your eyes as well. There's a trap built into the scope. If anyone else ever tries to look into it . . . well, they won't be very happy."

Kara nodded. "It'll explode?"

"More or less." He glanced at the clock. "Tomorrow, we can go out to the forest and you can try it, all right?"

Her face lit up—and it brought such a mix of fear and elation to Darius, he wasn't sure how to react. She nodded excitedly, still examining the weapon from every angle. Darius left her to it, only briefly reminding her to sleep soon or she wouldn't have much time to try it before class the next day. Kara waved him away, too busy learning every millimeter of her new weapon.

Darius watched from the door to his room, and he wondered.

Did I do the right thing for her?

*   *   *

Two months later, on a desperate night, Darius was holding council only a floor below. Kara lived just above the operations center in a secret home, the safest place Darius could imagine.

He and his trusted lieutenants were gathered around an array of monitors flickering between camera feeds. Each block showed another view of the city district and beyond as they desperately searched for their target. Every person clicked through feeds one by one, checking and double-checking, bringing fresh eyes, watching, hoping. They knew their quarry had to be in the district—it was only a matter of time before he appeared somewhere, and they could get people on him.

So far, though, it seemed Coburn had found a blind spot.

Despite their best efforts, they'd not yet gained a full blanket of surveillance over the district. Anti-surveillance laws and privacy laws had removed most legal camera coverage across the city, so Darius and his best hackers had no devices to hack into. The police were quick to trash any illegal cameras found, but the gang *had* managed to establish a strong secure net of cleverly camouflaged surveillance points, improved by a technology shared to Darius through his friendship with the Maclay company.

It wasn't foolproof. While they flicked through cameras, a police officer spotted one and threw a baseball at it. The feed cut out a moment later.

"If Coburn makes it out of the city, we lose our entire system," Darius reminded his men. His lieutenants all knew this, but a few of them could use the reminder of what was at stake. If Coburn got out, *everything* was out. They'd cut him off for now, but . . .

"I think I've got him," reported Michael, one of the newest of the leadership group. Darius hurried over and leaned in close. A possible match had been flagged by their facial recognition, and Michael had already cleaned up the footage by the time Darius got there.

He nodded. "That's Coburn. Southwest . . . Is he making for the ferry?" The pudgy man in the video was scrambling over a fence with surprising grace, some seven blocks from the piers.

"Looks like it. I can get someone there to shut it down in a few minutes."

"Do it."

Michael nodded and opened his phone, speaking almost immediately. His subordinates were prepared and effective. Darius was impressed. Michael's promotion was well earned. He returned to the feed, where Coburn was already changing course. The ferries had been a misdirect . . . *damn it. He knows we don't have enough boots on the street to corner him. But we have to try.*

"Can we get anyone into that area and flush him out?" Darius asked of the group. Two of his men practically scrambled over each other in their haste to reach their phones, dialing out to anyone they could raise at this hour. It was well past midnight, and most of their crews were probably asleep, or out clubbing or drinking.

Coburn had timed his theft well.

"I've got two guys within a couple of blocks," said Nathan, phone glued to his ear. "They're unarmed, but they can take him."

"Take him," said Darius. His eyes were still fixed on the camera feeds. He flicked through them again, focusing on Coburn's latest attempt to scale a fence. He wasn't *great* but somehow still managed to heave himself across in a minute or so. Darius shook his head. This pudgy, out-of-shape man was responsible for stealing enough secrets and evidence on their operation to get them all killed or jailed for a significant amount of time.

Coburn had been hired on as a security analyst for one of Darius's front companies, originally to test attack vectors on their network. He regularly penetrated low-level systems, but they were simple honeypots—designed specifically to allow intruders enough access and seemingly useful data to complete a counterattack. However, Coburn had leveraged that access into a back door for the whole network using forgotten debug controls, in a shrewd feat of reverse engineering that made Darius believe he *must* be a plant of some kind.

He only had access to the network in brief six second intervals, lest he be noticed, but Coburn was still able to leech a significant amount of data and build up a healthy archive of blackmail and configurations.

It was only by a lucky debugging session that afternoon that Darius even realized the breach. He'd noticed the server drives reading far more data than expected for a new program and dove into the logs, looking for anomalies. Coburn's leech on the server was plain as day, with his own access token attached. The man couldn't remove the token, but he *was* able to attach a flag to notify him if anyone ever checked the log.

The moment Darius opened the logs, Coburn disconnected. Within an hour, he'd fled his home.

He needed to die.

It should have been nothing. Darius's gang wasn't the most powerful in the city yet, not by a long shot, but they were respectable. They controlled a significant portion of the city, and better still, they did so with the cooperation of the police and the corporate security. Capturing a single man should have been easy. Yet . . . it had been hours, and the man still evaded them at every turn.

He's using our cameras against us . . . Darius knew he must have gotten a current surveillance map from his data dumping. Even so, Coburn *shouldn't* be so skilled. He was appearing on one camera heading in a direction, only to vanish and pop up on another camera two blocks over, moving the opposite way. The man evaded them like a master thief, and nothing in his background—which Darius had investigated *thoroughly* before hiring him—suggested this sort of expertise.

Darius's hands were itching. His instincts flared up. Something about the videos was definitely wrong. He leaned down over Michael's shoulder and paused the video they were looking at. Coburn had just finished climbing over a fence, and his jacket caught on the top. It looked . . . familiar.

He rewound the video. Sure enough, Coburn had climbed another fence in the exact same way, jacket caught on the top, but with a different background and mirrored to throw them off the scent.

"This is all faked," said Darius. His men looked up at him as Darius's adrenaline spiked in his blood. His head pounded with fear. "He's not on the streets."

"No, I'm not," Coburn said as he flung the door open, flanked by two hulking bodyguards.

Automatic gunfire raked through the operations center. Michael pulled Darius to the ground as the monitors above them shattered. The other men died before they could even get a shot off as the bodyguards sprayed the room with automatic rifle fire. Bodies collapsed to the floor, and Darius shut his eyes.

Kara . . . she's upstairs . . .

Michael scrambled for his pistol. Darius heard a few shots, nearly deafening him from the sheer pressure on his eardrums. One of the bodyguards grunted, and it sounded like they were taking cover. A few shouts of rage, but from the brief glance Darius got of them, they'd been wearing thick bulletproof armor. Michael's pistol wasn't nearly strong enough to penetrate. They weren't approaching just in case, but it was inevitable.

This was the end for them. His life's work, all his plans to improve the city, turn the decay around—lost. Michael still tried to land a desperate shot, reloading with incredible speed, but it wouldn't last. They'd already killed all the security outside too. Coburn was backed by serious muscle. *It's a takedown. We were getting too big. Someone up top wanted us gone. Maybe Black Thompson, maybe Jack, maybe the Nation. Does it matter?*

Footsteps were getting closer. Michael had stopped firing. Darius wasn't sure if he was out of ammo or waiting for a better shot, and evidently the muscle wasn't either. His imminent death brought new thoughts to Darius's mind, new fears.

What will happen to Kara? Nobody here knows she exists. Coburn wouldn't—I never typed her into a single computer. Rebecca knows, but

. . . can she really raise Kara? Could anyone possibly raise her besides me, knowing what she's gone through . . . what she is?

Darius's thoughts fled from his mind as the rear door—cut so as to appear perfectly flush with the wall—banged open. His eyes flew open.

The lights went out as a single bullet blew apart the ceiling lights. Michael, shocked, swung his aim around to the secret door that had swung wide, but Darius quickly shoved his aim aside. In the near-blackness, the only illumination coming from the flickering back-lights of bullet-ridden monitors, Darius could barely make out the silhouette of a young girl with a rifle. Coburn's muscle evidently hadn't thought to bring any light source or visual aids, as they hadn't fired yet either.

Kara, of course, had no such impediment. With her cybernetic eye switched to thermal, everyone was a brilliant white outline. She ducked behind a nearby chair, set the rifle on the armrest, and took aim.

Two shots burst through the room like twin cracks of lightning.

The bodyguards crumpled to the floor. One had just come around the corner to where Michael and Darius crouched, completely dry on ammo.

"Who the fu—"

Coburn's voice cut short as a third round blasted across the room. Another sound of crumpling as he fell to the floor. Darius held very still, watching the vague outline of Kara slowly sweep the whole room, scanning for more targets.

". . . I think that's it, Dar," she said finally.

Her voice, soft but perfectly clear and calm, broke the abrupt quiet of the room. Only Coburn's continued wheezing, the occasional crackle of a monitor, and the continued patter of rain on the roof above them reached his ears. Darius stood, with Michael next to him. His lieutenant vaguely swept the room with his pistol, looking for a threat, but Darius laid a hand on his wrist.

One of the monitors flickered back on, and suddenly Kara was perfectly visible—wearing a jacket and leggings with wet hair clinging to her cheeks. She'd just been taking a shower. Michael tried to take an uncomfortable step backward, but Darius held him in place.

"Michael, this is my sister." He didn't respond, still transfixed, so Darius continued the introductions, turning to Kara. "This is Michael Dunham, my best"—he paused, glancing around the room, and corrected himself—"my *only* lieutenant."

"Hello," said Kara.

Michael *finally* caught back up with the present at her greeting, seeming like a wave had just crashed into him as he stumbled a little. ". . . Has she always been here?" he asked carefully.

"Yes," said Darius. "She lives with me. I've never told anyone this, Michael," he added. He tried to inject as much gravitas to the phrase as he could manage, getting his point across with as few words as possible. Darius always felt implied threats carried far more weight than outspoken ones, and held less risk.

Michael, to his credit, caught up instantly. He gave a small nod and started to check the rest of the men, seeing if anyone had survived. Meanwhile, Darius walked over to the still-wheezing Coburn, bleeding out near the front door.

"Kill me and it all goes public," said Coburn, fighting through a bloody cough. "I've got a dead man's swi—"

"You don't," said Darius. "We already have several people at your home. Your net is disconnected, and you haven't had a chance to connect anywhere else, nor did you have time to copy all the data to a portable drive before you left. Nothing you own will ever be connected to a network again. You were smart, but not smart enough."

"We're clear," added Michael, a phone to his ear. "One of my teams is here and secured the perimeter."

Defeat and resignation filled Coburn's face. He wasn't an idiot—he knew when he'd been beaten. The man looked away, as disappointment and fear began to flood into his face.

"Who did you work for?" Darius asked quietly.

Coburn hesitated, processing. Darius knew that look. It told him everything he needed to know. He drew his own pistol and placed a shot directly between Coburn's eyes.

Michael flinched at the sudden noise, but after a look from Darius, simply returned a grim nod. He went back to work, beginning to recover from what they'd lost that night.

"Why did you shoot him?" Kara asked from her perch. She'd settled onto one of the arms of the chair across the room—she always preferred to sit on the arms, rather than actually in the seat of a chair. "Couldn't he have said something useful?"

Darius sighed. "Anything he told us would have been a lie, or outdated at best. He wasn't important enough to know anything valuable, and any access he had will have been revoked after he was discovered. They might have restored him if he was successful here tonight, but more likely, they would have just killed him. No one wants to work with a traitor twice."

"So . . . he needed to die?"

"Yes," said Darius. "He needed to die."

He crouched down and began to sift through Coburn's pockets. Inside, he found a handful of loose cash, a broken flash drive, a couple of magazines of nine millimeter rounds, and a folded up street map of Seattle. Inside, Coburn had marked dead zones, areas where Darius's gang had no surveillance so Coburn could pass invisible through the district.

Darius straightened back up, letting out a huge breath. He handed the map to Michael. "Well, at least we know what to work on."

A few hours later, Michael had cleared out the bodies. A few of his most trusted had come inside to assist, and every single one did a double-take at the sight of Kara—seated crisscross in the chair in the corner, rifle on her lap, her real eye closed, cybernetic eye perpetually scanning the room. She could be asleep, but Darius knew she was reading a book based on the subtle hand gestures from her hand on the surface of the chair. One earbud snaked up the side of her jacket, just barely visible as it burrowed through her dark hair. The faint music was barely audible in the near-silent room.

She refused to leave before anyone came in. Darius didn't insist—for the moment, he didn't want her out of his sight, and obviously, she felt the same.

Darius thanked the men for their quick response. He had a lot of rebuilding to do, and bonding with Michael's particular crew seemed a great start. Michael himself was an excellent lieutenant, and from the night's events, Darius already felt a strong bond and trust with him. He wouldn't abandon Darius, even in the face of a wholesale slaughter of leadership.

Likewise, Michael's men didn't seem to see the pile of bodies as a sign to abandon ship. If anything, they were more resolute. Darius was impressed. He relayed the thought to Michael as they shared a drink in the cleaned and rebuilt operations center, as the morning sun began to peek through the skylights.

"They're all good men and women," Michael said with a nod. "I don't deal with addicts or criminals. Security firms, ex-soldiers, mercenaries, cops, but only the ones I can trust." He fell quiet again, glancing at Kara with deep concern. "I have a daughter, you know."

"Yes."

"Around her age, in fact. Just two years older."

"Cassandra, right?"

"Cassie, yeah." Michael cleared his throat. "She gets . . . violent, sometimes. Rages, throws things around, tries to hurt people nearby. When she was younger, it just seemed like tantrums, but they never went away. She's sixteen now, and we had to cover up a *vicious* beating she gave a classmate." Michael shook his head in dismay. "It was some homeless girl, nobody really took notice of it, but it could have ended so much worse. I wouldn't put it past Cassie to end up doing something far worse someday."

Darius frowned. "What are you trying to say?"

"Anger, fear, jealousy. It drives kids to cruelty. Maybe it's revenge for a prank, or an insult, being inadequate. Jealousy of success or love, fear of the unknown, being different, being alone. Any kind of emotional stress. Your sister though . . ." Michael frowned. "I just don't see anything. She's . . . she's cold. She scares me." He paused, and glanced over at Kara. "Was that her first kill?"

"Yes," Kara said at the same time that Darius replied, "No."

Michael started. Evidently, he hadn't realized Kara was awake. Kara seemed surprised as well, opening her real eye and glancing at Darius, confused.

"She's shot animals on a hunting trip before," Darius said as calmly as he could manage. "A hunting trip in the woods. A few large deer and some smaller game."

"Ah," said Michael, obviously unconvinced. Kara seemed satisfied though, and returned to her book, her real eye closed once again. He turned back to Darius, voice reduced to a whisper. "What doesn't she know?"

Darius didn't respond. He'd take that secret to his grave.

Months later, as the rain turned to snow, Michael and Darius were once again gathered around a table, fearful for the future of their organization. This time, it was only the two of them, without any Kara upstairs—they'd long since divorced the operations center from Darius's home.

They'd rebuilt a great deal of their client base and reputation in the past few months, after the drama surrounding the Coburn incident. Michael's small, elite cadre was still the only group Darius truly trusted, but they had a solid network of runners and dealers mapped out, and the implants and sims kept flowing. The cash was flowing, the corporations were happy, and the cops were leaving them alone, but it was a precarious balance, and the two of them knew it.

The problem lay with the suppliers. Darius imported his implants from overseas, straight from factories in East Asia, without any government restrictions imposed by the mainstream brands. Theirs allowed for full nerve interception and interaction. Quality control was essential. If an implant was unstable, if it were tuned just slightly off, it could cause permanent damage to the nervous system. VR cripples weren't unheard of—and in fact, Darius had heard of far too many as of late.

It was their reputation and their entire business on the line. Michael doggedly followed the trail back to one of their middlemen, Lee En-Chih. Darius struck a deal with the man to bring in low-cost implants to handle their needs, but it seemed the Chinese black marketeer had other plans. After a *friendly* conversation with one of his underlings, Michael had discovered Lee was sabotaging a small number of their implants at the bidding of a rival, driving away Darius's customers.

Rumors were already spreading about the brain damage caused by Darius's product, the permanent loss of movement, cognitive function, memory loss, and other horrible effects. His men were sifting the product for faulty devices, but it wouldn't be enough. Their other suppliers were all well connected. They'd hear of the blow Lee En-Chih had dealt and would look to jump ship, or take advantage themselves and raise prices significantly.

Darius needed to send a message. Lee En-Chih needed to die, quickly and publicly.

"Yes," Darius answered finally, answering Michael's unspoken question.

"How do we do it?"

"Cleanly and in the open. There must be no doubt as to who killed him and why. You've been tracking him?"

"Yeah." Michael pulled up a few files on his screen.

Their organization may have been reduced to only a few core members, but Darius's network was still in place. They had extensive access to servers across the city, internet service providers, relay routers, cell phone towers, and more. It was practically trivial for Darius to intercept traffic and decrypt it thanks to back doors forced into the system by the government. The real trick was reassembling the traffic back into useful data. Luckily, Michael was diligent and incredibly thorough.

"Any opportunities?" asked Darius.

"He's going back to Taiwan in two days. But, before that . . . a charity event. Around seven o'clock at night in the convention center by the stadium." He brought up photographs of the area, as well as live feeds they could access nearby. "It's the only place I can be certain he'll be. No telling when he'll come back from overseas." Michael glanced at Darius skeptically. "There's no way we could get near it. Security's going to be tight. It's a high-class crowd."

Darius sat down next to him and examined the area. A few fire escapes across the road looked promising, but the angle was all wrong. The convention center was a solid building, for the most part, with the only windows above the doors facing the street. Any angle wouldn't afford much for a sniper, particularly if the event stayed indoors. The heavy rain forecast wasn't doing them any favors either.

"Does the center have any good back doors?" he asked, flipping through public blueprints of the building, now decades old.

"A few, but they're well known. There's no way we could get a gunman through, and definitely not fast enough to catch Lee off-guard."

"Hmm." Darius took off his glasses and cleaned the lens idly. He didn't need them, of course, but they felt right on his face. When he wasn't wearing them, his ears felt too light, his field of vision too wide. They helped him focus. "So we need to be there legitimately. The security will prevent weapons from getting in, and it can't be either of us. Lee would recognize us immediately." Darius paused. "What's this event for, anyway?"

Michael brought up the details. Darius read through them.

He read through it again.

"You've figured it out already," said Darius calmly.

"God help me, yes," said Michael, grim-faced. "I don't see any other way."

Darius stood up, turning to leave. "I'll be in touch soon."

* * *

"Kara?"

Darius opened the door to their loft, which was pitch-black. Rain pounded rhythmically on the slanted windows across the far wall. He rubbed his hands together, trying to get warm—their whole home was ice cold. He flicked the light on, squinting in the sudden brightness.

Their place was a wide-open single room—kitchen, living room, and bedroom all rolled into one, with a door to the bathroom set into the brick wall on the far side. Sprawls of computers, monitors, and various peripherals littered one side, full of half-finished projects. Their beds were on an elevated wooden platform on the opposite side, with one wide bed for himself and a small single bed for Kara, on which she currently lay with her tablet.

At the burst of light, she recoiled. Her cybernetic eye whirred around to focus on him.

"What are you doing?" he asked.

"Nothing." She shoved the tablet under the sheets and sat up. "What are you doing?"

She can have her secrets. God knows I've taken enough from her already. He pulled up a rolling chair and sat down. "How's your day been?"

". . . Fine?" Kara looked puzzled. "You're acting weird, Dar."

"I can't ask how my little sister is doing?"

"You *can*, but you never *do*. You just wait until I tell you at dinner. Or while we're watching TV. Or when I beat you in a game."

"Fair enough." He shrugged. "Want to play something?"

She smiled.

An hour or so later, she was smiling again as he fell into one of her traps. His general was far out of position, and Kara had snuck a few troops to strike at Darius directly. She'd win on the next turn. He conceded the game, as he had so many before. She usually beat him. He had trouble admitting it, but he really was getting beaten by his kid sister.

While she began to reshuffle the decks and set up the draft for another round, Darius pulled out his phone, checking for updates from Michael. As expected, Michael's man had gotten the rifle in place, neatly stowed away in an obscure corner of the convention center. Easy, when there wasn't any security in place yet.

As if on cue, Kara spoke up. "Did you take my rifle?"

He sighed. It was time. He was probably damning himself to an eternity in hell for this—on top of the eternity he'd already be spending there, of course.

"Yes. I'm sorry."

She frowned. "What did you need it for?"

"Something happening soon."

"Oh." Kara paused. "Are you going to kill someone?"

"Not me personally," said Darius. He felt himself on the edge of a cliff, gazing over the precipice, with his sister's curious face leaning over right next to him. He was about to hurl her over the edge. "Kara, I need your help."

He had no idea how she'd react. Darius wasn't even sure what kind of reaction he *wanted*. Eagerness would be horrifying. If she looked revolted, he could accept that, but he'd be even further into trouble. Confusion might be best, but it would subject Darius to even more torture as he explained painstakingly what he wanted Kara to do.

Instead, he got . . . nothing.

Kara's face didn't change at all. It was as if he'd said something about the weather. The lenses in her cybernetic eye whirred, refocusing as it changed targets to his face. He'd long-since gotten used to the look, but he understood why she could be so off-putting to people.

At the moment, her two eyes were pointed in entirely different directions. Her real left eye still pointed down, along with her face, focused on resetting the game, laying out the generals and the draft decks, carefully preparing according to the rules. Meanwhile, the slightly bulbous carbon-metal composite eye, with three lenses in a triangular formation, peered straight up at his face. If he looked closely, he could see the rings on the apertures rotating as they adjusted for a clearer picture.

She straightened another deck before finally answering. "What do you need me to do?"

He took a deep breath, all anxiety flowing away. Darius was over the edge—there was no turning back now. "There's a charity event two days from now for homeless teens at the convention center. A man will be there. We need him to die, in public, with a certain item in his possession, but none of us can possibly get in. The event is run by a high-class crowd and will employ the very best security."

He hesitated, as one final pleading voice in the back of his skull begged him to stop.

"You could get in. We've already planted your disassembled rifle inside the center. All you would need to do is walk in, plant the device in the man's coat pocket, put together your rifle, and hide in the rafters until you get a clear shot."

"And get out," said Kara.

"And get out," Darius agreed. He looked at her carefully, watching for a reaction. Her face was still calm as she looked over the generals, making her choice. "I only have one other person who could get into the convention center, and she lacks the . . . subtlety necessary to pull this off. I could send her in as a backup—"

"No." The response, so confident and direct, startled him. "I can do it."

"Are you sure?"

Kara didn't answer for a minute, and Darius couldn't tell if she was still thinking about the game or about what he'd just told her. Finally, she brought her whole face up to look at him, the white of her real eye a stark contrast to the dark cybernetic one.

"Does he need to die?"

Darius considered all the harm the man's sabotaged implants had already caused. There were already crippled sim junkies out there, many who could never walk, talk, or see ever again. Even beyond the impact to Darius's business, this could set back any form of neural interface research as the word spread. Lee En-Chih was a man unconcerned with the true damage he caused, working only for his employers and the highest bidder.

"Yes," said Darius firmly, no doubt in his mind. "He does."

Kara nodded. "Okay."

He was truly damned.

"Nobody else can hear me, right?" asked Kara, voice low.

"Just me, and they can't hear me either," said Darius. "Remember, don't play with the transmitter too much. It took a long time to get it hidden inside your arm properly."

"Got it."

On the monitor, Kara went inside the building. It was a strange view. He was seeing through Kara's eye, quite literally, on a one-way transmission bounced through the circuits on her arm. They'd spend the last day putting together a transmitter that could hook into her arm circuits and access the eye output. Normally, this was rigged to be impossible at the hardware level, but Darius had managed to hack it together in the last twelve hours.

Now, he could watch as she approached the entrance to the convention center, sliding easily into the crowd of homeless teens. A curtain of her hair hung over the cybernetic eye, obscuring it just enough that she wouldn't be noticed, but not so much they couldn't see. The eye's software was able to calculate around the strands with multiple lenses, filling in the gaps automatically on the feed.

Darius sensed her getting anxious as she got surrounded by the crowd. Kara had never done well with large crowds—she'd barely been in a single one in her life, even before all of this. The video stream got worse as her cybernetic eye jumped around more frequently, focusing on every single person around her one by one, marking them as targets.

He needed to help her calm down. "You know, I saw you cheat in the second game last night."

She laughed, a bit strained, but still—it eased his mind. "You're bringing that up *now?*"

"I demand a rematch."

"Fine."

"And no tracking heat on the cards this time."

". . . How could you tell?"

"I guessed. Thank you for confirming it."

"Dammit."

He laughed. She sounded much better already. He'd gotten her to relax. She could focus on the mission. The other men in the van looked around, confused. They were in a portable operations center, a block of monitors hooked up on the wall of the vehicle. They couldn't hear her, of course, but Darius had laughed louder than he'd meant to.

They were here to evacuate her if needed. These were Michael's handpicked men. They had no idea who they were protecting, nor did the other group Michael was with at the secondary exit. All they knew was that Darius had hired an assassin who could get into the event, and they were here to pick her up afterward. Tonight, they'd meet the newest member of the team, after she'd already proven herself—the best possible way to bring Kara into his organization.

She was inside now, looking through racks of free clothing the charity had set out against one wall. Kara had scanned the area without seeing Lee En-Chih anywhere. Now it was time to blend in, make her way to her weapon, and wait until she found an opportunity. Her arm reached out, spinning a rack of shirts around.

"Who the hell are we watching?" muttered one man nearby. Darius shot him a look, which shut him up instantly. He couldn't blame the man though—on the monitor, Kara's arm looked tiny, especially coming out of a loose hoodie sleeve. They'd do their jobs though. Michael's method of recruitment was slow, but it only picked up the very best—professionals.

"See something you like?" Darius asked Kara, returning to his own monitor, and using a low voice no one else could hear.

"Will you get it for me?"

"They're free, remember?"

"Right."

Kara wandered away from the shirts, making her way closer to the lockers where her rifle was stashed. She stopped at a table of jackets. One clearly caught her eye.

He smiled. It was entirely her—a dark green military jacket, too large, but warm and thick, with pockets for everything she could possibly need. It was something useful, something she could hide inside. She picked it up and pulled it on. The sleeves went well past her hands, but not *too* far.

"You'll grow into it."

"Mm-hm." She continued through the room, ignoring a boy who'd been trying to catch her eye. Darius wondered if she even noticed. "It's a little weird having you in my head."

"Do you need me to stop talking."

"No."

The view swiveled around—facial recognition had picked up their target. Lee En-Chih was surrounded by people, glad-handing important city figures. He spotted a major computer company executive, the head of the school board, a senator, a teenage girl he couldn't identity, the head of the charity, and other less notables.

"You see him?"

"You see what I see," Kara murmured.

"You've got the implant?"

"Yeah." She hesitated. "How do I do this?"

Darius considered for a moment, examining the scene on the camera. Kara was stalling at a table, looking down while her cybernetic eye kept the view on the group. As they shuffled around a little, people coming and going from the conversation, he spotted an opening.

"The girl he's right next to. Can you bump her into him?"

"Then what?"

"Look how she's standing. She's got a bad leg."

Kara nodded slightly, hair bobbing up and down as the cybernetic eye's stabilizers kept the view steady while she moved. "He catches her, and while he's distracted, I drop it in his coat pocket."

"Yes."

Without another word, Kara started her approach. She aimed for a table next to them, but at the last second, deliberately stumbled. Her shoulder rammed straight into the girl's back. She fell toward Lee.

The man caught her just before she fell. As Lee moved, Kara's arm flashed out, and Darius only barely spotted the implant drop into his jacket pocket. She walked away calmly as if nothing had happened, ignoring the girl ranting behind her and the gasps of surprise. Apparently, Kara was the rudest girl to ever walk the streets of Seattle, as well as many choice expletives Darius would rather never hear again, particularly about his little sister.

A few sighs of relief echoed through the van next to him. The men were relieved—and impressed. Kara had pulled off the drop perfectly. Darius hadn't doubted she could manage it, but she'd deflected suspicion so perfectly that nobody had given her a second glance, based on the other camera feeds inside the convention center. Even the girl was already back to the conversation as if nothing had happened.

"You remember where your rifle is?" he asked.

"Second locker on the left, the bank nearest the girls' restroom. South wall."

"Good."

She reached the locker, secluded in a corner. It was one of the few spots out of sight of the cameras. They only had her vision to monitor from here out, as Darius had deliberately knocked out every camera between this spot and her firing position. No record of her presence would exist from this point onward.

Kara glanced around, making sure for a third time no one was watching. The lock was simple, coded to a digital key Darius had provided. She picked it out of her pocket and plugged it in, unlocking the electronics in an instant. The door popped open and there was her bag, totally innocuous. She picked it up, nonchalant as could be, and proceeded to the rear stairwell nearby, hurrying up to the rafters.

"Doing okay?"

"I'm fine. I'm trying to listen though."

"I'll be silent." He didn't like it, but he understood. Kara relied on every sense she could. While she was shooting, her both eyes were focused on the target, leaving only her ears to warn her of incoming danger. Any sound he made could potentially cover up an approaching threat. She'd be on her own now.

Kara reached the top floor, where the maintenance workers had access to the roof fixtures above. She peeled off a ceiling panel and slid it aside, dropping herself onto the wide upper surface of the lights. They'd provided her with a layer of insulation to protect against the heat of the huge light fixtures, but even so, Darius could tell it was already sweltering. Kara pulled off her new jacket and laid it aside for the moment, and then set to assembling her rifle.

The front of the light fixture was just ahead. With her rifle's barrel extended and a magazine loaded, she crawled up to the edge, set the bipod out, and settled in. The barrel didn't extend past the edge, but she was lined up for the stage where the speeches would be given later in the night. She couldn't be sure where Lee En-Chih would sit, but they knew he was an honored guest and would be up front. All that remained was to wait.

She relaxed and laid down flat on the light fixture.

"I think I'm good," she said quietly.

"Not too hot?"

"Feels kind of nice, actually."

"All right." Darius glanced at the clock. "You still have plenty of time. The speeches don't start for twenty minutes, if they hit their schedule. So, half an hour at least. He won't be on the stage until then."

"Okay." Kara's cybernetic eye screen switched away from the range finder and up popped a virtual book—a story he didn't recognize, but it seemed to be science fiction from a glance.

"Mind if I read over your shoulder?"

"It's more like you're reading through my brain."

"Don't be pedantic."

"What does pedantic mean?"

He was about to answer, but the cybernetic eye beat him to it, popping up a definition floating beside the book. "When did you add voice recognition?"

"A few weeks ago. It doesn't work very well yet."

"Voice recognition never has. People have been working on it for decades, but it's always a mess. Nobody ever seems to get it right."

"Maybe I will."

"Want me to help you out?"

"Sure." Her hair moved slightly, and Darius assumed she'd just shrugged. "I'm just following guides online right now anyway."

Darius laughed. "That's how all programmers learn."

She flipped through the pages of the books. The software didn't display the title anywhere, and the next few pages didn't help much, either, in identifying it. "What are you reading?"

"It's an old sci-fi book. It had people with cybernetics in it, and I was interested. It's nothing like the real thing though."

"Hm. You would know, I suppose."

"They mention stuff like their leg getting painful when it gets cold out. And the guy with cybernetic eyes just sees stuff. His eyes don't do anything." Darius was surprised by the sudden passion in her voice. "It just seems like such a waste."

"No one knew how far technology would go back then. Or at least, not how fast. Even so, your eye is unique."

"Cool."

Kara went back to the book, and only the faint hum of the lights reached his ears. Every minute was agonizing for Darius as she kept reading, calm as could be. He assumed she was calm, anyway—he could only see what she saw, after all. He had no idea what the expression might be on her face, her body language, her real eye. She could be feeling any number of things, and with only the steady feed of her cybernetic eye, Darius had no context to build from.

After a few minutes, a loudspeaker announced the speeches would be taking place in ten minutes. A few windows flashed up on screen as Kara started a timer in the corner of her vision for eight, before she went back to reading again. Darius could barely make out the stage behind her book, but it was directly in the center of her vision, so he concluded she must be watching it with her real eye.

Am I doing the right thing? He'd been entrusted with his sister's life and well-being. He was raising her, educating her, keeping her healthy and sheltered. Darius was the only person in the world for her at this point. She had no friends, beyond anyone she might speak to online. He'd instilled a healthy paranoia for the internet though, and she presented herself as a male high schooler or college student whenever possible. The only person she truly interacted with outside beyond himself with any regularity was Michael.

This was a way to get her out into the open, but with all the necessary tools and resources she'd need to survive. If she had a place in their world, the underbelly of Seattle, with a reputation for herself and a connection to an organization like theirs, she could survive. With the cybernetics and her missing memories, she'd never make it as a normal girl anyway.

I'm doing what's best for her.

Justifications and self-reassurances pounded through Darius's head, one after another. He'd chosen this life for himself over many years, time and again. He knew the stakes; he knew the dangers. She was just a kid. How could she even understand life and death, the magnitude of what she held in her hands?

Of course she can. After what happened, she knows it better than you do.

"Darius," Kara hissed in his ear, startling him.

The timer had just hit zero, and right on schedule, the stage began to fill. Her cybernetic eye zoomed in on Lee, and a faint red box outlined his head, following him as he moved. It swiveled, and armed guards were marked with yellow boxes. Her software kept them highlighted and tracked their movements. Darius had even added predictive algorithms recently, to approximate their locations if they left sight, behind cover or the like.

"When do I take the shot?"

Darius looked up at the man responsible for communication with the other squad and gave him a hand signal. The man returned a thumbs-up a moment later.

"We're ready," he reported.

Kara didn't answer, but the gun barrel began to extend. She leaned forward, and it just barely pushed past the edge of the light fixture. The steady rise and fall of her chest slowed as she controlled her breathing. Lee En-Chih stood up, hand reaching out to shake with the mayor. Her vision became perfectly still.

She exhaled. An instant later, Lee En-Chih's head burst open. He fell to the floor.

For a moment, nobody seemed to react. The mayor was frozen in place, his hand still extended, waiting. Everyone else was looking at him, waiting. Everyone . . . just waiting.

Pandemonium broke out. People screamed. Kara fired a second bullet into Lee's chest on the deck of the stage for good measure, then began to break down her rifle. Panic flowed through the crowd like a wave. From the other cameras, they could see people sprinting for the doors, heedless of one another. Guards were already searching for a target, but no one had looked up into the rafters. By the time someone did, Kara was already crawling back into the ceiling.

More shots echoed through the building, accompanied by screams. On the feed, holes burst into the ceiling. Someone had noticed the light fixture shaking.

"Are you—" Darius started, but Kara cut him off.

"On my way," she said, her voice still incredibly calm. As she made it back out of the ceiling tiles and into the maintenance area, her arm scraped against the side. The video feed went blank.

Panic flooded his veins. Darius felt like he was part of that crowd, infected by the same abject fear. "I've lost video," he said, struggling to keep his voice calm. "Are you still there?"

"Still here. I think I broke the transmitter cable." The audio was on a separate channel, to Darius's relief. He let out a sigh.

"Okay. Make your way to the exit." He was still anxious. She had a fair distance to go until she reached the stairwell, then the fire exit on the side, before she hit the ground floor. Kara wasn't likely to run into anyone though, thank goodness.

Of course, the moment he considered the possibility, it had to happen.

"There's someone on the stairs," Kara whispered. "I'm switching to the second exit."

"Got it." Darius waved at the communication man to get them ready. He started talking immediately to Michael's team. "They're waiting."

A slow, painful minute passed. He agonized through every moment of it, desperate for any sound beyond Kara's quiet breathing. Darius heard the slide of a pistol—*I didn't even know she brought one with her* . . .

"What's happening?"

A muted gunshot rang out. Kara's suppressed handgun. "One guard. He's dead."

"Are you all right?"

No answer. The feed from Kara's radio sputtered into white noise.

"Are you hurt?" Darius asked again, knowing it was futile. After another try, he switched his feed over to their net, listening in on Michael's communications. "Michael—"

"We have her." *Thank you* . . . Michael's calm voice gave more comfort to Darius in that moment than anything else in the world. "Snipe is secure."

Darius let out a deep breath, then— "Snipe?"

"The first thing I could think of. We can change it later."

"Okay. Is she all right?"

"She took a scrape jumping down from the fire escape, but she'll be fine."

"Good. Tell her she did well." Darius relaxed in his chair, his anxiety ebbing away, replaced not by relief, but by dread. Kara had done it.

Damned, damned, damned.

CHAPTER 8

I woke up with my pistol still in hand. The barkeep hadn't come back. I was still totally alone, metal shutters in place on the door and windows. My half-eaten pizza was over on the bar. I'd slept in the same booth he'd originally set me down in, not seeing any better options. I listened carefully, but there wasn't any noise from outside.

Time to go. No use sticking around any longer. I put the safety back on my pistol, dropped it in my bag, checked my rifle again just to be safe, and went to the door. There was a "closing time" function for the metal shutters, where I could leave and have them close behind me. I used it—better safe than sorry, and the old man had been nice to me.

As soon as I stepped out into the street, I heard a gunshot a few blocks over. There was *still* something going on. *Good thing I locked up, then . . .*

I hurried down a nearby alley and pulled up my hood. The streets were covered with a thick fog in the early morning. I could barely make out anything more than a few dozen feet away. My other eye did a little better once I brushed back my hair, but it wasn't great. The streets seemed to be devoid of people. My software highlighted the few, still in combat mode from the night before, but I ignored them. Nobody here was a threat.

I sat underneath a loading dock one street away and rummaged through my bag. A few things had gotten loose from their pouches and were jangling together in the center. I strapped them back in, not wanting to make any more sound than I needed to, then grabbed my burner phone, checking for messages.

Nothing. Not that I expected any—the only person who knew my new number was Faith, and after I'd sent her away the day before . . . she wasn't likely to get in touch.

Good. I'm confused enough already. I can't handle anything else right now. So I told myself, at least, but there was still a pang of regret for sending her away so roughly yesterday . . . If she'd taken everything from my hideout and split, I wouldn't blame her. I wouldn't likely be going back there either. I needed to track down Jerome first.

He usually worked out of a computer repair shop, a little dump of a place between the train station and our district. The station was a spot nobody controlled—by unspoken agreement, everyone left the transit to and from the city alone. I didn't expect it to last, but for now, that part of the city was relatively neutral.

But after last night . . . who knows what's neutral anymore?

It *had* to be Jack, didn't it? I wondered what he was playing at. He'd put a hit out on my brother, with the strong implication I was taking it. Right now, I honestly wasn't sure I wouldn't kill Darius and take the money if I saw him. After what I'd seen in that video . . . No matter what Darius said, he'd done something unforgivable.

Nobody could want this. Even if I did ask for it, it's too much. He turned me into a killer with nobody else I can turn to.

I sat back against the cold concrete wall and tried to relax a little. I needed to get some air before I went to see Jerome—scum that he was, the guy was still dangerous enough. I couldn't let my guard down around him, and with how the rest of my life was falling apart, I needed to keep our relationship strong just in case.

Everything I do is criminal, Darius. Is that what I wanted? Did you do that to me because I asked to?

It was ridiculous. Darius hadn't driven me into this life—I dove in headfirst, willingly. Truth be told, I didn't mind what I did either. Sure,

I only killed those who needed to die, but . . . I still killed. It didn't bother me. It never had. I held to that vague sense of moral justice like a lifeline, the idea that I really was making the world a better place in some indirect way.

More importantly . . . I was good at it. I got satisfaction from pulling off a job. It wasn't tied to Darius anymore—it was me. I did plenty of jobs without him around. I'd been able to survive on my own without him for over a year now, no matter what came my way. Case in point . . .

Someone was coming out of the fog. Someone armed.

His approach was direct. I had no way to get out of my spot without being spotted. I wasn't sure he'd seen me yet, but I was just sitting under a loading dock—any step, in any direction, meant I was right in the open with no cover. I pulled out my rifle and pressed the button to extend it. If I had to shoot . . . I was gonna make sure it counted. One shot, no chances.

He came out of the fog, little by little, pistol in hand—and stopped. He was looking right at the loading dock. My rifle eased up, finger inside the trigger guard. If that pistol moved . . .

"Snipe?"

Instantly, I pulled my finger away. I knew that voice.

"What's going on?"

He took another few steps closer as I lowered the barrel. I doubted he could see my face, but he knew my rifle—and knew nobody else in the whole city was likely to have its ilk. It was Alex Dunham, the son of my brother's second-in-command. He had a wiry figure, tall, but not remotely intimidating. The only signal of danger about him were a few tattoos, poking just up out of his shirt and onto his neck—but to be fair, he spent a lot of time in Portland. *Everybody* has tattoos in Portland.

Or so I've heard. I've never been there . . . or anywhere else in the world. I've never left Seattle, except with Darius into the forest to shoot.

I knew how dangerous Alex could be though. Appearances were deceiving. I'd seen him take down men three times his size easily. He used his apparent weakness against them and he didn't leave anything to chance, just like me. I appreciated that about him. He'd been a useful partner more than once.

Sometimes, on jobs for Darius—and even a few of the other ones too—Alex had acted as my spotter for targets. He'd be on the ground while I moved across rooftops or walkways, giving me locations, getting me into a good spot to take down a target. He was smart, he was capable, and he could be *very* charming. On top of that, he'd inherited his father's absolute professionalism.

We had a 100 percent success rate together. I enjoyed working with him. I wouldn't consider him a *friend* by any means—I didn't have any of those, especially not after I ran Faith off the day before—but he was an ally, and right when I needed one.

This connection was going to pay off big-time today. Alex had been out of town for *weeks*, down south visiting his boyfriend in Portland. He wasn't due to arrive in Seattle until this morning, and he'd probably have no knowledge of the events of the past two days if he'd just showed up this morning on schedule and wandered the street rather than reporting in.

I could use him.

"I don't know," I called back. I took a risk and waved him forward, lowering my rifle completely. He hurried forward and crouched down near me, watching out as I started packing up again. "There's been a ton of gunfire all night. My phone got hit. I haven't been able to contact anyone yet." I took another chance, asking an important question up-front to gauge his reaction and verify my trust. "Did you just get home?"

"Yeah," said Alex, and I suppressed a sigh of relief. "I was just heading to check in and heard an explosion. I ran into two of Jack's crew. What are they doing in our district?"

I glanced up and down the street, more to play for time than anything while I processed the info. They *were* Jack's guys. Alex would definitely know. So . . . if he put out the hit, why was he suddenly pushing for open warfare in the street? How was I supposed to kill Darius if Jack got him into a lockdown, all-hands-on-deck state? Jack wasn't an idiot, and this didn't play into any game plan I could see yet . . .

"Jack put out a hit on Darius," I said carefully. My own involvement had to stay a secret, until I knew just how far I could trust Alex. "We went into lockdown after the first attempt was prevented two nights ago."

Which wasn't an attempt . . . but Darius believed it was . . . He was supposed to be down in Portland. I don't understand . . .

"He was at station three the last time I contacted him, but that was before *this* started up," I added, gesturing at the scatter of bullet impacts on the wall in front of us.

Alex looked puzzled—and I *completely* sympathized. "So Jack puts out a hit, and Darius retaliates with . . . this? That doesn't sound right."

"It doesn't," I agreed, all too happy to speak my mind. "Something else is going on, and I don't know what it is yet." I glanced back at him. "Do you have a secure phone?" *If he does, and he doesn't give it over, I'm going to need an exit strategy here . . .*

"I didn't charge it enough before I left Portland. It's dead." Alex checked the magazine on his pistol and glanced down the street as well. "You got a plan?"

"Survive," I said, shrugging.

Alex smiled faintly. "You always do. Anything more substantial than that?"

"I've got one contact a couple of blocks away," I said. "He's an info broker that runs an electronics store. We could get to him. I don't think anyone from Jack's crew knows about him." *Except Jack himself, of course, and Darius* doesn't *know him . . . but Alex doesn't need to know that.*

He gestured at the street. "After you, then?"

I nodded and got to my feet, resisting the urge to wince at the pain from my skin scraping together over the bullet gashes. The bandages seemed to hold though. I didn't want to tell Alex I was already wounded, just in case he *was* playing me. Like I said, he was really good at his job.

My rifle had to go back in my bag, and Alex's pistol back inside his jacket. Now that it was morning, the coffee drones *were* starting to fill the streets again, getting their morning nectar before they crawled off to whatever office job filled their waking hours. More importantly, if we were openly carrying, we'd attract way more attention. Our best bet was to blend in—the two of us alone couldn't possibly take on Jack's crew, and he sure seemed to be throwing bodies at the district without any reservations.

The cold air chilled my skin. It wasn't raining anymore at least, but my breath came out in soft clouds. I wrapped my scarf tighter around me and pulled my jacket close, doing my best to keep a low profile while I followed Alex. I'd given him a basic idea of where to go, but I always let him scout ahead when we worked together. It made for the best movement pattern—he presented a target, whereas I, with my other eye, could spot threats much more quickly and easily than he would.

It wasn't chivalry or anything. Alex was better at hand-to-hand combat, so him being in front just made sense. Beyond that, he wore a set of body armor under his jacket—Kevlar, carbon fiber, lightweight ceramics, and a few other materials the military kept a tight secret. Michael got it from somewhere, and offered me a set, too, but it didn't move well with me. Besides, if I was getting shot at, I'd probably screwed up somewhere along the line.

I tried to scan every window, every doorway, every *shadow* as we walked. More than once in the past, I'd spotted someone leaning out, about to take a shot at Alex. Every time, I'd gotten them first, or at the very least, gotten them to miss and duck. Today, I was watching for anyone, friend or foe, terrified someone could jump out from any direction.

If you do not make allies, everyone is your enemy. Our world is life and death, Kara, and your greatest strength comes from those you can trust.

But, Darius, what about when *you're* the one I can't trust? When I don't know who's really my ally, because you took it all away?

We were moving between the shadows cast by the slowly rising sun in the east, peeking through the buildings. The street continued to fill up with more and more people, especially as we moved closer to the train station. With how many civilians filled the street, we didn't really need to be so far apart anymore. Alex came to the same conclusion as I did, and fell back to join me just as we rounded the last corner.

There it was—Jerome's shop. I stopped Alex with a tap on his shoulder, and we ducked into a side alley.

"I should go in alone," I murmured.

Alex popped out a vape and lit up, leaning against the wall. He nodded. "Your contact, your rules. I'll grab a paper and take the bus bench?"

He gestured to the bench, which was just barely out of sight of the store windows, but could easily see most approaches. Just close enough for a quick intervention if I needed it. Alex had done this for me before. He knew I had contacts outside the scope of our gang and wouldn't necessarily take kindly to outsiders. In fact, Alex had never let slip my outside affiliations to anyone in the gang before either—one of the reasons I trusted him now. He respected my privacy and my independence. Right now, I *really* needed that.

We split up. Cold raindrops splashed on my forehead as I crossed the street. Alex took the bench, puffing the vape and pretending to browse his dead phone while I made for the door. It wasn't open, but I had the code stored in my password vault on my eye. I scrolled through as I walked, picking it out just as I got to the barred door. With a quick wave to dismiss the interface, I punched in the code and let myself in.

The little bell jangled as I walked in. A thump in the back room told me I wasn't alone.

The prickles on my neck returned tenfold. I was in danger. I drew my pistol and dropped behind a shelf of desktop speakers, crouched low between them and the security shutters on the windows.

"Jerome," I called out. I waited, but no response. There wasn't any movement at *all*.

I edged forward, moving closer to the door behind the counter. There were four shelves packed to the brim with merchandise between me and the sales counter. I could approach from either side—the left had a slight disadvantage since I'd be visible through the partially open door, but the right didn't have much protection if they were at the far door. Of course, if they had anything heavy, I was dead already. None of this stuff was *bulletproof.*

I took a small stone from my pocket and chucked it at the door, loud enough to make a *crack* echo down the street. Alex would know my signal and start making his way around to the back.

Pistol at the ready, I started moving toward the counter, staying as low as I could. My arms were out at length, steady aim on the doorway. It twitched slightly.

I tensed up, finger on the trigger.

A small cat wandered out. Its tail brushed against the wood frame. The cat mewled at me, then sauntered away, ignoring me entirely. I let out a breath, removing my finger from the trigger, and kept moving forward. I slowly rounded the corner, still low, trying to come from an unexpected angle.

All that greeted me was a corpse.

Jerome was seated at his office chair, monitors live behind him with the last email he sent. He was dead, and who knew for how long? I stepped forward to examine him, after checking every corner of his little office in the back. There weren't any physical marks, but he wasn't exactly in bad health either. My first thought was poison of some kind. There was another door in the back, leading to an inventory room and a locked rear exit.

I checked both, just to be safe, then went back to the computer and bent over the keyboard, doing my best not to touch Jerome in any way.

His last email was to Jack Monroe, demanding payment. I clicked in further, curious. It was no surprise he'd been a broker to Jack, obviously—I'd figured out that much last night. I didn't begrudge him either. Jerome was a neutral party; he could work for any paying customer he liked. I was still disgusted by him, but I couldn't blame him working every angle.

I did wonder what Jack would *kill* for though. There wasn't any doubt in my mind Jack had gone after Jerome. His security was lax at best, so breaking into his emails didn't take any time at all. I just used a few of Darius's simpler tricks and I made it inside in minutes.

Alex walked in while I was typing. I'd opened the rear door for him. He still had his gun drawn, but I waved it down. We were secure for now. He walked up to join me, looking at the dead Jerome with a slightly sick expression.

"Your guy?"

"Yes," I said, distracted.

I was hunting for older emails in the chain with Jack. The most recent was exactly as I expected—demanding payment for supplying the video. Jerome had a frustrating lack of labeling, a disabled search box, and he'd deleted inbound and outbound addresses, so I had to do a lot of manual trawling to determine which emails were actually relevant. Mostly, I was working off time stamps added by the operating system, which Jerome *hadn't* cleared out.

"Jack?"

"Probably someone working for him, yeah," I answered. "Poison, I think."

The next email had a bunch of inventory receipts. Nothing useful, probably just laundering money. This was taking too long. Darius had made sure I knew my way around most operating systems, and it was time to start breaking out the real tools. I didn't have time to waste here.

I exited the email application and started writing a quick program— a script to convert all his emails into a simple plaintext format that I could search more directly. It was a complete hack, and Darius would have shaken his head in disgrace at how ugly my code was and how many shortcuts I used, but it worked. Within a few minutes, I had an entire archive of data to work with.

Simple phrases to start off. My first instinct was to try myself—under "Snipe," of course. I found a few emails *from* me almost immediately, quick clarifications on details from meetings we'd held in person. Jerome was never completely clear when we spoke, and I often had to follow up with him. I also noted, with some disgust, that he'd left my private encryption key right on his desktop for anyone to pick up.

I deleted it, but I wasn't worried. Nobody else would be able to access my emails, besides the ones I'd sent to Jerome himself—and those were innocent enough devoid of context. I used a unique key pair with everyone I ever communicated with. The compromised keys died with Jerome.

Emails emerged chronologically, beginning with the earliest, and I started skimming. I was looking for *anything* to explain what Jack was doing. So far, I'd only encountered one message I didn't recognize—a note from Jack inquiring about my whereabouts, which Jerome never answered. I felt an odd note of sympathy for Jerome realizing that. He'd maintained *some* code of loyalty to his customers, myself included.

I reached the last two instances of my name, barely glancing over them, when another one caught my eye.

In the second to last email, Jerome had offered Jack an authenticated, time-stamped video file, smuggled out of a Maclay Technology lab. He'd commanded a massive price and a clearance of all previous debts.

Ice shot through my body. There it was again. *The* video. The one that showed everything Darius had done to me. I didn't want to look at it again. I never wanted to *think* about it again . . . but it dominated every waking moment of my life. I couldn't *stop* thinking about it.

My hand seemed to have a mind of its own. The cursor slowly drifted onto the file.

"Alex, watch the front?" I asked.

He looked surprised, but nodded, and quickly exited the room. My eyes remained fixed on the screen as he walked away. I clicked on the file.

The video flickered on, exactly as expected. The sound skipped occasionally as one of Jerome's hard drives began to click. I'd just seen it yesterday, but once again, my knuckles gripped tight, fingernails digging into my skin and cutting circulation short.

Everything faded away as the video crackled to life once again.

The rain had stopped by the time I finished watching it again. The silence in the rear of the shop was absolute. I could hear passing vehicles sloshing through puddles in the gutter. I vaguely remembered they used to carry loud, roaring engines, but those had all vanished as Cascadia mandated advanced, quieter electric engines on every car, alongside the self-driving software. It was a rare privilege to drive one's own car these days, expensive and *very* difficult to license.

Everything moved faster, ran safer when they relied on the network. Every car knew where everyone else was, everything could be tracked, collisions avoided. People could just sit back and enjoy the ride while computers did all the work.

I still stood in front of the machine, with Jerome's corpse sitting just behind me, transfixed by an empty black window. The first time I'd watched it, my left eye had been fixed on its mirror. The frozen expression on my face, conveying so much fear and pain through a single weeping eye. There were open gashes along my arm and neck, a monitor showing the process of deleting my memories. The rest of the video had practically become a haze, details faded and lost.

This time, I watched Darius instead. His expression was usually so dispassionate, but this time, he'd been rife with worry. I'd never seen him so upset. He was a master of dissembling, of dealing with any situation while keeping his true feelings buried deep inside. The only time I'd ever seen him truly upset was . . . last night, when I called him.

And now again, in this video.

I'd always felt some familial love to Darius. It was respect, and loyalty, and sure, *some* enjoyment out of the games we played together, but I don't know if I'd call us *close*. Maybe we were close by default, since he was the only person I knew. I trusted him and I guess I loved him, but still—I'd always wondered how much Darius saw me as a sister and how much he saw me as an asset.

Watching the screen, watching his face, I was less sure than ever before.

The speaker pinged. Jerome's system had just popped up with an alert. His network *was* wired up with some solid basics. Somebody had just started trying to break into his firewall, and I recognized the address—it was one of ours. The time stamp was almost five minutes ago. They'd tracked down this IP, and with geolocation and mapping Darius had done for the city, they'd have the physical address any moment now.

"Alex, time to go," I called out. I plugged in my drive and started copying everything off as fast as I could. To my relief, it was finished by the time Alex walked in—plaintext emails weren't exactly large.

I drew my pistol and put two bullets through Jerome's hard drive. There was no guarantee he didn't have server-side backups somewhere, but at the very least, I'd be slowing things down. Sparks exploded outward as the bullets punched through the casing and destroyed the drives with a wrenching sound of metal.

"We've been traced."

Alex nodded, no stranger to cyber warfare. "Exit strategy?"

"Rear door, down the alley and east three blocks. We'll be close to one of my safe houses from there," I said hurriedly, stowing my flash drive back in my bag. "If we get spotted, split up and meet later," I added, fully intending to deliberately give Alex the slip at some point, before he realized I wasn't officially on his side anymore.

Alex drew his pistol and nodded. He led the way again, as usual, and I followed—back out into the street, back into potential danger, where

I had no clue who I could trust. Enemies could be anywhere, and they could certainly look like former friends . . . or family.

I couldn't stay where I was. All I could do was trust that the filled city streets, packed with people on their way to work, to shop, or whatever else filled normal peoples' lives, would keep any of the people hunting me at bay.

We only made it two streets before I spotted a threat.

CHAPTER 9

Three guys at the end of the street," I murmured to Alex. "Don't look."

He was walking beside me, holding my hand. We sometimes posed as a young couple. Everybody ignored the young inseparable couple holding hands everywhere they went. It blended into a crowd perfectly and gave us a simple excuse for Alex to be close by if I needed immediate backup.

Today, it meant I could redirect him before he noticed the three guys at the end of the street were *our* guys.

"Let's go there," I added, gesturing to a retail chain store nearby that took up the entire bottom floor of the nearby block. We were too exposed on the street, and this part of town only had dead-end alleys to duck into. The three guys trailing us were good—they stuck to our trail like hunting dogs. We needed obstacles to lose them.

I made for the entrance, dragging Alex behind me, keeping up the charade. I wasn't *totally* sure they were following us yet, so it was worth trying, and it kept anyone in the crowd nearby from getting suspicious or causing a panic. A chorus of chiming machines greeted us as the advertisements everywhere flickered to life. A huge gust of hot wind blew my hood off my face and my hair back as we crossed the threshold, vents built to keep out insects and debris from blowing into the store.

I brushed everything back into place to hide my other eye, and to my relief, nobody seemed to have noticed. The store was mostly empty. A few checkout stands pinged disharmoniously, automated boxes while the one attendant stood half asleep nearby. In contrast to the overcast gray skies outside, the whole store was lit up with a dense array of fluorescence befitting any major retail store. Bright primary colors assaulted us from every direction.

As we hurried down a set of aisles, avoiding the odd glance of an early-morning customer or bored employee, my other eye swiveled up to glance at a mirror mounted on a ceiling corner. I spotted the three men enter the store, not one minute behind us. They were following us—and one of them clearly had a pistol in his jacket.

I know him. One of Hammer's guys. He'll definitely shoot, even in here.

They were splitting up to cover and sweep the entire store. Worse, one of them was beelining for the other exit, putting him squarely on a path to intercept Alex and me. Our options were thinning rapidly. I couldn't engage any of them with Alex nearby, since he'd recognize them immediately—but if we split up, I'd be on my own again, and I *really* needed allies right now.

My phone buzzed.

I slammed it to my ear so fast, it cracked against my skull a little. Faith's voice crackled out, an angel's voice in my current panic.

"Get to the west exit, no matter what. Make for the curbside."

The phone clicked off.

I shoved it back into my bag. There was no time to wonder how Faith knew what was going on. Alex glanced at me quizzically but went back to scanning the store for threats. My mind accelerated as the world seemed to slow down around us. Plans and ideas raced through my brain, as I assessed and dismissed them as quickly as I could.

I needed to get out, unharmed, preferably with Alex at my side. We had to get through at least two men, both larger than either of us. Ideally, we needed to do it without firing a shot. I also needed to do it *now*, because one of the men had just rounded the corner to our aisle.

My mind collapsed inward as I moved, complex thought giving way to raw instinct and reaction. I forced myself to stay calm. I'd never been built for a straight fight in close quarters. They were all stronger and faster than me, and they outnumbered me three to one—likely with reinforcements already on the way. My one advantage was that they wanted to kill me. I only needed to escape.

"Sorry, Alex."

I grabbed him from behind before he could react. The barrel of my pistol poked between the seams of his armor, where I knew a shot would penetrate without fail.

He dropped his own gun immediately, startled, but not inexperienced. I wondered briefly what was going through his mind. Maybe he thought this was all part of some elaborate plan, that I was going to get us both out okay. I could work with that—but then he spotted Hammer's man, with whom we were both acquainted, and he knew.

"To the west exit," I muttered. "Right now."

"What's going on, Snipe?" Alex asked as we backed down the aisle toward the west side. Hammer's man had drawn his pistol, aim steady. The other two were approaching quickly, but Faith had chosen the direction none of them had taken, so their path to get behind us was much longer than expected.

I didn't answer, concentrating on holding the gun against his side while we stepped backward. My other eye was tracking the two men as best it could, predicting where they moved as they dodged between aisles. Indicators tried to follow them, but they were unsteady and flickering as the software lost confidence. I felt the impending pressure of action, of violence about to erupt within the store.

The only thing keeping us alive was Alex himself. They wouldn't dare shoot the boss's son. Michael was the number two, and they knew it.

We were twenty feet from the door when I made my move. I couldn't risk it any further. I swung my arm out wide, straight down the aisle one of the men was about to enter parallel to us, and fired a few rounds. He ducked away before I came close to hitting him—but the damage was done.

I'd opened the floodgates.

Hammer's man in front of us opened fire. Two shots landed directly in Alex's chest, knocking both us backward. Alex grunted, but the armor seemed to have held—until a third bullet came in. His arm burst in a dark crimson puff as the bullet flew through.

People were screaming. *Again . . .*

As customers scattered for cover, I fired a few shots back, just to keep Hammer's man down, but I was running low on ammunition. I felt Alex's stance weaken from the bullet he'd taken. I emptied my magazine, blowing apart an ad fixture on the end of an aisle and keeping Hammer's man down a few seconds longer, then turned.

We bolted forward as fast as we could, me half dragging Alex through the automatic doors and out onto the street. Right on cue, a dark car with thick windows pulled up to the curb. More shots impacted the store doors as they closed behind us.

The car door burst open. Faith was inside. She threw herself forward, arms outstretched.

I shoved Alex toward her, and Faith helped me get him onto the seat. She had to dodge out of the way as I flung myself on top of him.

"Go, now!" I shouted, scrambling around for the door handle.

The driver had already stepped on the gas, merging with the early morning traffic smooth as you please, while Hammer's men came sprinting out of the door. They lowered their guns as the car sped off. Firing in the store was one thing, but even Hammer's men weren't stupid enough to fire into traffic.

I managed to pull the door shut, then turned to look at Alex. His arm was covered in red, sleeves soaking, blood leaking out onto the seats. I glanced at Faith, who already had a first-aid kit in hand.

"I hope you know how to use this better than I do," she said, glancing uneasily at Alex.

I nodded, grabbing the case and turning back to him. "Hold his arm up above his head. We need to keep pressure on and make sure it doesn't release too much blood."

I grabbed out cloth bandages and started to wrap the bullet hole. It went completely through. We could clean, bandage, and tourniquet it until he could get some real help. Alex groaned, returning to his senses after the shock of taking three bullets finally began to wear off.

"Snipe," he said groggily, "weren't those our guys?"

I continued bandaging him without answering, but Faith decided to fill in the silence for me.

"Yeah, they were. You missed some bits while you were down in Hipsterville, Alex." She let his arm down gently as I finished tying up the tourniquet. "Don't worry. You're not the first person to bleed on these seats this weekend." She laughed sardonically. "Your gang's decided they don't much like Snipe here anymore."

"Faith—" I started, but Faith cut me off.

"Hey, he's taking bullets for you, so he should know *why* at least. Hell, you've kicked off a war across the whole damn district with your shenanigans. I never thought I'd see open gunfire in a *supermarket*." Faith paused, a slight grin creeping onto her face. "You just gave those poor retail drones the most interesting shift of their lives."

Alex coughed, his gaze shifting over to me. "What did you do?"

I didn't answer, sitting on the floor of the back seat. Faith's car was nice—*really* nice. I had my own questions to ask, but right now, I was coming off a huge adrenaline rush, and the weight of everything happening around me was still sinking in. Faith was watching me, concern etched into her face.

"Look," Faith said carefully, "I already know. It's all over the streets." She got up and took the seat next to Alex, leaving me alone on the wide floor. "Hammer's not exactly *discreet*, and with the war we started overnight here, you're not gonna have many allies left. Since you didn't just drop Alex here during your daring escape, I'm guessing you care about him at least a *little* bit."

I nodded.

"Right. So he deserves to know too. He'll know sooner or later, unless he kicks it from that gunshot."

Faith cocked her head to the side, perfectly in time with a sudden burst of light as the sun peeked through the gap in the skyscrapers around them. It was off-yellow due to the tinted windows, but it still bathed her in light while I sat down in the shadows at the bottom of the car.

"Besides that," Faith went on, "I'm still looking to know the why myself. I'm investing the personal property of somebody *very* close to me here to get you out alive and the life of a very kind Japanese guy in the front seat. I'm putting all that on the bet that you're actually a good person worth helping. So," she concluded, tossing her hair out of her face, "are you?"

I took a very long time to respond. My left eye watched the passing cars in the street behind her. Our driver was obviously taking a substantial detour but still heading back to the hideout I'd given Faith in what somehow seemed like a different lifetime altogether. Once we made it back there . . . where was I going next? What were we going to do *then?*

Alex was bleeding out. I was being hunted by all my brother's men, and some of them would shoot at me in broad daylight. Everyone believed I was trying to kill my brother, and I wasn't even sure I disagreed with them.

What we do stays in the shadows. The public wants to believe they live in a safe place, and as long as we stay out of sight, it's true. Safety is a belief, not a fact.

Doesn't work, Darius, when the shadows are pushing back. Where does our world end if you're having people shoot at me in the middle of the light?

"I'll tell you," I said finally, not meeting their eyes. I swept my hair down to hide my other eye and closed my left one, wanting nothing more than to shut out the world. At least for now, in this car, I believed I was safe. "As soon as we get to the hideout."

*   *   *

We got there without incident. The sun was high in the sky by now, as time marched onward toward noon. There weren't any shadows to be found anymore. The world looked like a washed-out picture to me after the last few days. I hadn't slept properly since Friday night, after my last job, and even *that* wasn't great since I'd still been wary of Faith in the next room over. Meanwhile, the constant bursts of adrenaline were *really* starting to wear me down.

The area looked clear enough, but Faith's man checked every alley before opening their doors. Apparently, Faith had opened up the bottom-floor entrance at some point since moving in. I had no idea when she found the time, but obviously she'd kept busy since yesterday. The driver grabbed a crutch from the front seat and handed it to Faith.

"Thanks, Tanaka."

Faith accepted it with a grimace, avoiding my eyes. She clambered out with some help and headed straight for the front door. Alex climbed out next, handcuffed. Faith had decided that until they'd had a good talk, he'd be restrained for everyone's safety. To my relief, he'd accepted it without complaint.

Faith made her way inside, looking far more delicate than I'd ever seen her. She was avoiding putting *any* weight on her bad leg and looked far worse than the last time I'd seen her. I spoke up for the first time in minutes, stepping out behind them.

"What happened to you?"

Faith glanced over her shoulder. She seemed surprised. "I ran into an old friend yesterday after we split up at the mall. We had a . . . difference of opinions." She began to make her way up the staircase to the top floor, Alex and Tanaka close behind.

"Was it someone I know?"

"Depends," said Faith, "you gonna do anything to them?" She made it sound like a joke, but I caught the faint undercurrent of real concern.

"You seemed fine last night," I said, dodging her question with one of my own.

Faith shrugged and nearly missed the next step as she did. She winced. "I was in a better mood. Thrill of the heist or something. Plus, let's be honest, you were *super* distracted. I'm touched you're concerned for my well-being though."

She sounded completely sincere, to my surprise. I didn't get it, given how I'd treated Faith last night. I couldn't think of anything else to say, and so we kept moving up the staircase in silence. As we reached the top floor, I felt an odd sense of familiarity and comfort. This *was* a home, for better or worse. I already felt more at ease, here in a place of my own making.

Of course, with what Faith was about to ask, and what I'd be telling her, it wasn't going to last long. Her curiosity was practically tangible, bubbling away just behind her eyes like a pot about to boil over. I walked into my makeshift bedroom. Faith hesitated, glancing at Alex.

"Alex, be a *dear* and go wait in the kitchen with Tanaka, would you?" He nodded, and seated himself there—the opposite end of the building from my bedroom. "Want a snack or anything?"

Alex shrugged. Faith rolled a glass bottle over to him. He caught it despite the cuffs, wincing from the pain. Faith winced. "Tanaka, got any painkillers for the guy?"

Tanaka hurried out. Faith nodded, then turned and followed me back into the bedroom. I knew I should probably have done a lot of that, it being my place and all, but . . . I couldn't. Dread filled my stomach like an unpleasant weight pulling me down to the ground. Every step felt painful, not helped in the least by the bullet wounds I'd sustained. I walked over to my bed and sat down.

I'd found a reasonably intact mattress and sheet combo from a nearby thrift store, along with a good reading lamp and a few other small comforts. I could afford better, of course, but this fit the decor, and it was easier to sneak in without assistance. There was only a single window in the apartment, but I'd blacked it out for security. I preferred the dark anyway.

The only light in the whole room was that reading lamp. It cast huge shadows across the walls, amplifying every little object into teeming masses, making even the smallest thing seem huge. I'd once put together little dramatic displays, carving out dioramas to hang on the light and cast interesting shadows on the wall.

I reached down and pulled out my laptop from under the bed and plugged it in, letting the battery charge up. Faith closed the door, then walked over and sat down on a stool I kept over by a small table, where I usually ate whenever I was here. She watched me but didn't say anything, waiting for me to open the conversation. I would have waited until curiosity got the better of her—but for once, I had a question of my own I was dying to ask.

"Where did you get a car?"

Faith's eyes darted away. She looked suddenly *shy* and full of guilt. "Before you jump to conclusions," she said, obviously uncomfortable, "I'm not secretly rich or anything. I'm pretty much exactly like what you first met: crippled, homeless chick extraordinaire." She leaned back against a dead refrigerator I kept near my table. "I just have a few good friends who sometimes do favors for me."

"The former yakuza bodyguard out there, for example?"

"Employee of a friend," said Faith. I raised an eyebrow, and she shrugged. "How'd you know he was yakuza?"

"They've got an air about them. I've met enough to recognize it. He wouldn't be working for you, though, if he was still actively involved."

She grinned slightly. "You're what, eighteen, and you can recognize a yakuza on sight, but *I'm* the suspicious one because my friend lent me a car?"

"A *nice* car, with a well-trained bodyguard. And I'm sixteen."

"Fair enough." Faith leaned forward again. "That's not why we're here though, K." She cleared her throat. "We're here 'cause the street thinks you're trying to kill Darius. Your *brother*," she added, and the floor seemed to fall out from under me.

". . . What?" I said stupidly.

Faith shook her head. "Don't worry. Nobody else knows that part. Hell, I only put it together yesterday."

"But . . ." I shook my head. "You can't know. Nobody does."

"Nobody knows your name either, K," Faith said with a shrug. "There's a *lot* I'm not supposed to know that I do. That's kind of my deal. Yours is killing people. So let's make a trade, yeah? You tell me why you're trying to kill your brother; I'll tell you how I know that you are."

I looked away toward the window, covered in a solid layer of black foam. I was still shocked, but at the same time . . . it made a strange kind of sense. Faith was clearly way more than she appeared, and she already knew the deepest secret of my life. She'd somehow made her way into every piece of my world in only a couple of days. What was one more, weighed against *that*?

"He did something to me," I said quietly.

Faith nodded. "I figured that much. Normally, I'd say tell me when you're ready, but we're kinda in the middle of a war all of a sudden, and I'm *pretty* sure it's all centered on you somehow. I'm gonna need more detail here, K."

"I wish I had more," I whispered.

". . . Huh?"

I cleared my throat and reached down to boot up the laptop. As it warmed up, I fished through my bag for the flash drive—the one that now contained a copy of the video, the emails Jack had originally sent me, all of Jerome's emails, the other files on Jack's laptop . . . everything.

While my laptop booted up, I stared at the corner of the room. I couldn't look Faith in the eye.

"Jack Monroe contacted me four days ago on Tuesday, telling me to check something within the software of my other eye. He said I'd find evidence of tampering, and that I should know about it. I wasn't sure what he meant and I figured it had to be a trick, but . . . nobody has access to my eye. It's not possible."

"Okay," said Faith. "I'm not a computer gal, but I'll trust the expert here."

"He didn't say what. I think he knew if he told me, I wouldn't believe it. So when I found it . . . when I found what Darius did . . ." My voice choked up. "He'd done something, using the implant on my neck."

"Done . . . *something?*"

I couldn't say it aloud. The laptop finished booting up. "I didn't do anything about it for two days. I was still trying to figure out what it meant. I had a job on Thursday night and I did it, and then . . . I couldn't get in touch. Everything started falling apart from there. Jack put out a hit on my brother, they believe I *already* tried to kill him, and . . . I'm still not sure if I *don't* want to."

Faith looked seriously concerned at this point. I turned the laptop toward her, every file open, the video already selected and ready to go. I handed it over, then lay back on the bed. I was dead tired, exhaustion threatening to swallow me whole. With my whole life laid bare in front of her, I trusted Faith completely at this point. My eyelid slid closed, and every memory, every pain over the past few days resurfaced.

The gunshots that tore across my skin.

The shock of watching Darius erase my memory.

The confusion of confronting him.

My flight from Jerome's, and the impact of gunshots against Alex right in front of me.

Faith now knew more about me than any living soul on the planet besides my brother. I'd given her my trust completely now and I'd only done that once before. Faith had saved my life, with no apparent benefit to herself beyond a confused friendship I didn't understand yet. I felt raw and exposed as I drifted to sleep. My other eye shut itself down.

A faint clicking across the room was the last sound I heard as I fell asleep as Faith began to plumb the depths of my life. Maybe she'd find a solution. All I saw was blinding light in every direction—too much exposure, too much pain. Either Darius had done this to me, or I'd done it to myself. Either path seemed too painful to accept. I needed to find my brother and I needed to hear the truth.

One way or the other.

CHAPTER 10

I snapped awake.

As far back as I could remember, I'd always woken up like this—it was just how my body and my brain were built. Sleep was a vulnerability I *absolutely* could not afford, so I always slept light. When I needed to wake up, my body didn't waste a second. The transition was quick, seamless . . . and a little panic-inducing, every time.

My eye slid open. I wasn't sure what I expected to see, but the room was still dark. After Faith learned how I wanted to kill my brother, how I was in league with one of the biggest drug pushers in the city, how I'd just casually used a supposed ally as a human shield . . . I'd half expected her to be long gone, along with all the cash she could carry. Sure, she'd shown some kind of loyalty before, and rescued me out of the retail place, but . . . a lasting bond? With *me?*

Certainly, I didn't expect to see Faith sitting right next to me on the bed, legs propped up on a pillow, quietly typing away on my laptop. Not only that, but a black line trailed out of my vision—she'd plugged in my other eye at some point too.

I mentally kicked myself for forgetting it *again*. It had been perpetually low on power all weekend, and I'd finally gotten an opportunity to rest and recharge . . . but I'd forgotten. It was bound to cut out at the worst possible time, and that'd probably end with a very dead Kara.

Instead, Faith—who'd always cringed at the sight of my deformity, who looked away whenever I plugged it in—had taken care of it for me. She'd overcome that, for *me*. I felt a weird rush of affection, unfamiliar and almost painful, compared to the swirling feelings of betrayal, anger, fear, confusion, despair. It was something I hadn't felt in such a long time, an emotion I barely remembered.

My left eye was twitching. I could feel the tear duct giving way, the only one I had left. Moisture was building up. I forced it back, steeling myself, willing away the tears. My sudden stiffness must have alerted Faith though, as the gentle typing abruptly stopped. The room was silent, only the faint wind and the never-ending patter of rain on the roof above our heads filling the space.

I wasn't sure what to do. I held still, waiting, letting Faith speak first, as I knew she would.

"Rebecca Maclay was the closest thing I ever had to a mother," said Faith, her voice soft and quiet. I felt a huge thrill of confusion and shock at her words—*the doctor*. "She was brilliant and kind, and she gave me a ton of crap about everything I ever did, but in a nice way, you know?"

Faith set the laptop aside for a moment. She stretched out her leg and massaged it a little, working out the aches, before leaning back against a pillow and staring up at the ceiling.

"She once told me that she got into experimental medicine and bio-technology to solve the problems people took for granted. 'Shortcomings of random selection,' she said. Becca wanted to make life better. Easier. More worth living."

Faith looked down at her leg, and even out of the corner of my left eye, I could see just how frustrated and angry she was—at herself, at her leg, at Rebecca, I couldn't be sure.

"I think she was gonna try and fix me. I hadn't wanted her to, because I'm stubborn and prideful and all the other crap. My leg was part of me. If I wasn't the crippled, homeless girl, who was I? So I refused, I said no over and over for a *year* . . . until it was too late. The opportunity was gone, just like that, and all because of me."

She shook her head. "Sounds like a neat little tale, right? 'Girl's pride becomes her downfall.' Just like yours, 'girl kills boy for mind-rape,' nice and straightforward, if you boil it down to a single sentence."

Faith sighed. "Becca was the one who kicked me out. Ellie begged her not to, but she'd never persuade them. Arthur was on the warpath, and his wife was even worse. I can't blame 'em. Their beloved, precious daughter, goddess of the earth on which she treads, was maimed. Marred for life. She could have died, and they reminded me that endlessly. All their money and all their expertise couldn't restore her back to normal."

The rain seemed to pick up just as Faith's voice got more intense. I was still silent, laying on the bed, unmoving, listening to her speak. I didn't know where she was going with all of this, but I didn't want her to stop either.

"It was a permanent reminder. Every single day, I'd look at her face and see every stupid mistake I made that led to up to it. I'd remember every moment in my past where I could have changed things, every interaction where I could've done something different, said something different, and maybe it doesn't happen. Maybe Ellie doesn't end up in that alley, trapped in with a spurned-suitor-turned-homicidal-psychopath."

Faith finally looked over at me, her eyes hard. "I didn't do anything to stop the one who threatened my family and I lost all of them for it. Now it's your family on the line. What happens next?"

"I don't know," I said softly, sitting up. The cable trailed way from my other eye, dragging down slightly, snaking off across the edge of the bed. I glanced around, and the door was still shut, the room lit only by the lamp and the laptop. Faith's face was half cast in shadow, with the other side almost totally black.

"Do you want to kill your brother?" Her tone was completely flat, giving me no clue what she thought of the idea.

". . . I can't trust him anymore," I said. "I can't trust anyone anymore, because of him."

"Does that deserve death?" she asked, unrelenting.

I hesitated as my thoughts struggled to form into cohesive sentences. I wasn't a talker like Faith. I didn't know how to just vent my thoughts at the drop of a hat.

Faith's eyes kept flickering over to the laptop screen, as if watching for something, but she never took her focus away from me. Finally, I worked up an answer . . . or at least, the best I could come up with.

"He took my self away," I said quietly. "I don't know who I am. I feel like I'm just a product of Darius." I took a breath before going on, my heart pounding in my head, but with an odd sense of relief, finally getting to voice the thoughts which had been stuck swirling in my mind for so long. "It's like there's a song on the tip of my tongue, except it's *everything*. My whole life, just on the edge of my brain, but never close enough to touch. It's a puzzle with half the pieces missing, and I don't know where they are, or how to get them back."

My left eye narrowed, and a bit of anger and frustration tinged my voice unintentionally as I went on. "Darius did that to me. He went inside, he changed me, he made me into his . . . his puppet. I don't know if this is what I wanted, what I'm supposed to be, what I . . . I don't know. I just know I'm never going to get it back."

"Maybe," said Faith, and a fresh burst of confusion rushed through my mind. "After you fell asleep, I started doing some digging. I got in touch with a few friends, got some database dumps—schools, hospitals, shelters, clinics, so on. I figured if I could narrow it down to this area and what I *assume* to be your age, I could find some info on who you were up against. Found something interesting instead."

She typed a few sentences, then slid the warm computer over onto my lap. She pointed at a file she'd brought up on the screen.

It was a temporary residency slip, just a routine check-in. The address listed an abuse shelter in Tacoma. It had photos, dates, and times, but no names. There was a middle-aged man and a young girl on the slip, listed as ages forty-one and nine, respectively.

The man was looking away from the camera, bruised and with a cut on his forehead and his neck. His hair was dark brown and receding, and he wore glasses, bent and taped across the middle, slightly askew on his face. He carried a book under his arm, thick and leatherbound. The girl wore a hooded sweatshirt, pulled low over her head. Her eyes were narrow, her face taut with anger. Brown hair spilled out on one side, partially obscuring her right eye. Her arm was hooked around the man's, holding close, stance defensive.

"Except for the bogus CID you've got," said Faith quietly, "this is the only photo that exists of you anywhere on the net, as far as I can tell. The shelter took people anonymously, so I can't tell you who the guy is, but I've got a pretty good guess."

I couldn't stop looking at them. His face was . . . uncomfortably familiar. He reminded me of Darius. Not *identical*, but . . . definitely related. The girl wore her hair in the same way I did, though she didn't have anything to cover up like I did.

"Who raised you?"

I glanced back at Faith, momentarily confused. "Darius. He taught me everything I know. I've always lived with him. I didn't even have to go to school, since he put me in the registry so I don't show up truant." I looked at the screen again, more closely. "Is this Darius's brother?"

Faith sighed. "That's some piece of work. No, Kara, I think it's your dad."

My mind skipped a beat, like a corrupted song. Faith's last sentence took several moments to comprehend . . . and even then, it still sounded wrong. "I don't have a father."

"I think this is what he erased," said Faith. "I don't know why, but I'm sure as hell gonna find out. You deserve to know who your parents are."

She put her arms around me and hugged me, but I was still too transfixed by the screen to notice.

Every instinct in my body told me Faith had to be wrong. Darius raised me. Darius had *always* raised me. He'd trained me, sheltered me, cared for me, taught me. We'd always lived together, and since that night when I was thirteen, we'd worked together. We ate dinner together every weeknight until I was fifteen, when we'd both become too busy to keep it up. It had always been us together against the world.

Who is that man? And why am I with him?

I had no doubt the girl in the photo was me. Her hair, her eyes, her stance, her choice of clothing, *everything* seemed exactly like me. Except . . . I had two real eyes. No cybernetics in my face, nothing in my arm, just a normal kid.

"I couldn't find anything else on him," said Faith. She pulled the laptop back. I started for it, as if she were somehow taking something precious from me, but I shook it off. My focus was coming back as Faith closed the pictures. I had bigger things to worry about.

A gunshot in the distance, faint but distinct, punctuated the thought. It was far enough away that I didn't feel threatened, but nonetheless, the street war continued. We were well past midday, and both the police and the corpo security were undoubtedly mobilized by now. Even their cautious tolerance of our gang had its limits. They couldn't possibly ignore bodies dropping in the streets in broad daylight.

Faith spoke abruptly, her voice suddenly firm and brisk again. "Kara, I'm sorry about this, but it's important—" She looked at me, back to business as usual. "I listened in on your phone call with your brother."

I sat up straight, torn between betrayal and surprise, not sure if I was happy she'd come back despite my awful treatment, or furious she'd broken my privacy.

"Yeah, you were pretty distracted and I snuck back in." She shrugged, looking slightly embarrassed. "I wanted to make sure nobody else came by . . . and honestly, I can't help myself. Sorry."

"It's fine," I said, and landed on forgiveness in the same moment. I'd already been regretting it, and if Faith was willing to let it slide, so was I.

"Anyway, point is, you apparently *wanted* to forget everything. *Asked for it.*" Faith cocked her head slightly. "I'm not saying you shouldn't try to get them back, because I sure as hell would, but just think about it. Be sure. What if he's right, and you're better off not knowing?"

"I have to know," I said without hesitating. That much, out of everything in my confused life, I knew for certain. Living without knowing, with the massive holes in my life, was far worse.

Faith nodded. "Okay."

A flood of relief, but it was coupled with more stress and fear about what might be coming for me. I decided to switch topics, eager to get back to something where I felt more confident. "Who started the war outside?"

"Technically we did, plus Hammer. Jack's the real instigator though."

Faith took a deep breath before continuing. Her hands tensed up for a moment, but she soon started typing again. I leaned over to see what she was doing—and she had a few phone texting apps open, plus a map of the city, and some other research tools, along with all the contents of Jerome's emails I'd grabbed yesterday.

"Hammer killed my friend Kevin. One of the pickpockets from yesterday. He tracked him down and beat him to death." Faith's voice was still calm and professional, but I could hear the anger just under the surface. "I don't think Hammer realized he was on Jack's turf at the time, or who Kevin worked for, but that's what kicked everything off. Alex is fine, by the way," she added, glancing over for a moment. "Tanaka drove him to the hospital while you were asleep. I figured he's probably not gonna talk, even if you *did* nearly get him killed."

She paused. Something in the email chain I'd grabbed from Jerome's had just caught her eye. She scrolled through quickly, skimming the contents faster than I could follow.

"What?"

"Ahh," said Faith, satisfied as if she'd just figured out a puzzle. "Okay."

"What's going on?" I asked. I leaned over to read the email. It looked relatively innocent, just an inquiry from one of Jerome's fake online handles, looking for more information on Maclay Technology's ocular replacement programs. Maclay had revealed a few early prototypes, not dissimilar to what I had stuck in my own eye socket, but there wasn't anything substantial yet. They'd claimed a few more years required before the designs were fully tested and certified for safe operation and implantation.

Of course, didn't stop Darius and the doctor from putting one in me . . .

"I've been trying to figure out the power balance between Jack and Darius," said Faith. "Trying to track down hideouts, numbers, allies. Hell, I even got Jack's personal residence—somewhere I'm gonna steer *way* clear of, for sure. But I couldn't figure out why Jack was so willing to head into open war."

She glanced out the window. We'd heard another few stray shots through the rain, but it'd been quiet for a while now. The sun was already far in the west, dipping much deeper, casting long shadows out across the city, and swathing huge portions in darkness.

"Jack's got a slight edge in numbers, sure, but this attack was *right* on top of the plan to kill your brother. He's gotta know that on your turf, with your heightened security and the support of the cops and whoever else, he can't possibly win. Jack's got a terrible relationship with Seattle. Plenty of people would be more than happy to see him gone."

"So what's he after?" I asked, catching up. "Because if it's not Darius, but it isn't territory or taking us all out . . ."

Faith pulled up another email, one Jerome had picked up from Jack himself. Inquiries about ocular enhancement, cybernetics, black market values, potential of the technology.

"He wants my eye," I said bluntly.

She nodded. "He's after the Maclays for sure. Distracting Darius's people will pull any protection they might have, even inside your turf." Faith hesitated, her expression uncertain. "I know this is a rough time for you, K, but I need your help right now," she continued, more tentative than I'd ever heard her. "You don't owe me anything, but I owe *them* my life, and more besides. Jack's after them, and I can't protect them."

I'd already unplugged my other eye before she stopped talking. I packed the cord away. The display flashed up a battery level, still uncomfortably low—Faith must not have plugged it in until fairly recently. I had to hope it'd be enough, along with the nap I'd just been able to take.

Faith had fallen silent, watching me, confused and hopeful. I stood up and walked over to my bag in the corner. Rain kept pounding on the windows, like a foreboding drumbeat signaling the danger I was about to throw myself headlong into. I pulled out my rifle, glanced over it briefly, and turned back to Faith.

"Where to?"

By the time we were a block away from the Maclay estate, the sun was already completely gone. Dusk settled in, and the sky grew darker with every passing moment. Clouds still hung thick in the sky, and with the wind blowing thick storm clouds in the distance, it only looked to get worse the night through.

I got out of the car before we were in sight, picking the best of the buildings I'd scouted online before we go there. The thing was locked, but just as before, it was a simple piece to hack. After another couple of minutes with the keygen, I was inside. I hurried up three flights of stairs to the roof, back into the rain again as I crawled across the gravel to the edge.

There wasn't anyone in sight. I pulled out my rifle and set it up. The Maclay household was directly in front, its walls shimmering back at me. Colors shifted as I trained the scope on each window in turn, cycling through, looking for potential threats. I saw Rebecca through one and her daughter, Eleanor, through another. They looked calm . . . unsuspecting.

As I scanned, my other eye began to filter out the colors, adjusting from the sheer spectacle. The wall shifted to its true form—millions of tiny panels slanted at every conceivable angle. Soon enough, it simply appeared as a plain, grayish surface, unremarkable and far less distracting. I did one final sweep of the surrounding streets, but there wasn't a soul in sight. That alone was a little unsettling, but for now, I'd take it. I pulled out the burner and texted Faith.

K: Clear.
F: Thanks. Omw

I shut the phone and went back to my sweep. My hood was down to give me more peripheral vision, despite the rain starting to soak into my hair and the back of my neck. I had the rifle set on a bipod, mounted just behind the lip of the roof so the barrel didn't extend over the edge. For now, it was retracted, but a single button press would extend it out. With the longer barrel, I got more velocity and accuracy on the bullet, since the increased length meant more time for the charge to explode and the trapped gases to propel the projectile.

Combined with the dynamic range finding I could get between the scope and my other eye, I was practically guaranteed to hit any target within about eight hundred meters. Still, I hated relying on it. I practiced as much as I could with all the assisting tools disabled, sometimes even without the scope. I never wanted to rely on something that could potentially fail at the worst possible moment, especially with my other eye already at risk of such a disaster.

Tanaka's car pulled around the corner. I tracked it down the road for a moment, scanning it just out of habit. Two occupants, no surprises. I went back to watching the house, where the front light had just flicked on. The gate automatically opened as the vehicle approached, with a bright white light flashing it as it passed through.

As the car curled around the garden, the front door opened. Eleanor stood in the flood of light, and I got my first look at the scars Faith had described. They didn't seem so bad to me, but then again, I hung out with a very different crowd than the wealthy Maclay family.

Faith clambered out of the rear seat of the car, cane in hand, and made her way toward the stairs. Eleanor rushed down and buried her in a hug. Faith gestured vaguely toward the open garage, which Tanaka had just pulled into. After a few moments, they hurried inside, and I followed them in with my rifle all the way, finger far away from the trigger. I swept the garage, just in case, but I doubted anyone was inside. As everyone disappeared, I went back to my scan of the streets surrounding.

I tried to relax a little. It could take a few minutes for Faith to persuade the family. Even beyond the drama between them, the Maclays had *always* been safe in our district. Darius had a solid working relationship with Rebecca—I was evidence of that, obviously, but still, they were one of the biggest streams of revenue in our territory. Darius had even talked about bringing our programming core into the Maclays' company, working on legitimate software projects.

The Maclays were reluctant though, given Darius's work. We sold black market sims and implants, and though we did our best to avoid damage, we had our fair share of deceased or permanently crippled junkies. Beyond that, addicts got lost in the simulation, drawn in by such rich, intense feelings that the real world felt pale and empty by comparison. If I were being honest, Faith's rants about the world retreating into virtual space were as much our fault as theirs. Arthur Maclay was the strong holdout. He'd agreed to work with Darius on products to improve lives and he saw the sim business as permanently damaging, even without the physical afflictions.

I scanned across the building and the streets again. I couldn't see anyone in the windows anymore, and the streets were still quiet.

Even the best advancements in procedural generation and randomized content could only produce so many scenarios. Patterns became obvious over time, and sim junkies would lose their immersion, rendering the sim useless. Thus, we had a market. They were always looking for new sims, and that kept our programmers and designers hard at work making new experiences for the implants we sold them. It was an effective feedback loop that made us a *lot* of money.

I never worried much about it, but the rampant escapism was the root of the argument between Darius and the Maclays. To me, judging from history, it seemed like the same thing as always. Instead of TV, movies, books, whatever, they now had sims. Sure, it was a lot fancier, using the mind's natural impulses to create stories to fill out gaps in the programming, drawing on lucid dreaming states for controllable heightened senses, but it ended up the same, didn't it?

Arthur argued that Darius was consigning sim junkies to an exiled life in a false world. Rebecca was on the fence, eager to explore the technology, but torn between Arthur and Darius. Eventually, I stopped seeing her and I'd always assumed a rift had grown between them too insurmountable to break.

Of course, this was all secondhand. I'd never met Arthur. Everything I knew about the Maclay family was through Darius, my own research, or overhearing conversations with Rebecca whenever she came over to install updates in my other eye.

One of those very updates they'd installed just clicked on. I usually stuck to normal vision, but the small third lens above the two primary lenses was never *off.* I now had the ability to have it alert me if any new, human-sized signatures entered my field of view.

Two just had. Outlines sprung to life in my scope, drawing squares over their estimated positions even though I could barely make them out yet. Two men, cautiously approaching the house, carrying concealed pistols in their jackets. They looked like an advance team. Jack's previous operations usually involved a pair who secured the perimeter and ensuring the target didn't leave before his main force arrived to securely capture them.

By my estimate, it'd only be twenty minutes max before Faith got interrupted by some very unpleasant company.

I tapped the button on my rifle and extended the barrel to full length, then screwed on a suppressor. It couldn't do much to quiet the sound, but it would hide the muzzle flash and reduce echoes from the buildings near me. I hoped that'd be enough to hide my position. I pulled out my phone and dialed Faith.

Straight to voicemail. I sent a text.

K: Incoming, two men. More soon.
F: Need more time.

I mentally cursed, but set to planning. I'd keep them safe, no matter what.

If Jack's men found a clear area, they'd report back immediately. One of them had a headset on and was in constant communication with the main group. If I killed either of them, though, Jack would be aware instantly. I needed to make them *doubt*. Not threaten, but make them uncertain, delay, buy enough time to get the Maclays out.

The men were circling around the front of the house now, nearest my side of the street. We were running out of time. I had to make a move.

I grabbed some gravel from the rooftop and hurled it at the men while yanking my rifle away from the edge. The crackling rocks all around them was enough cause for alarm. My other eye could still make them out clearly between the streetlamps, even in the fast-dimming dusk.

The man on the headset was still talking. They'd both drawn pistols but hadn't raised them. Alarmed, but not to the point of attack just yet. They both crouched, glancing around the street.

I grabbed an empty beer can and chucked it into the alley nearby.

That did it. The men turned and approached the alley. I waited for them to get near the entrance, then tossed another handful of gravel at the chain-link fence halfway down the alley. It made a perfect faint metallic rattle—just the right impression of somebody climbing over as fast as they could.

The men bolted down the alley, chasing their nonexistent quarry. *No witnesses allowed, of course.* I tracked them for a few moments, verifying they were truly leaving, then tossed my rifle back into my bag and made for the street.

The staircase let out on the front, right between two shops. I opened the door a few inches. *Nobody else on the street yet. They're waiting to move in. Good.*

I sprinted across, running for the Maclays' front door as fast as I could. The security fence flashed me but didn't try to hinder me in any way. *I guess I'm on the list . . . huh.* I didn't stop to think about it, because Faith was out of time. I'd drag her out if I had to.

Tanaka emerged from the door, moving to intercept me. I blew right past him.

"Get the car ready," I called over my shoulder as I went up the stairs, two at a time. "They're coming."

He nodded. I was impressed—the man knew when not to bother with questions. He went to the garage immediately.

I entered the house through the front door, up on the second story. The hall split three ways from the entrance. To the right, stairs led down to the lower floor and the garages, next to a door for the master bedroom. The left hall led to several more rooms, with a wide living room at the end. I heard raised voices echoing down that hall—Faith shouting, and the Maclays matching her right back. The door was slightly ajar, and I could just make out Faith, standing but leaning heavily on the couch, favoring her good leg.

Straight from the front door, I saw a dining room and a sliding door to a balcony, lined with an elegant wooden railway . . . which a masked man was currently rolling himself over.

A black balaclava covered his face; he had a suppressed pistol in hand, and body armor thickened his physique. I slid to the side, into the left hallway toward the living room and the voices, and ducked into one of the bedroom doorways. I crouched just inside, peeking out so I could see the hallway. Every door was open, but the only illumination came from the living room.

A slight creak echoed through the house—the floorboards in the main hall. My adversary was moving and moving *quietly*. I didn't hear a single other sound, no rustling or footfalls. This man was *good*. I hoped by his approach he was still moving toward the Maclays. I'd need the element of surprise.

I drew my knife from its belt holster. The German-manufactured black blade had served me very well over the years. I'd found it in the personal belongings of a target, a soldier who'd taken up with a now long-dead rival. I'd taken the rival out from more than seven hundred meters through a frosted-glass window, my bullet shattering the toilet seat cover behind him as it passed through his heart, but the soldier had required me to get up close and personal.

Michael trained me. We'd gone over basic attack and defense maneuvers, how I could use the weight of a larger foe against them, using pistols and knives in tight spaces. He'd stressed I should *never* get in a stand-up fight if I could avoid it. My size and weight were just too great a weakness. I barely stood over five foot four. I had muscle, but not much else. Against a fully-grown man, I didn't have a chance of physically overpowering them.

My only option was quick, merciless brutality. I had to end a fight before it started—which, to be fair, is exactly what I preferred.

The masked man had just passed my door. I watched through the crack in the hinge. He checked my room, but didn't go far enough to spot me—*sloppy*. I remained hidden, and I was able to take a better measure of him. Thicker armor protected his vital regions, but his neck and legs were exposed for ease of movement. I had an opening.

Arthur Maclay was now shouting about recklessness. I smiled grimly and set my bag down on the floor. It was as good a cue as I was going to get.

I moved.

Into the hallway, two quick steps, right up behind the masked man. I ducked low as he began to turn and kicked the rear of his knees.

He stumbled forward. I leaped onto his back, bringing my knife to bear—but I'd misjudged how far he'd made it down the hallway. My momentum carried both of us right into the living room.

Shocked shouting greeted us, but I had no time to pay attention to anything else but my opponent. The man was twisting around underneath me, trying to gain leverage. I took the knife and plunged it into his neck. Spurts of warm red blood sprayed out.

The man gagged. His lifeblood was leaking away.

He threw me off, but the knife still stuck in his neck widened the cut as it came away in my grip. I rolled to the side, returning to my feet coincidentally next to Faith. The man raised his pistol, aiming wildly, trying to hit me, but his arm was shaking too much.

I flipped the knife over in my hand, grasping the blade, and threw it end over end.

It flashed in the light as it spun. With a sickening sound, it planted into the man's face. His mouth opened wide, as if trying to scream. He dropped the pistol and stumbled backward, tearing the balaclava from his face.

I dove forward, snatching his gun off the floor and twisting around to aim back up at him.

One round, right between his eyes—and my shock suddenly matched his own.

I recognized him. I'd worked with him before. He was one of *our* assassins, another hitman employed by my brother. I *knew* him. What was he doing *here?*

Without a word, he slumped to the floor—dead.

JACK

He opened his eyes, but at the sudden sting, closed them again immediately.

It was too bright. The sunlight streamed in from the window nearby, adding a layer of warmth to the blankets they were already wrapped up in, but visually it only intruded on their space. He rolled over, facing the woman next to him, someone he loved beyond compare. She was his guiding star, the light of his world, the anchor of his life. She was beautiful and pale, with snowing hair cascading down her cheeks.

He smiled. His hand reached out and tenderly brushed her face.

Her eyes fluttered open, deep icy landscapes hiding mysteries he'd never fully understand. Every time he looked at her, he felt like he was discovering something new about her, and as his curiosity never waned, every moment spent with her was joyous.

The woman's own smile cracked into being. It was a quiet smile, miniscule compared to his own wide grins, but it was warm and compassionate, and bespoke a happy, loving soul behind its outward beauty. As the sunlight struck her, she, too, closed her eyes, the direct light a far more painful sting than the mere irritation it caused his own.

He spoke to the room. "Close curtains."

His voice was firm and clear, that the computer would understand him better. A soft beep acknowledged his command, and small motors whirred into life. Heavy curtains slid over the window, plunging the room back into darkness. "Lights," he spoke next, and soft lights at discreet locations brought the room to a dim glow.

"Piano, please," came the voice he so loved. It was gentle, sweetly asking the room as opposed to his own direct, imperious tone. He never much saw the distinction, as the software had no knowledge of manners or tone, but the room never failed to answer her commands while often misinterpreting his own.

Ah well. He couldn't possibly begrudge the computer's preference of user.

One of her selections emanated from the speakers set into the corners, filling the room with a light melody of soothing music. It was a piece she often awoke to. Long ago, such music had bored him, but after listening to the many compositions in her collection, he'd grown an appreciation for the smooth melodies of these solo pianists. It was a stark contrast to the bombastic symphonies he typically associated with classical music, a side of the genre he'd never encountered.

Lately, her morning routine had included as many of his musical discoveries as her own.

He leaned closer and kissed her on the cheek. She giggled. He sat up, vaguely indignant.

"What?"

"You're always such a romantic in the mornings," she said, her eyes twinkling as they opened. "Thinking of the mysterious white beauty again, right?"

He laughed. She knew him. She was the only one who truly did.

"You let me know when you meet her, yeah? She sounds fascinating."

He grabbed a pillow and tossed it at her, but she'd already raised her arms, expecting the throw. He followed it in, landing atop her and planting a kiss on her lips. She happily returned it, but soon pushed him aside.

"Come now, we've things to do today."

She sat up, reaching for the white robe that hung from her bedside table and slipping into it. Her feet found the floor, and she stood to walk over to the desk where her laptop sat waiting. She tapped a key to wake it, letting it progress through the usual welcome messages with perfect, patient tranquility. Soon, it pulled up the work she'd left open the previous night, still in mid-sentence—her novel, as yet unpublished.

It grew every weekend, whenever he came to live with her. During the weekdays, she corresponded with clients—listening to their fears, their hopes, their dreams and despair—and tried to help them as best she could. Many came to see her in person, in this very home. She took them each one by one, providing an ear, lending a hand, doing what she could. Every client was special to her, and she never forgot a single one.

He was once a client, in a way—in a different life. She'd met him in a bar, alone and friendless, and she'd talked to him when no one else would. His empire had crumbled and he'd fled his home, but he had nowhere else to go. He'd been on his last legs, ready to depart the world, and she'd given him a reason to stay.

His resurgence from that day was almost miraculous. He'd rebuilt his holdings, gained control of a new home, a new world, and he never forgot who had pushed him back into the light.

He sought her out and asked her to dinner. They spent a lovely evening on the waterfront, just wandering the market. She never let go of his arm throughout the night, alternating between letting him lead and tugging him away to the sounds of something new and exciting. They repeated the excursion many times over the next few months. She loved the ever-changing cacophony of the market—the fishmongers tossing their catches with wild shouts, the constant bicker and barter of every vendor on the strip. The smells, the sounds, the palpable energy in the air itself were intoxicating to her.

As she put it, "Life, infinitely variable and unstoppable."

Soon, he was taking her all over town. They'd attend a show or a concert one night, then spend the next just talking alone. She had a keen understanding of conversation, of its flows and ebbs. He'd almost call it a science to her, if it didn't sound so dispassionate. Everything from her lips sounded like her soul, bare, welcoming, and wholly truthful.

In turn, he could not imagine lying to her, even for a second. He poured out his whole life to her, all the rights and wrongs, every moment he'd set the world in motion toward a better place, and every failing he'd brought down upon himself. He spilled his weaknesses, his fears, his hopes and dreams.

She helped him understand his true purpose. Before, all he cared about was wealth and power, empty pursuits in the greater symphony of life. He'd been fighting for the same tiny notes as everyone else in the city's underbelly. She showed him he was destined for the grander design, the composer. The city would be rejuvenated under his direction, and every person within would thrive. Every day of the last ten years he spent with her renewed his soul.

Over the last month, due to his business, he'd only managed to find his way out to her home a scant few times. It pained him to spend so much time away, but his work was paramount. She understood this and never thought less of him for it. She admired his dedication and drive, his refusal to back down under strife. No matter how long he waa gone, she always welcomed him with the same warmth and joy as the first time they'd been together.

The music clicked over, and the next track opened with a more somber and intense melody. He still liked the piece, but the pause in atmosphere was enough to remind him of his own duties. He swung his feet off the bed and stretched himself to wakefulness. The cold wood floor was an intrusion, and he once again reminded himself to bring some kind of slippers.

Regardless, the mood was lost. He took the chair at the other end of the desk, where his own computer sat waiting. He pressed his palm to the screen. It read his fingerprints and DNA, unlocking the device. Not one to trust a single method of security, particularly with the opposition he faced, he then typed in his password to fully unlock the laptop. Two messages appeared, both recent since the previous night.

One was a report on the household his men currently surveilled. The security system was strong but not impregnable. He did his own quick analysis, then drafted a few ideas for the operation, detailing exactly what he wanted and when. It wouldn't work without a little outside help, but he was confident he could come up with something. He sent it back to his men in the field, with ironclad instructions not to proceed until notified. The men wouldn't dare, of course, but it didn't hurt to be thorough.

The second email was more interesting. It seemed one of his low-level street urchins had been killed, and his men took the excuse to start killing—right on schedule. He thanked the world yet again for sending him intelligent and opportunistic underlings.

He shut the laptop. He was ever reluctant to leave her side, but these events required his direct involvement. If everything didn't proceed exactly as planned, all his work over the last few months, the bribes, threats, and ticklish little piece of information about his main rival would be for naught.

He packed up his laptop. "Gwen," he said aloud, "I'm sorry, but I fear I must depart early today."

"That's quite all right, Jack," Gwendolen answered, speaking at the wall. He walked over and touched her shoulder, letting her know where his hand was. She reached up and grasped it firmly, rising to hug him. "Will you be back later?"

"I'm afraid not. However, if all goes according to plan, I should be free tomorrow, and so many more to come."

He leaned close and kissed her cheek. She brought a hand to his own, pressing him back until their lips met once more. He could have stayed in that kiss for ages, but his mind was already rushing ahead, like a conductor frantically directing his orchestra. Every layer, every piece of the symphony had to come together perfectly in his mind, until the path ahead became clear.

Jack finally broke away, giving her another brief hug before he walked to the door. She sat down again, her eyes focused on nothing and everything at the same time.

"Hurry back," she said, smiling. "I'll be waiting."

She turned back to her laptop, asking it to read back the last few sentences she'd written. A synthesized voice, not dissimilar to her own, began to echo her story back to her. Jack walked out the door, with a final glance at his beloved, before he returned to the streets, back to business.

The crunch of bone greeted Jack as he entered the room.

Hammer had just put his fist through a man's face, crushing him into the wall. The man crumpled, but the two behind were not so easily cowed. They rushed Hammer, each grabbing an arm and pinning him to the opposite wall. He struggled, but it wasn't long before they'd chained the brute down, hard stone unyielding to his desperate thrashing.

It was a small, square room, tucked in a long-forgotten basement deep in a business structure deemed particularly unremarkable by the city. Jack owned the building, though none would ever connect his name to it, and used the lower levels for all sorts of ventures. The building above was a legitimate business, of course—accounting services, a law firm, various other institutions. He had no involvement with those beyond as their proprietor.

The true purpose lay below, in the network of basements and tunnels that provided Jack all the room he needed to explore the darker half of his composition.

In the middle of the room sat a table, surrounded by gray stone walls, with plan metal chairs on each side. In one wall, a one-way window would allow Jack or others to observe unseen, a mirror to the brightly lit room. It was perfectly reminiscent of a police interrogation room, except for the location. Anyone walking by would never think twice about it. Certainly, they'd never imagine the many, many horrors that had taken place in the room over the years.

Jack took the seat opposite Hammer, one foot up on his opposite knee. He projected an air of ease and security while everyone beyond his two bodyguards left the room. Jack waited patiently, watching

Hammer with a silent, curious stare. The brute continued to strain against his chains, cursing mightily and swearing all sorts of horrible violence upon him.

Jack took it in stride, never allowing a single hint of fear to cross his face. In truth, Jack was intimidated by the man's sheer strength. He'd be a fool if he wasn't. Hammer was huge and vicious, and his reputation was not unfounded. Jack had personally witnessed the man beat several of his minions to death with a street sign. Granted, the sign hadn't actually been embedded in the ground when he'd taken ahold of it, but still . . .

He shook the memory away. Focus was paramount in this moment. He had limited time to achieve what he wanted here today, and it had to be orchestrated perfectly if Hammer was to play his part. Jack's mind delighted in the puzzle laid out before him. He always preferred the indirect approach. People around him were tools to bend to his will, a million different parts of the grand symphony. He could take out each instrument, move them around, change their parts, alter their notes, but only careful composure could create the piece he wished to accomplish. He had to be meticulous and thorough, lest his orchestra fall to a cacophony of chaos and discord.

This encounter, with this brute, was the beginning of the crescendo. His men had captured Hammer not long after he'd killed the poor young pickpocket. They'd corralled him into this building, forcing him back room by room until he'd been confined to this chamber. It was important he remain alive and not incapacitated if Jack's grand design was to play out.

Karl "Hammer" Ryzhkov, an adopted waif from Russia at a young age, abandoned on the streets to live as an urchin for many years after his new family couldn't stand him any longer, but the foster system could not find another home to place him in. A rough childhood led into an even rougher adulthood. His foster home had kept slim records, and his child services representative even less. Jack often wondered if Hammer's abrasive personality had surfaced on day one, or if his life tied to the streets created the man. He suspected the former, but it was a question Jack doubted he'd ever truly answer.

To get someone to do what he wanted, there were two routes Jack could take. The target could be told, unequivocally, his fate if a task were not carried out. Fear would snap into obedience, but it would be a timid performance, lacking in initiative and passion, with little chance of a repeat.

Jack avoided that coarse approach whenever possible—too crude, too wasteful. His preference was more subtle and had far greater effect over the long run. He would simply present his hapless victim with a measured, reasonable scenario and allow them to play their own part. Jack's contribution was at the periphery, always one step removed, but in truth, he carefully steered them toward fulfilling each piece of his greater design.

With the week Jack was already having, this was just icing atop the cake. Darius's gang was already fighting among themselves, even at the highest levels. Hammer was already confused, striking without permission, off the leash. It would be a simple movement to redirect his rage to more productive outlets.

"Just kill me and get it over with," growled Hammer, finally ceasing his struggle. He fell against the rear wall, breathing heavily.

Jack smiled, relaxing as best he could. In truth, despite all his confidence, his own heart beat a heavy tempo. While Jack had every appearance of the upper hand, Hammer was physically intimidating like none other. Simply being in the same room as the man, openly hostile and only barely restrained, was honestly terrifying.

"In due time," he said lazily. Jack produced a document from the wide folds of his jacket, opening it and giving it all the appearance of reviewing it. In fact, he had read it many times over, but the play was the thing, as it were. Careful consideration, quiet movements, striking crescendos—combined with his considerable reputation—would light the fuse for this particular rocket. "Seems you've started a war outside, my friend."

"I knocked off some punk who had the balls to take my phone," he grunted, a discordant noise that nonetheless filled the space Jack required. "So what?"

His confusion seemed genuine. Jack marveled that such a stupid man had progressed so far in their organization. His respect for Darius diminished daily.

"Ah, but that young man was in my employ," said Jack, his voice practically purring, "and on my land. Surely, you didn't expect me to let the offense stand?"

"You didn't care about him. You just wanted a damn excuse." *Not entirely an idiot.* He'd picked up some concept for the machinations of politics from his time around Darius. Jack decided it was time to throw the rabid dog a bone.

"True enough, just a minor piece of the puzzle. Still, without every piece, the puzzle ends a fractured mess instead of the lovely picture intended by its creator. I cannot abide incompleteness," Jack sighed— perhaps a little too dramatically, but he was enjoying himself, and he doubted Hammer would catch the subtleties of performance. "Mr. Ryzhkov, I wonder if you've ever partaken of the VR simulations that are so popular these days with the addicts?"

Hammer snorted. "Why bother when I get all the ass I want for free?"

Jack winced inwardly, disgusted, but kept his face calm and serene. "I suspected a man like yourself would see past the illusions of fulfillment. What you may not know, however, is how a simulation diminishes over time. You see, like any good market, you require repeat customers to keep business booming. Why would a customer return when they have a perfect facsimile of reality at their fingertips?"

Jack raised an eyebrow for effect. Hammer looked unimpressed, but from the way he sat, Jack knew he was listening intently. Jack's reputation was strong enough to command attention, even from this fool.

"Acclimation, Mr. Ryzhkov," he went on, digressing from what was strictly necessary for the moment, but Jack enjoyed the topic. "Those worlds aren't perfect, no matter how they might seem. They only create things at random, or by a specific set of rules pre-programmed by a developer. After some time, the mind will grow more sensitive to any imperfections in the simulation, be they flaws in graphical design, bugs in the software, so on. Impurities surface, the illusion is broken, and the simulation no longer sustains reality.

"The brain, impeccable tool it is, can recognize something falsely pushing on the edge of reality, particularly when it appears precisely the same every time. The world is too random and chaotic for such constant perfection. Thus, you stay in business. Your . . . *customers* run out of their sims, and they need fresh untamed worlds to lose themselves in. Given government limits on direct nerve interfaces, they come to you for black market software, a reliable source that won't fry their poor brains."

"I already know all this shit," growled Hammer. "Get to the point."

Jack smiled. He was baiting the hook, and Hammer was almost *too* eager to chomp at it. Jack's reputation for grandiose speeches was playing off the hapless hulk perfectly. Hammer hung onto every word, as Jack was known to drop useful information even to his worst enemies when he got onto a tangent.

All intentional, of course—only information calculated to be of little true worth, but valuable enough to be noticed. Jack played into their presuppositions, nurturing his "tendency" carefully over the years precisely to use it in moments like these.

"Thus, we come to cybernetics, Mr. Ryzhkov. A whole new world of highs, for addicts who will never experience such a pure feeling as what I'll be delivering. By skipping the VR link and going directly into the brain, I can provide them something your feeble software can only dream of, and all without the expense of the programmers and designers who drain your resources day by day. It will be . . . revolutionary."

Jack's eyes sparkled at the word, though of course the revolution he planned was quite different from the one he spoke of. Hammer would never catch the subtle irony he placed on his words, but it tickled Jack to no end how obvious his deception should have been.

"You think we didn't already try that, dumbshit?" Hammer sneered. "Brain knows it's false, just like you said. It doesn't work."

"Ahh," Jack said with true satisfaction, "but see, I've solved that problem. Or rather, some good friends of mine solved it for me." Jack smiled, as Hammer's eyes widened.

It was all too easy. He'd barely had to do anything. Jack could see the connections forming in his head already. Talk of cybernetics would lead him to the Maclays, and Snipe's link to the Dunhams and her assassination of Darius would provide the weight of the connection. Hammer would escape, shortly after Jack left the room, and Darius's gang would soon be aligned against one of their most important and influential allies.

If only Snipe had gone after Darius herself, instead of needing additional incentive. Jack had believed the initial evidence more than enough—she was a smart girl—she should have drawn the necessary conclusions without the video. The video could potentially engender more sympathy of Darius. Evidently, her legendary lack of empathy wasn't quite true, just as with the legends about himself, but so far, he'd seen no evidence she was back in the gang's good graces.

The crescendo continued to build.

Jack stood up, the smile still plastered on his face. "It was a pleasure talking to you, Mr. Ryzhkov." He nodded to one of his guards, subtly flashing a signal to his man as he rose. "He need not suffer."

He smiled one last time at Hammer before exiting the room. The man would be unchained and dragged toward the exit, in preparation to be dumped into the incinerator—no need to bloody the room, after all, when he wasn't to be left alive.

However, the guard would be distracted by a sound down the hall, and Hammer would find a chance to escape. The guards would be conveniently be overtaken, and Hammer would find his way through the line of open doors leading to the streets. The GPS tracker Jack planted on Hammer's coat would give a neat map to wherever Darius and his men were assembling. Meanwhile, Jack estimated it would only be a few hours before Hammer would mobilize something to eliminate the Maclays, and certainly without bothering to run it by Darius himself.

Jack's own men would be nearby, watching for the result, keeping a safe distance. Meanwhile, Jack himself had other work to be done. His orchestra had a few final preparations, a few more players still missing his notes. The Maclays would soon either be dead or in his hands, and Darius's influence in the city greatly diminished. Jack's men would be ready to move in and take control, and steer the city toward a better future.

The symphony played on.

CHAPTER 11

Blood pumped through my brain, pulsing at the edges of my skull. My mouth was bitter with adrenaline and the taste of blood—I'd accidentally bitten off a piece of my tongue at some point. Close quarters fights were the worst. They were always messy and brutal.

I reached forward and pulled the knife from the man's face with a bit of effort. After quickly wiping it down, I sheathed the knife behind my back once more. I examined the man's pistol, but I disliked the weight of it immediately. It was definitely more powerful, but I preferred the familiar grip I'd practiced with. The difference in weight and recoil could mean life or death in a pinch.

Rearmed, I leaned forward and examined the body. It was definitely one of Darius's other hitmen. I only knew them by face, since they, too, preferred to keep their names and identities private. I felt something of a kinship to them, a shared experience and occupation. In fact, this man had actually recommended the pistol I now used, an upgrade to the one Darius originally gave me. He'd brought it up after we crossed paths hunting the same contract, and I'd missed a few shots with my old handgun.

Embarrassing to no end, while he'd gotten the target easily. To my shock, though, he gave me the credit—which honestly might have saved my life. It preserved my reputation, and in my line of work, reputation can hold off any number of would-be usurpers.

What was he doing here? He'd only come here if he intended to *kill* the Maclays. Darius wouldn't send an *assassin* if he wanted them protected—*except me, maybe.* But then again, Darius wouldn't want them killed at all. They were his most important business partners. This man's presence made no sense. My mind struggled to put together the puzzle here, but I came up empty. I finally looked away, with no more clues to be found on the dead man.

I was suddenly *very* aware of how silent the room was. The four other occupants were pale as death, staring at me. I stood up, lowering the pistol, trying not to look threatening. I thought about saying something, but no words came to me. They were silent as the grave.

My gaze wandered, avoiding their faces. I couldn't bear to look at Rebecca. Memories threatened to push into my mind, mixed with the videos both of my past and of the surgery she'd performed. It wasn't the time. We were still in danger. I refocused, and found something to land on—Faith.

Her face was flashing through so many emotions, it was difficult to keep up. Shock, horror, desperation, gratitude, happiness, despair, confusion—all of them mixed together in her expression. I only hoped Faith would come to her senses quickly. I knew *I* couldn't talk to the Maclays and I had to hope she could persuade them to leave, right now.

To my shock, though, it wasn't Faith, but Eleanor who spoke first. "Dad, we need to leave."

My other eye moved to her. Her own eyes were determined, expression grim. She was already past the shock, as focused as I was. I mentally approved of Faith's choice of friend. Eleanor reached out and grasped Faith's hand firmly. Her eyes widened, but even so, she still said nothing.

Instead, Arthur spluttered to life. "Who—who was that man? Who is this *girl?* What the hell—"

I noted the second question with interest. Apparently, Rebecca had never informed her husband about our shared history. *I guess that's a point in her favor . . . she never gave me up.*

"Art. Arthur. Calm down, please." Rebecca was also quick to regain control, just like her daughter. She grabbed his shoulders, pulling him into a tight hug. "Someone just tried to kill us. She saved us. The rest doesn't matter yet. We need to leave, right now."

Rebecca looked away, toward me. Recognition dawned on her face—we hadn't seen each other in years, but I certainly had a . . . distinctive look. I flinched, despite myself. She brought only painful memories now.

She looked hurt by my reaction, but she pushed through, nonetheless. "Do you have a plan?"

I glanced down at the man. "Hide from Jack," I said simply. I assumed they were aware enough to catch the implications of that name. It would save us some time, rather than introduce even more intrigue by revealing the assassin's true origin, which *I* still didn't understand.

". . . Oh god," gasped Rebecca.

"Jack?" asked Arthur. "Why would he want to have *us* killed?"

"I don't know," I answered truthfully. I walked to the doorway and glanced down the hall, just to reassure myself. It was still clear, but I had no doubt Jack's men had come back by now. If the assassin was from Darius, we probably still had time. Jack's men were here to observe, and Darius wouldn't send another after the first failed. They were too valuable, especially in the current situation.

I leaned against the wall, watching the hallway, checking my pistol's magazine and making sure it was fully loaded.

". . . That's all you've got? You *don't know?*"

Arthur's voice was getting more furious by the syllable. He took a step forward, but I stared him down. My left eye matched his glare-for-glare while my other eye scanned the room again. I'd watch every single corner I could manage, with what we were up against.

The assassin's blood seeped across the wood, staining the white rug nearby a deep red. Eleanor was silent on the couch, seated next to Faith, holding her hand firmly while watching her parents. Rebecca stood next to Arthur, holding him back. Faith . . . was still silent, her eyes fixed on the assassin sprawled on the floor.

It bothered me. Faith, who normally couldn't shut up to save her life, was perfectly silent. It was wrong, so very wrong.

I took a step forward.

The room reacted to my movement. The Maclays froze, eyes fixed on me, terrified what I might do next. Rage still filled Arthur's expression, fear Rebecca's, and . . . jealousy in Eleanor's? I didn't understand, and my step had obviously made things worse. I stopped, and let my other eye keep scanning, trying to make it seem like I'd only been examining the room further.

Arthur only now seemed to notice the whirring metal in my face. "That's my tech . . ." he murmured. "Becca?" He pushed away from his wife, glancing between the two of us. "Trinocular-lens in a silicon-polymer construction, direct nerve link. But . . . you solved the brain damage issue from attaching directly into the brain bypassing the optic nerve?"

His eyes narrowed. "You took my ideas and used them to make . . . *this?*" Arthur gestured to me as if I were an object. His hands fell away from his wife, anger shifting focus. I glanced away, looking back into the hall, listening as best I could for movement. This was a waste of time, but how was I supposed to get them focused? I was the subject of their argument.

While their voices rose again, I did wonder—I'd never really been bothered by my cybernetics. They were tools and useful ones. I didn't have a particular attachment to my original body, as long as I was myself inside. I'd cultivated this look, with my long hair and the outfits I wore, mostly to conceal identifying marks rather than because I was ashamed over the things which made me different. I wore my other eye almost like a badge of pride, something which made me unique—and deadly, of course.

With the revelations about my memories, though, I did wonder what it was like to have two eyes. I'd never known anything else, or what my arm was supposed to feel like without the hard metal sheath lining the skin. I couldn't remember a time before Darius, so I had no idea what a normal body felt like—but now I knew I *did* have one once, thanks to Faith.

Was I always a killer? Would I be so okay with what I am, with the changes to my body, if I could remember what I'd been before? I never had a choice in any of this . . . unless Darius is telling the truth. Unless I really did ask for it.

If I got my memories back today . . . would I still be me?

"Arthur, please," said Rebecca, her eyes welling up with tears. "It's not the time. We're in danger."

"She looks like a high school girl, and you turned her into a killing machine!" Arthur's voice rose with every word. "What *else* did you do to her?"

"She would have died, Arthur!" cried Rebecca, now clutching her daughter's hand since her husband has broken away. "It was this or permanent blindness and her legs crippled! We had the tech; she needed it. What else was I going to do?"

. . . Legs? I lifted one of my legs experimentally, trying to sense something strange, but I didn't feel anything. Either Rebecca did her work remarkably well . . . or I had no clue what a normal leg was supposed to feel like anyway.

Arthur was silent now, still fuming, but without a response. Rebecca was quietly crying, standing next to her daughter on the couch, clutching onto her hand like she might float away if Eleanor didn't hold on. Meanwhile, Eleanor was looking at me, the product of her parents' work, sizing me up. My other eye flicked over to her unconsciously, and she flinched, just for the briefest moment.

She recovered quickly enough, but it made me uncomfortable again. I looked away, sweeping my hair down over my other eye, watching the doorway—but a movement on the couch turned me back immediately.

Faith clambered to her feet. The room fell silent, *every* eye fixed on her. She let go of Eleanor's hand, walked straight across the room—carefully sidestepping the body—and wrapped me in a hug.

I didn't know how to react. My hand still held the man's pistol, and my other eye was desperately trying to keep watch on the whole room through both my hair and now the sudden obstruction of Faith—but nonetheless, I appreciated it a lot more than I could express.

"Thank you," she murmured.

For a very long moment, I didn't move . . . but finally, I put my arms back around her in return. It just . . . felt right. I fought away the anxiety and the fear in that moment. Faith needed the gesture . . . and if I was being honest, so did I. It lasted a few seconds, before Faith finally broke away and turned back to face her adoptive parents. Her voice was low, hurried, and back to the usual confidence I hadn't realized how much I missed.

"We gotta go. Ellie, call Tanaka and get us rolling. He's probably already in the garage. Grab some first-aid stuff, load it in the car, just in case. Art, get anything you want from your room. You've got five minutes." Faith paused, then turned to me. "I know you've got a lot of questions for them, but it's not the time, okay?"

I nodded, though of course I hadn't planned to ask anything yet.

Faith smiled, but it vanished as she turned back to the Maclays. "Becca, get your stuff. We're probably not coming back for a while."

Rebecca nodded. Arthur was finally caught up too. All three of them recognized the sheer danger they were in. They left the room, leaving me and Faith alone with the body.

Faith looked at me, face hard. "So."

"So?"

She gestured at the man on the ground. "That's not one of Jack's, is it?"

"How did you know?"

"The way you looked at him. You knew him, didn't you?"

I hesitated. "Yeah. He was nice to me. I didn't know it was him until I was pulling the trigger."

"Shit, Kara . . ." she sighed. "I'm sorry." She put an arm back around me, a sort of one-armed hug. I felt a weight on my shoulder as she instinctively used me for support, taking the edge off her leg. It wasn't really a burden and it made me feel a little better that I was helping her. It felt right. "Are you okay?"

"I'm fine. It was him or me."

"Yeah . . . it was. Him or us, probably," she added. "You saved my family. I think I owe you my firstborn now, too, on top of my life a few times."

I shook my head. "You don't owe me anything. That's what friends do, right?"

"Oh, we're friends now, huh?" said Faith, a weak smile creeping onto her face.

". . . Yes?"

She laughed. "Shared our darkest secrets, saved each other's lives a couple of times, and now we're two girls against the two scariest mobs in Seattle. Yeah, okay, we can be friends." I laughed, and we shared the moment, a respite from all the drama and stress we'd been dealing with. "Becca said legs . . . You been holding out on me, K?"

I shook my head. "I didn't even know. My legs always just felt like . . . you know, my legs."

"Your original legs were crushed," said Rebecca, reappearing in the doorway with a bag over her shoulder and another in her hand. *There's no way she packed that much so fast . . . She had a go-bag ready.* "You have an extremely advanced composite material comprising both the muscles and bones, combined with a natural skin covering. It pulls power from the battery bank in your arm and should grow naturally as you do, adjusting for height." Her voice was clinical and measured, the voice from every diagnostic I'd ever had. "They're much stronger than the average sixteen-year-old female and they will never feel pain. They'll also take a considerably larger amount of force to break."

She stopped, and her voice caught in her throat. ". . . I was working on another version for Faith," she added quietly.

Faith fell silent again. I looked at her, waiting for some kind of reaction, but nothing came. Her face was blank. Rebecca waited in the doorway, watching us. Finally, she spoke first, breaking the silence.

"Faith, I think Ellie needed your help with something downstairs."

Faith nodded. She left the room, still silent. Rebecca turned to face me, and all softness was gone from her voice—this was business, the attitude she took with Darius when they weren't happy with each other.

"You saved us, and I'm grateful, but you and I both know that man was from Darius. So, you'll excuse me if I don't exactly trust you at the moment." Her voice might be calm, but I saw the fear in her eyes. I was shocked—Rebecca's involvement went way beyond me and technology, if she knew one of Darius's assassins by a face alone.

"I don't trust you either," I replied, which was entirely truthful.

"Fair enough. You're here for Faith, Faith's here for my daughter, and Ellie's not going to leave without us, and I'm the target here. Does that sound right?"

"Essentially."

"Good." Rebecca walked close, looking at my other eye carefully. I resisted the urge to take a step back. ". . . This needs cleaning."

"We don't have time," I said impatiently.

"No, we don't." Rebecca sighed. "Lead the way, then."

We left for the garage level. I grabbed my bag from the bedroom as we passed, dropping the assassin's pistol inside and grabbing my own, grateful for the familiar grip in my hand again. I strapped on a holster and stowed it, then pulled out my rifle and checked it.

The click of the magazine echoed through the empty hallway. Rebecca grimaced, but she didn't say anything. I slung the rifle over my shoulder, ready to use, and drew the pistol again. I tightened a suppressor on the end, just in case. It'd be better in the tight hallways, where my rifle was too large and unwieldy to aim quickly.

Their house was quiet. A light at the far end flickered, shadows dancing on the walls. Arthur was moving around inside, probably packing as fast as he could. Rebecca led the way downstairs, with me only a few steps behind. The staircase curled around as we descended. I heard a faint murmur from below, voices I presumed belonged to Faith and Eleanor. We turned the corner and emerged into a room packed with shelves, full of every manner of gadget, objects with purposes I couldn't begin to discern.

In the middle of the room stood a man whose purpose was all too clear.

Jack Monroe was right in the center, standing just behind Faith, a pistol at her head. One of his men was nearby, another gun trained on Eleanor, seated on the couch. A third stood near the garage exit while a fourth stood in the near corner, evidently waiting to snatch whoever came downstairs next.

My hand raised like lightning. Before he could react, I'd already aimed and squeezed the trigger twice. Two quiet shots echoed through the house, the impact of the bullets louder than the pistol itself.

The man collapsed against the wall. My second shot had punched through his neck. He wheezed as he began to bleed out, completely removed from the fight.

The man near the garage was already turning to aim at Rebecca while Jack's aim on Faith tightened. I dropped to base instinct, doing the first thing that came to mind.

I grabbed Rebeca and pulled her back, moving up the staircase so my entire body was hidden behind her. My pistol snaked up until it rested next to her ear, the barrel pointed directly through her skull. Rebecca was tall, almost as tall as her daughter, but the height of the staircase step made it possible. My threat was clear.

"Mom!"

Eleanor started to rise, but her guard forced her back down. A brief moment of shock flashed through Faith's expression, but it was quickly replaced by grim understanding. Jack hadn't won yet.

I still had a few tricks left.

"Hello again, Snipe," said Jack, his smile widening.

He mirrored my own move, forcing Faith to her feet and holding her between us. I couldn't get a clear shot, not from my angle.

"See, my friends tell me that this little bird is an ally of yours. You've been seen together a few times, far more than any other companion I can recall." He laughed. "I must thank Darius's man for opening up the security and letting us in tonight. The Maclay house is such a marvel. I've always wondered what it's like inside."

Jack glanced around the room like a gleeful child. "I wish I had time to examine all the wonders doubtless contained herein, but alas, I've many duties that await, some which require your services, Dr. Maclay."

Rebecca shook her head.

"Oh, come now," said Jack, sounding disappointed. "You're really not in a position to bargain. You've got a gun to your head from your erstwhile ally at the same time I'm holding your daughter and her lover hostage. Think rationally, please."

"Lover?" snorted Faith, and I felt an incongruous burst of joy that she hadn't been totally suppressed. "Check your facts next time, Mr. Supervillain."

Jack paused, looking genuinely confused. ". . . Did I not just chance upon the two of you sharing a moment? It touched my heart to witness. I even let it continue as far as I could before I had to move things along."

Eleanor's face was getting redder by the second while Faith fumed nearby. Jack was practically giddy, his glee palpable.

"How do we resolve this?" I asked, tired of the head games. I knew the longer we talked, the more it put Jack at an advantage, both from his men *and* from his voice.

"Well," he said with a sigh, "to be frank, Snipe? You're not leaving alive. Nor is anyone else, save Rebecca. You've been soundly cornered and you've no allies left. So please, just send Rebecca over, and I'll make it quick."

While Jack spoke, Rebecca turned her head slightly, whispering from the corner of her mouth in a way that neither Jack nor his remaining men could see.

"Thermal."

She didn't need to risk anything more. I tapped her on the back twice, letting her know I got it. I made a slight gesture with my hand out of Jack's sight, selecting the option in my other eye's menu to swap lenses, and I tensed up—waiting.

Jack sighed again. "I really don't want to risk Dr. Maclay's health here, Snipe. I can assure you, she'll be dealt with after I've gotten what I need from her. In fact, if you have any requests, I'll do whatever you like to her. We can all agree—what she did to you was quite monstrous."

Rebecca twisted her head around fully to look at me. "You *know?*"

I didn't respond, except to move slightly to keep myself in cover from Jack, using her body as a shield. Jack filled in the silence for me, quite eagerly.

"Yes, Rebecca, she knows. She saw the whole thing on video. Terribly convenient of you to keep recordings for even your black market surgeries."

Eleanor spoke up from the couch, confused. "Knows what, Mom?"

Jack chucked. "Ah, the drama in this room could fuel an opera. I wish I had time to digest it all."

"Trouble, Jack?" Faith asked snidely.

"Hardly," Jack replied, glancing down at his captive. "Just pleasant company, and even more pleasant activities waiting." He glanced at his watch, taking his eyes off Rebecca for *just* long enough. I tensed up, and she didn't let me down. Rebecca seized the opportunity.

"Now!" she shouted, diving for the nearest shelf and grabbing a canister in midair. She tossed it into the center of the room, landing with a grunt as the object arced through the air. I shifted my other eye into thermal, right before it landed.

It pulsed a piercing white light several times, filling the room. A moment later, the lights all went black, plunging us into darkness. My left eye was completely blinded by the jarring shifts of extreme contrast, but my other eye told a different story.

Jack's men were suddenly perfectly outlined, white silhouettes stumbling about from the painful shifts of light. Jack himself had dropped out of sight, but I wasted no time on his other men. I dropped to a crouch and opened fire.

My first shot dropped the man standing over Eleanor like a sack of rocks. I dove forward before I tried for the other man, and it saved my life—he opened fire blindly where I'd been only a moment before.

Bullets snapped by overhead, as the man's gun—far louder than my own—fired again and again. I crawled to the end of the couch, flat on the ground. His legs were just barely visible, but I had a clean shot. I put a round through his ankle. He screamed and crashed to the ground.

My next bullet found his skull.

I turned. Rebecca wasn't where I'd last seen her. I rose up just high enough to see above the couch, barrel of my gun leading the way as the lights flickered back to life. Faith was sprawled out on the ground. Eleanor crouched nearby, cradling her head. Both looked as disoriented as Jack's thugs had been.

Rebecca was caught. Jack now held her tight, his gun on her head in much the same manner I'd done only a minute earlier.

Another one of Jack's thugs appeared in the doorway to the garage, a pistol at the ready. I trained my arm on him, ready to fire, but he ducked out just in time.

"I'll be leaving, then," said Jack, his voice husky and breathless. He jerked Rebecca slightly, and she began to move toward the door while Jack kept her squarely between himself and me. As much as I hated it, I couldn't get a clear shot—the Maclays were all too tall. "Relax, Snipe. Your friends are still alive. No hard feelings, just business."

He backed out of the doorway, and the rifle poking around the doorframe was enough to dissuade me from following.

"Sorry about upstairs!" he called out before he fled the house.

I rushed the door as soon as the room was clear. Jack's man tried to aim for me, but I put two clean shots into his chest before he ever had the chance. *Four bullets left.* A counter on my other eye helpfully kept track, as the sensors detected my trigger finger movement. As I rounded the corner and exited the garage, a car engine revved outside.

Jack was already pulling Rebecca into a waiting vehicle. His man in the driver seat revved the engine again and pulled away. I took a shot at the tires, but it pinged off the metal on the front. The back door slammed closed on its own as the car squealed out of the Maclay compound through the wide-open gates and past the disabled security system.

I let out a deep breath. We'd survived. We'd lost Rebecca, but . . . we'd survived.

I went back inside. Eleanor looked up, worry and fear splayed across her features. I slowly shook my head.

A brief note of panic crossed Eleanor's face, but to her credit, she drove it off remarkably fast. She turned and helped Faith get back onto the couch.

"Are you okay?" I asked, reaching into my bag and pulling out a fresh magazine. I reloaded calmly, then moved to check the bodies of Jack's men still lying around the room. I kept my other eye watching Faith while my left eye examined the corpses, verifying they were dead and nothing was on them that might explode or send a signal back to Jack, or something.

"I will be," said Faith. "Shit, that stung." She massaged the top of her head gingerly. "He hits like a freight train."

"I think you'll be fine," said Eleanor, examining her head. "It doesn't look bad from here." She glanced over at me just as I finished checking the last of Jack's three men. All of them had expired. "Who *are* you?"

I looked up, but my left eye found Faith instead. She understood, without any further prompting, what I wanted.

"She's a friend, Ellie. One with talents we *seriously* need right now." She looked up at Eleanor. "Do you trust me?"

"Of course I do."

"Then you can trust her. She's here to help." Faith got to her feet, stumbling a little, but Eleanor helped her stay upright. "So what's the plan?"

Before I could reply, we heard a thump from the ceiling. Something had just dropped onto the floor upstairs.

Faith and Eleanor both sprouted the exact same terrified look.

"Jack said something about upstairs . . ." Faith said cautiously.

A beat of silence—and Eleanor took off. She bolted for the staircase, and I followed only a moment behind, my pistol at the ready. The staircase and hallway above were still dark, the only light coming from the master bedroom down the hall.

I managed to grab Eleanor's arm as we hit the upper landing, stopping her in the hall. She turned to protest, but I held a finger up to my mouth, then gestured with my pistol. Understanding flooded her face, and Eleanor stood back. I raised the gun and walked forward, slow, quiet steps down the hallway.

My movements were nearly silent, the house even more so. The Maclay house was apparently nearly fully soundproofed from the city engulfing it, something I hadn't noticed earlier. I approached the door, step by step, my arm steady.

It was partially ajar. Light spilled into the dark hallway, but I didn't see any more movement in the shadows. I couldn't see inside from this angle—only the headboard of the bed and an end table. A faint dripping noise was audible as I got closer . . . and then a gasp.

A painful wheezing cough.

The sound of a man drawing desperate, final breaths.

I thrust the door open, but I already knew what I'd find.

Arthur Maclay was on the floor, his neck sliced open. Blood ebbed out of him, a trail leading down from the top of the bed to his place on the carpet. His hands desperately clutched the open wound. A suitcase lay atop the bed, half packed and splattered with red.

I entered the room, still cautious. I checked the corners and the closet, but I didn't find anyone. Jack's men were already gone.

A strangled cry like a dying animal from behind me. I whipped around, alert, but dropped my aim immediately.

Eleanor rushed past me into the room. She collapsed next to her father, grabbing the sheets from the bed and pressing them against his neck to stem the bleeding.

"Call an ambulance," she cried, her voice thick. "I can't save him on my own."

"We can't," Faith said before I could respond. "Any medical responders in this area are owned by Darius, and that assassin in the living room was his. We can't trust them."

"Who's Dar . . . never mind." She cut off mid-sentence at another painful gasp from her father. "A private clinic then," she said determinedly. "One *I* trust," she added when Faith seemed about to protest.

". . . Give me the number," said Faith, pulling out the burner I'd given her.

Eleanor rattled it off. I walked out of the room while Faith made the call, taking up a better position to cover them. Crouched in the doorway with my pistol trained on the entrance, I'd be able to take out—or at least scare off—anyone who showed up, but I doubted we'd see anything else. Jack already got what he wanted . . . didn't he?

Unanswered questions swirled in my mind. *Why would Jack have taken out Arthur? Wouldn't he be way more useful alive, as additional leverage? Why was Darius suddenly turning on his allies? Why did Rebecca give me the implants and not Faith?*

What happened the night my memory was erased?

I refocused myself as a private ambulance pulled into the drive. Its lights and sirens were off, probably at Faith's instruction. Another point of admiration from me—she had smart instincts.

A man and a woman rushed inside, carrying a stretcher. I ducked into a side room before they saw me, watching closely as they hurried past. Some rustling sounds, and then they were rushing back, Arthur loaded up, Eleanor at his side. Moments later, the doors outside slammed closed, and the engine roared away.

Silence crept back through the house once more. I emerged into the hallway, where Faith leaned against the wall. Her eyes were hard, face covered in tears, expression full of determined rage.

"Where to, Kara?" she practically growled.

I considered for a moment. ". . . We're not going to find him by trying to track him directly. He's too smart for that. We need to lure him back."

"With what? He got what he came for?"

Did he though? What was so important about the Maclays that he burned all of this tonight just to get Rebecca? "You said you found his personal residence, right?"

"Yeah," said Faith, frustration creeping back into her voice, "but it's not like anybody'll be there."

"He's mentioned company twice now," I said carefully. "Someone *we* can leverage."

Understanding dawned on Faith's face—grim, reluctant understanding. "Fight fire with fire?"

I nodded.

CHAPTER 12

"Not sure what I expected," said Faith.

We were looking down at the home, crouched behind a window in a second-story apartment a few blocks away. Faith had binoculars while I relied on the scope of my rifle. So far, we hadn't seen a single living soul even glance at the place.

It had only been an hour since we left the Maclay estate. We'd run into Tanaka on the way out. After getting the car ready, he'd seen several of Jack's men outside the perimeter and . . . dealt with them. He'd come back just in time to see Jack speeding off with Rebecca and put a few bullets in the car himself, but he hadn't any more luck than I did.

Tanaka had attached himself to us in the meantime, following Eleanor's last order. After confirming Jack's address from her notes, Faith had him drive us near the house.

We'd stopped as soon as we got close—no use risking setting off any guards Jack kept around his personal residence. The apartment guard was kind enough to let us in, after a pointed conversation with Faith while I simply stood nearby with my hood low, idly fiddling with my pistol in my pocket. Despite the pressure of our current situation, Faith still clearly relished her role. The man was seriously intimidated by the time we left.

"It's too plain," Faith continued, scanning across the building.

I had to agree. It was a one-floor squat house, and worse, it didn't stand out—plain roof, plan door, plain windows, plain mat in front of the door and mailbox at the end of the walkway. For all intents and purposes, it was utterly ordinary. It didn't fit my image of Jack at all.

"Are you sure it's the right place?" I murmured, still scanning through every opening I could find. There was *nothing*—the house might as well have been a tomb.

"Sure seemed like it . . . From the emails, this is the only place that makes sense. You said Jerome *is* a reliable source, right?"

I nodded. "He never let me down. Not someone to *trust*, but his intel was always solid. He always kept his word."

A look crossed Faith's face. Something like . . . shame?

"What is it?"

"Nothing." Faith quickly refocused on the house down the street. "So, we storming the castle?"

"Is it even worth storming?" I asked, frustration audible in my voice. "He could be watching the place, and we've got no reason to believe we're going to get anything useful. We need better info."

Faith sighed. "Yeah, we do. My turn, I guess. Time to go." She stood to leave.

"Hm?"

She grinned. "Don't worry, K. You're gonna love it. It's the most talkative place in the city."

An uncomfortable feeling dropped into my stomach—but nonetheless, I followed her out.

Tanaka drove them deep into the main downtown district, a block bordering both Darius's and Jack's territories, but not controlled by either. This was a contested zone, and my paranoia was only getting worse with every minute we spent here.

Our car was one of the only vehicles on the road not running autopilot. I'd insisted on manual drive. One of Darius's pet projects had been to try and co-opt the driving network—mostly for records of destinations, especially on autocars—but there wasn't any reason the system couldn't be turned into a full-control trojan. We hadn't ever actually *succeeded*, as far as I knew, but . . . I'd also stopped paying attention. It could have happened.

Thus, Tanaka had a chance to show off his driving skills—and he was *good*. Since we weren't hooked up to the network, other cars couldn't use predictive algorithms to determine our path and velocity, nor have an idea where we were going. Anything in our way would be relying on visual sensors.

We had to give them plenty of leeway but still appear to be driving on autopilot. Manual control in this part of the city was strictly illegal, for good reason—there weren't any traffic lights. Every car knew exactly where every other vehicle was going to be, after all. They didn't need to stop, ever. Except . . . Tanaka was relying solely on reflex and intuition.

Suffice to say, we were barreling through intersections with rapid cross-traffic, dodging cars by centimeters, all to give the impression we were still on autopilot. He was perfect, and nobody noticed. After all, driving like you were going to crash into everything was exactly how autocars were supposed to work.

Tanaka finally pulled off onto a side street after reaching the forest of skyscrapers that marked downtown. He stopped briefly to let us out, giving us a slight nod of farewell. I helped Faith get out quickly, before Tanaka started holding up traffic. As soon as I closed the door, he smoothly merged right back into traffic, and I lost track of him a few seconds later.

Faith led the way into the alley, covered in huge puddles from the downpour. The rain had dropped to only a drizzle in the last few minutes. I pulled my hood off, letting my hair free for a bit. Faith went straight down a staircase built into the concrete, where a heavy metal door was set into the basement level.

She walked up and rapped on the door with her knuckles. The moment she did, a camera at the far end of the alley turned to look at her. I stayed out of its line of sight, but Faith looked right up at it. As the camera came into view, Faith gave it a wink.

The door immediately swung open.

Faith turned around and gave me another wink. "Welcome to my lair, Cyclops." She limped her way inside, favoring the crutch.

What on earth . . . I hesitated, still eyeing the camera with some apprehension, but I followed her inside.

As I rounded the corner and went in, the door swung closed. A man had been sitting just behind it, sitting on a stool and calmly reading a book. He had an old wired telephone next to him, with soft red indicator lights glowing beside a reading lamp. The man didn't give us a second glance.

I hurried forward as Faith had already disappeared down the hallway. Around the next corner, there was a heavy thick curtain, which Faith walked through as if it weren't there. The moment she did, I heard a chorus of muffled shouts.

Was that surprise? Joy? . . . Fear? I tried to listen, but I couldn't make out any of the words. *Who is Faith . . . ?*

With trepidation slowing every step, I walked through the curtain, favoring the edge, trying to displace it as little as possible.

Noise assaulted my ears from every direction. The room was a *cavern*, stretching outward for the whole length of the city block. A few other curtained doors ringed the main floor. Long picnic-style tables and benches filled the main floor, and at one end, a huge open buffet sat laden with food. Behind it was a busy kitchen, with several aproned men and women bustling about behind, preparing dinner.

Large vats of soup, ovens wafting the smell of baking bread over the crowd, a pile of vegetables, and more, all waiting to be served. The tables were lined with people of all ages—men, women, children, all obviously showing the strain of homelessness and hunger. Tattered clothes and weak faces filled my view, but as soon as Faith walked in, they were full of joy.

She was the center of attention and she clearly adored it. Nearly every table raised their cheap plastic cups to toast her arrival. Even the cooks stopped and waved a brief greeting, before hurrying to meet the demand of the crowd. Several in the long, *long* serving line looked confused, but I could just barely make out their friends hurriedly whispering explanations—and soon enough, they were toasting to Faith as well.

I slipped in unnoticed, with all the attention on my companion. My clothes weren't high enough quality for me to stand out, to my relief, and I'd also had the foresight to stow my weapons in my bag before we walked in. My hair was still thick over my other eye, so nobody was likely to spot it either.

With the lack of attention, I started making my way along the wall, getting out of the entryway. I didn't feel a single eye on me, though I did get the occasional odd glance. My other eye stayed locked on Faith, watching her move between two of the largest tables. She was greeting a few specific people as she limped by, giving a hug, a fist bump, whatever.

She was . . . beloved. What did she do for these people? How did she inspire such a display?

Faith finally stopped by a lone couple, a man and woman eating together near the end of a table. The man stood out in the crowd by his sheer bulk, especially once I looked more closely. He sported a huge beard, and while at first glance, he seemed to be buried under a huge patchwork coat, I realized he was even larger than Hammer.

His companion, on the other hand, was a willowy young woman with short-cropped hair, rimless glasses, and small beady eyes that darted back and forth with impatient intelligence. Both were in their late twenties, if I had to guess. Neither of them *quite* fit the scene, even with the sheer variation present at every table.

Must be who we're here to see.

My suspicion was confirmed a moment later as they both stood. Faith limped over to one of the doors at the edge of the room. Her eyes crossed mine just briefly, and she threw a subtle hand motion, gesturing for me to follow. They exited through another thick curtain.

I waited just a moment, making sure no one was watching, then circumvented the crowd as quietly as I could.

Through the curtain, Faith was sitting on a ragged couch, her legs propped up on a beaten old wooden coffee table. The beady-eyed woman sat nearby in a cheap office chair, rotating back and forth with her feet every few seconds. Meanwhile, the huge man stood in a corner, waiting for me to enter.

As soon as I did, he drew the curtain closed. I glanced at him, with just enough threat to make sure he knew not to try anything.

"Hey now," said Faith, "these are my friends. We're all good here."

I didn't *actually* have any intentions, but the guy looked ready to pounce on me. He reminded me of a lion, with the huge mane of brown hair. At Faith's word, though, he sat back on his stool, pulled out a vaporizer and lit up. He seemed to be totally uninterested after that, leaning back and breathing deep.

"*Thank* you, Sebastian," Faith said dramatically. She turned to me. "Take a seat?"

Without any other options, I took the spot next to Faith on the couch.

Faith smiled, then turned back to the woman. "All right, Ames. Let's get down to business."

The chair spinning stopped. She leaned forward, elbows on her knees, and her beady eyes twitched rapidly as they bounced between the two of us at light speed.

"Hol' up, Faith. Who's Miss Dark 'n' Mysterious? Don' like workin' wit' people I don' know."

Her accent twanged, and it took me a moment to actually understand what she said. Faith glanced at me, obviously uncertain how to answer.

"Snipe," I replied without hesitation. Faith raised an eyebrow, but she didn't say anything. *Better to just save time and use my reputation here. We're in a hurry, and Faith trusts these people. It won't leak back . . . probably.*

The woman whistled. "Well, aw righ' then. Seems i's tha' kinda week. Hell you doin' with my Faith though, girl?"

"Told you, Amy, we're friends," said Faith.

"Sheeeeit, girl. You been movin' up in the worl'." Amy smirked, leaning back. "Well, what kin I do ya fer?"

"I need you to put the word out," said Faith. She adjusted slightly on the couch to shift her leg, trying to get more comfortable. "You might've noticed I'm not walking too great right now. Can't really get to my guys, so I need 'em to come to me."

"You go' it." Amy pulled out a stick of gum. She unwrapped it and tossed the gum in the air, then caught it easily in her mouth. "What 're they lookin' fer?"

"Jack Monroe."

At the name, the air in the room seemed to sharpen. Everything dropped by a couple of degrees. Sebastian leaned forward, his eyes focused and steady. Amy stopped chewing, her eyes narrow.

Faith simply waited, saying nothing.

". . . Tha's dangerous game, Faith," said Amy cautiously. "Wha's the play?"

"He took someone." Faith's voice sounded remarkably calm, but I saw the tremor in her hand. Despite their rocky history, she clearly still cared for Rebecca. *A mother figure,* I presumed. *Something I've never known.*

A wave of melancholy rolled through me at the thought. I suppressed it. Now wasn't the time. I needed to pay attention. Faith was talking again.

"I need to know his hideouts. His home. Who he hangs with. What I had was a bust. If I can get his current location, that'd be best, but he's gotta be way in hiding by now."

"Hm." Amy frowned. She didn't sound too reluctant. I took that as a good sign. I'd wondered if I should chip in, but I decided against it. This was Faith's show—she'd prompt me if I had a line. Concern crossed Amy's face, but it was soon replaced by a crooked grin. "Dammit, Faith, you know I can' turn y'all down. No' affer what you done fer me."

"Glad to hear it." Faith returned the smile, her face lighting up with real joy.

Amy pulled out a pad of paper and a pencil. She scribbled a note, too fast for me to see, and held it up. Sebastian swooped in and took it. He left abruptly, without a word, straight out through the curtain.

"Who 're you fixin' t' use?"

"This is urgent. Pick up everybody who's not busy. Let 'em know it's an emergency. Leave the trickers and the guys we got on Darius's turf though. For now." Faith threw a sideways glance at me. "No telling what they might be up to. We'll need updates out of there."

"Sounds good," said Amy, scribbling a few more notes. "You wan' reports 'ere, or somewhere else?"

Faith shook her head. "Too slow. I've got something else for this run." She reached into the paper bag and pulled out a burner phone. "There's a dozen of these, thirty minutes loaded on all of 'em. They can text anything they find back to me, or call if they don't read and write well."

Faith stood as she finished, dropping the phone back into her bag. Amy stopped writing, and handed the note to Faith.

"Give that to Seb."

"All righty then. I'll be in my office." Faith threw me a wink as she walked out. "Play nice, Snipe."

I rolled my left eye. It was silent for a few moments, as both Amy and I watched the swaying curtain Faith had just passed through. Unconsciously, my hand slid back to the pistol holstered in my bag. Amy, meanwhile, was picking at a piece of bread stuck in her teeth. The dull background noise of the kitchen continued unabated.

"You hurt 'er, I'll end you," Amy said suddenly, fixing me with a glare.

My grip on the pistol tightened, but Amy's threat didn't seem to hold any urgency. I was startled by the level of sincerity. The loyalty Faith commanded here was fierce. Curiosity got the better of me once again, as I spoke up.

"Why?"

Amy looked taken aback. "Why wha'?"

"She's homeless, penniless, and crippled. How did . . . all of that happen?" I asked, gesturing vaguely at the window.

"Though' y'all were frien's," Amy said suspiciously, and her beady eyes dropped to my bag for a moment.

I took my hand out and folded my arms. My legs moved up to the couch. I was trying to appear as unthreatening as possible. It'd take Faith a while to get everything we needed, and I was truly interested in her. Amy seemed like a close friend, and maybe the best source of information I'd ever find—except, perhaps, the departed Maclay heir.

I'd entrusted Faith with a great deal of my life—I needed to learn more about her if this was sticking around.

"To be honest," I said, trying to sound more gentle, "I only met Faith a couple of days ago. She helped me with something, and since then, we've kinda gotten tangled up in each other's lives."

Amy sighed. She leaned back in her chair, returning to her idle rotating with her feet. "Mm, I getcha. Faith go' a knack for trippin' 'er way straigh' inno people's lives. Thin' she migh' a bi' off more 'n she kin chew here though? You bein' an assassin 'n' all?"

I shook my head. "I don't know. Things are getting complicated."

" 'Ell of an understa'men'. There was a shoo'in' all over las' nigh'. Plenny o' bodies dropped, dozen a' least. No' jus' gangers either. Los' a frien' las' nigh'." Amy frowned, darkness filling her expression. "Is tha' war abou' you?"

"It's about a lot of things."

"Gimme a straigh' answer, dammi'," Amy growled. "Faith's puttin' a lo' on the line 'ere, plenny o' souls tha' owe 'er their lives. Y'all are kickin' this inno gear righ' as the sun's dropped. Guns 'll star' blazin' up soon 'ere, and they're gonn' be in danger."

I hesitated. I wasn't sure how much Faith compartmentalized—would Amy know her personal life? For that matter, how much did *I* really know about it? I only had what Faith had given me in that one conversation, plus what I'd seen in the Maclay house. I didn't want to reveal Faith's secrets, especially when I wasn't totally sure of them myself.

I settled on something as safe as I could come up with. "Ellie's mother was taken," I said carefully. *Just vague enough, I hope.*

Amy rewarded me with wide, shocked eyes. She was in the know.

"Oh, 'ell . . ." she murmured. "No won'er she's off her rocker."

"What?"

"You didn' notice?" Amy sounded genuinely surprised. "You know abou' Faith's family, but ain' got a clue 'bou' the network?"

I shook my head.

"Faith buil' this place. Charity work ain' really in style for the big corps, y'know. All they care 'bou' is profits, and we ain' even a tax incen'ive anymore. 'tween Silicon Fores' down sou' and the Web giants up here, no one gives a shit for the little guy."

She shook her head. "Why should they? Easier to au'omate every-thin', 'n' a 'ell of a lo' cheaper in the long run. Soup kitchens 'n' food banks were valuable server space. So, 'course, since people ain' stopped poppin' out babies lef' 'n' righ', 'n' apartments 're packed to the brim, we go' a lo' of homeless on our hands."

Amy spun herself around in the chair. She was a frequent fidgeter, as I'd already noticed. Impatient, impulsive.

"And Faith built a kitchen for them?" I asked, skeptical. *She's pretty capable, but . . . that's a huge stretch.*

"No' tha' simple," said Amy, "but yeah. Faith foun' a revenue stream. Seems our corp'rate overlords needed some spy'n' to be done, but with all the facial recognition da'abases, their own goons coul'n't pull it off without gettin' tagged. Bu' see, a stree' beggar's prolly no' in school, or on the Web. We ain' been pu' in networks yet. So we get around totally unnoticed. Faith got contacts, dunno how, 'n' she started gettin' deals with the highest bidders. Soon she had ears all of the city. Then, some-one in housin' tipped her off abou' this."

Amy gestured all around us at the building. "A glitch in the system. This floor's still shown under an exec who died years ago. All cleared out, but nobody ever noticed it, basemen' floor in a buildin' too unimportan' to care 'bout. Faith brough' in a crew, paid 'em well, cleaned it up. She got the cheapes' furniture she could lay hands on, lined up the tables, 'n' bought the whole kitchen piece by piece. Said she had t' give back to the street wha' raised her."

"She grew up on the street?"

"Yeah." Amy cocked her head to the side. "Far as I know. Never in a foster home. System's packed anyhow. She prolly would've go' los' in the shuffle. Faith's been ou' here a long damn time."

I nodded. "And now she's got a stable of employees."

Amy shook her head. "No' the righ' word, darlin'. She don' pay no one. Folks wouldn' know what t' do with the cash anyhow. Prolly drop it on cheap blow from the damn waterfront. Faith jus' asks favors. Gives 'em out in return too." She laughed, a short, unpleasant bark. "Way more loyal tha' way. She ain' gotta worry 'bout people outbiddin' her."

The practice was common enough. When only money was offered, low-level thugs often switched sides for a quick payoff. I'd bribed a few myself in the past. They could never be trusted past the initial betrayal though. I'd offered favors myself before when I wanted something more serious, since money was so easily outbid. Jack still held one over me, technically, with the promise to kill Darius, though I doubted he really cared if I fulfilled it.

Darius used other methods to keep our people in line. Others relied on numbers and brute strength, so that a few traitors wouldn't thin the ranks, but we focused on information control and gaining what Darius might call *true loyalty*. Blackmail, favors, and a sheer level of constant surveillance to intimidate any would-be traitors to submission.

Legend held that Darius know of your betrayal before you'd even finished making a deal. Your imminent death by sniper rifle would soon follow. Most didn't believe the rumors completely, but the fact remained, we had far less turncoats than the other gangs.

I, of course, didn't have to believe anything. It was my rifle.

The curtain rustled. I couldn't quite see it from my angle, and shifted for a better view. Sebastian came back in, with a folded note in his hand—but as my head turned, my hair swept out just a little too wide.

Amy gasped. "Now . . . wha' was *that?*"

"What?"

"Yer eye, darlin'."

". . . What about my eye?" I asked, playing for time, hoping Faith might return, or something else would happen.

"Damn well ain' normal. Whaddya go' hidin' in there?"

Amy sounded curious, but not exactly threatening. Still, I was on the defensive. I didn't want to reveal so much to people I had just met. Sure, it turned out okay with Faith . . . but I wasn't about to toss the dice *again*.

"Nothing."

"Like 'ell."

Sebastian chose that moment to interject. He stepped between us, holding up a folded piece of paper right in front of me. I recoiled a little, but took the note. Sebastian stepped back as I unfolded it. A rapid, barely legible scribble greeted me.

S: think I found jack's ladyfriend. reports of a woman he has dinner with a lot. stay tuned for loc

-f

ps - ames is great with tech. might have some ideas for your eye. i trust them

"Thank you." I crumpled up the note. Faith had remarkable timing, for sure.

"Wha's up?" Amy asked expectantly.

"Nothing yet," I said, leaning back on the couch a little. "Faith thinks she might have a lead on someone Jack is close to. We're waiting on a location."

I tried to relax a little. This stage of the plan would take some time, based on past experience. We were actually already going faster than what I was used to.

Faith's network was undeniably efficient. Darius relied almost entirely on computers and networked resources for intel, with far less boots on the ground. While it gave us a huge volume of data in neatly indexed archives and plenty of automatic alerts for threats, it did have a distinct disadvantage against the technologically-averse.

Jack was a prime example. He did most of his work on hard copies. We'd found out years ago that Jack ran nearly the entire business on paper and phones, without computers. It prevented a lot of Darius's usual tactics for dealing with competitors, either by undercutting costs and going after suppliers, or gathering evidence and leveraging a loyal judge or prosecutor.

His gang was the primary driver for Darius co-opting the phone network and getting access to the cell towers, and even *that* didn't help us out much. Meanwhile, on-hand work was a lot more difficult for us, since we had fewer members and a higher propensity to be on a hit list when exiting our district.

Faith's network didn't have any of those disadvantages. They weren't affiliated with any gang, they'd been overlooked by every player, they didn't use anything beyond the absolute basics. The whole group was practically invisible.

"Back on topic, then," said Amy, eyes narrowing again as Sebastian left the room, "wha' the 'ell's up wit' yer eye?"

I hesitated. I'd been about to brush off the question again, but a thought echoed in my head—why *had* I trusted Faith so readily, and not this beady-eyed hacker? Sure, I hadn't exactly *intended* for Faith to enter my life. It was fatigue and carelessness more than anything, stumbling into the bathroom before I actually cleared the building. But . . . I'd made no move to hide myself. I'd trusted Faith far more than anyone else I'd ever met, right away.

Because she treated me like a person.

It hit me like a wave finally crashing home after days of cresting at the edge of the ocean. My life was filled with people who'd treated me as a tool or a curiosity. I was an experiment for Rebecca, a weapon for Darius, a knife for Jack to stab into Darius's back. To most of my contacts, I was a force of nature, unknowable, to be feared and respected.

Faith knew exactly who and what I was before we'd spoken a word to each other, and *still* she pushed her way in. I'd only known Faith for a few days, but I already felt closer to her than I'd ever been with Darius. Every memory with Darius tainted and foreign, and even the few benign ones were covered with the signs of him shaping me into what he needed.

I resented him now, for pushing me into this life. His world was filled with secrets and shadows while I flitted around the edges. In the last couple of years, we'd grown more and more separate as I got more independent from the gang . . . and this was the last straw.

Darius clearly cared about me to some degree. He'd taught me more than was totally necessary, went out of his way to protect me, even risked his gang to do it. I was independent . . . or so I assumed—if I could even trust that wasn't just another manipulation. Was all of it just calculated steps to keep me, his weapon, in check?

I trusted Faith, someone who'd asked so little of me, but already given me so much. Faith told me this person, Amy, could possibly help me. I wasn't sure *how*, but maybe Faith knew something I didn't. Besides which, I was confident if I needed to, I could destroy Amy.

Any reluctance I had dissipated. I sat up and brushed aside my hair, tucking it back behind my ear. My other eye whirred about, a bit extra deliberately for effect, and finally refocused on Amy. The software surrounded her in a pale white, outlining her against the dark backdrop of the room. Next to her head, a faint number appeared, giving me a rough distance estimate from the depth perception of the double lens.

Amy's eyes widened. After a few seconds of staring, she suddenly lunged forward. The office chair squeaked wildly as she rolled across the room.

One wheel was missing, and Amy nearly knocked the whole thing over in her haste. I flinched as she approached, but I managed to hold it in.

Her face shot up in front of mine. She tore off her glasses and peered close, inches away from me.

"Wow," Amy murmured. She whistled again. "Now *tha's* somethin' special." I willed myself to sit still, waiting, as Amy's beady eyes darted all about. After a minute or so, Amy spoke again, and I could feel her breath on my face. "Seb, ge' my kit, will ya?"

Sebastian made a short clicking sound, which Amy appeared to take as an acknowledgment. She sat back as he departed through the curtain, and I let out the breath I hadn't realized I'd been holding.

I glanced at the still-swinging curtain. "Can I ask—"

"Yeah," said Amy. "Implan' malfunction. Burned righ' through 'is brain, demolishin' the poor sap's speech 'n' language centers. Seb'll never talk again." Amy spoke matter-of-factly, but I could sense the smoldering rage in her voice. "Sons of bitches," she added, muttering. Her eyes were still darting all over mine.

"When did it happen?" I asked, with another vague memory resurfacing as I did.

"Dunno, 'fore I met 'im. Fact is, I ain' never heard tha' bird sing. Be' he had a real pretty voice on 'im too," said Amy wistfully. "Still, I love tha' lunkhead. Speakin' o' which," she added as Sebastian returned through the curtain with a black metal case, "pass me the thing, lunkhead."

Sebastian opened the toolkit and handed Amy a small handheld microscope. She leaned in close and began to examine my other eye in more detail, squinting and *hmm*-ing to herself frequently as she did. I held still, but after a minute or so, Amy was already leaning back, shaking her head.

" 'less I'm mistaken, tha' ain' s'posed t'exist yet."

"No."

"Where'd y'get it?"

I fell silent. Sure, I trusted Faith, but I was gonna draw the line somewhere, and starting to connect things back to the Maclays and my history was too much.

Amy nodded. "Fair enough." She tossed the microscope over her shoulder to Sebastian, who caught it easily enough. They'd obviously done this many times before. "Well, 'splains why Faith'd wanted us t' meet. I'll bet she figgered I coul' give you a tune-up or somethin'."

I shrugged.

"Well, good as I am, that looks *way* beyond me. Sure, I fix up the cheap-ass bionics some of us got on us, but tha's a perfectly integrated system, and it's gotta be tied to your brain direct. I wouldn' want t' fiddle with it, no' embedded in yer skull like that. Too much risk." Amy rolled the chair back, and I finally relaxed my shoulders. "Maybe some-day. Or if you're on yer deathbed or somethin'."

"If I'm dead, you're welcome to it. I doubt it'd be intact though."

Amy laughed again. "Faith's heart's in the right place, but girl don' know her tech at all. Well, mayhap I kin do somethin' else for ya."

"You're already helping us find Rebecca. That's all I need right now."

"All righ'." As she spoke, my stomach grumbled quite audibly. Amy cocked her head to the side. "Hungry?"

It suddenly occurred to me, I hadn't eaten all day, and with how much we were doing, it was seriously dragging me down. The last sub-stantial meal I'd had was with Faith at the food court . . . and even that got interrupted. No wonder I'd been so slowed down.

I nodded.

"Whaddya in the mood fer?"

"Anything."

"We go' a few options, girl. Anythin' you like?"

I hesitated. ". . . I like cheese," I said finally, glancing away embar-rassed. She'd put me on the spot, and honestly, I didn't think about food that often.

Amy stared at me for a moment, dumbfounded, before breaking into a not-unfriendly laugh. "All right, cheese it is. Let's see wha' we kin do."

She got up and left the room, leaving me alone. I leaned back, trying to relax, taking the opportunity to get *some* kind of rest after how crazy the day had been. A moment later, Amy poked her head back through the curtain.

"Comin'?"

"Oh." I felt stupid. Obviously I should follow, nobody was here anymore.

Amy laughed again. "Don' worry 'bou it. I'll find you some food. Why don' you go see how Faith's doin'? Her office is way over behin' the line. Lets people ge' in and ou' withou' bein' spotted 'cross the way."

"Right." I nodded. Amy glanced at me curiously, before shrugging.

"See you later then," she said, and ducked out again.

I made it around the room without attracting attention. Luckily, it was still the middle of the dinner rush, and the huge line snaked around the outside wall. I followed it back, sticking to the outside. Before long, I found another curtained doorway, with a small handwritten paper sign taped in a beaten up picture frame next to it.

The Proprietor Is IN.

I grinned. Inside, Faith sat behind a desk, legs propped up on a padded stool at the perfect height for her. Several maps were spread across a wide table, along with a beaten-up old laptop. Her phone sat open to the side, buzzing frequently. Every time it rumbled, Faith glanced over, then grabbed a colored pin from a basket and pinned it to a map of the district laid directly in front of her.

A green pin marked our location. Blue pins circled inward to a central location, and Faith was changing these with every report that came on. Yellow pins were scattered inside while red pins dotted throughout the district, both inside and out. I spotted several marking places where I'd been the last couple of days. Finally, there were two black pins—one near the center of the encroaching ring, and another well outside. Both had small initials written in blue ink nearby.

"Blue is you narrowing it down, yellow is a possible confirmed contact, and red is gunfire reports," I said, taking a guess. I sat down in front of the desk.

Faith grinned. "Sharp as a pin, Cyclops." She tossed one in the air and caught it. Another report buzzed into the phone, and she glanced over. "My people are closing the circle, bit by bit." She grabbed another blue pin, closing the gap on the north side.

"Black is where you think he is?" I asked. It seemed inconsistent, given the distance between the two, but I didn't have any other ideas.

"No," said Faith, and her expression got dark. "Black is a phone getting cut off." She continued after a quick deep breath. "Sorry. Anyway, yeah, we're closing in. Finding out about his girl was a lucky break."

"Who is she?"

"Not sure." She shrugged. "A friend helps take out the trash at a restaurant downtown in exchange for meals and the after-dinner mints. Loves 'em to death." Faith rolled her eyes. "Anyway, he says Jack was there a few times with a woman. Same person every time, wispy and snow-haired. Kind of an odd duck. His words," she added quickly. "Not sure what he meant . . ."

She glanced down at the black pin. I grimaced.

Faith shook it off before continuing. "Anyway, I got a good enough description to pass on. We caught a break on the location too. He overheard once she'd never left the district since she moved here. Odds are, she still hasn't, so all we gotta do is narrow it down. Can't be that many white-haired young women around here, right?"

I nodded. "This is really good."

"Glad you're impressed with my operation," Faith said as the phone buzzed again—and kept buzzing. It was a call this time. She snapped it up.

"Go . . . All right. Thanks."

Faith hung up and set it back on the desk, then grabbed up a huge group of the blue pins. The south border of the circle shrunk by half. "DK does his job well, for an illiterate gorilla."

"A . . . what?" I asked, raising my eyebrows.

"What, no Nintendo with your brother? Sheesh." Faith laughed. "Nah, his name's David Kettleman. But we have like eight Davids, so he ended up DK. He hates it," she added with a snicker. "Anyway, DK's coordinating a group and moving through buildings pretty efficiently. I should reward him."

"With what?"

"Trade secret," she replied instantly. I rolled my left eye. ". . . You know, it's pretty interesting how different that is when you've only got the one eye."

"Huh?"

"I dunno," said Faith, cocking her head to the side. "I can't decide if it's got less of an effect or *more* of one. Like, maybe there's more emphasis 'cause you've only got the one, or maybe there's less since you only need half the effort to roll your eyes as the rest of us." She grinned. "You sure do it a lot around me."

I started to roll my left eye again . . . then stopped myself with a laugh. I was glad Faith seemed okay about it now. Normally, I hardly cared what someone might think of my appearance, Faith's reactions before had been seriously disconcerting. I wanted Faith to be comfortable around me. If she was making jokes about it openly, that was a good sign.

Faith grinned, before the phone buzzed again. She glanced down, read the text, then moved a pin on the west side a little bit closer.

"Not near the water. That's good," I said, examining the circle. "Away from Jack's territory."

"You think he'll have her heavily guarded?"

"I don't think so. Most of his men are tied up right now anyway. I doubt any of them even know about her, since we never did. Jack's people are usually really easy to follow. I sometimes track them for fun when I don't have a contract pending."

Faith snorted. "We're *definitely* gonna have to change your definition of fun, K. Or broaden it, at least."

I shrugged. "I like the practice."

"Whatever you say." Faith looked up at the door, where the curtain had just swayed open. Amy had arrived, bearing a plate of sandwiches, along with a fair-sized bowl of steaming tomato soup.

"Grilled cheese special order," she announced.

Faith glanced at me, amused. "Grilled cheese?"

I looked away, embarrassed even more.

Amy chuckled. "Girl said she liked cheese."

Faith smiled. "Mind setting them aside for now, Ames? No room here."

With a deft movement, Amy hooked a chair by the wall with her leg and dragged it over next to me, setting the plate and bowl down. "Anythin' I can getcha t' drink?"

"Water, please," I muttered.

"The same, m' dear," Faith added with a fancy voice. Amy looked a little disappointed, and Faith quickly dropped the affectation. "Sorry. I'd love to drink the night down, Ames, but this is too important, and it's a school night."

Amy ducked back through the curtain. I glanced at Faith, surprised. "School night?"

"Didn't I tell you I was still attending public high school?" Faith sighed. "It's really gonna suck tomorrow. I get the feeling this is going to be another long night." She rolled her head around, trying to loosen up.

"You go to school *and* handle all this?" I was seriously impressed.

Faith nodded. "Haven't found anyone else to run the place, and I've tried. Believe me, I'd love to be done with the whole corporate espionage and gang politics thing. Too much hassle. Life threatening situations *really* aren't my thing."

"You've handled them pretty well."

"Says you," she replied, a hint of exhaustion finally leaking into her voice. "I'm out on the skin of my teeth, usually. I'm seriously lucky it's been the weekend here and that I've actually found safe places to sleep."

"Do teeth have skin?" I asked, trying to lighten the mood.

"Hell if I know. For the sake of my idiom, they do."

A pang of inconsistency flashed into my mind. I gestured out at the wide cafeteria beyond the curtain. "When we first met, you said you were living on a single school lunch a day."

Faith sighed. "Wasn't lying . . . not exactly. I don't get much. All that?" she said, gesturing to the curtain. "Mostly volunteers, donations, and funds from the jobs we pull. Even then, it's barely enough to cover two nights a week. Thank god, people are so willing to help out on Sundays."

She grinned. I chose to ignore the bad joke.

"But yeah, that's why I'm going to school. Having the diploma and the degree on record still matters if you want to make a serious living. I'm going to get into a good college, make some real money that isn't under the table, and bring it back here. We could use some proper dishes and silverware, for one," she said, nodding at the chipped plate which our four sandwiches sat on. "By the way, you'd better take at least a bite out of that before Amy comes back. She made those herself."

"Really?" I asked, surprised. Amy hadn't struck me as the cooking type.

"Yeah. Ames loves to cook. No way she'd have one of the volunteers make it when she can do it herself. Of course, she doesn't have much to work with here," said Faith with a sigh. "The cheese is good, straight from Tillamook, but the bread's really plain and sometimes a bit stale, and we don't get much in terms of variety. That's something else I'd buy, real ingredients for Amy to whip into something special."

Faith sighed again. She leaned back in her chair and closed her eyes. "It's been a *long* weekend."

"Yeah," I agreed quietly.

Both of us were running on naps taken whenever possible, little food, and bursts of sheer adrenaline. I picked up a sandwich—cheddar cheese on white bread. I took a bite. It was delicious. Amy had grilled it to golden-brown perfection. It might have been simple, but I loved it, and I savored every bite.

I devoured it in a minute and grabbed up the next one. Meanwhile, Faith's phone buzzed, bringing her out of her brief respite. She closed the eastern side by the circle a fair amount, then glanced over at me. "Pass me one, yeah?"

I handed the plate over, and Faith started munching through a sandwich. Amy returned through the curtain with two cups of water and a huge pitcher full of ice, and set them on the floor. Faith gave her a thumbs-up, her mouth completely stuffed, and Amy left us alone again.

We enjoyed the sandwiches in silence for a few minutes. I found myself, in spite of everything happening around us . . . comfortable. Content, almost.

"What are you going to school for?"

Faith smiled. "It's just public high school, so nothing specialized yet. But I'm looking at engineering. Electrical, probably."

"I would never have guessed."

"No one ever does." She grinned. "I love designing systems. I love figuring them out, making them more efficient, solving problems holding them back. If I do my job right, it should just work, and I don't need to keep it working. Of course, electronics and physics are a bit different from running an underground intelligence network, but . . . the goal's *kinda* the same."

"I guess so," I said, finishing off my second sandwich and savoring every last bite.

She shrugged. "I'm probably not describing it very well. There's only been time for a few things so far. Working a community college into my schedule and my budget next year will be the real challenge. High school's been bad enough, but at least it's free, you know?"

"I've never been."

"No?" Faith seemed momentarily surprised, before realization dawned on her. "Oh . . .yeah, I guess you wouldn't. You'd stick out like a sore thumb, for one."

"Something like that."

She shook her head, and finished off her own second sandwich. "Don't worry, you're seriously not missing out. High school sucks, but it's free and it'll get me into a good university if I can keep my grades up."

I fell silent for a minute, sipping on the ice water. Faith downed her glass in a single go and poured another from the pitcher.

"I wonder if . . ." I trailed off.

"If what?"

"Nothing." I glanced at the curtain, uncomfortable again.

"It's cool, K. Nobody's gonna come in. Sebastian will make sure, and Amy won't come back again." Faith was sharp, as usual. She'd picked up on my reluctance and found a way to reassure me without missing a beat.

". . . I wonder if my parents would've wanted me to go to college."

Her eyes widened a little. "Do you remember something?"

I shook my head. "Nothing. But . . . I've stopped feeling like parents are something I never had. Darius raised me, and he's my brother, I'm sure of that. But I'm obviously not his child. So . . . I have to have parents *somewhere*."

"Fair enough." The phone buzzed again. Faith checked it, then set a red pin near the waterfront.

"Trouble?"

"A guy shooting at seagulls apparently." Faith rolled her eyes. "How do lunatics like that get guns, anyway?"

"In Jack's territory?" I pointed out.

Faith snorted. "Right. Duh. Well, it's worth marking, just in case. Anyway. Did Darius teach you, then?"

"Every weeknight. He started with some private tutors, but I guess I scared them." Faith snickered, and I rolled my left eye. "I take online courses from a curriculum Darius chose. It's all under someone else's name."

"So basically, you're already in college while I'm still slumming my way through public high." Faith laughed. "Rub it in more, why don't you?"

"Sorry."

"Don't worry about it, K. I'll catch you yet." Faith gulped down another glass of water. "Besides, I'm clearly smarter than you already."

"Oh?"

"Definitely." She made a grand gesture at the maps scattered on her desk. "Look at all my shiny pins here. I'm *clearly* the mastermind."

I laughed. Faith smiled as the phone began to buzz again. She moved a few more blue pins, closing the circle even further. I fell silent for a few moments, thinking.

"I'm surprised," I said finally.

"Also *very* talkative tonight," Faith said with a wink. "Go on, what's surprising?"

"You."

"Moi? Dites-moi, s'il vous plaît."

". . . What?"

"French." She shrugged. "I picked a useless language. Anyway— why am I surprising?"

"You're dealing better than I expected. Better than I am, I think."

Faith suddenly got very quiet. Her expression fell, and I worried I'd said something *very* wrong. "Trust me, K, I'm not dealing."

"But—"

"I'm terrified."

I didn't say anything, unsure how to respond. Faith seemed to be working herself up to something, like a dam threatening to burst—and then it did.

"I'm desperately trying to find the mother of my closest-friend-slash-adopted-sister, who got kidnapped in front of me earlier today while I was on the ground beaten and crippled. My closest ally is a girl I only met a couple of days ago, who's a *hell* of a nice person despite her reputation—but again, I've only known you two days. I'm not usually like this."

Her hand was trembling on the desk. Faith glanced down at it like it were someone else's, totally alien to her.

"I've got this much influence and *this* much authority, both of which are entirely voluntary. That's the whole of my ability to save her. You're my only trump card in this, and I have no idea how you'll act. Especially after that cold-as-hell reunion with Rebecca."

Faith paused, taking a sip of water. "I trust you. She clearly doesn't. We have no idea what Jack's doing with her. So, cards on the table—I'm *terrified.* And it's only getting worse. We're not even close to finding Jack himself, we're just tracking down some mistress he *might* have. Who we *might* be able to leverage into *maybe* luring out a response from Jack. We're nowhere close to Jack himself or Rebecca."

She sighed, taking another sip of water and a deep breath, then leaned back and closed her eyes again.

I sat very still, processing . . . then I stood up, walked around the desk, and put a hand on Faith's shoulder.

Her eyes flew open. She glanced up at me, startled, but I didn't say anything. Faith took my hand, clearly grateful for the contact. Hers were warm, and I could feel her shaking in her very bones. After a short time, she finally broke away, and I walked back to my seat. Faith was silent for a few moments—then finally, she smiled.

"Thanks."

I nodded. "I'll do whatever you ask me to."

"Like hell," said Faith with a chuckle. "I'm not some master strategist here. I've got ideas, sure, but you've been doing this at a professional level just as long as me. Longer, actually. We're partners, all right?"

"Partners, then."

Faith smiled. I returned to my last sandwich, finishing it off in short order. The phone buzzed again, another call. Faith picked it up.

"Go . . . What? . . . Stay on her. Do you have backup? . . . Send me updates. Thanks." Faith snapped the phone shut.

"Tagged her?" I asked, getting to my feet.

"Yup. She's walking around downtown, not a care in the world." Faith started to get up, and I rushed over to lend her my shoulder. She grabbed her cane and began to make her way out, tossing the phone to me. "Call Tanaka and get our ride out front? I gotta talk to Ames for a sec. The number's under 'star-star-heart-sword.' Don't ask."

Faith disappeared through the curtain. As I thumbed through the contacts, another text came in, from a contact labeled with another incomprehensible set of symbols. The woman had entered a house, street address included. I found Tanaka's number and dialed.

He answered on the second ring. "Yes?"

"It's Snipe."

"What can I do for you?" He sounded polite, but vaguely surprised.

"Can you bring the car around to the front? We'll be leaving here in a second."

"Of course, ma'am."

"Thanks."

I hung up, and right away, another text came in. Faith's people seemed to have surrounded the house and were currently keeping watch on it. I could only hope they were surreptitious enough to avoid Jack's notice. If they got spotted . . . I shuddered to think how badly this could go, if this woman really was his mistress or companion in some way.

Faith poked her head inside the curtain just as I snapped the phone closed.

She grinned. "That's why smartphones suck. You can't snap 'em shut dramatically. Anyway, you ready to go?"

I nodded. We walked back out past the still-lengthening line for food. Faith greeted several regulars along the way, and I held back, making sure my other eye was well hidden. Before long, we'd exited the way we came in. Tanaka's car pulled up to the curb right on time.

Faith clambered into the back, I followed, and we were off.

CHAPTER 13

I t's still too plain, but I guess this isn't *his* house," said Faith.

We were once again in a complex a couple of blocks away, surveilling a house, in much the same positions we'd been in hours earlier. Tanaka was on the way to the hideout to retrieve some items while Faith's people had all cleared out. It was just the two of us.

I watched the house through my scope. It wasn't as dead as before—through the window, I saw a woman moving around. She picked up a glass of water and brought it back to her kitchen table where a snack waited. As she sat down, she stared directly at the far wall, which was totally bare as far as I could see. It was a simple one-story place, with no garden and little decoration. Even *I* decorated my home more than she did . . .

"Something's off here," I said uneasily.

"What?"

"I'm not sure."

"Does it feel like impending doom?"

"No, not really." I scanned across the house again, but there still wasn't another soul to be seen. "It's just unsettling."

Faith grimaced next to me. "If you're unsettled, I'm terrified."

"Don't worry. I can protect you."

She grinned. "All right, Guardian Angel. Are we going in, then? Should be totally clear, at least from DK's team."

I retracted my rifle and retreated from the window—even though I doubted anyone was watching our particular vantage point, I still took the usual precautions. "As good a time as any."

We made our way downstairs and back out onto the street. Faith pulled out her phone and sent Tanaka a message to let him know we were on the move. I walked a few paces ahead of Faith, checking the corners before we crossed *any* opening. I wasn't taking any chances, and Faith couldn't move as fast as I could.

It wasn't that I didn't trust Faith or her own confidence in her network of informants. I just knew they couldn't possibly spot the same sort of threats I was used to—and with the sort of person we were about to approach, a close personal friend of Jack, I was expecting anything.

Our approach ended up completely uneventful. We reached the front door, I picked open the lock, and Faith walked straight in.

The woman glanced up as we entered, but more in the general direction of the door than anything else. Behind her on the table sat a book, but there wasn't a single word on the pages, just raised bumps in the paper. As soon as I saw her eyes, icy white and unfocused, I got it—she wasn't looking at us because she wasn't looking at *anything*. She never would.

I closed the door slowly behind us. As soon as it snapped shut, the woman nodded slightly, and a smile cracked her face.

"Hello," she asked in a firm and unafraid tone, "may I help you?"

I was taken aback. Either strangers dropping in totally unannounced late in the evening wasn't unusual for her, or she was *supremely* confident. *Expect anything . . .*

Faith took the lead. "Hi. We're just looking for a friend of ours. Tall, handsome guy, name of Jack."

"Oh. I see." She paused, and carefully marked the page she was on by folding a corner before closing it and turning to us. "Well, I can't say if I know the man you're looking for. I know more than a couple of different Jacks. Could you be more specific?"

Faith faltered. I couldn't blame her. The woman seemed so honest and open, neither of us were quite sure what to say. Besides which, Faith had never actually met Jack.

I stepped in. "Smooth voice, British accent, used to live on the Oregon coast?"

It was nearly imperceptible, but my other eye caught the tiny sharpening of her expression as I described Jack. Her voice, however, didn't give a single sign. "I'm still not quite sure, sorry. Is your friend a client of mine?"

"He might be." I glanced down at the book on the table, which thankfully had an English title visible on the cover above the braille. It was a journal on mental illnesses. "You're a psychiatrist?"

"A psychologist, actually," she said with a slight smile, "but it's not too different."

Her voice was inherently comforting—soft and inviting, ready to listen and to help. I felt a compulsion to confess my secrets, my pains and fears, to lay bare my whole life before this pale angel.

I forced it away. "You wouldn't discuss any clients with us even if we asked, would you?"

"I'm sorry, but no. I cannot divulge anything said to me in confidence. That'd break the trust my patients have in me, not to mention I'd lose my license." She paused and turned to look at me more directly. "May I ask your name? I'm not accustomed to strangers in my home so late in the evening."

I shrugged, then remembered she couldn't see it. "My name's not important."

"Oh, I think all names are important. Names have power in them. Everybody has a name they can point to and say 'this, this is me.'" She smiled. "My name is Gwendolen. My parents didn't decide to inflict the name 'White' on me, but when I found out who I was and what it meant, I found the name I was destined to have. When I became an adult, I adopted it."

"Faith," came the voice behind me. I glanced at her—she seemed oddly uncomfortable. I wondered if there was a history there with psychiatrists. Darius had brought one to see me once, a brief session that hadn't lasted long. I think I scared him. "My name is Faith."

"I see. Hello, Faith."

"This is the part where you tell me it's a beautiful name, right?" *There's the Faith I know.*

"I wouldn't presume to know what a beautiful name is. If it's yours, if it fits you, then that's something like beauty, isn't it?"

Faith shook her head. "And if it doesn't?"

"Then maybe you're not quite sure who you are just yet. You've got plenty of years ahead." She smiled, and it was as sincere as any smile I'd ever witnessed. "You'll find your name, I'm sure."

"We might not have many years," I interjected. This conversation seemed to be getting off-track, and we still had something to accomplish tonight—more than a few things, in fact. "If your friend Jack has anything to say about it."

"Ah." Gwen's lips tightened, and her posture straightened up. "From your tone, I feel you intend to take me hostage. Is that correct?"

"Yes," I answered right at the same time Faith said, "No."

We looked at each other, confused. Wasn't that the plan . . . ? He takes Rebecca; we take the person he cares about. Fire with fire, like we said.

Gwen smiled again. "If you need to come to an agreement, please feel free to step outside. I promise I won't move."

Her voice was so patient, so full of sincerity as before, I believed her. Besides that, I was confident we could run her down if we had to, and the house only had one other exit on the side, which we could see. I opened the door and led Faith back to the front step.

"She's a blind albino therapist," Faith stated the moment the door clicked closed. "Are we *seriously* gonna do this?"

"She knows Jack. Probably very well, actually."

Faith frowned, obviously not convinced. "You sure?"

"She reacted when I described him. It was subtle, but I definitely saw it. She knows him and she's protecting him."

Faith kicked a pebble on the porch with her good leg, sending out into the street. She winced as it sent her a little off-balance. "I just don't see it."

"Do you trust me?" I asked quietly.

She sighed and kicked another pebble stubbornly. Her eyes lifted up to the dark sky, where the clouds hung thick, gray, and ominous. A car turned the corner and lit up the asphalt all around us—Tanaka, returning with what I'd needed.

"Yes," Faith said finally, "but this still doesn't feel right."

"We need her," I said impatiently. "This is how we get to Rebecca. We talked about this."

I glanced down the street at the sound of a faint gunshot in the distance, back toward the border between our district and Jack's. The evening's fighting was getting underway. Despite everything, despite all the confusion, anger, and fear I felt, I hoped we were doing okay—that we were winning.

Either way, we were running out of time. I looked back at Faith pointedly. She sighed again, then pulled open the door and limped back inside.

Gwen looked up from her book expectantly. "Shall I pack a bag?"

Faith glanced at me with a significant look before answering. "We've got a few things to take care of first."

"I understand." She picked up her snack and took it to the sink, moving very slowly and deliberately, but with far more grace than I expected for someone who couldn't see the floor or the objects around her.

Faith took her by the arm once she was done and led her down the hallway to the bedroom. I walked outside and picked up the bag Tanaka had just dropped off. At my request, he'd also written out a brief report of the gunfire and anything else he spotted on the way back.

The battle lines were moving, headed deeper into our district. I was getting worried. We shouldn't have been giving in so easily. What was

Darius playing at? I knew we had more at our disposal. He needed to crush Jack's incursion and discourage a larger investment of resources if we were going to keep our territory.

I shook the thought away. Gwen and Faith were still walking down the hall. I had plenty to deal with here, and worrying about what was going on in the gang I was no longer a part of was just a waste of time and energy. Instead, I pulled out Alex's phone, which I'd plugged in to charge that morning. It was back to full and linked up to Darius's network.

Alex was still at the hospital where Tanaka dropped him off, outside town and without the ability to communicate with anyone yet. I had full access to our network with my backup password, as long as nobody realized Alex wasn't on his phone anymore.

I checked the bag Tanaka brought. Inside were the blackout curtains, a video camera—a model that didn't save any location or ownership details—and a harsh bright lamp. The curtains would make a great backdrop to hide any details of our location, as well as present the threatening atmosphere I wanted so Jack took the threat seriously.

He's a bit theatrical . . . If I match that, will he respond more harshly, or will he play by the "rules"?

We needed immediate results. I wanted to hit him emotionally, make him react faster than he might think, give in to the threat.

I walked into the bedroom. Faith guided Gwen to a stool she'd found while I set up the curtains behind her. I set up the camera and the light and turned it on. Everyone winced from the harsh glare, even Gwen.

I raised an eyebrow. Faith shrugged. She sat back on the bed, watching me carefully.

"So, what now?" asked Gwen, unnervingly calm about the whole situation.

"We're going to send a video to Jack," I explained. "Can I trust you to stay silent? It won't be live, so there's no way for you to get a message through."

"If you say so," she replied. "I'm happy to help."

Faith glanced at me quizzically. I felt the same way. This woman was strange.

I turned off the hallway lights and closed the door. Faith and I were plunged into darkness, and all we could see was the illuminated circle of Gwen, patiently sitting on her stool, her eyes pointed somewhere over my shoulder.

The camera was ready to go. I handed it to Faith, prepped to record, then pulled out my pistol, standing just out of sight from the viewfinder.

Faith clicked the button. The camera beeped softly.

I held up the pistol in view of the camera, unloaded it to show the clear live ammunition stocked inside, then loaded and racked the pistol. Gwen winced at the sound, looking around in confusion. I held the pistol up to her head and clicked the safety off, waited a few seconds, then nodded to Faith.

She held up a piece of paper I'd written in front of the camera, where it would be clearly visible. It requested a trade: Gwen for Rebecca.

After a few more seconds, I nodded again. The camera beeped, and the recording was over. Simple, to the point, dramatic. Jack would get the message fast and clear.

I flipped the safety back on for my pistol and stowed it in my bag. Faith passed me the camera, and I reviewed the video several times, watching Gwen closely for any sign of a message or signal. I found none. After I was certain, I rendered a final copy and passed it to Alex's phone, prepped to send through our proxy system and away to Jack's personal number. Thanks to Darius, it was virtually untraceable—certainly not within the time frame we were operating, anyway.

"All done," Faith said to Gwen. She turned off the spotlight and flicked the bedroom lights back on.

"Ah. Thank you," said Gwen. She stood up and felt her way to the bedside, sitting down on the edge facing us. "I take it you have a video now to send off to Jack?"

"Yes," Faith said apologetically. "Sorry to have involved you."

She sounded sincere. I wasn't so sure this woman was as innocent as she seemed, but I didn't say anything. We'd be done with her soon enough. I set to repacking the materials and the camera, making sure we didn't leave any trace behind. Gwen wasn't exactly part of the game— the police weren't likely to overlook anything here.

"That's quite all right. It'll avoid bloodshed in the long run, I hope." Gwen was still so eerily calm. Everything about her bothered me. "Jack will react appropriately."

"You're no longer hiding that you know him," I noted aloud as I zipped up the bag.

"It just seemed . . . exhausting. Jack once told me he'd make enemies with what he was doing. By association, I expected they might come for me. He wanted me to hide our relationship, but I never could. I'm a terrible liar." She smiled—a small, sad smile. Her face was remarkably expressive. I felt like I could read every emotion passing through her mind at a glance.

"Isn't half of psychotherapy lying to make someone feel better?" snapped Faith. She'd sat down on the bed against the wall, her leg propped up to rest. I was surprised by her sudden hostility, as was Gwen it seemed. She looked taken aback by the harsh words.

"I suppose for some it might be," Gwen answered, suddenly pensive. "I've never liked that approach. I want to make a connection with my clients and I think that can only be done honestly, by building trust. I tell them anything they want to know and I let them decide if they want to trade that for knowledge of themselves. Together, we reach some kind of understanding."

"*Anything* I want to know?" Faith said sarcastically.

Gwen continued to stare straight ahead at the wall, her expression quite calm. "Well, you aren't exactly a client, but I can make an exception. I'm being held against my will, after all." She smiled, and her tone was quite light. I thought it was probably a poor choice to antagonize Faith, but I stayed quiet. We were waiting for a response, I had nothing better to do for the moment.

"Straight to the point then," said Faith. She sat up. "What's Jack's plan here?"

The woman shook her head. "I couldn't tell you." She continued even as Faith opened her mouth to interrupt. "Not because I won't. I simply don't know it. Jack only tells me his inner thoughts, his desires and fears. The specific workings of his empire are for him alone."

"All right, fair enough. Didn't expect anything from that anyway," Faith said with a shrug. "What about his desires then?"

"What are you trying to find out, Faith?" asked Gwen, her voice quite gentle compared to Faith's hostility. "Jack is only a man. He has some power and he uses it how he sees fit. He's trying to make the city a better place."

"He's murdering people left and right and he started a street war between gangs," Faith growled. "How is that better?"

Gwen shook her head. "Jack does not murder people," she replied simply.

"You're wrong," I cut in quietly. "He's a killer. A brutal one. I've seen him shoot someone point-blank in the head and complain about the mess a moment later."

They both stared at me—Gwen's focusless eyes boring right through to the wall behind me while Faith just looked horrified.

I winced. She doesn't need that kind of detail . . . not while Rebecca's still missing.

"And what were you doing?" Gwen asked pointedly.

Normally, I wouldn't indulge a question like that, but some semblance of cooperation might get us more information. Besides, it didn't really matter in the end.

"I was there to back up my brother when he made a deal."

"A deal for what?"

"Territory, borders, treaties."

"And you were there when Jack shot this person?"

". . . Sort of."

"What do you mean?"

"I was a few blocks away and four stories up."

Briefly, I flashed back to that night. It was rainy, as usual. They'd met in an alleyway, bodyguards everywhere. Jack revealed he knew about the spy we'd planted in his organization and shot him, right there on the spot. Darius hadn't been pleased, but in the end, we still won the negotiation.

A few well-placed unexpected sniper rounds do wonders against enemy morale.

"Do you know why Jack ended their life?"

I shook my head, forgetting again the futility of the gesture. It was a difficult habit to break. I was used to communicating in short phrases and physical motions, not so much talking. Faith was by far the most I'd ever spoken to anyone outside of my home. "Does it matter?"

She nodded. "As I said, Jack does not *murder*. That's not to say he doesn't kill. But when you speak of murder, what do you think of? Passion. Rage. Blood shed for blood's sake. Murder serves no greater purpose. It's selfish. It brings only pain."

Gwen took a deep breath. Her voice had cracked at the last few words, breaking with emotion for the first time all night. "Jack might kill a man, but he does so for the sake of everyone. He's trying to improve the city. Some people can't understand that, and they're too stubborn to be persuaded otherwise. Only once he's out of options does Jack resort to killing."

The sincerity never left her face. Gwen clearly believed every word she spoke. I glanced at Faith skeptically, and she looked unnerved.

This woman's insane.

"So how's he gonna fix the city, then?" asked Faith.

"I don't know," said Gwen.

"Getting tired of that answer already," grumbled Faith. "Fine. What does he think's wrong with the city then?"

"The city's become too passive," started Gwen. She was getting less emotional now, more analytical. "People slumber in virtual reality and forget about the world around them. Neglect sets in. Our roads and buildings are crumbling, piece by piece. Institutions that were once the pride of the city have been closed or abandoned, replaced by their digital counterparts. We've grown worse every year, hollow introverted shells, never participating in the world or trying to make it a better place together."

"And how does Jack stop this?"

"By cutting the problem off at the source, I expect," said Gwen. "Virtual reality has always been a short step away from physically damaging, right from the start. Early versions often left users with significant eye strain and other physical symptoms, and with the development of nerve implants, there's a far greater risk of permanent impairment."

Faith grasped the implications immediately. "That's sick."

Gwen's expression softened. "Yes, it is. But the eventual self-destruction of our city and beyond would be much worse." The softness went away, replaced by some kind of crazed devotion. I wasn't sure how to describe it. She was like a fanatic to the cause she'd adopted from Jack. "Our society doesn't react to theoretical dangers. We only move once the tidal waves are already encroaching on the land. If the dangers of this delusional escapism aren't made more apparent, I fear we'll never recover. If a few must be sacrificed to force the public to action . . . that may be for the best."

Alex's phone buzzed. There was a text with a picture attached: Rebecca, standing over a laboratory table, a gun casually pointed at her head. A clock was visible on the wall behind her right next to a Maclay Technology logo, showing the current time. Beneath it, Jack had included the address.

It'd be closed on a Sunday night. Rebecca was there with Jack, working on . . . something.

I pulled up an analysis program from our repo, just to be sure. After a few moments, it declared the image genuine. Rebecca was definitely there, with Jack or a gunman, being forced to work on *something*. I tossed the phone to Faith, who glanced at it and nodded.

"Time to go," said Faith, getting to her feet.

I reached into my bag, finding the handgrip easily enough.

"That's it, then?" asked Gwen, still seated. Her expression sank. She knew what came next. Gwen might claim ignorance about Jack's empire, but she certainly knew enough about the machinations of these sorts of deals to realize her life was effectively over.

Witnesses are risks. Every time you expose yourself, you take a risk. Weigh them carefully, and if anyone might have learned too much, do not hesitate to secure your own safety.

"We got what we came for," said Faith. She started toward the door.

I raised my pistol.

Faith's eyes widened. She dove for the gun and knocked my aim aside. I moved my finger away from the trigger just in time, avoiding a possible misfire.

"What are you doing?" I asked, confused.

"Me?" Faith shot back. "What the hell are *you* doing?"

"You said it yourself. We got what we came for."

Her eyes widened in horror. She took a step away from me. The movement hurt more than I expected. *We have to do it . . . She needs to die. We can't leave a trail.*

"What?"

Faith didn't answer. She just stared at me, mouth slightly open. I wasn't sure how to answer. Gwen obviously knew what was about to happen, but Faith had been a step behind the room for once.

"She's not from your world, dear," Gwen said quietly. She looked right at me, somehow, with her endless gaze. "She's a next-door neighbor at best."

"We're done here," said Faith, her voice shaky. "Let's just go."

I felt uncomfortable, confused, in pain. Faith looked frightened of me, and it bothered me more than I cared to admit.

"We can't leave a witness," I said carefully—but out loud, it just sounded hollow and empty.

"She's not a witness," snapped Faith. "She's *blind!*"

"She knows your name. She knows my voice. What if Jack or someone else uses it against us? Against *you?*"

"So we kill Jack. He deserves it. Hell, maybe she does, too, I don't know. But not like this. She hasn't done anything."

I shook my head. "It's an unnecessary risk. We can't . . ."

Faith glanced at Gwen, whose face was downcast and trembling slightly, but remarkably composed for someone who knew they were about to die. She looked back at me again. "Please," Faith whispered.

My whole mind was conflicted. This was against procedure, against what I expected to do coming here. I'd made a plan. I executed it. I got what I needed. The woman sitting there, no matter how harmless she might seem, knew more about us than we could say, particularly as a psychologist. I knew full well how useful an overlooked witness could be—even more so now that I'd seen Faith's network in action.

It didn't feel right to leave her alive, but the look on Faith's face pained me more than anything else. I hesitated, my gun still trained toward her, uncertain. *Maybe . . . maybe it'll be all right. Gwen doesn't necessarily need to die. Besides, if we deal with Jack . . .*

A light *tap-tap* on the door.

I froze, my heart racing. My aim spun around toward the doorway. Faith, likewise, had twisted around in shock.

A muffled voice called out.

"Mom?"

Gwen spoke before either of us could react. "Elsie, sweetie, go back to bed."

"What's going on?"

I moved to the door as silently as I could, still gripping the pistol. Sweat beaded on my hands. I was more anxious than I'd ever been in my life. Something about this suddenly felt so wrong. I couldn't stop my heart from pounding in my skull, overwhelming every sense, focused solely on the shadows of small feet through the bottom of the doorway.

"Nothing, sweetie," said Gwen. Her voice trembled, far more than the slight amounts it had earlier. She sounded terrified. I shot her a warning look, but there was no way she could control the sheer level of fear filling her expression. "Just talking with some friends."

"Can I come in?"

"I'll be out in a minute, Elsie. Go back to bed, all right?"

"But there's a guy by the door. Is he one of your fri—"

I flicked the lights back off and slammed the door open. The girl's eyes opened wide.

I grabbed her by the shoulder and pulled her in, shutting the door closed behind her as quickly as I could. The room was dark, only lit by the streetlamp through the now-uncovered window. I drew up my hood, hiding as much as I could, while Faith retreated to a shadowy corner.

The girl was as pale as Gwen, with equally snow-white hair spilling about. Her eyes were focused though and darting about in fear. I guessed her to be nine, if not younger. She looked at me and tried to shrink away in fear.

She wasn't blind.

"The man by the door," I asked, lowering my voice as much as I could, "was he Japanese?"

"What?" said Elsie, confused. "Umm . . ." She glanced at Gwen, who nodded frantically.

"Tell them anything they want to know, sweetie."

Elsie swallowed and looked back at me, still scared. "Yes, I think?"

"And he was alone?"

"Yes."

Faith sighed in relief. I felt the same way. It was just Tanaka. We hadn't been discovered yet. Still, it was a harsh reminder—we needed to get moving.

"Okay." I let go of Elsie, who hurried to her mother and grabbed on tight. A deep, fierce pain flared up inside me at the sight. I had no clue what it was, and I didn't have time to figure it out. I pushed it away. "We're leaving now. You two are going to stay there, facing away from the door, for ten minutes. After that, I suggest you leave town."

"What about Jack?" asked Gwen.

I didn't answer. After a few seconds, Gwen nodded. She held on to Elsie as tight as her daughter held on to her. They turned away, as instructed. I looked at Faith, still lurking in the corner, her expression torn between relief and fear.

There wasn't time. I swung the door back open and turned to leave.

"He's doing what's best for everyone," Gwen said quietly as we left the room.

Tanaka was standing by the door, ready to go. Faith handed him the phone with the picture Jack had sent. He nodded. Together, the three of us made our way down to the car on the sidewalk. The rain began to pour down on us just as we reached the street. We piled in, Faith and I in the back, Tanaka up front, and off we went.

Faith pointedly stared out the window as we drove, speeding through the emptier streets of Sunday-night Seattle. The silence stretched out awkwardly. I busied myself with checking and rechecking my weapons, refilling magazines, testing my knife—preparing for anything Jack might have up his sleeve.

The response had come quickly enough that I wasn't too worried. Jack probably went straight to the lab with Rebecca and the couple of men he had left. He needed her for . . . something. I wasn't *quite* clear on what, but having seen Jack's pseudo-family, I was getting a pretty good idea.

Given the Maclay building's security, Jack probably couldn't bring too many of his men inside without drawing attention. Rebecca's ID would get them in unhindered, but the place operated 24-7, and the onsite security should still be around. I had no doubt Rebecca was cooperating after what he'd done to her family . . . *We might have to get past Maclay security ourselves.*

Except . . . I had Tanaka and Faith. They were both important members of the household, and at least based on their home security, both were definitely in the clear. As long as Tanaka knew where the particular lab in the photo was, we could probably cut Jack off.

"Look," Faith started finally. My tactical mind dropped away as I shifted to focus on Faith entirely. She was still staring at the window, watching the raindrops make trails as they rolled down—*just like I always do* . . . "I get it. That was just standard procedure, right?"

I didn't answer. I wanted her to get her thoughts out first, before I said something stupid again, sent her away, whatever.

"Were you really going to kill her?"

I hesitated. ". . . You changed my mind," I said quietly.

Faith still looked uncomfortable, and still refused to look at me. "So if she hadn't been blind, you still would've killed her? Even with her kid just down the hall?"

A waterfall crashed through my brain, floodgates opening wide. "I didn't know she had a daughter."

My voice cracked. I didn't understand the sheer emotions flooding through me, any of them. The sound surprised Faith as much as it did me. She looked around and saw my face—saw the tears suddenly rolling down my cheek.

"I didn't know she was there. I didn't . . ." I choked up a little. "I didn't know they loved each other. I didn't know." My voice fell to a whisper, barely getting the words out, but I needed to. I needed Faith to understand. "I didn't know. I didn't know. I didn't . . ."

"Hey . . ." Faith pulled herself across the back seat and wrapped me in a hug. I let her arms envelope me, closing my eyes, still muttering over and over as Faith murmured into my ear.

We stayed like that for the rest of the ride.

It was well after hours, but Tanaka's car was allowed through the automated gate and the guards shortly after. We drove straight into the underground garage, sloshing through deep puddles from the runoff above.

The whole garage was brightly lit from every angle. There wasn't a shadowy corner to be found. Only a few other cars were present. Tanaka identified three of them as belonging to the regular night janitors, leaving only one which was obviously Jack's. By some pure luck, the bullet holes we'd put in it earlier were at an angle that placed them just out of sight to the guards as they came in.

We hurried to the entrance, Tanaka and I checking alternate pillar all the way there while Faith moved as quickly as she could.

Glass double doors blocked our way. Tanaka flashed his phone over the pad near the wall, and a light flashed green. The doors clicked open, and we hurried inside. A set of elevators and a staircase awaited.

Faith moved toward the elevators, but I touched her on the arm to stop her.

"Never take the elevator."

"Right," said Faith. She glanced warily at the stairs. "Goddammit . . ."

I glanced at her leg involuntarily. Faith shook her head.

"I'll make it. Third floor, right?" she asked, glancing at Tanaka. He nodded. "You two go ahead, secure it, and whatever. I'll catch up."

"Not a chance." I looked to Tanaka. "He's with you. I'll go circle around to the opposite stairs and come from the far end, cut off any escape routes. Watch your fire," I added, though I had no doubt he could handle himself.

He nodded again. Faith shrugged. "Fine, okay. I'm with strong-and-silent." She took my arm as I turned to leave. "Be careful."

I pulled together a smile. "Always." As Faith began to climb the stairs, I hurried down to the other end of the hall.

The lights were dim. Only every third lamp was on. Rain pattered against the huge glass front windows on the floor above, echoing through the empty corridors and stairwells. As I advanced, the rain became a roar, pounding on the rooftop with a fierce vengeance, as though it wanted to tear the building down. I kept a tight grip on my pistol, moving between every shadow and corner, listening out as best I could.

I needed anything I could get for an advantage with how little I knew about what we might be going into. The rain drowned out all but the loudest footsteps. I reached the opposite stairwell, a back-and-forth spiral up to the technology labs, and began my climb.

Obsessively, I went over my pistol as I went, reassuring myself it was loaded and ready—and trying to keep my mind occupied. It was a small black design, given to me by a former Secret Service agent who now worked for Darius. Through his old connections, I even had access to Kevlar-piercing cartridges, beating the more common types of body armor.

I wondered what Faith would think of all this. Suddenly, I was far more self-conscious than I ever had been for my whole life. I knew I had an unusual obsession with guns—more than a few people commented on it, but it never bothered me. It came with the job.

Still, I had model numbers, ammunition types and calibers, cartridge types, attachments, and so much more in a huge mental index. I wondered if I'd be happier with that space filled by thoughts of school, gossip, games, whatever else normal people would be talking or thinking about. The "normal" world and I had never really interacted.

Climbing a staircase in a research lab in the dead of night with two different pistols and a personally customized sniper rifle, a German combat knife, and a fresh intent to kill still lingering? Totally normal for me.

I forced it all away again. I couldn't deal with it right now, not when I might be in a life-or-death fight at any moment.

The third floor was just ahead. I stepped out carefully. It was just as dimly lit as the rest of the building. Light spilled out from a tiny window only a few doors down, very close to me. I approached cautiously, pistol raised.

It was a tightly shut lab door with a tiny slit for a window. The lab itself was completely windowless and sealed. I stepped up to the door and carefully peered through the window as best I could, always staying at an angle, never directly in-line with it.

I couldn't see anyone.

Faith and Tanaka were just reaching the top floor, arriving at the opposite end of the hallway. I pointed at the door. He nodded, his own pistol drawn and ready.

Tanaka walked forward and tapped his phone on the pad next to the door. The locked clicked open. He took the handle and pulled it outward.

I still couldn't see anyone inside. Slow, careful steps forward, my gun leading the way, leaning around each corner. The lab was brightly lit, instruments littering various assembly tables in rows, technology scattered everywhere. It stung my left eye for a moment, the bright white walls, floors, and ceilings a sharp contrast to the dimly lit hallway.

The room had no other exits. At the opposite corner, tied to a chair, sat Rebecca. She was awake and relatively calm. I met her eyes.

"Jack already left," she called out.

I started forward, still cautious, but Rebecca seemed to be correct.

"Why would he do that?" I asked as I walked forward and pulled out my knife. Rebecca winced as I started working through the ropes binding her to the chair.

"He got what he came for." Rebecca paused. Her voice was shaking a little. "You saved my life."

"How?" I asked, still trying to cut the rope. It was thick, and the serrated portion of my knife wasn't particularly effective.

"Whatever you sent. He was about to shoot me when he received it . . ." Rebecca stared at me, eyes glistening. "You've saved my life twice in one day. *After* knowing what I did to you. Why?"

I didn't answer. The ropes finally gave way. She was free. Faith had caught up by now and took a chair nearby. With me silent, Rebecca turned to Faith.

"What happened at the house?"

"Arthur's hurt," Faith said bluntly. "Neck sliced open."

Rebecca took it far more calmly than I expected, though she was still obviously upset. "I know. Jack let that slip. Is . . . is he—"

"He's alive," Faith said with a nod. "I think. Ellie took him out of town with what's-his-name. The doctor who came around for Thanksgiving."

". . . Dr. Johansson. That's good. He's very good." Rebecca was calming down. I decided that might as well be the time to jump back in.

"What did Jack get?"

Rebecca swallowed hard before answering, and her eyes fell a little, as if ashamed. Faith got up and began pouring a glass of water from a nearby sink.

"Your cybernetic eye," she said quietly. "This is the prototype lab where we developed it. High-grade ocular implants. Like Arthur said, though, we're years away from anything commercial, but the materials and the research are all here."

"Wouldn't he need you to implant it?"

Rebecca barked a short laugh. She took the water from Faith and drank deep before answering. "I'm good, but I'm not the only neuro-ocular surgeon around. There's a couple others, one here in town, and I'm sure Jack could find more if he needs to."

"And he wanted it for himself?" I asked, though I was pretty sure it wasn't the case.

Rebecca shook her head. "Didn't seem like it. The measurements he had were way off." I glanced at Faith, and she nodded. "What?"

"He's got a wife and a daughter," said Faith. "They've both got severe albinism. Mom's completely blind, daughter had at least a bit of sight."

"Ah," said Rebecca. "That explains it. He kept asking about pigmentation and the nervous system. There's never been an effective method to correct visual impairments caused by extreme albinism. Normally, it isn't so severe, but I've heard of edge cases . . . Replacing the eyes entirely *would* be a solution." She frowned. "Drastic though."

"People do drastic things," I said. I hadn't meant it to sound so accusatory, but it was out there.

Rebecca gave me a strange look—shame, guilt, regret, and a good dose of fear all rolled into one. Minutes dragged on, with Rebecca staring at the floor, Faith fidgeting, me staring at Rebecca.

I had so many questions to ask, the woman who might have the answers was right in front of me, and finally, I actually had time . . . *Where do I even start?*

The answer was simple, once I finally thought about it.

"Can you restore them?" I asked abruptly.

Rebecca hesitated, still afraid to meet my eyes. ". . . I don't know. We saved a detailed neural model from before and after our alterations, but it's all theoretical. The map of your neurons allowed us to pinpoint where the specific memories were stored and erase them, based on Darius's description. They're completely gone from your brain."

"And the backups?"

"Like I said," she continued, still nervous. "It's all guesswork. Your neural network is still in place, but it's not possible to remap neurons in that way without extremely invasive surgery, and I couldn't guarantee success."

Her voice was getting more clinical as she spoke, back to a scientist instead of a terrified mother who'd just been through a serious ordeal.

"The method we used simply overwrite the existing neurons with counterbalanced electric wave pulses piggybacking on your active brain waves through the implant. It's similar to how a noise-cancellation system creates counter-sounds to nullify the existing sound waves already bouncing around." She paused for a drink. "Your brain is creating and updating your neural network constantly—dumping short-term memories during active states, then analyzing and storing long-term memories during passive states like sleep. To give you new memories, I'd have to create entirely new sections of your neural network and attach them *while* you're awake. I don't think it's possible without killing you or causing permanent extreme damage."

I sat down, taking it all in. *I'm not getting it back.* My mind was desperately trying to process it, a huge wave slowly flooding in, just like the tsunami still fresh in my mind from Gwen. What Darius did to me—what my *brother* did to me—couldn't be undone. My memory was gone, forever.

They were both watching me. I was silent, still processing, still trying to figure out what to do. Should I be angry? Sad? Regretful, dive deep into despair? In some strange way, I felt . . . relieved. The complicated mix was starting to overwhelm me. I needed something else to focus on.

There were more answers to get.

"You said Darius described the specific memories. What does that mean?"

Rebecca looked away before answering. ". . . It means he told me in detail what to look for. So we could target it properly."

A thrill rushed through me. *Is this a good idea? Do I actually want to know?* Doubt crept into my mind . . . only to be banished a moment later. I needed to reclaim myself. I *had* to know who I was, so I could start becoming who I actually wanted to be.

I had to know.

"Tell me everything that happened that night."

"If I told you that you were better off not knowing?" Rebecca was practically pleading with me. "That you asked to forget?"

"I was wrong," I said simply. "I have to know."

Rebecca finally looked at me again, saw my resolve. She nodded. A brief glance at Faith—a doctor asking for the room.

Faith started to get up. I reached out and touched her arm.

She sat back down without a word.

Rebecca swallowed down the rest of her water and cleared her throat. "I'm so sorry."

KARA

A knock on the front door—gentle, cautious.

She stood on the balls of her feet, just outside the hot beam of sunlight poking through the trees. Her ears strained for any sound inside, as the whole world came to a stop. Even the birds in the trees seemed to stop singing, waiting with bated breath. Her hand pressed against the chipped paint of the apartment wall, as if she could feel a presence inside.

Nothing yet.

The ground-floor apartment was a cramped two-room place, but it was quiet and out of the way, and their neighbors never seemed to be home. It had a creaky, old front door, the lock stuck when it was cold, ants regularly made an unwelcome visitor, and the rear windows were forever stuck in a locked position . . . but it was home. It was a precious thing.

She very carefully pushed open the front door. A long squeak echoed through the apartment. She winced at the loud sound . . . but still nothing.

Shadows filled the dark entryway. Her eyes squinted inside, hoping, praying for nothing. The light played tricks on her, dancing illusions that flitted in and out of existence—was that truly just their beaten old coat rack behind the door, or something worse?

She walked in. It was a slow, deliberate process. Two steps forward at a time—stop, listen, wait, two steps again. The main room was empty.

Just the furniture she expected to see, between the beat-up coatrack, the patched couch, and the small kitchen area with the gently humming refrigerator. Except for the ants, there wasn't a single bit of movement.

It wasn't enough. She had to be sure. The bedroom door awaited.

Anxiety built up in her chest. She felt muscles tensing up and a hint of blood in her mouth. The door loomed in front of her, scratched and painted two colors in haphazard layers. She glanced over her shoulder ever so briefly for strength, for reassurance—and she leaped for the door.

The handle turned. She flung the bedroom door open.

It was empty.

Relief flooded through the girl. It was safe. *They* were safe.

She practically danced back to the entrance, leaping through the door and around an unkempt wall of rhododendron bushes. A short walkway out front led her down to the street and just around the corner out of sight, there waited her father. She grabbed his hand, spouting a stream of comfort and reinforcement as she pulled him back to the house.

"It's okay, Dad. It's all right. She's not here. Come inside. It's okay. It's dinnertime."

Her father smiled at the last sentence, timid as he was. He tightened his grip on the book under his arm while she pulled him inside the apartment. The door creaked closed behind them, and she made sure it shut nice and tight.

She walked him over to the old ratty couch and sat him down. He winced as she glanced over his bruised, cut face, dabbing at dirt near his old wounds. Her father tried to fob her off, muttering about being okay, but she insisted. His daughter—his brave, beautiful daughter, fierce determined fires burning behind her blue eyes. At only ten years old, she was already capable and independent, taking more care of him than he did for her.

He teared up. She was the real head of the household. He hadn't been a good father to her.

"You're the best, Dad," she said, answering his thoughts as she checked on the bandage around his forearm. Or perhaps did he imagine the comma in that sentence? "I love you."

He smiled again, stronger this time. "Thanks, Kara."

"What? It's *true*." She kissed his forehead and stood back. "All right, you passed. What's for lunch?"

Her father raised an eyebrow. "It's already four o'clock."

"We didn't have lunch yet. Lunch can be at four."

"I guess it can," he conceded. "Go see what we have."

Kara got up and ran to the refrigerator. The entire machine rocked on its feet as she yanked open the door exuberantly. From his angle, he couldn't see inside—but her swiftly fallen face told him more than enough. Undeterred, she closed the door and began digging through the pantry.

"Spaghetti?" she asked, poking her face around the pantry door, holding a box of noodles miraculously unopened.

"Sounds good." He laboriously got to his feet to help.

She waved him off. "I got it, Dad."

"You sure?"

Kara was already pulling out a pot and filling it with water. She'd grown so fast . . . she didn't need the stepstool anymore. When had she last needed it? He couldn't . . . he couldn't remember.

"What?" she asked. She hadn't heard him over the clang of the pot as she dropped it onto the stove.

He sighed. "Do you know how to turn on the stove?"

"Yeah . . . I think so."

The click of the ignitor, the faint hiss of gas release, and the stove lit up. Their apartment was old-fashioned enough to still use a gas stove. Technological advance was slow in Tacoma, especially compared to the leaps and bounds in Seattle just an hour north. They'd only just gotten their self-driving car network in place last year— nearly a decade late.

"See? No problem."

With the pot on to boil, Kara set to cleaning up their table as best she could. It was a nice, solid wooden table—probably the nicest thing in their entire apartment. The legs were elegantly hand-carved, each shaped into the vestiges of different Greek deities. He'd carved it himself, a lifetime ago. It had followed him for so long, even as all his other possessions were sold off or pawned. That table, plus the book sitting on the couch next to him, were truly the only things he had left.

The book wasn't even his—he'd borrowed it from the library ages ago and never returned it. He couldn't afford to buy a new copy. It was a reminder of what he loved, more than anything in the world.

Well, almost anything. Kara had just returned to the couch. She dropped onto the cushion next to him and leaned over, setting her head down on his lap. He put an arm around her and held her close as he picked up the book, holding it in front of her.

Kara's finger traced the author's name on the cover. "Dad, why'd you write such a boring book?"

He laughed. "Ouch . . .You read it?"

"Only a little. I liked some of the pictures." She twisted up to look at him. "Did you pick them?"

"No. The editor picked them out. I helped."

"Huh."

Kara opened the book and began to flip through. Pictures of ancient structures, photographs of preserved weapons and replicas, depictions of clashing armies—the book was an overview of European and west Asian history, from the beginnings of the Achaemenid Empire through the Middle Ages. On every page, he winced at another mistake or improvement that could have been made.

She stopped on her favorites, and it soon became clear to him that his daughter didn't care in the slightest about history. "Sorry. It's not really meant for kids."

"But I can read it!" she answered petulantly.

He ruffled her hair. "You're a really good reader. This book's for adults though. It's to help them learn."

"Why do they still need to learn?"

Kara's father sighed. "To stop making the same mistakes over and over."

"Oh." She thought for a moment. "Does your book do that?"

"It tries to."

"How?"

"Well, I think if two people can look at how the last generation messed up, maybe they can avoid doing the same. Of course, every time they do, they usually end up screwing up in a new way instead."

"So it's no good?"

"Maybe. I think we're doing better. We're not screwing up as badly. This book is about things from over a thousand years ago, you know. We're doing a *lot* better on some stuff."

"But not everything." Kara glanced over at the kitchen, where the faint sounds of popping bubbles and churning water were beginning to form.

He closed the book. "No, not everything." Kara got up and hurried over to put the spaghetti in, and he felt just the briefest sense of loss and fear as she left him.

He'd begun to relax—slowly, and with anxiety still coiled in his stomach like a viper ready to strike—and he was feeling far more comfortable. Kara looked back at him from the stove, where she stirred the pasta with a long spoon.

She smiled.

He smiled back. They were home; they were safe. Nobody was going to hurt them. She wasn't coming back.

Kara pulled out the taller stool and sat down in front of the stove. Her legs just reached down to the lower rung. He leaned back on the couch and opened his book. There, just inside the front cover on the dedication page—the ink that declared the most important things in his life forevermore.

To my children, D and K

They both wondered how Darius was doing. His son had left four years prior when he turned eighteen. They'd had a fight—Darius was involved in the drug trade, and he'd gotten hurt.

He'd been too afraid to confront his son's growing involvement in gang culture. The police never got involved, but Darius had never reconciled with his father either. Every day, he went over the things he wanted to say to his son, but he never brought himself to words. A scant few times, he'd mentioned addictions and alternatives—such as the growing virtual marketplace and emerging technologies—but Darius had never imprinted on the ideas like he'd hoped. He hadn't gotten through to his son.

Now Darius was in Seattle. They talked about once a month by public phone, but their relationship was strained and painful. Darius might be doing anything, as far as he knew. They never talked beyond simple pleasantries. He had a vague idea that Darius was becoming more important and influential, but besides that . . . well, he loved his son, without question.

He just didn't know what to do for him. Every failed conversation reminded him how he'd failed as a parent. He couldn't protect either of his children—he couldn't even protect himself. His daughter helped them scrape by on their own.

Even worse, he was afraid he needed Darius's help. His son could probably provide for Kara far better than he ever could, as bitter as the thought might be. A life like that wasn't ideal, but compared to this? Surviving off social safety nets and the occasional royalty check from his book, bouncing between jobs he couldn't hold . . . If she went to Seattle with Darius, she'd be safe.

"I think it's done?" Kara asked, glancing over at him. "Can you come and check?"

Laboriously, he got to his feet and walked over. Leaning over her shoulder, he pulled out a few strands with the spoon to test them.

"Seems perfect to me." He patted her on the head. "Can you go get a colander?"

"Yeah!" Kara hopped off her stool and dug through the cabinet next to them. "I thought you were supposed to throw spaghetti at the wall to check if it was done."

He laughed. "No, that was something made up. Somebody started a practical joke that spread all over."

"Oh, okay." She came back up with the green plastic colander and dropped it into the sink. He turned the stove off and poured in the spaghetti, letting the water drain away. As it steamed in the sink, he checked the refrigerator.

"No cheese or sauce . . ." he trailed off, thinking aloud.

"I could go get some!" said Kara. "The Corner's got cheese, right?"

Only at the end of the street . . . "Yeah, it would. Let me get my coat."

She shook her head. "You're tired, Dad. I'll get it. I'll only be a couple of minutes."

He sighed. "Okay. Straight there and back, right?"

"Yeah, yeah. I know."

She grinned as she pulled on her own jacket. He fished into his pockets and grabbed his wallet. Only a few crumpled bills were inside. He handed over the whole thing, and she dropped it into her pocket. With her hood drawn up and hair spilling out onto her face, he could barely see her eyes.

"I'll be so fast it'll still be steaming. Just watch."

He smiled. "I'll be right here."

Kara threw a hug around his waist as he started pulling out a few dirty plates and began to wash them. A moment later, a scamper of feet across the floor, the click and scrape of the front door opening, and the wooden creak as it shut again.

The apartment seemed just a little bit darker.

"Kara? Is that you?"

She was waiting in line. *Why is there a line? It's the middle of the afternoon on a Saturday! Nobody comes here!* At least it was moving fast. All she could think about was the spaghetti waiting for her back at home.

She had the small block of cheddar cheese in hand—nice and cold compared to the hot summer sun outside. The store had air-conditioning, but she was dreading the run back home.

The sound of her name froze her in place. She took tight hold of the knife in her jacket pocket, a knife she now carried with her everywhere. Her head turned, very slowly, carefully peering around the edge of her hood.

"I knew it!"

Kara relaxed instantly. One of her friends from school, Nina, was just a couple of places behind her in line with a box of candy. Nina pushed forward, ignoring the muttered protests of the people she cut past, and threw a one-armed hug around Kara's shoulder.

"Why are you wearing a hoodie? It's so *hot*."

"Hi, Nina." Kara shrugged her arm off, not wanting the weight on her shoulders.

"I haven't seen you in *forever*. Why haven't you been at school? The year's almost over, silly!"

"I already know enough."

Nina laughed. "Just 'cause you got the best grades doesn't mean they won't get mad when you miss four weeks in a row."

The man behind them grunted. Kara hadn't noticed the line moving forward. Nina shot him a dark look, but they took a step—only one person left between Kara and spaghetti.

"You missed out on so much! We got to play fun games in gym and we did this whole pioneers and Indians thing. Not that you care, I guess," she added flippantly. "Why don't you ever join in? Where have you *been?*"

Kara shrugged. "I had other stuff to do."

"You're so cool," said Nina. "You *know* . . . Kelen was asking about you."

Her face heated up. She turned away.

"Aha! I knew it."

"No," said Kara.

"You *totally like him!*" Nina nudged her. Kara deliberately ignored it, stepping forward to finally pay for her cheese. Nina glanced at it curiously. "Just cheese?"

"Yeah, so?"

"It's so *gross!*"

"You're just saying that 'cause you only ever have cafeteria stuff." Kara tore a small chunk off the top while the cashier got her change. "This is Tillamook sharp cheddar, it's the best. Try it."

Nina bought her candy, then gingerly picked up the little bite, eyeing it like it might be poisonous.

"Go on. Trust me."

"If you say so." Nina took a nibble. Her face twisted in an uncomfortable way. "*Eww.* Still awful." She quickly threw some candy in her mouth to overwhelm the taste, rolling her eyes, while Kara eagerly ate another chunk. "Weirdo."

"Whatever." Kara shrugged. "I gotta go."

"What? But we just—"

Kara felt nervous. She wanted to, but . . . if Nina held her back too long . . . "I'm sorry. My dad's waiting."

"Aww, come on! We haven't talked in ages!" Nina held up her candy. "Here, have some. Get all that gross cheese taste out of your mouth."

A couple of minutes. Nothing's gonna happen. Spaghetti stays hot for a long time. "Okay. Just for a little bit."

"So where have you been?" Nina asked as they walked outside to a bench near the front door. It gave them a little privacy, but still put them in the path of the AC blasting through the entrance, keeping away the heat.

She's relentless. "I went away with my dad."

"What, like a trip or something?"

"Kinda, yeah." *Not one we wanted to take . . .* She glanced away. "I don't want to talk about it."

Nina's voice got more subdued. "Are you okay?"

"Yeah. I'm fine." She forced a smile. "All good."

"If you say so . . . oh!" Nina grabbed her purse and dug through it. "Here. I got you something."

"You did? But I didn't—"

"It's special. You desperately need one." She pulled out a cell phone—a simple old-school flip prepaid. "You can't afford one, right? Here."

Nina pressed it into her hand. Kara winced.

"It's already paid, and I put my number in it. You can use it as much as you want. My parents said so." She smiled. "Now we can talk anytime. Plus it's got internet and other stuff too. And I put a flower sticker on the inside. You'll love it."

Kara wanted to give it back immediately. She wanted it, sure, but she couldn't have something like *this* at home. Not around her dad, who'd feel guilty about not affording even simple things like phones, and especially not around *her.*

She's not coming back. A cell phone would be useful, especially since their home service had been cut off months ago. Kara turned it on reluctantly, glancing through the system and making sure she knew how to use it. It wasn't a bad model—cheap, but reliable.

"I'll pay you back, okay?"

"*Pshh.* No you won't. I won't let you. It's a gift, okay?" Nina gave her another hug. "It's got Kelen's number in it too," she added slyly.

Despite herself, Kara giggled. "Are you serious?"

"Yeah! I felt bad asking him though. He thought it was for me for a second. But now he knows he's got a secret admirer. You better not let him down."

"Okay, okay." Kara pocketed the phone, which bumped against the knife in her pocket.

She stood up suddenly.

"Huh?" asked Nina, confused.

"I'm sorry. I really gotta go."

"Aww . . . okay." She stood up too. "Are you gonna come back to school before it's over?"

"Maybe." Kara pointed at her pocket. "I'll let you know."

Nina grinned. "You'd better." She gave Kara another hug. "See you later!"

She turned and walked away toward the bus stop. Kara waved good-bye, then darted down the street back to her home, suddenly light on her feet. The sunlight was so much brighter, the warmth not quite so irritating anymore. Her day was looking up. Maybe the spaghetti wouldn't even be too cold. She'd probably taken too long though.

It'd be okay. Spaghetti was still good lukewarm, and she could warm it up in the microwave. Her dad would be happy she'd gotten to talk to Nina. And she had a *cell phone!* They could use that for all sorts of things! Especially if it had internet access. Her dad would be okay with it.

Today was *definitely* looking up. She was practically skipping as she rounded the wall of rhododendrons . . . to find the front door wide open.

Her heartbeat skipped, then accelerated like a furious drummer in the midst of a solo.

Dad never *leaves the door open.* He was too careful for that. Every-thing always went back into its proper place when he was around. Even if she'd forgotten to close it when she left—which would have been totally unlike her too—he would've gotten it.

The door open could only mean one thing.

And I left him alone.

She sprinted inside. Her ears caught the voice of her nightmares long before she crossed the threshold.

Kara grasped the knife in her pocket tight.

He'd just poured a couple of glasses of juice for the table. The spaghetti wasn't steaming anymore in the colander. Kara wasn't back yet. It con-cerned him a little, but she could definitely take care of herself. *If noth-ing else, I got that right.*

It was still warm. If she got back soon . . . and as if on cue, the door clicked and creaked open. He turned to greet his daughter.

The scent of cheap alcohol wafted in.

His entire world darkened as all the light was sucked away. The terrible visage that haunted his every waking moment was drawing it all in, just as she wiped her drool on her arm.

"What's cooking?"

The woman's speech slurred as she walked in. Her arm was pocked with track marks, dirty bottle in hand, and her shirt torn at the side. He backed away she entered the kitchen. Her eyes shot to the sink.

"Spaghetti? I hate spaghetti."

She dropped the empty bottle into the sink. It shattered. She overturned the colander, strands spilling amid broken shards of glass. His face fell. She continued to the refrigerator without missing a beat.

"Cook me somethin' real, will ya? I'm starvin'."

The woman tore open the fridge, pulling out a fresh bottle. She popped the cap off with the edge of the countertop—one lined with many, many chip marks from her previous bottles. Without taking her eyes off him, she shoved the fridge door closed with her foot. Fridge and woman wobbled in equal measure from the awkward movement.

She wandered the room, downing gulp after gulp of the drink. Even now, somehow, he could still see traces of the intelligent, passionate beauty he'd once loved. Her eyes betrayed the depths to which she'd fallen. Where once her eyes held the same blue spark of life and joy that filled Kara's, now she seemed a walking corpse, with only two different emotions: desire and anger.

The empty rage now within her eyes sent him scurrying back away—into the refrigerator, as it happened, which started wobbling once again.

She glared at him with utter disdain. "Are you gonna cook somethin'?"

"There's nothing to cook," he mumbled.

"Wha' you say?"

"There's nothing to cook," he repeated, finding a little courage somewhere.

"Bullshit." She walked toward him, turning at just the last second to open the pantry. "There's gotta be something."

As she moved, she crossed through the sunbeam filtering through the window in the kitchen area. His eyes involuntarily scanned her body, reminding him of how she used to look. He quickly averted them, hoping, *praying* she hadn't noticed.

As if that ever worked. She notices everything.

"Oh, I see how it is," she snorted. "You want something first, do ya?"

She placed a hand on his arm. Her fingers walked up, one by one, light strokes all the way up to his face. She caressed his cheek, gliding across his skin, wrapping around to the back of his head.

He fought the urge to recoil, her foul breath filling his lungs, rough skin scraping against his own. The stench of whatever alley where she'd passed out last night nearly overwhelmed his senses.

As she leaned forward, it became too much to bear. He instinctively pulled away . . . but he forgot the wall behind him. His head thumped hard and immediately began to throb—nothing compared to what was coming next.

The woman's voice slid from sultry to dagger-sharp in an instant. "I'm not good enough?"

Her hand, still behind his head, grasped tight and slammed him back into the wall. She winced, but it was nothing compared to his sudden blurry vision as sheer pain wracked his skull.

"What, you found some *slut?*"

She punctuated this with another slam, this time against the fridge and without her own hand as an inadvertent cushion. It wobbled against the wall, then leaned forward over them at a precarious angle, but somehow held steady. Bottles shifted and rolled around inside it, knocking about. The fridge was the least of his concerns though, as his head began to coarse with somehow even *more* agony.

"I'm the best damn thing that *ever* happened to you," she snarled.

The woman shoved him away, toward the couch. He stumbled and tripped, but somehow stayed upright. She turned away, mercifully, to start digging through the cabinet.

"Where's my shit? Hey, asshole, did you take my stash?" She glared at him. "I need a hit. You got any?"

"N-no, I d-don't," he stammered desperately. "P-p-please."

"Don't lie to me! You have some!" She started toward him. "Give it over!"

The woman shoved him down onto the couch. She leaped on top, straddling him. Her hand came down hard across his face, once. Twice. Again and again.

All he could feel was pain. All he could hear was her ranting above him, the slap of her hand, the creak of the door.

Suddenly, she was knocked flat into him, practically bouncing off the ratty cushions. As she twisted around, he realized what had happened—Kara had tackled her from behind.

She sprang up, looking around. He rolled away as best his could, following his instincts, trying to hide, but his eyes were drawn in the same direction as the woman's.

Kara stood in the center of the room. She reached into her pocket and withdrew a short black object. A click of a button and the blade flicked out. It locked with a satisfying click. *Where did she get that? She's too young to have a knife,* he thought irrationally. *I'll have to talk to her about that later.*

The woman raised an eyebrow. "You even know how to use that, brat?" she slurred.

Kara's voice, by contrast, was steady and even. "You won't hurt Dad anymore."

She cackled. "She's adorable, hon," the woman shot over her shoulder mockingly, before turning back to their daughter. "Come here, Kara. Give Mommy a kiss."

The woman approached cautiously. Despite her words and her obvious inebriation, she still took the threat seriously. Kara's hand was trembling, but she *was* armed. As the woman took another step forward, Kara's hand was suddenly steady.

Kara moved forward. Her short arm began to swing.

Too slow! Even he could see that.

The woman stepped in quickly, hand outstretched. Kara's wrist was caught before the strike could ever land. The woman twisted her wrist, and the knife dropped out of Kara's hand.

Not deterred, Kara swung her foot upward. She struck her mother between the legs. She groaned and stumbled backward as Kara dropped to the ground scrambling for her knife.

"You little *bitch*," she half slurred, half snarled, kicking out. Her shabby tennis shoe slammed into Kara's descending face. Her daughter's head snapped away, and the amount of force flipped her completely over onto her back . . . but she had the knife.

The woman's foot came for her again, but Kara managed to roll away. Her face, half hidden behind her hair, was visibly contorted in pain—as was her mother's. Kara struggled to a crouch and pulled the knife just as the woman lined up to kick her once again.

Blood sprayed. The slash had connected with the woman's leg. She yelled in pain, but her kick still followed through. Kara was once again on her back, crumpled. She let go of the knife, trying to crawl away. The woman reached down and picked up the knife.

He tried to open his mouth to warn her, but he was still frozen by pain and fear. If he spoke up, she'd come for him instead, and she was armed now—and she stood between both of them and the only exit.

"You need some manners," she growled. The woman stumbled forward on her bleeding leg. Kara was still desperately crawling back toward the kitchen, but it was no good. The woman reached down and flipped her over.

Kara's eyes widened, panic-stricken. The woman sat down next to her, knife in hand. Her daughter tried to fight her off, but she was too small, too weak. The woman's eyes narrowed in abject hatred and disgust.

"Stop looking at me like that!" she shrieked. Her arm, knife in hand, plunged down—into Kara's eye socket.

Screams erupted from both sides of the apartment. Kara writhed in pain, a stream of red on her face. Her father was on his feet, barreling forward with a burst of energy through overwhelming pain.

He rushed the woman, knocking her aside. His hand wrenched the knife out from Kara's eye. He prayed he hadn't hurt her worse, but it was the only hope they had. He turned to swing at the woman . . . but she was quicker.

She kicked him away. The knife clattered to the floor. *How is she so strong?*

He crumpled against the wall, coughing. He tried to struggle back to his feet, but pain kept him down.

Kara was up again. Blood trickled from her unrecognizable eye. Her face was a mask of fury and pain. She opened her mouth and let out a bloodcurdling scream, barreling forward. The woman, too surprised to move, didn't react as Kara grabbed the knife and plunged forward.

It found her stomach in a long, deep stroke. The woman crumpled, wheezing heavily. Kara's knife didn't stop, again and again. She kept slashing and stabbing, tears streaming down her face, screaming in pain and fear. The woman crawled toward the refrigerator blindly, trying to escape Kara's wrath.

She ran into it headlong, sending the already-wobbling fridge over the edge.

He saw the danger. It was telegraphed, plain as day. Her name ripped out of his throat, screaming out, as if he could somehow change anything.

"Kara!"

It was all in slow motion. She looked up, far too late. She turned to run, tried to dive out of the way, but down it fell.

The huge appliance fell with a crash on top of them both. Kara's legs were trapped underneath.

Her head twisted around awkwardly to face him, covered in blood and tears.

"Hey, Dad," she asked, coughing. "You okay?"

Kara's face fell against the floor. Too still. Too quiet.

He crawled forward, desperate. "Kara. *Kara.* Wake up. Kara!"

The man wasn't sure if he should move the refrigerator—if he even *could.* He couldn't think straight. A hand reached for his daughter, as if it wasn't even his own . . . but it stopped. Something else had clattered to the floor, beside the bloody knife.

A cell phone. *A cell phone?*

He grabbed it, praying desperately. Nine-one-one was no good . . . He couldn't possibly afford it. There was only one number he could call.

The phone was already on and connected. He dialed.

Darius picked up before the third ring. Like he always did.

"Darius. Help."

CHAPTER 14

Rebecca took a sip of water. Faith had refilled her several times by now. She'd calmed down considerably since she began speaking.

"Darius called me later that night. We'd been working together for a while by then, on a few different projects. I think I might even have called him a friend." She visibly darkened, her expression pained. "I've never seen him so upset. It terrified me—that a man like him could be *that* afraid.

"We tried . . . we tried to just take out that single event, but the brain doesn't work like that. Memories are linked to one another relationally in a web of connection and understanding. In order to remove that night entirely, we ended up erasing all memory of the people involved as well."

Rebecca's voice had shifted to clinical again. "Your legs were crushed beyond repair. We took you into the operating room and managed to replace your bone structure with an experimental alloy I'd been working on with my husband. Your brother collaborated with us on the design process, providing all the software and funding we needed. It was a prototype, but you took to it far quicker than we expected."

While she spoke, I was stock-still on my seat. I hadn't moved in what felt like *hours*, though my other eye stubbornly insisted it had only been a few minutes. My left eye was still fixed on the wall somewhere behind Rebecca's head. Her words washed through me—slow, inexorable waves that crashed in, one after another, never quite staying around, but always leaving an imprint.

My mind didn't want to believe what I'd just heard. I couldn't see any reason for Rebecca to make this up, but . . . I hadn't processed it yet. It felt like somebody else's story. Not mine. As far as I knew, I'd never had a mother or father. All I had was Darius.

Now . . . maybe there was something else waiting for me. *Someone* else.

"Your eye was trickier," Rebecca continued. "We didn't attempt to replace it until—"

"Is he still alive?" I interrupted. It was the first sound I'd made since Rebecca began.

She faltered. "I . . . I don't know. I never met him, and Darius never told me anything. I don't even know *your* name. Darius was very determined to keep your privacy."

I was surprised. Darius had always insisted my name was totally secret, and on the surface, I'd believed it . . . But at the same time, she was the doctor. She'd been so otherwise involved in my life, I just assumed she already knew me.

Apparently, this woman, responsible essentially for *creating* me, didn't know who I was. It was bizarre, and in a way, it endeared me to my brother. Even in such a moment, he'd cared about my privacy, my identity. He'd tried to help me have the option to ignore my past, however misguided it may have been.

And . . . it was misguided, wasn't it? I wanted to know this. I *needed* to know this. Having such a massive hole in my life, where anything could have happened, was too terrifying. I hadn't expected . . . well, I wasn't ready to confront what Rebecca told me just yet. But I knew I couldn't live totally in ignorance.

"Where were we?" I pressed.

"It was an apartment in Tacoma. We went there on Darius's call, stabilized you as best we could, and brought you back here for more operations." She shuddered. "When I got to your home, it was still covered in blood."

I was quiet again, thinking, my mind desperately trying to process this event, which I had no memory of, but had shaped my entire life. Silence passed for a few moments, until finally, the silence was broken—by the person I'd almost forgotten was in the room.

"How long ago was this?" asked Faith.

Rebecca glanced at her, seemingly just as shocked by her presence. "About six years ago."

My mind instantly fell back into memories again. Six years ago. Lessons from my tutors, one after another, until Darius finally gave up on them. Enrolling in online classes at his behest. The many, many nights he'd not come home until well after I'd fallen asleep—only to wake me the moment he opened the door. I was far too light a sleeper for him to ever sneak into our little home.

The game we'd played together. The meals we'd shared. Days when I'd fallen sick and he'd sat at my bedside reading to me, bringing me food and water, caring for me.

The night I'd heard shouting and gunfire below the floor and dropped everything to protect my brother. The first time I'd killed someone for Darius—a man responsible for ruining the lives of hundreds and crippling people forever with faulty machinery, but still a person, nonetheless.

My growth in the organization as I took on more jobs for Darius. How I spread out from our gang and took even more, building my reputation, gaining influence, gaining power. The fear I commanded from a room as I entered, how even the largest and dangerous on the street would watch carefully if I were ever in attendance.

The way Darius would smile, the relieved expression on his face when I came back from a job safe and successful.

How it all came crashing down in the last week.

I had work to do now. Faith seemed to come to the same conclusion. We both broke the silence simultaneously, with the same thought.

"Time to go."

". . . Go where?" asked Rebecca, confused.

"Well, *you* gotta go to your husband. Ellie would be pissed if you didn't return the instant you could." Faith turned and called out the door. "Hey, Tanaka!"

The man, professional as ever, appeared instantly in the doorway.

"Take Rebecca to Johansson's, yeah?"

"And you, Miss?"

Faith glanced sideways at me. "I'm staying."

I shook my head. "You should go with them. Eleanor would want that."

"First of all, she hates it when people call her Eleanor," said Faith. "Just a heads-up. Second, no way in *hell* am I leaving you alone right now. Rebecca needs to go, and Tanaka's the only one around to take her."

"Will you be safe?" interjected Rebecca. Faith looked taken aback, and words failed her. Rebecca sighed. "Yes, Faith, I do still care about you."

Faith smiled weakly. "I'll be fine. This is my turf, and now I've got ol' Cyclops here."

She grinned at me. Rebecca cleared her throat. "Come home when you're done, all right?"

Emotion flooded Faith's face. It took her a few moments, but finally she choked out a simple, "Yeah."

Tanaka stepped forward and offered Rebecca his arm. She took it gratefully, and together, they stepped out of the room. Silence fell once more. Faith was staring at the wall determinedly, looking away from me. I wasn't sure how to take that.

". . . You okay?" I asked tentatively.

"Me?" asked Faith. From the sound of it, she was holding back tears. "After what we just heard, after what *you* just went through, you ask if *I'm* okay?"

"Yes?"

Faith laughed. Sure enough, her eyes were red and swollen, and a few tears were already leaving streaks down her face. "I'm fine, Kara. My erstwhile mother figure just casually invited me back into the family I got myself kicked out of years ago. No big deal." She dabbed at her eyes with her sleeve. "But seriously, it's your turn. Are *you* okay?"

"Yeah."

"Okay, one word answers not allowed. I know you better than you think."

I hesitated. ". . . I don't know how I am. Not yet."

Faith nodded. "*That* I can understand. Do you want to talk about it?"

"I . . . don't think so. Maybe. But you said it yourself, it's time to go."

"Right." Faith shook her head a bit. She stood up and leaned against the wall for support. "So, what do you want to do?"

"Darius. I need to talk to him, so I can get answers."

"Okay, yeah. Sure. We'll find a way." Faith got pensive, hand to her chin in thought. "You said he's still in lockdown, right?"

"Yes. They won't lift it for a while, not until Darius is sure they've regained control of the district from Jack."

"What's a lockdown look like?"

I involuntarily glanced around, despite being completely certain we were still alone. Darius had drilled in a health paranoia about security procedures over the years, and it wasn't a habit I ever broke. "Depends. By now, they've probably switched locations again. When I called Darius yesterday, they were at station three."

"Ominous."

"It's just a place. An old nuclear fallout bunker from way back when that was a thing."

"Sounds nice and impossible to get into. Where would they go from there?"

"Well, it isn't very well connected. Darius probably would decide he needed a better setup, so he can track everything going on. He could have gone to a few different places from there. I have no idea which one."

"Hm." Faith drummed her fingers on the wall. "We need someone who'd know where he is, then. Hammer again?"

I shook my head. "After I stole his phone, plus all this stuff with Jack, there's no way Hammer would be trusted at that level again. We need someone higher up, but also somebody Darius would still trust enough to be out in the field at a time like this."

"You guys sound more like a military than a gang," said Faith, raising an eyebrow.

I shrugged. "Militaries are usually more efficient."

"Well, you know 'em better than I do. Who would we want to go after, then?"

I raised an eyebrow. "I figured you'd know who I was talking about."

"I don't know *everything*," said Faith, rolling her eyes. "Sheesh."

"Well, I need a favor from you," I said, hoisting my bag onto my shoulder as I stood up.

"Name it."

"Your network. I need them to track somebody down again. Can they do that?"

"This late? Probably not. Check the time."

I'd been aware of it, obviously, but even so, it hadn't struck me just how late it really was by now. We were well past midnight. Normally, I had a pretty good internal clock, but my sleep schedule had been all over the place the last couple of days. Suddenly, I realized I was hungry again too. I sighed.

"Don't worry about it, Cyclops," said Faith, her expression softening. "He's probably not going anywhere fast. I'll get them on it first thing in the morning, before I head to class."

My brain skipped a beat. "Class?"

"Tomorrow's Monday, remember?" Faith laughed. "Believe me, after *this* week, there's no way in hell I'd be going if I didn't have to. I won't pass if I don't take a test tomorrow morning. It's up first though. I can cut the rest of the day."

I shook my head, exasperated. It was so . . . *ordinary*, compared to what we'd been dealing with. Normal life just kept happening around us, despite how crazy our lives had become.

"Okay. Tomorrow, then."

Faith grabbed a clipboard and pen from the nearest shelf and passed it over. "Write the guy's name and any details you've got, and my expert team of wannabe PIs will be on the case come sunrise."

I took it and started jotting down notes. "Michael Dunham," I answered aloud as I wrote. "He's my brother's second-in-command. They're rarely in the same place, for securi—"

"Dunham?" interrupted Faith. I looked up at the sharp edge in her voice. Her eyes were narrowed to needlepoints.

"What?"

"This guy. He wouldn't happen to have a daughter, would he? Around my age?"

"Um . . ." I considered for a moment. "Yes, I think so. Yeah, he does. I only met her once or twice though, a long time ago. What's up?"

Faith didn't answer for a long moment, her face blank. ". . . I'll find him. But when you go get him, I'm coming with you."

"Are you sure? It's going to be pretty—"

"No arguments," Faith said abruptly.

I set aside the clipboard. "What's going on?"

"Don't worry about it. It won't affect you and Darius at all."

"Faith . . ."

"Trust me, all right?"

I considered. Faith looked frighteningly determined. But, after everything she'd done for me . . . "All right."

"Good." Her face lightened up a bit. "Are you hungry? I'm starving. Those grilled cheeses really didn't do all that much."

"Yeah." I started toward the door, and Faith followed. "Where to?"

"Know anywhere good that's open this late?"

"Uhh . . . not much, I guess. Not on a Sunday, anyway."

"Overnight fast food it is."

I made a face.

"Oh, it won't kill you. Come on." Faith started limping her way forward to the stairs. "There should be one a couple of blocks away. Won't take long."

I followed, a hint of a smile forcing its way onto my face—until a second later, as my mind snapped back into remembering what had just happened. Everything Rebecca had told me.

My mother stabbed me in the eye.

I'd killed my own mother.

My father had done nothing to help.

I'd begged to forget everything, a few days after my legs had been repaired.

Suddenly, I was reexamining every decision I'd ever made, every action I'd taken over the last few years. How had I become the killer, the assassin of Seattle? From the sound of it, I'd only killed to protect my father, but was there more than that? Was I a killer all along?

I didn't take pleasure in killing. Not exactly. There was a lot of satisfaction in being efficient and effective. I enjoyed the sense of power, especially in the way I'd become infamous to foes and friends alike. I held a powerful reputation. Every time I came home from a successful job, it was another notch on my belt, another accomplishment. Darius would go over every mission with me, showing his approval, expressing his gratitude and appreciation, and telling me what I did wrong.

There it was. Darius had created me. It always came back to that. I understood why he'd erased my memories, and to a degree, I could sympathize with his choice. Now, though, I had so many new questions. Why, after such trauma, would Darius reintroduce me to violence and death? Give me weapons, push me into that life? What prompted him to push a thirteen-year-old girl into the life of a deadly assassin?

My list for my brother grew by the hour.

Faith and I were the only two people at the restaurant. It was totally empty and completely automated. Simple touch screen menus allowed us to place our orders. Cheap bulbs lit the whole place, styled to look like a retro diner, with chrome wall sidings on the booths and checkerboard patterns everywhere.

A maintenance tech was probably hanging around in the back somewhere, watching a show or carousing in VR, but we'd ordered and had our food delivered automatically, loaded on a tray and ready to go. Even so, I felt like we were being watched from somewhere. A quick scan using my other eye caught a few cameras in discreet corners, confirming my suspicions.

I promptly led us to a table where we'd be invisible from every angle.

We ate mostly in silence. The air was filled with faint, incessant, inoffensive pop radio. I sat with my back to the wall, watching the door to the street. Faith was unusually quiet, with only a few weak jokes here and there before she lapsed back into silence.

Both of us were exhausted. I had no idea when Faith had last slept, given how much we'd been running around all day *and* the night before. I was surviving on the nap I'd taken that morning in my hideout, which was plenty uncomfortable due to my injuries. A painful twinge from the gunshot wound reminded me again as I ate.

I wondered what was going on between Jack and Darius now. I wasn't used to having so little information. Right now, I was working off tidbits from the conversations with Gwendolen and Rebecca, plus my own observations of the streets as we'd rolled through. The open shooting gallery seemed to have been an isolated event. Since then, the occasional burst of gunfire was audible, but I'd only seen police on the streets—various corporate badges worn in the open.

They'd finally had to respond, no matter what deals Darius might have in place to keep their eyes averted.

In fact, at this point, my brother would probably welcome them. Jack's group was rougher, but far more numerous. With their willingness to gun down in public, Darius would find plenty of allies among the businessmen looking to preserve the status quo. As long as the police and our gang stayed out of each other's way, we'd probably come out with even better relationships. I'd never be able to work alongside the cops, but Darius kept a friendly open channel with most of the higher-ups.

Jack knew all of this. He'd known it for a long time, and it was a major reason why he'd never made a play for our territory before. So what changed?

It couldn't be the eye tech. That was just a bonus, something Jack could pick up while taking one of Darius's major allies off the board in the Maclays. Even if he came up empty, he'd still have them gone—a major blow to Darius's finances and influences in the medical technology sector.

I briefly flattered myself with the notion that having me disconnected from the gang was significant enough, but I soon dismissed it. Jack and Darius had been at it since before I'd become a major player, and I wasn't *totally* aligned with my brother. I'd always tried to present myself as freelance, albeit never taking a job against Darius. It was a way to further dissuade attempts to discern my identity, by throwing up another layer between myself and my brother. Our public relationship was strictly professional.

Jack wasn't going to win on the streets. That was clear. He'd lose just as much, if not *more,* from a drawn-out fight with Darius. The only win for Jack was a direct blow to the command structure. Without leadership or coordination, we'd be easy to overwhelm. Jack needed to go straight for the head—for Darius.

My brain went into planning mode. I tried to approach it as an exercise for myself, as if it were any other job I'd taken.

If I were Jack, how would I take out Darius?

My brother was known for using hideouts with plenty of surveillance and multiple exits. It was nearly impossible to get the drop on him, unless you could land a shot from a *very* long distance. You'd have to set up well beforehand, with a gunner who wouldn't be on any of the alert lists for Darius's facial recognition. Plant a weapon in a window, have the gunner arrive separately, and set up where you could be assured a good angle on Darius.

From there, it was a waiting game. Simple enough. It all came down to location, which was the one step I couldn't figure out.

"How could Jack get Darius's location?" I asked aloud.

Faith started. She'd been lost in thought as well. Her head cocked slightly as she refocused on me. "Huh?"

"Jack's going to try and kill Darius. Very soon."

"How do you know?"

"Just trust me on this one. It'd take a while to explain."

"Okay. Uhh . . . . I really don't know." She looked embarrassed. "Sorry."

"It's okay."

"All right." Faith glanced down at her food. "Can Darius trust everyone around him?"

"At this point, he'd only trust people absolutely closest to him. *Everything's* been compromised, as far as he knows. That just leaves Michael, Rebecca, and me."

Faith shook her head. "Probably not you anymore." She winced. "Sorry."

I swallowed, forcing down a burst of emotion that had rumbled up in my chest. "Yeah, probably not . . . wait."

I stopped dead. Something was wrong with that list.

"What?"

"Rebecca."

"What about her?"

"Why would Darius have her killed?"

Faith's head snapped upward. "That's . . . I didn't even think about it."

"Darius wouldn't. He had no reason to go after Rebecca. Even if he thought I was turned, so far as he knew, I would've put them on the same side for sure."

"So it had to be somebody else."

I nodded. "Someone with rank. Not just anybody can send out one of our assassins. There's only three besides me. But they also had to be someone who wasn't clear on the Maclays' loyalty."

Faith snapped her fingers. "Rank, motivation, and dumb as a box of rocks."

It hit me. "Hammer."

"Bingo."

"He sent the assassin. After killing one of Jack's men on Jack's turf—"

"Jack must have picked him up," continued Faith.

"And then leaked something to him to set him on the Maclays," I finished.

Faith frowned. "Could he track Hammer?"

"Not easily. Hammer's not *that* stupid. If Jack got a good GPS tag on him though . . ."

"And Hammer would just lead him straight to Darius?"

"He's Darius's bodyguard. Darius wouldn't put him out in the field after that screwup, but he's still worthwhile on defense."

"Okay." Faith stood up. She took the food tray and slid it into the trash. The machine buzzed to life, clearing the tray, cleaning it, and sending it back for the next customer. "So we can assume Jack's going to make a move soon. Maybe even tomorrow."

"That's what I said."

"I think aloud, okay?"

I winced. "Sorry."

"We're tired." She shrugged, starting for the door. "There's not much we can do for now. We don't know where anyone is and we don't really have a way to find them until morning."

I followed her out. A raindrop smacked me in the face right as I hit the street. I glanced up, and the blanket of clouds had once again blocked out the stars with a sheet of black. More raindrops fell, one by one, trickling out of the sky.

"Time to call it for the night," I said, drawing up my hood.

"Damn it," muttered Faith.

"What?"

"The rain's gonna wash out my plans for the night. I wanted to go do some more snooping." She yawned. I glanced around.

Faith was leaning heavily on the wall underneath the restaurant awning. For the first time, I noticed she wasn't just avoiding her leg—she looked totally dead on her feet. Her eyes drooped closed every few seconds, before snapping open again.

"When did you last sleep?"

She shook her head. "I'm fine."

"When?" I asked again, insistent.

"Uhh . . . after we split up at the mall."

"Faith, that was almost two days ago."

"Yeah, and you woke me up too."

I pulled out my phone and brought up a map.

"What are you doing?"

"Finding you a place to sleep for the night."

Faith sighed. "Okay, okay. Fine, I'll sleep. No need for that." She glanced around, eyeing the nearby alleyways.

I shook my head. "A real place to sleep, with a real bed."

She sighed again. "Cheap motel okay with you?"

"The best option, actually. They tend not to have networked surveillance or dedicated security guards."

Faith smirked. "You and I look for very different things in reviews, don't we?"

I shrugged. "I assume you've got somewhere in mind?"

"There's a cheap motel a block away from my school. Owner owes me a favor." She grinned. "More than one favor, actually."

I didn't want to know. "How far?"

"About a mile."

Faith didn't exactly walk a fast mile. It was another half an hour before we arrived at the poorly lit two-story motel, with aging yellow walls and a foreboding air filling every crevice of the dingy room. The front office seemed to be open, despite the time. Faith barged right in, dragging her feet over the threshold.

"Evening, Jeff."

The man behind the counter nearly fell out of his chair. He took the VR set off his face, glancing around confused.

"Is that . . . Faith?"

"No, it's Hope."

"Huh?"

"I'm here with my friend Charity"—Faith jerked a thumb at me— "and we need a room. Just until the morning."

Jeff was only beginning to catch up. *Not the brightest guy around*, I noted. To be fair, though, I wouldn't want to deal with a tired and angry Faith's wordplay this late at night myself.

"You need a room. Okay. Let me see." He pulled out a keyboard tray from his desk and lit up the old desktop next to him. "We got a couple open. Only singles though. Just one bed." Jeff glanced back at us with a lewd expression. "That good for you?"

"Oh, grow up," growled Faith. "The key?"

"Hang on, you gotta pay first."

Faith raised an eyebrow. "Say, Jeff, rememb—"

"Okay," I interrupted. I stepped forward, pulled a small wad of cash from my bag, and set it on the counter near the bulletproof turntable.

Jeff's eyes narrowed. "Who are you?"

"Believe me, Jeff, you don't want to know," said Faith. She held out her hand. Jeff swung the cash around, then dropped in a key to the room and spun it back to them. "Go back to your porn."

Jeff continued to stare at us all the way out the front door. Faith made her way down the line of rooms to theirs, pressing the key against the door lock. It clicked open and they went inside. I flicked on the light switch.

"You don't turn off, do you?" Faith commented idly. I realized I'd unconsciously scanned the entire room for signs of an intruder, hidden cameras, or anything that could pose a threat.

I shook my head. "Keeps me alive."

"Right." Faith sighed. "I'm sorry. I'm not very nice tired, am I?"

"It's fine. This is better than I expected," I said, gesturing around.

There was one bed, as promised, but it was surprisingly clean given the shabbiness affecting the rest of the place. The entire room was actually much more cozy than I expected. There were a few chairs set against the wide, curtained window, and they looked plenty soft, with thick cushioned arms. A bathroom and a small closet comprised the far end; a cheap TV sat on a wooden media stand opposite the bed.

"Yeah. He might be a sleazebag, but Jeff keeps a decent place."

Faith collapsed on the bed, reaching down to toss off her shoes before she pulled up the sheets. She stretched out, giving a wide yawn. I turned to the door, but Faith stopped me before I could leave.

"Hey."

"Yes?"

"Look, I . . ." Faith trailed off. I turned back to look at her. She was already wrapped tight in the blanket, pillows propping up her head. "I'd feel safer if you stuck around."

I just looked at her for a moment. Finally, I nodded, and flicked off the light switch, settling into one of the chairs next to the window. I drew the curtain out to cover it entirely, leaving only a tiny slit to see through from my spot. Satisfied nobody was outside, I pulled out my rifle from my bag and began my usual cleaning routine.

Patience was something I had in spades. It wasn't uncommon for me to spend hours in a single position, waiting for the perfect shot. Faith, on the other hand, obviously wasn't built the same way. She tossed and turned in bed for several minutes while I carefully polished my scope. Finally, Faith spoke up, breaking the silence.

"What are you going to do?"

"What do you mean?"

She sat up, leaning against the wall. "You're gonna be face-to-face with Darius soon, assuming everything goes right here. And now you know the whole story."

"I don't know everything yet."

"Point being, what happens when you two are in a room together?"

I hesitated.

"Don't kill him."

Her voice was resolute. I looked up. It was hard to make out her face with so little light spilling through the window, but after a moment, she became clear as my other eye compensated for the low light much faster than my left eye could.

"No matter what he's done, or his reasons, he's still your family. He clearly cares about you, too, even if he's an asshole. Might be the only family you have left. You can't throw that away."

"I don't know what I want to do," I said quietly.

"So don't. Get all the answers you need. We'll find your dad, there'll be a happy reunion, and then you can—I dunno, find a job as a professional woodcarver or something."

". . . Woodcarver?"

"Shut up, I'm tired."

I laughed.

"Don't make fun."

"It's not that." I smiled. "Darius actually did teach me woodcarving."

"You're messing with me."

"He really did. We'd make things to decorate our place with. I used to carve little pieces on some jobs while waiting for a shot. Then, somebody found wood shavings and started linking them to me."

Faith shook her head. "You're making this up."

I reached into my bag, found one of my pieces and tossed it to Faith. She barely caught it in the semi-darkness. "I made that a few weeks ago."

"Huh." Faith examined it as best she could. "You know, this isn't half bad. Really does look like a rat."

I frowned. "It's supposed to be a beaver."

She laughed and tossed it back. "Seriously though, woodcarving?"

"I always have a knife on me, and it's pretty quiet. Why not?"

"Fair enough." Faith laid back down, still grinning. "Make something for me next, uh-huh?"

"Sure. Do you have a request?"

"Nah, surprise me. It'll be fun to try and guess."

I rolled my left eye. "Thanks for that."

She cackled.

"Shouldn't you be sleeping?"

"I wish." Faith was suddenly dead-serious. It nearly gave me whiplash how fast the mood in the room died away. "Too much on my mind."

"What's going on?"

She looked away, hesitating. "You've been sharing your whole life, I guess it's my turn." Faith took a deep breath. "I sort of have a history with the Dunham family."

"I guessed as much."

"Right. Well, it's one Dunham in particular."

"Not Michael, then?"

"No. It's his daughter, Cassie."

I thought back. I'd never interacted with Cassie much. I knew of her existence, sure, and I'd met her at least once, but the girl was a blank in my memory. I tended only to focus on the higher-ups when dealing with my brother's lieutenants. Cassie was *way* below my pay grade. "What did she do?"

Faith sighed, then gestured to her leg. "This."

"I thought you said a drunk—"

"Yeah, I lied. I'd just met you and I didn't want you running off to kill her. The rest was true though, dragging myself to an emergency room and all that." Faith shrugged. "Cassie's been the terror of my existence for years."

"Why'd she do it?"

"Not important. Let's just say I embarrassed her. Anyway, she thrashed me, and being the homeless wonder child I am, I never made it past the ER. Thus, cripple girl was born. Made my high school years *real* fun."

"This was before high school?"

"Freshman year, yeah. But I got over it. I started it that time. I could live with it. Besides, some people *do* treat you a lot better on the whole when you've got a handicap. It sucks, but hell if I wasn't going to use that to my advantage."

I picked up on the hint. "*That* time?"

Faith swallowed hard before she continued. "Yeah, that time. Cassie came back for round two, three years later. She was near to graduation and she'd mostly gone quiet on me. It was pretty confusing, actually. Cass isn't really the forgive-and-forget type. That girl holds a *grudge*. All year, though, she barely said a word to me." She paused again. "Then, one night, in a big stupid dramatic gesture, I found out why."

She seemed restless and uncomfortable. I raised my hand. "You don't have to tell me if you don't want. It's okay."

"Nah," said Faith. "Somebody oughta know everything beside Ellie. We were walking around downtown one night. I was showing Ellie the places I used to live. Pretty stupid and reckless, in retrospect. We could've been attacked by *anyone.* Instead, we got Cassie, trapping us in a one-way alley with a knife, declaring her love for Eleanor Maclay to all the street trash."

"She thought you—"

"Yeah, exactly. So I was the obstacle. Dunno what she was thinking she'd accomplish. Like, Ellie's not gonna go out with a girl who just sliced up her faux-sister. It was so ridiculous." Faith shrugged. "But that's how it ended up."

"So Ellie's scar was Cassie?"

"And that's the reason I got kicked out." Faith sighed. "Deservedly."

I looked out the window again. A car rolled by with nobody inside. The pathfinding software took it cleanly around the bend, sloshing through rainwater filling the curb. It was probably on its way to pick up some drunk from the bar and take them safely home. Rain started to fall more heavily, and a slight breeze sent it pattering against the window. As it grew heavier, it echoed through the roof and the thin floor above them.

"You didn't deserve that," I said, still staring out the window. "You weren't at fault."

"If I hadn't been there, Cassie wouldn't've attacked."

"If not there, somewhere else. Cassie's the only one to blame here."

Faith didn't bother to argue further. "Look, it's past now. I'm over it. Mostly. Just promise me you won't do anything to her."

I turned, a little surprised. "Why are you coming along, then?"

"Oh, I want revenge. But it'll be on my terms," said Faith, her voice dark. "She won't be a problem."

"What are you going to do to her?"

"Can't spoil the surprise."

"Should I be afraid?"

Faith grinned wickedly. "Maybe."

I returned the smile, although Faith probably couldn't see it with her normal eyes. She was resourceful and motivated. I had no doubt Cassie was going down.

"*Are* you in love with Ellie?" I asked tentatively.

Faith sighed. "Ellie's in love with *me*. I don't really know what to do with that. I mean, I love her—just not like *that*, you know?" She shrugged. "I've never actually been in love. At least, I don't think so. I dunno. I'm usually too busy. Running my network's kinda a full-time gig."

"Do you need any help?"

"Nah." Faith tapped her pocket. "As long as I've got a working phone, I'm already way better than normal." It buzzed suddenly, startling them both.

". . . Expecting someone?"

"Nope." Faith grabbed it out and read the message. The faint blue glow illuminated her face, casting a huge shadow on the wall behind her. "Huh. Seems Amy's up late. She's already started a few of the overnighters on our search." She tapped on the phone, sending a reply. "Damn, it *is* late. Or early, whatever." She set the phone onto the bedside table and wrapped herself back up in the covers. "You should probably sleep, too, while you can."

I glanced pointedly around the room. The floor was a very thin carpet, and the chairs not exactly the best shapes for comfortable sleep.

"Yeah, yeah, I got us a crappy room. Sorry, Cyclops Girl." Faith's voice was getting drowsy. "You know, if you wanted, I wouldn't mind sharing over here. Promise you won't tell Ellie."

"Go to sleep, Faith."

". . . Yeah, you're not good enough for me anyway . . . too short . . ."

Faith trailed off. Before long, her breathing had steadied out. I returned to staring out the window. Sheets of rain were now pounding the roof and the walls. The light above the parking lot flickered, casting a ray of light through the drops of water.

I went back to work on my rifle, making sure it was still as perfect as the day Darius gave it to me.

CHAPTER 15

Hey, Kara."

I jerked awake. My face had been pressed up against the window, rifle held close to my chest sitting on the chair. From the light outside, it seemed still early, the sun just beginning to rise, and the clock in my other eye confirmed it. Faith was standing over me, a curious look on her face.

"What?"

"You look pretty badass like that."

"It'd be better if I hadn't fallen asleep." I rubbed at my left eye briefly, trying to get myself properly awake. For some reason, I hadn't woken up instantly like I usually did. I felt . . . oddly safe.

"Relax, we're still alive." Faith began to make the bed.

"Don't they usually do that for you?"

"Oh, right, you paid this time. Normally when I stay here, Jeff lets me take a room off-book. I just make it look like I was never here and we're good. This is one of the better spots to crash for a night, but it's occupied way too often."

I packed away my rifle and stood up to help her finish. "It looks better than when we got here."

"Yeah." Faith nodded. "And now I've gotta get to class. It starts in half an hour. What are you going to do?"

"I'll be fine. Did your people turn anything up yet?"

"Michael's at his home right now. I sent someone there first thing after I woke up to stake it out. Seems like he'll be there all morning, and if not, we've got eyes on him."

"You know where he lives?"

Faith grimaced. "I know where Cassie lives."

"Ah."

"I'll have someone on him all day if I need to. Got a few friends with nothing better to do." Faith opened the door and stepped outside. I followed her and closed the door silently behind us. "Well, I should get going. What are you going to do for an hour?"

I glanced around, getting a bearing for where exactly we'd ended up. I'd been really out of it the previous night and hadn't paid attention to where Faith was taking me.

"The hideout isn't all that far from here," I said finally. "I'm going to go get a few things we might need."

"Gotcha." Faith raised a finger as if to scold me. "Remember, don't start without me!"

"I promised, didn't I?"

"Technically no," Faith said with a smile, "but I'll count it."

She started walking away. I felt like I had to say something else, but I couldn't figure out what it was. As Faith was just nearly turning out of sight, I finally called out, "Good luck on the test."

Faith gave me a thumbs-up, then rounded the corner and was gone.

I sat a block away from the school entrance. It was a fenced-in compound, with automatic scanners at every entrance for weapons or unauthorized persons. A stream of students walked in, apparently a group off whatever schedule Faith followed. I doubted anybody would look toward the shadowed alleyway I was perched in, but I still kept my hood drawn and my hair low over my other eye.

Better I wasn't noticed.

I'd gone to the hideout and back without incident, picking up a few odds and ends. While normally I carried enough supplies in my bag for any daily needs, there were a few more specialized tools generally too bulky or heavy to be practical. If I was going up against Michael's home, I expected good security. I wasn't sure what I'd be going up against exactly, so I brought a bit of everything.

Despite his status, I'd never been to Michael's; I wasn't even sure where his house was. We'd only ever met in the field, in meetings with the gang, or a few times at Darius's home. Michael had always treated me with respect, if not an actual modicum of kindness. I had the feeling he didn't approve of my brother's choices for my life.

My life.

I watched a few girls around my age going into the school, talking and laughing. They looked like they didn't have a care in the world. I wondered if I could ever fit that kind of life. Mentally, I conjured up an image of walking into the school, side-by-side with a friend, joking and gossiping. For the first time I could remember . . . I wanted it.

Not just that, I wanted to be normal—go to a normal school, hang out with normal friends, talk about normal topics. Maybe meet a normal guy, go do some normal things, have a normal romance. The normal kids standing around at the front of the school sure seemed to enjoy it.

I was still daydreaming when the idyllic picture in front of me . . . changed, ever so slightly. My other eye picked up on it before I did. An outline of a gun in a man's pocket showed up on my infrared. The software had detected it and swapped over automatically, marking him as a possible threat with a faint box. He was walking steadily toward a group of kids just under the school sign. I zoomed in on them and noticed a faint tattoo on one and a knife in the pocket of another.

They were definitely gang members, younger ones, possibly associated with our organization. The man approaching could be anyone. I'd be willing to put money on him being with Jack. His intent was plain as day, but they hadn't noticed him yet.

I pulled out my rifle and set up on an empty barrel. I was prepared to engage if needed. My other eye overlaid all of them with indicators, marking friend and foe. I was hoping they'd notice him first and get inside the school grounds. They'd be safe inside. The school's security wasn't foolproof, but it was good enough to protect them from a single gunman. Due to tighter restrictions on the area government buildings could affect, however, its protection didn't go beyond the gates.

If they didn't notice the danger soon, they were all dead.

I tracked the man as he moved closer and closer. His hand reached inside his pocket, grasping something.

My other eye switched modes, giving me direct view through my scope. I was ready to take him out the moment he drew the gun. He'd never get a shot off. Our people would be safe.

He was getting closer, step by step. They still hadn't noticed him. Why weren't they paying attention? Didn't they know what was going on right now in the city? Anyone could be in danger.

The man was within a few steps. My finger slid along the trigger, a hair's breadth from firing.

He was staring straight ahead, but I was ready for him. His head would turn, his eyes would narrow, his hand would snap out—and I'd put him down.

I took a breath.

He walked past.

The kids continued to talk, totally unaware. He kept moving. My hands automatically tracked him all the way to the end of the street. He waited for the light, then crossed in front of the waiting cars.

I gently eased my finger off the trigger.

Adrenaline was slowly subsiding in my blood. I laughed aloud, a bitter, dead laugh that echoed in the alley all around me. *This* was why I'd never be normal. I'd nearly executed a man for nothing, right in front of a school. I pressed the button to retract my rifle's barrel, then carefully packed it away.

I settled back into the shadows of the alley, watching the school again. It wasn't enough though. I needed to take my mind off of it. While I still kept watch on the building with one hand in my bag, I started digging through my old recordings again. Something was in there, some clue to the questions swirling in my head, but how could I pick out the right one, when I hadn't even known I was missing anything until now?

Eventually, I just picked the happiest memory I could find. Yes, it involved Darius, but I wasn't so sure I hated him anymore. I definitely hadn't *forgiven* him, and I still wasn't sure if he needed to die or not . . . but I had to give him a chance. This memory seemed like a fair compromise.

I'd started recording without Darius knowing. It was just the two of us, lugging boxes out of the van and into the house. My rifle was leaning up against the inside of the door, ready just in case, but neither of us expected to be disturbed. Not a soul knew we were here.

"What's *in* this?" he grunted as he nearly dropped it.

I smiled. "Ammo."

Darius raised an eyebrow. "You need this much ammunition for your *apartment?*"

"You never know."

He set the box down with a sigh of relief. "The whole point of this place and why we don't have any help right now is that nobody will ever know about it," he said, frowning. "You shouldn't ever need to defend yourself."

"Yes, but this way, I have it for when I go out too."

"Couldn't you just resupply at one of our armories?"

I shrugged. "I might not be able to get to one."

Darius hesitated, torn between exasperation and what seemed like . . . pride? He was impressed I'd thought of the exceptional possibilities. I don't think I realized the second emotion in the past, as I responded even more harshly.

"You said I'm always supposed to be ready, no matter what!"

In the present, I winced. I'd forgotten how bratty I could be. The clip was a little more than a year ago. I was fifteen. By what I'd learned, it was pretty young for a normal person to be living on their own, but I was anything but normal.

My brother nodded. "That's a good way to think. I just . . ."

"Just what?"

"Never mind." He picked up the box again with another grunt of exertion. "Where do you want it?"

"Upstairs, the empty room next to mine."

Darius nodded and started lugging the box upstairs. Meanwhile, I set to arranging the curtains around the two downstairs windows—they were custom made, a material that would be completely opaque to normal human eyes, but almost transparent to my other eye.

This went on for a while. Darius would bring in boxes of my things, whether they were for my budding career or just to make the place more cozy and livable, and I'd direct him on where to put everything. It was a whole day's worth, just the two of us, putting things in order.

There wasn't anything else important to the memory, and it ended with the two of us playing a round of cards on the floor of my new apartment—we'd gotten too tired to bring the two small couches in, and for whatever reason, the floor just seemed more appealing than the table. I had a terrible draft, and Darius ran my deck out in short order. After that, he left, and I ended the recording.

I'd originally recorded it just because I wanted to have a way to find anything that might've been misplaced. Today, I'd selected it as my happiest memory, but I wasn't exactly sure *why* I considered it the happiest. There wasn't anything particularly special to it. It took rewatching it—while still surveilling the school and waiting for Faith to return—to finally figure out why it was so important to me.

That apartment had been the first time I'd really started feeling like *me*.

Darius had agreed I'd become self-sufficient enough to live on my own. He'd helped me get a place for myself, and it truly was just mine.

It was in my name, paid for by my own money, filled with my things and arranged as I wanted it. The only thing Darius had done was carry boxes and offer the occasional suggestion.

It was just . . . mine.

I'd never had something like that.

Faith emerged a few minutes later while I was still lost in thought. I called out to her, and she made her way across the street after a few moments.

"All set?" asked Faith, looking a little nervous.

"Yeah." I frowned. "You okay?"

"I'll be fine." Faith glanced back toward the school. "For some reason, I feel like I'm never gonna see it again," she added ominously.

"Don't be ridiculous. You'll be back tomorrow."

"Yeah." Faith shook her head. "Okay, let's go."

She tilted her head, indicating I should take the lead. I hesitated. "Umm . . ."

"What?"

"I don't know where he lives."

Faith raised her eyebrows. "Seriously?"

I glanced away, embarrassed. "Shut up."

"Oh, this is going *great* so far." Faith laughed. "Well, come on. It's a couple of miles away. Let's roll."

Faith started limping away. I checked the map on my phone briefly, tightened the strap on my bag, and followed.

"Shouldn't there be more people around?" Faith asked cautiously.

"After the last couple of days, they're probably laying low. No one wants to be caught out on the street right now between the cops or rival gangs."

I glanced out from the alley where we were crouched. Same as Faith, I didn't see anyone of note. Michael didn't seem to have a single guard posted, and the only visible people were too far away to be of real consequence. This was going to be way easier than I thought.

We were a block away from his home, which was a trio of unremarkable apartment buildings. Michael supposedly owned the entire complex, renting apartments out for some extra cash flow. He lived in the central building with his family. I doubted we'd run into any trouble from the other two buildings, but the center one likely had at least a few of Michael's best men. If he was home, I had no doubt there'd be extra security in place.

More importantly, scanners would lock the place down if anyone on the blacklist got near, and I had no doubt I'd made that list by now. If I got in range, it'd activate the remote defenses. I spotted at least three spots in the brick walls where a small gun mounted on a turret could be concealed—easy to pop out and fire from terminals inside.

Luckily, I had ways to beat those. I knew our security inside and out.

I dug into my bag and pulled out the small laptop I'd gotten from my hideout earlier. It took a few moments to boot up, a curious Faith watching over my shoulder.

"What are you doing?"

"Hacking." I logged in, turning on the wireless adapters.

"Jack of all trades, aren't ya?"

"Something like that."

The laptop was still registered as one of ours, since it was just a generic terminal not assigned to me, so the wireless network let me in as a limited guest. To get more access, though, I needed proper credentials or a back door—but to my disappointment, the usual one Darius and I used was shut tight. I'd need to log in legitimately, which would send out a ping due to the admin access, so I'd have to work fast.

I pulled up the log-in page for the router and noted the model number listed. Next, I opened a text document and typed out the password I'd memorized from Darius, then began shifting the characters based on the model number to get the login for this particular device. I had to trust Michael hadn't reformatted his network *completely*, but I doubted he'd bother. Michael was the more hands-on of the pair, and Darius handled the digital end of our organization.

" 'Those who have forgotten history are doomed to repeat it. Those who remember history and repeat it intentionally are truly evil,' " Faith read aloud over my shoulder. ". . . Huh."

"Darius's password unencoded. Exactly a hundred and twenty-eight bytes."

I finished encoding it, then returned to the router prompt and typed it in. The device granted me admin access, to my great relief. I brought up a list of devices connected to the network. In a stroke of luck, they were even still labeled correctly. *Darius would be ashamed.*

With a few clicks, I disconnected the turrets from the network and blocked them entirely. The security alert system would be trickier. While the turrets were programmed to go into standby when disconnected—to avoid firing on invalid targets—the cameras and facial recognition alarms would send out an alert if they didn't receive a ping every three seconds. After ten missed checks, the system would notify all users of a possible fault.

I found the address of the machine running the cameras and opened a terminal to it, which got me another password prompt. The default didn't work, and the interface for the cameras didn't provide any kind of model number. I sat back and thought for a few seconds.

"Problem?" asked Faith, who'd noticed my sudden stop.

"Just a second."

I rubbed my left eye, mind racing to find a new vector of attack. My other eye flitted over the top of the screen, checking the whole street again. There was still no sign of activity, to my relief. I returned to the laptop.

The camera feed interface wasn't one I recognized. It didn't look like a standard one from Darius. I opened the source code of the default page I was sent, looking for anything I could use—and I found the address for the database of the system, plain as day.

I laughed aloud. Darius would be *furious* at this gaping hole in security.

One simple exploit and I was downloading the database. I found the listing for the user passwords, and they were encrypted, but I had the decryption key—it was our own system, and Darius and I held all the private keys. With that, I could decrypt any password we needed, and all I had to do after that was keep using them until one gave me an admin login.

I set up a script to do just that, then set aside the laptop.

"Success?"

"Yeah, probably. Give it a minute."

I scanned down the street again. There was an old drunk sitting in an alleyway, much like we were. He lay under a sheet of cardboard, but if I zoomed in, I could see his eyes were alert and focused. I nodded in his direction.

"Is that your guy?"

"Good catch," said Faith, impressed.

The laptop beeped. It had a valid login. I now had access to the security controls. I found the alert system and turned it off with time to spare, as well as locking down internet access to all channels for the network.

A pop-up notified me that the alert had to be turned back on within six hours or an automatic notifier would be sent to leadership. I had no way of disabling that function without rewriting the system itself, but I certainly didn't expect to be sticking around that long. I opened the feeds for the interior, but I only saw one man near the front hallway. Most of the rooms didn't have a camera feed.

"You ready to go?" I asked, still typing.

"Yeah," said Faith. She stood up and stretched out her leg.

"Go, now. I'll be right behind you."

I sent a message to the man at the door, prompting him to leave. He'd just received a valid order to head down the street and do a sweep of the adjacent block—a pretty standard request, or so I hoped. I figured that'd give us enough time.

Once I saw him step outside, I shut down the laptop and put it in my bag. Faith was already crossing the street, but he paid her no mind, immediately heading in the opposite direction as I'd instructed. After he'd moved far enough away, I sprinted across the street and arrived at the front door nearly at the same time as Faith.

I walked up the short staircase and went straight inside. My wet shoes squeaked on the wood floors. The entrance opened into a tight hallway, with doors on either side, and a staircase leading up at the far end. I didn't see a soul around.

Faith closed the door behind us as quietly as she could. I drew my pistol and began walking down the hall, checking every door as we passed. The kitchen and living room were totally empty. We climbed the staircase to the second floor and found another hallway with a new set of four rooms.

The first on the left was a wide office, with the wall to the adjacent apartment knocked down to widen it even further. *Owning the entire building has perks.* A rug covered most of the floor, with a set of chairs around a low table. Bookshelves lined the edge of the room, so stuffed I half expected them to collapse under the sheer weight of heavy tomes.

A huge screen was set into the side wall above a crackling fireplace. Behind the wide oak desk at the other end, staring at several computer screens, sat Michael Dunham.

As the door opened, he began to rise. I was faster.

I stepped to the side as soon as I was in. My pistol was already trained on his face.

He raised his hands in surrender immediately.

"Snipe?"

"One of the chairs, please," I said with a slight jerk of my head. There were four, forming a neat square around a coffee table near the fireplace.

Michael walked very slowly across the room and sat down, his hands still raised and his back to the door. Faith sat down opposite him while I walked around the both of them—pistol still trained on Michael along with my other eye—and sat down in Michael's desk. I scanned the screen as fast as I could.

He was in the middle of writing a message to Darius. Most of it was about me and questioning whether I had any real motivation to break ties with us, or kill him, and if they were chasing the right target.

Michael doesn't know. Darius never told him either.

I shut the computer down, then joined them at the table, sitting in the chair next to Faith, where my other eye could keep watch on the closed door.

"So," started Michael.

"I need to see Darius," I said bluntly.

Michael let his hands drop and relaxed a bit in his chair. "I won't bother saying I don't know where he is. But . . . what do you plan to do to him?"

"I just want to talk." For now, that was still true.

"You understand why I might find that hard to believe, right?"

"Yes."

"Look," cut in Faith, "this has been a crazy weekend, all right? Somebody's gotta clear the air. She needs to talk to Darius, and *I* need to talk to *you*."

Michael looked at her, surprised. "Who the hell are you?"

Faith looked honestly taken aback by the lack of recognition. I couldn't blame her. She'd been building up to this confrontation for *years*, and this was something of a letdown. Nobody spoke for a few seconds, each of us glancing between the others.

A knock at the door.

My pistol was already rising as it swung open to reveal . . . Cassie Dunham.

"Hey, Dad, when are we going out?" Cassie asked as she walked in. She stopped dead. "What the fu—"

"Morning, Cass," said Faith. "I brought Snipe, as promised."

CHAPTER 16

Cassie looked from Faith to me, and then back again. Her mouth opened and closed a few times. Nothing came out. She seemed to have completely frozen up.

"Sit down please, Cassie," Michael said finally. I gestured toward the other chair next to him with my pistol.

Her eyes narrowed on Faith. "What the hell are *you* doing here?"

"I stopped by for a snack," Faith said with a shrug.

Cassie launched herself at Faith, snarling with rage. I was about to stop her, but Michael beat me to the punch.

He stood up, and in one quick combination, he'd dropped Cassie to the ground. She sprawled out on the floor but scrambled to her feet in an instant. Michael still had the jump on her though, and he was considerably stronger. He put her into a hold with practiced ease.

After a few seconds of struggling, she relented. They'd obviously done this more than a few times in the past. Michael released her, and she moved, subdued, into the chair. I relaxed once again, but my pistol was still pointedly trained on Cassie—and ready to swap back to Michael in an instant if need be.

"Glad you got that out of your system," Faith said brightly.

Cassie stared daggers at her, matching the bladed tattoos sprawled across her neck. "Screw you, bitch."

"Scintillating." Faith turned to Michael. "Your daughter is just so *charming!*"

Michael frowned. "Cassie, who is she?"

"She's nobody," growled Cassie, never taking her eyes off Faith for a second. "Street trash."

"Street *treasure*," corrected Faith.

She's enjoying herself way too much. Cassie looked ready to throttle her, damn the consequences. But . . . this was Faith's moment, so I said nothing.

"She's worthless," Cassie continued. "Nobody would miss her. Let me get rid of her." She started to stand up. I tensed, but Michael intervened once again.

"Cassandra, you will not leave that chair again." The tone in his voice was so icy, even I felt a chill. Cassie dropped back down without a word, eyes locked on Faith.

Michael glanced at her as well. "Do I know you?"

"No, you don't. But you really should," said Faith. She picked up a pen from his desk and played with it idly. "Think back a few years. It'll come to you." With Michael obviously blanking, Faith began to tap the pen against her leg rhythmically.

Michael's eyes narrowed for just a moment . . . then went very wide. "The homeless girl."

"Yahtzee." Faith tossed the pen aside.

"What do you want?"

"That's so sweet of you! But no, I brought *you* a present." Faith turned. "Can I have your laptop, Snipey?"

I sighed. "Only if you promise never to call me that again."

Faith grinned. I passed my bag over, still keeping a close watch on Cassie with my other eye. Faith dug out my laptop, which was still logged in from earlier, and accessed the net. She pulled up a file storage site I wasn't familiar with and logged into her account.

"Hey, how can I put this on that nice big screen?" she asked, glancing at Michael.

I leaned over—my other eye still locked on Cassie—and pointed out the right buttons to press. After a few moments, a set of videos popped up on the wall.

It was dozens of short camera phone videos and pictures, many of the same events from multiple angles, and all of Cassie Dunham. I could barely take them all in, especially with how brutal some of them got. Cassie beating on innocent bystanders, knife in hand, or far worse. Several full-on kills—some legitimate actions I vaguely remembered, others obviously committed for personal reasons. Faith had a cavalcade of evidence.

"There's plenty more besides this, and not just visuals. I've got tons of people lined up willing and ready to testify. *Way* more than you could intimidate or buy off—and trust me, they aren't getting bought." Faith shut the videos off. "You're going to prison, Cassie."

She laughed. "Didn't work last time, bitch. Why would it now?"

"You're not a minor anymore," countered Faith, "and I've got some good friends in the Justice Department these days who are *very* interested in what I've got to say." Her tone was deadly serious now, all mirth gone, and getting colder word by word. "You shouldn't've attacked one of the Maclays. They're very important in this city."

Cassie got very quiet. She wasn't a *complete* idiot.

"Don't worry. I'm sure your dad's got some kickass lawyers, since you slithered away so easily last time. You'll probably only get fifteen years. Twenty, tops. Plus I hear prison girls are *definitely* your type." There wasn't any glee to be found, no trace of the Faith who'd walked in with me. A quiet, controlled anger had filled her voice. "You screwed up the moment you laid a finger on my sister."

"Dad—" started Cassie, but Michael raised a hand to silence her. Everyone turned to look at him.

He closed his eyes. "I assume this evidence is already on the way to the authorities?"

Faith nodded. "They'll have it soon."

Michael sighed. "Cassie, you are going to go down to the police station on Twelfth Street and turn yourself in. I'll have Mr. Renalds there by the end of the day. Do not say a *word* until he arrives."

"Dad, wait, I—"

"Do it now, Cassandra, before I change my mind and send you there for life," Michael said quietly.

Cassie stood up. She shot one final glare at Faith, then left, leaving them alone once more. Faith watched her go with a mixture of satisfaction and sorrow in her expression. I lowered my gun, letting it rest in my lap, ready but unobtrusive. I was pretty sure Michael wasn't a threat to us and I'd rather we had him as an ally than an enemy.

He sat back in his chair, expression inscrutable. Silence followed for a minute afterward while they heard Cassie furiously packing a bag in the next room. A door slammed downstairs as she left.

"She'll try to run," Faith said finally, once the echoes of her abrupt departure had faded.

"Probably," agreed Michael, opening his eyes. "But she doesn't have any friends left. You already sent it, didn't you?"

"This morning."

"So public transit's off-limits. She's locked out. They'll pick her up before too long." Michael glanced at her, curious. "You're the classmate, aren't you? The girl she put in the hospital."

"Yeah."

"This is probably worthless at this point, but I'm sorry for what she did."

Faith shook her head. "Look, catharsis is great and all, but my part's done here. We have other business to attend to." She glanced at me, and Michael followed her gaze. "You're gonna take us to see Darius."

Michael frowned. "It's not that simple."

"So simplify it."

"Do you know what she did?"

"What she *allegedly tried* to do."

"I just want to talk," I interjected.

"Snipe, you're not exactly convincing me here," sighed Michael. "Will you tell me why you want to kill him?"

I hesitated. "No. I need all the answers first."

"And her brother is the only one who has them, and we already wrecked your security system, so we can probably do his as well," Faith continued. I privately disagreed with the idea, but there was no point mentioning that aloud. "You'll make it a lot easier, and with less damage and death all around. So let's skip to the end, okay?"

Michael looked surprised. "You know who she is?"

"Oh, I know everything," smirked Faith. "You have a son too. Alex, right? He was supposed to get back in town yesterday." Michael nodded, now a little nervous. "Bad news, he got shot. He's okay, but he's in a hospital outside town. I'll give you the address after we're done here."

Michael's face creased with worry. He looked at me. "Did you see him?"

I nodded. "He'll be fine."

He relaxed at the words. "Thank you." Michael's eyes closed again for a moment as he took a deep breath, then opened again and found mine. "Can you promise me right now that you don't plan on killing Darius?'

"I don't plan on it," I answered truthfully. I had no idea what I would do, except that I had to get answers.

He sighed. "Fine. I'll get in contact with him." He pulled out his phone, but of course, the network rejected his outgoing traffic.

"Sorry," I said. "I may have gone overboard locking down your network."

"This is nice and all, but remember the other bit we wanted to bring up?" cut in Faith. "The Jack business?"

"What about Jack?" asked Michael, raising an eyebrow.

"He's going to try to kill Darius again," I said. "Probably today."

"How do you know?"

"Hammer's with Darius right now, right?"

"He should be, yes."

I nodded. "Hammer got picked up by Jack on Saturday, after he killed the pickpocket. Jack probably got a tracker on him and set him loose, so he could get Darius's location."

"Damn it all," muttered Michael. "How did we miss that?"

"I was wondering the same thing," Faith added mildly.

Michael stood up. "We need to move." He walked behind his desk and picked up a gun concealed in one drawer. I didn't feel even remotely threatened by him anymore.

"Where to?"

"Your home, actually," said Michael. It took me a moment to remember he really meant Darius's place—he didn't know where my home was. "Darius wanted the full network access."

I was surprised. It wasn't the most secure location. I'd expect Darius to be somewhere a little more protected than *that*. Maybe he had another reason to go back home. It had an extensive set of local resources and multiple lines of fiber access, sure, but so did a few other, more secure locations.

Why did he go home?

I shook it off. Michael was right—we needed to move. I stood as well, opening my bag and tossing out some of the more weighty useless contents, including my laptop.

"What's the plan?"

"Jack will already be on the move. This time of day is awful. It's completely bright and no concealment anywhere. Worst conditions for us, so Jack will want to take advantage of it." Michael ejected the magazine from his gun and checked it. "I'll call a few guys, but we won't have much backup. You'll have to cover the street until we can secure the front door."

"The building at the south end has a good fire escape I can shoot from."

"Sounds good. I'll approach from that end underneath your cover."

"Do your men have automatics?"

"Not that they could bring in time."

"We'll make it without. Just remember the signals."

"Don't worry, I've drilled those in."

Michael started for the door, and I followed right after him. My blood was already starting to pump harder, and we hadn't even left the room yet.

"Uhh," Faith said suddenly. We both stopped, and in unison, glanced over at her. "Sorry . . . what should I do?"

I didn't know how to answer. I didn't want to say it, but there really wasn't a place for Faith in this. She was too slow and completely untrained. Michael spoke up before I did, to my relief.

"You've done enough. We've got it from here."

"Right," said Faith, but she didn't sound happy about it.

I turned to Michael. "Go. I'll catch up." He walked out without another word, already on his phone and typing out a message to send as soon as he could.

Faith looked at me with a painful expression on her face. "Sorry I'm slowing you down."

I didn't say anything. Instead, I stepped forward, lifted my arms, and wrapped Faith in a tight hug.

Her eyes widened. "Okay, okay. I get it. Sheesh."

"Thank you," I said, not letting go.

"If you say so," said Faith, her voice muffled in my hood. "Get out of here. I'll be fine."

I broke away. "I'll call you as soon as it's done."

"It's a date." Faith followed me down to the street and pulled out her phone. "I'll be with Ellie. Don't do anything I wouldn't do." She paused. "And . . . Kara?"

I stopped. "Yeah?"

"He's your brother."

I nodded. Faith turned and began walking away. She was already talking to Tanaka. I watched my friend walk away for a few seconds, her distinctive limp carrying her down the street, step by rolling step, back to her family, and for a moment, I wished I could go with her.

Time to go. I turned and followed Michael the opposite direction, toward my only brother, and the only childhood home I'd ever had . . . the only family I'd ever known.

Michael and I were heading down a side street. We'd already encountered one of Jack's crew, well inside our territory. It wasn't a good sign.

"What's going on between us and Jack?" I asked.

"He's been hitting us hard. Most of our dealers are holed up after a few got shot out in the open. The security teams were out looking for you, so we couldn't respond in time. Jack outnumbers us by so much we can't really go toe to toe."

"And Darius?"

"He shut himself off completely," said Michael, voice hard-edged. "He's been hiding out, refusing to talk to anyone. I've been trying to run everything, but I can barely keep up. I never really knew just how much he did behind the scenes until now." He shook his head. "Police have been getting on us way more too. I think they realized he isn't calling the shots."

We both looked up as a few raindrops started to hit. The clouds were rolling in again, blotting out the sunlight.

"Figures," muttered Michael.

I drew up my hood and double-checked my bag to make sure it was zipped. "What about your men?"

"Lost a few good ones in the firefights. I only have three coming right now, but they're well armed. It should be enough, I think. Jack's not crazy enough to send everything he's got. He still has a business to run himself, and it's the middle of the day. He'll only send what he can afford to lose."

"He's already got the Maclays' tech. Darius is just a bonus at this point."

Michael's eyes widened. "He does?"

"Yeah. He kidnapped Rebecca. We got her back, but he has the tech and he got away."

"What the hell have you been *doing* all weekend?"

"Things," I replied, feeling distinctly Faith-like as I did—and enjoying it.

We turned another corner. Our old home was only a couple of blocks away now—the place where I'd originally met Michael, and the home of so many memories with my brother, good and bad. The rain was picking up now, darkening the sidewalks. We sped up, ducking into the alleyway we'd designated as our staging ground.

Michael's men were already there. One was watching the street, and the other two sat under cover. Both stood as we entered the alley, weapons raised and trained on me. Before they could do anything, Michael stepped in front of me, blocking their aim.

"She's with us."

Their guns lowered slightly, and both men looked confused. The lead spoke up. "What changed?"

"She wasn't really against us."

"If you say so." He still looked suspicious, but Michael's tone brooked no argument.

"Movement down the street," cut in the lookout. He was watching around the corner to the left.

I leaned over him, peeking out just enough for my other eye to get a good view. With a quick hand motion, I zoomed in and marked five targets. They were milling about the end of the road, but with a clear focus on the two-story house in the center of the street—my old home.

"Five guys, armed," reported the lookout.

"Five for me too," I agreed. "I don't see anything big."

"Five is too few for Jack," murmured Michael. He checked the opposite direction. "Shit."

Sure enough, as I turned to match his eyeline, I spotted at least three more approaching from the right side. I marked them as well.

"Okay. James, Mikey, you two are going around. Flank the guys on the left. Snipe, you and Mitch have the right. Thirty seconds."

They nodded. The two Michael had named left the alley the same way they'd arrived. They'd move along the next street down, get behind Jack's men, and set up an ambush as fast as they could.

"No way to get you to the fire escape," Michael added apologetically. "Sorry."

"It's fine."

I pulled out my rifle and got set up. As I did, the five men on the right suddenly made a break for the house. I lined up my scope, but I hadn't had time to prepare.

My first shot went wide. I adjusted, and my second went through a leg.

He tumbled to the ground. My third went into his head. The others dove for cover—behind parked cars, solid fences, anything they could find.

Unfortunately for the hapless men, my software kept up with them. The markings I'd laid on each one followed them, bright squares clearly marking their likely positions by calculating their momentum and angle of descent. I put a round through the fence where my other eye guessed one had landed—and was rewarded with a hole through both the fence and the man's shoulder.

More shots from the street. Michael's men were moving in to flank. Another man sprawled out dead, his head falling to the pavement next to the car where he'd taken cover.

Gunfire from behind. Mitch had taken out one of Jack's guys, but the other two were returning fire. I didn't have a clear angle on any of them. Taking a chance, I fired a few shots experimentally toward places they *might* be hiding, though I couldn't expect to hit anything through the thick material. One of them was stupid enough to fall for it.

He rolled out into the open. My next round blew through his torso.

I felt a rage building inside me, unfamiliar and raw. I didn't want to kill these men. I didn't want to kill *anyone* anymore. It was all part of a life that had been forced on me. This insanity, all this death, it was a choice made for me. I didn't really have a say in it.

But they were trying to invade my home and kill my brother. I didn't have a choice here either.

I put another round just past the head of a man who'd popped up to try and spot me. He ducked immediately.

They know our angle. This isn't working.

I tapped Mitch on the shoulder, pointing in the man's direction. "Go."

He understood without explanation and broke into a sprint directly at the man's hiding place. I put another round over his head to keep him down and unaware. Mitch got close enough and put his gun around the corner. A few rapid pulls of the trigger, and another of our targets was gone.

I cleared them from my software and turned to the original five. For an instant, I saw one rise, beginning to sprint for the front door—and suddenly, everything in the world became very flat. Color and detail blurred. I could barely see anything.

For a split-second, I gagged, as if I was about to be sick. It took me a second to realize what had happened. My other eye's battery, after so many days of neglect and frequent use, had finally run dry.

I tried to recover. My first shot went wide, but I got the man to duck. I cursed and tried to adjust my aim, but I heard the telltale click of my magazine running dry . . . and the man was getting close to my home.

A guttural scream tore loose from my mouth, rage, despair, and helplessness rolling off my tongue in one primal noise. I stood up.

"Snipe, wait!" called Michael, but his voice might has well have been another raindrop.

That man was not allowed inside. It was my home. Every good memory flashed through my mind in an instant. He didn't belong there. My instincts overwhelmed me, pushing me to act.

I threw caution to the wind and broke away from the alley. Bullets flew past as I sprinted forward, heedless of the danger. The man kicked in the door and fired a few shots into the entryway. Hammer had been behind in cover, but one lucky shot went through his skull. He collapsed.

The man walked through the front door. I was only a few steps behind. I threw my empty rifle to the side and leaped forward. My entire body connected with his back.

He fell. He'd been lighter than I expected, and we tumbled forward into the front hall. His foot kicked out blindly and connected with my face.

I rolled away dazed, ending up in the kitchen, trying to avoid a second strike. My bag clunked against my side. The man struggled to his feet, raising his gun and firing blind. I crawled out of the way just in time, and the bullets struck the kitchen floor. Half-blind, I dug into my bag, trying to find my pistol, but all I found was something round, with a metal ring at the top.

It would have to do. I was desperate.

As the man rounded the corner, still stumbling, I pulled the pin and let go. The grenade rolled toward him. I scrambled to my feet and sprinted into the next room, putting as many walls as I could between us.

The explosion was deafening. I felt like my ears had burst open. The entire house shook. I was thrown off my feet, with no idea if any of the fragments had pierced me. I couldn't tell what was going on anymore. It felt like the end of the world. My vision was swimming, my head pounding . . . and the world through my one remaining eye faded away.

I felt someone pick me up. I tried to protest, but I couldn't find the strength. My left eye was still struggling to make sense of the world as I was taken up a flight of stairs.

The arms holding me were strong, but gentle. They bore me to a familiar bed, where everything finally started to come back into focus. I still only had one eye, but it was working again. There were blue eyes, behind slim glasses.

Darius pulled up a chair next to me. He was watching me very closely, his eyes thick with emotion.

He didn't say a word while I recovered from the explosion. My ears were still pounding, but I was beginning to hear sounds again. As my mind finally seemed to restart and bring itself into working order, I felt around the bed—and found my bag still strapped to my side.

My rifle, too, leaned up against the bed, within reach. Inside the bag, I found my pistol, and by the weight I could tell it was loaded. I looked at Darius, trying to read his expression. It looked so much different without the benefits of my other eye. I couldn't make out the tiny details I knew were there.

Was my left eye always this bad?

His own eyes were inscrutable. I had no idea what he was thinking. I didn't even know what *I* was thinking. What was I going to say? My entire focus had been solely to confront him and get answers, but now that I was here, the way forward was lost. I had so many questions that I couldn't figure out where to start.

Finally, Darius broke the silence. "You left a huge dent in the kitchen."

My mouth opened slightly, then closed again as words failed me. Whatever I'd expected, it definitely wasn't *that.* To hear him make light of what I'd gone through, however indirectly . . .

I grasped the handle. My hand whipped out, and the pistol was in Darius's face, barrel between his eyes. He didn't react in the slightest, except to sit back slightly.

"It's loaded," he said quietly. "If you want to, go ahead." His voice was so calm, so *accepting.* It was infuriating.

"Why?"

"Specify, Kara. Please." Darius took off his glasses, cleaning them with the little blue cloth he always had on him.

"Specify?" You. I. *We,*" I stammered. I stopped myself, trying to gather my thoughts. I settled, finally, on the least loaded question I could find. "What happened outside?"

"Jack's men are gone. We took care of them. Michael left, but his guard is still outside. We won't be disturbed."

I relaxed a little at that, but then the next thought hit me. "How long was I out?"

"A few hours."

Suddenly, my injuries seemed to catch up with me. My arm was too weak to keep the pose. I lowered the gun, still gripping it, but without a real sense of aiming it at Darius. My vision felt so poor without my other eye. It made me feel too vulnerable. I tried to steel myself, taking a deep breath.

"No more lies. Is Dad alive?"

Darius sighed. "I've never lied to you."

I laughed. It was a hollow, short sound, devoid of any mirth. "How can you say that with a straight face?"

"Not once. That doesn't excuse what I've done though." His eyes were still so calm. It grated on me. "I pushed you into this life, and for that I have no excuses. I made you into a killer."

"According to Rebecca," I said softly, "I already was one."

"She told you?"

"The whole story."

Darius nodded. "The story she knew, at least."

"What does that mean?"

"You did kill your mother, Kara, but you did it to protect someone. You were defending our father, a helpless man. It was love for your family, not pride, rage, or whatever drives you now."

"But I still became a killer," I said, a little insistent. "It's all I think about, Dar. Tactics, methods, defense and offense, strategies. Even before you recruited me, I was doing that. It's my whole life."

"I think that's my fault as well." He sighed. "Memory removal is . . . experimental. We had no data on the possible side effects or long-term changes to the psyche. I was trying to target everything I could related to Dad, the fight, your mother, your childhood. Everything I thought might let you start over with a normal life, but all it left you with was a harsh paranoia and the fight-or-flight instincts, you'd built up. Any kind of emotional development was damaged, maybe lost."

"So I'm like a really smart, really scared little kid?"

He shrugged. "Like I said, I'm not certain."

My mind finally processed the smaller tidbit Darius had revealed. "You said *your* mother."

"She wasn't mine. Dad's first wife died when I was seven. I don't remember her perfectly, but she was kind and she was smart." His eyes glazed over. "Her death hit him hard. It was a long five years of drinking, drugs, and whatever he could use to escape. I ended up staying out of the way, hiding out at friends' houses, school, wherever. Then one day, I came home, and I found him with a woman."

"Mom?"

"Yes. She seemed intelligent, charming, passionate. I was too young to understand at the time how she was playing him. You were born less than a year after they met. It was so good to see Dad happy again, I just assumed everything would be all right. You were such a joy to be around too. I loved having a little sister."

He smiled, but the expression was filled with regret. "It didn't last. I got older and I saw what she was doing. She was draining him, month after month, sneaking cash away. She was a kleptomaniac and a drug fiend. If it wasn't bolted down, it was pilfered and pawned for her addictions. Little by little, I watched anything and everything of value disappear from our house. I didn't want to destroy Dad's happiness though, or yours, so I found my own way to help."

I was still quiet, letting Darius speak, but my hand hadn't yet left the pistol. I didn't trust him anymore, but his words . . . I could believe those still.

"By then, I already had friends in the trade. I started helping out, doing odd jobs for cash, buying back whatever she sold to the pawnshops. Dad might notice something missing, but find it only a couple of days later after I'd snuck it back in. She was too high to realize she'd sold the same things repeatedly. It worked for a while, until Dad caught wind of what I was doing."

Darius winced. "I'd never seen him like that. It was the only time we ever fought. I lost my temper. I called out your mother on everything she'd been doing, but he refused to hear any of it. He told me how ashamed he was, how he hated what I was doing. I told him I was the only reason he was still able to live in that house."

He sighed. "I ended up leaving that night. You were only eight. I didn't even say goodbye." He coughed, clearing his throat. "That's when I moved to Seattle. I kept track of you, though, when Dad moved up to Tacoma. He'd finally wised up and gotten you away from her. You had an apartment, you started going to school. It went well for a while, until she followed you up there."

"I know the rest," I interrupted. I didn't need any more. A huge breath escaped my lungs. I felt like I'd just come through a very long, very tight tunnel. I hadn't even realized I'd been holding my breath through most of the story.

"When he called me that night . . . god, Kara." Darius shook his head. "Seeing you like that, I couldn't take it. I just wanted you to be whole again. Rebecca had the solution, after we'd done everything we could."

"And you gave me my cybernetic eye."

He nodded. "The legs first, but yes. Your right eye was completely nonfunctional. I wanted you back to your old self, as much as I could manage. You'd always loved watching things. You were mesmerized by waterfalls, crowds, cars passing in the street, even just the rain. You could sit and watch things moving around forever. When you first woke up after we fixed your legs, all you said was how hard it was to see anything. I couldn't bear it. Rebecca wasn't sure it would work, but I decided it was worth the risks.

"You took to it so naturally. It was the right choice. Once it was installed, you almost seemed like your old self again, what I remember from years ago. Except all the joy was gone. You were so much quieter. We lived together like that for a week. Then, at dinner, you finally begged me to make you forget everything."

"And you just did it?" I asked, my voice thick with pain and rage. "Just like that?"

"Of course not!"

Darius's own voice was harsh and broken. I was startled. It was the first time he'd really reacted to me since I'd woken up. He'd been talking for a while, but it was like I was barely there. He could have been talking to a statue.

"I didn't want anything like that. But you had heard Rebecca talking about memory experiments, and you were *way* too smart for a ten-year-old. I argued with you, so many times."

"Why did you do it, then?"

"You went around me," said Darius, his lip cracking slightly, the barest hint of a smile. "The next time you went in for a checkup with Rebecca, you brought it up yourself. You pleaded with her, begged her, persuaded her. She came to me, and we argued about it for days. Between the two of you, I finally caved in." He sighed. "We erased your memories the next day."

Everything he said rang true. I had plenty of reasons to doubt him . . . but plenty more to trust him too. For whatever he'd done, he *was* my brother. Neither of us spoke for a long while. I was still digesting, processing, figuring out exactly what he'd just told me.

"Why bring me into the gang?" I asked finally.

He sighed. "Maybe I really had no choice, after that night with Coburn. Maybe it was survival." He hesitated. "Or maybe I wanted you with me. I didn't want more secrets between us. I thought if you were part of my world, you'd be safer. Happier even." Darius shook his head. "It was stupid and reckless. You could have died so many times."

"But I didn't."

"You didn't," he agreed, "and every time you came home alive, I felt more secure in my decision—and damned myself even further."

"I could've chosen to stop. You weren't forcing me to kill."

Darius raised his eyebrows. "Would you have though?"

I didn't have an answer for him. I wasn't sure myself. There was definitely something inside me, a willingness to kill, that had prompted me to accept his request that very first time. It was the same darkness that kept my hand firmly gripping the pistol on my bed, ready to kill my own brother.

The pistol reminded me where this had all begun, the most important question—the one that Darius had avoided from the start.

"You never answered me. Is Dad alive?"

He closed his eyes and nodded. "Yes."

My heart skipped a beat. I cleared my throat nervously. "Where is he?"

Darius gestured to his desk. "May I?"

I nodded, still firmly grasping my pistol, strength returning to me with every passing second. Darius stood and took a scrap of paper off his desk. He scribbled something out, then tore it off and handed it to me, neatly folded. I could see a name and an address in Portland, but I couldn't quite make it out.

"You have it memorized?"

"I've kept track of him and I've tried to provide for him discreetly. He found a decent job there, after a good amount of persuasion and money I sent their way. We haven't spoken since . . ." He trailed off.

"Since?"

He coughed again. "After you told me you wanted to erase your memory, I told Dad you hadn't made it off the operating table. He doesn't know you're alive."

Darius sat back down, folding his arms. He looked pointedly at the pistol in my hand.

"So, Kara. What happens now?"

I didn't know what to do. The mental image of Darius in my head had been revised so many times in the last week, I barely had a clue who he was anymore. To me, the guy sitting across from my bed barely resembled my brother. My arm still held the gun, loaded and aimed at his chest.

Betrayal and disgust filled me—at what he'd done, at what I could never get back. There was a hole in my mind that could never be filled, a childhood I'd never be able to reclaim. I had a father who thought I was dead, who was erased so thoroughly from my mind that I hadn't even the slightest notion he might exist. My whole life had been fabricated by Darius, right up to the night I'd decided to kill him.

And yet . . . I created my own life out of it all. I had more than what just Darius had given me. Since learning the truth, I'd found an independence I'd never truly felt. I'd made a true friend. I knew who I was and where I came from, questions I'd never realized I needed answers to, but had become fundamental foundations of my being. In a few short days, I'd become so much more than just my brother's agent.

I realized I didn't need him anymore. A weight lifted from me, relieving all the stress and pain. I had all the answers I'd been looking for. My life no longer centered around my brother. I had my own path to follow now.

It hadn't come in an ideal way, and I had no idea what my life was going to look like now, but at least I had an idea of where to go next. There was a path to walk, and people to walk it with.

And it didn't include Darius.

Ten minutes later, I snuck out of the house, bag under my shoulder, rifle tucked securely inside, with the address slip clutched in my pocket, straight into the bright afternoon sun.

EPILOGUE

Unfortunately, his life was cut short before he could complete what he'd set out to accomplish, leaving the battle to his son. In October 486 BCE, he was embalmed and entombed at Naqsh-e Rostam, near Persepolis. He was sixty-four. Xerxes, his son, took control a few months later, in a smooth transition prepared by his father. Almost immediately, Xerxes crushed rebellions in Egypt and Babylon, and within a few years, he had grown the empire larger than it had ever been at his father's peak. Of course, Xerxes had yet to invade the Greek mainland, where his most famous battles would occur. I'm sure you've all heard of the Spartans," he added with a wink.

Someone in the back of the class shouted a movie quote. A few kids chuckled, but many more rolled their eyes.

He smiled. "But we are out of time. Finish the readings assigned in your syllabus. I expect write-ups in my box by Friday. No more weird file formats either. *Or* deliberately corrupt files, Jessie." He smirked as her jaw dropped. "Nice try, by the way, but you'll have to do more than damage the header. Your essay was pretty good for the first few paragraphs, but I found the rant about my unfair grading and assignment schedule *very* illuminating. I'll be sure to take it under advisement." He winked again. "Just so you know, it had a *lot* of typos."

Jessie's face turned bright red. One of her friends had to practically drag her out of the classroom. He took quite a bit of joy in surprising his students with his technical knowledge. Just as he'd tried when he was in school, so, too, would every class from the advent of computers until the end of time attempt to claim technical difficulties to avoid a deadline.

The rest of the students filtered out, trickling away one by one. A few stayed around to ask questions about upcoming assignments or clarify a recent grade. He was patient with every student, taking as long as they needed to understand everything. Luckily for him, it was the last class of the day, so he wasn't in a rush. Soon enough, it was just him and his TA, Connor, left in the room.

"Aren't old people supposed to be worse with technology, Mr. Portman?" asked Connor, smirking. He was collecting old papers and sorting them. "I mean, you still print out assignments and return them by hand."

"I find some students do much better at remembering where they went wrong when it's written in bold red ink."

"I always found it annoying, personally."

"You were never one of my students, Connor."

"Good thing too. These are thick as hell. I wouldn't want to write this much weekly."

"Language, Connor."

". . . Sorry."

He sighed. "It's fine. It's all a part of the vernacular. You wouldn't be a proper member of this time period if you didn't use every word colloquially recognized by our society."

Connor raised an eyebrow. "Do you really try to relate everything back to history? That was pretty awkward."

"I was trying to be the clever professor."

"Ah."

"Whereas *you're* too smart to be a student." He waved a hand at the stacks. "Go on, I can finish those. Don't you have a date tonight?"

His eyes widened. "How did you know that?"

"Professors with nothing better to do tend to gossip a lot. I listen in sometimes."

Connor grinned. "Well, they're right."

He smiled. "Go on then. Be a romantic. Embrace life."

"You got it, boss."

"And don't talk like that. Your date won't like it. You sound like an old mobster."

"You got it, Boss."

"Get out of here," he said, waving him away again.

Connor gave him a lazy salute, then headed out the door. He shook his head, then sat down to finish sorting away the assignments. Before long, he reached Jessie's. As expected, she'd turned in a perfect paper. She was bright, but too stubborn and headstrong. The young woman fell into a camp of students who could spend a night coming up with an entire well-reasoned essay explaining why they shouldn't have to do a particular assignment, even when doing so took *more* work.

Jessie would make it eventually. She was smart enough to come back around and finish the class properly. Her grades would drop for a little bit, as a wake-up call, but she'd ace the class in the long run. In the meantime, he'd focus on the students who actually needed his help and keep an eye on her to make sure she didn't fall too far off the wagon.

He glanced up at the clock. It was getting late, and he was *running* late.

The last paper went into his files. He locked his cabinets, grabbed his coat, and headed out. The door swung shut behind him, and the lights flicked off automatically. He pulled out his phone and tapped the button to call a car. The college paid his fee automatically. Within a few minutes, the city had routed the nearest available car to him.

The door popped open. He sat down, and as soon as the doors were secure, the car whisked him off to the destination he'd requested, merging neatly back into traffic and setting off downtown.

"I am so sorry I'm late," he started. She waved him off before he could say another word.

"It's fine, really. We don't have a table yet anyway." She gestured to the seat beside her. He sat down and leaned in. His head fit perfectly with the crook of her neck. She put an arm around his back. "You're cold."

"Heat in the car was broken," he murmured.

"Those companies really don't keep them in shape, do they?"

"It's not worth it to them," he sighed. "The cars mostly survive on subsidies anyway, since the workers who use them can't afford more than bare minimum fares."

"Maybe we can get our own car someday."

"That'd be nice." He closed his eyes. "Have you ever driven out in the countryside?"

"Once, when I was little. I don't really remember it."

"We drove out to Yellowstone once. I remember it so vividly. Once we left the city and got control of the car, my dad zoomed along the roads. There wasn't a car for miles around, and he'd drive far above the speed limit. It felt like the car was floating over the road."

"You know, they're working on those."

"What, floating cars?"

"Yes, using magnetic levitation. They'd float along the roads frictionless, so it uses less energy."

"Huh. Will it work?"

"It'd cost a fortune to redo all the roads. Still working on a way to solve that."

"Mmm." He kissed her cheek. "I believe in you."

She smiled. "Thanks, but people have been working on this for decades. I'm just one piece of the puzzle."

"Well, once you solve it, we'll get that car, and I'll take you to Yellowstone. You, me, the kids, we'll have a blast."

She frowned. "The kids?"

He gulped. "I uhh . . . I didn't mean to say that."

Her phone buzzed. Their table was ready.

She set down her drink. "It was just sudden, that's all."

He didn't say anything, just staring at his empty plate.

"Hey." She leaned forward and tapped her fork on it. "You can't eat the plate." He glanced up, and to his relief, Julia didn't seem upset. She sat back again. "I do want kids, if you were wondering. Someday."

"Oh."

"Not right now, of course. We're not married yet, and I'm just start-ing my job, and we can't possibly afford another member of the house yet. And, by house, I mean shitty, run-down apartment."

"Yeah." His eyes started slipping down again.

"What's wrong?"

"It's nothing."

"Hey, it's me here, remember? You can trust me." She peered at him. "You didn't screw up, okay?"

"Okay." He cracked a smile.

"We've still got plenty of time ahead of us to try kids. Decades. His-tory yet to be written." She grinned at him.

He laughed. "Someone else will have to write that one. The system rejected me as an author."

"Aww, is your book not doing well?" she teased. She knew he didn't mind it coming from her.

"Not the most vital of college reads."

"Maybe you should've included more battle scenes."

"I dedicated an entire chapter to the Battle of Thermopylae!"

"Oh, that's the easy one." She rolled her eyes. "Everyone knows that one. You need to bring up the more obscure ones."

"Like what?"

"Dammit, I'm an engineer, not a historian!" She winked at him. "Come on, there's probably some other desperate couple waiting for our table. Let's head home. You can tell me all about those battles."

"Who the hell's knocking at this hour?" she grumbled. Her face was pressed deep into a pillow, and he barely understood a word she was saying.

"Want me to get it?"

"I want them to disappear. It's past eleven."

"So . . . yes?"

The next set of knocks started. She grabbed his pillow and used it to cover her head. "Yes. Go. I'll catch up."

"No, it's fine. Stay in bed. I won't be long."

He stood up and pulled on a robe. His mouth was parched. Before heading to the door, he filled a glass with water. Sipping it as he walked, he shuffled out of the kitchen area, down the hall, and out to the front door. As the next set of knocks started, he pulled it open, ready to press the security call button if he needed to.

The girl's fist stopped in midair. She leaned heavily against the door-frame, favoring one leg. Behind her, back against the railing, stood another girl—swathed in a thick green military jacket too large for her, a sweep of hair covering half of her face, with a dark bag at her side.

His glass shattered against the floor.

". . . Hi, Dad."

AFTERWORD

So long, *Snipe*!

This novel was built out of the first full-length work I ever produced, though it has been *heavily* revised. I originally wrote this version in a sprint for the Royal Road 2019 National Novel Writing Month competition. In the process of eventually finishing this book, I tossed out the start a good five times. The only element to persist mostly unchanged was Faith, who sprung fully formed from her first words. I don't believe I've ever changed a word of her dialogue, except when necessary to update specific story details.

Unlike her cheery best friend, Kara went through multiple versions: everything from a Joker/Harley Quinn-esque cackling psychopath to a brooding angry misanthrope. Eventually, though, I found that something more subtle ended up stronger. The result provided a perfect foil to Faith, and someone whose mind I find fascinating . . . and a little disturbing! I hope you enjoyed the end result.

In my life, I hate to repeat work of any kind. Losing progress in something is brutal for me. I'm a bit ashamed of it, but I've completely dropped video games if my saves got deleted, or if I lost too much progress in a bad fight. Likewise, I've given up on many aspects of my life that probably could have produced something worthwhile, if only I'd kept up my pursuit.

Writing's where I finally turned that around. In writing, to produce the best story you can, you *must* be willing to sacrifice what you've already created. "Kill your darlings" is a popular phrase, and it holds true. If something isn't working, no matter how much you might love it on its own, it must go. Stories get written and rewritten; they are never truly completed.

Likewise, *Snipe* is not truly completed either. I've written a full story up there, don't get me wrong—Kara and Faith both got full arcs—but is the journey *really* over? Of course not! What fun would that be?

My sister once shared with me a quote (which for the life of me, I've never been able to attribute): To produce a great tale, once you've written your story, start at the end and write another one. I don't think it applies everywhere. However, for both this story and my other works, I've always been fascinated with what-comes-next. For *Snipe* here, there are new relationships to explore, new intrigues to unravel, and a dynamic friendship that's only just begun to blossom.

Come join me, won't you?

—etzoli

Lily Lashley

etzoli.mail@gmail.com

https://etzo.li

https://discord.gg/yY6738dAUK

ABOUT THE AUTHOR

Lily Lashley, aka Etzoli, is an IT girl in healthcare from Oregon who loves to write long-form sci-fi and fantasy in her downtime. Lily loves cyberpunk, magical realism, and all other sorts of complex genre fiction. She also watches far too much TV, and she's hopelessly addicted to pretzel sticks. There's nothing Lily loves more in the world than cuddling up on a warm couch with thick blankets and disappearing into another world for the day.

Podium